ALL TO PLAY FOR

Other Books by Josie Juniper

Coming in Hot

Double Apex

ALL TO PLAY FOR

JOSIE JUNIPER

ORION

First published in Great Britain in 2026 by Orion Fiction,
an imprint of The Orion Publishing Group Ltd.,
Carmelite House, 50 Victoria Embankment
London EC4Y 0DZ

An Hachette UK Company

1 3 5 7 9 10 8 6 4 2

Copyright © Josie Juniper 2026

The moral right of Josie Juniper to be identified as
the author of this work has been asserted in accordance
with the Copyright, Designs and Patents Act of 1988.

All rights reserved. No part of this publication may be
reproduced, stored in a retrieval system, or transmitted
in any form or by any means, electronic, mechanical,
photocopying, recording, or otherwise, without the
prior permission of both the copyright owner and the
above publisher of this book.

All the characters in this book are fictitious, and any resemblance
to actual persons, living or dead, is purely coincidental.

A CIP catalogue record for this book is
available from the British Library.

ISBN (Paperback) 978 1 3987 2465 5
ISBN (eBook) 978 1 3987 2466 2
ISBN (Audio) 978 1 3987 2467 9

Printed and bound in Great Britain by Clays Ltd, Elcograf S.p.A.

www.orionbooks.co.uk

*For my Grandma Josephine.
Thank you for telling me about the
little world underneath the dandelion,
and for sharing your name with me.
(Sorry about "all the cuss words" in this book!)*

ALL TO PLAY FOR

1

PORTLAND, OREGON

SAGE

I focus on the target, cocking my arm back, assessing the trajectory: right into the middle of that clown's face. Release the breath slowly with an underhand snap of the wrist, and—

Bull's-eye.

I can't hold in my laugh. "That's for 'mouthy little hoyden with more ink than talent.'"

Beside me, Priya hands over another hefty wooden ball. "Get it out of your system, girlfriend." Her tone is half motherly soothing, half impatience.

I toss it up and catch it—weighing the mass, balancing, integrating it as part of my arm—then launch another straight into the high-score ring.

Bam!

"And *that's* for 'pint-sized poppet with more assets in the seat of her trousers than in her helmet.'" Lights flash and bells chuckle. Another string of tickets spits out of the game, just below the start button.

Priya leans to tear it off before draping them around my neck with the piles of others. "I know this is therapeutic, but how much longer? I'm starving."

"Go get some of that stale popcorn." Eyes locked on the Skee-Ball game, I jab a finger at the coin slot. "Gimme more. I'm not quitting 'til I beat the high score." I nod toward the clown face. "Looks a little like him, doesn't it?"

My PA and lifelong best friend drops nickels into the slot, sighing, then tips her head and gives the target a glance. Her glossy, dark hair slips around her shoulder. "Maybe the bow tie? Alexander Laskaris seems like the kind of guy who'd own one."

I grab three balls from the return gutter and launch them into the air, juggling. "I'd like to make him *eat it*, the misogynist dickbag."

"Um, language?" Priya scolds. "This place is full of kids."

Behind me I hear a child's giggle. I carefully turn, keeping the paint-chipped balls in motion. A little girl with hair pulled into a ponytail on top of her head is watching me.

In a grand finale move, I toss the balls high and do a 360 spin before dropping to one knee and catching them. "Ta-daaaaaa!" I sing out.

"You're a good juggler," she tells me.

"Aww, thanks. Wanna take over my lane? I just put in new coins, but my whiny friend here says it's time to go."

The girl takes the balls from me, eyeing one of the curls

that's escaped from my seventies trucker cap. "Why's your hair blue?"

"Grew that way." I stand and brush off the knees of my jeans, which are dusted with popcorn shards from the dirty floor. "My mother's a mermaid, and my dad—"

"Don't lie to children!" Priya hisses.

Lifting the prize tickets from my shoulders, I drape them around the girl's neck. "Here—get something big. Don't go for the lava lamp, though. I got that once and it was a piece of—"

"*Sage!*" Priya snaps.

"I was gonna say 'junk'! Chill out, babes." Waving goodbye to the little girl, I hook an arm through my best friend's and drag her away from the Skee-Ball lanes.

Just before the exit doors leading out to a rainy Oregon afternoon, I stop at a bank of candy dispensers. I love how everything in this arcade is a time warp from my childhood. This place—the whole funky, artsy Southeast Portland neighborhood, really—has barely changed since I was a kid.

My parents' house, a mile from here, is the same one I grew up in. We could've afforded fancier—my dad made a fortune in the late-nineties dot-com boom—but my parents have always preferred experiences to "stuff." We went on tons of family vacations: Mom, Dad, my brother Julian, and me. And my karting was a major investment, along with Julian's mountaineering.

The only thing Jules has to show for his efforts is a missing toe from frostbite when he climbed K2 and a string of brokenhearted women around the globe. Sounds mean of me to say, but…we're not the best of pals. As for me, all the money and time my parents shelled out set me on the road leading to this year's dream drive: second seat on the Emerald F1 team, the sole woman driver in the sport.

"You shouldn't eat that junk," Priya scolds as I feed a quarter into a machine full of ancient-looking Good & Plentys. "Dagna will strangle you."

"That's why I'm having it *now*. All season she'll be giving me the stink eye if I touch a cocktail or a candy bar."

"She's an amazing physio. You're lucky to have her."

I twist the dispenser knob and cradle the spill of purple and white sugar pellets. "Yeah, well. When I told her I was craving chocolate, she sent me a recipe for whipped tofu with cacao nibs." As Priya tries to lead me to the door, I protest, "Wait! I need Hot Tamales…"

"What you *need* is self-control."

She drags me into the rain, shooting a cranky side-eye at me as we walk down the street to where my restored 1974 Triumph TR6 is parked. "I should've gotten a video of you talking to that little girl," Pri says. "Social media *gold*. Better than a rescue-puppies post."

I tip candies into my mouth and awkwardly talk around them. "Cynical photo op," I mumble, transferring the mound of stale licorice to one cheek.

"Maybe a pic of you with your car? Fans must be curious to see what a Formula 1 driver gets around town in." Priya pulls her phone from a back pocket as we walk up.

"Meh. I don't need strangers to know that." I hop into the driver's side.

"Phaedra told us to get fun pics for Insta," Priya insists, climbing in. "Gotta 'build your brand' and all that."

"No thanks." I mop the condensation off the inside of the windshield.

"You're *so* weird about social media. Anyone who's met you would think you'd be live streaming every time you brush your teeth, and your dad made a zillion bucks off the internet, but you act like I'm trying to steal your soul if I hold up a camera."

"Yeah, but my mom was adamant about 'being present' for experiences. It's part of what gave me the focus to excel at racing. 'Make memories, not content,' she always says."

"Well, *your boss* sees it differently. Taking pictures of you is part of my job. And you know who cares the most about your socials? *Sponsors.* Which is exactly what Phaedra will say."

"The season hasn't even started yet. Let me enjoy one last month of *not* having a camera up my ass." I start the car, the engine coughing before it roars to life. "Soon enough I'll be back in the snake pit, my privacy all kinds of invaded by dickweed journalists like He-Who-Shall-Not-Be-Named."

"That's my point. It's not helping that two of the bloggers who talk about you the most do it because they hate you. We need to create content that makes you fun and relatable. Get ahead of the narrative. According to that Carol-Jeanne lady on *Sports and Tortes*, you're a conniving villain who sabotaged her precious daughter."

"CJ Ardley is a delusional sports-mom who happens to have a big following. Mostly because she posts those cougary cheesecake pics along with...like, actual cheesecakes. No one takes her seriously." I rev the engine not only to encourage it but also because I'm irritated and enjoy the aggressive sound. "Her own daughter thinks she's cringe. Maya Ardley and I were super supportive of each other in karting."

"Sure, but lots of people read her blog. And you know who has even *more* influence? This guy." Priya holds up her phone: Alexander Laskaris's dumb, smirky face in the profile pic beside the banner of his *In the Mirrors* blog.

"Whatever. Alexander *who*?" I put the car into gear and screech onto the road.

It's a shame that he's been dragging me for months, because I used to be a fan of his writing. He's smart, funny, and... okay, kinda handsome—I can't deny that. I used to follow his blog. But after I got the Emerald seat, he started posting all this snarky shit. What a disappointment, discovering he's just another insulting, clickbait-generating douche.

Priya scrolls down his latest post, skimming the content. "Uh-oh..." she groans.

I look over after navigating a turn. "What?"

She rotates the phone to face me again. I can only afford a brief glance while I'm driving, but it's enough to see an unflattering pic of myself climbing out of a car outside a club with a flash of crotch.

"Oh, fuckbuckets. What's it say?" I demand.

"The headline is 'Putting the "Cock" in "Cockpit,"' and the lede is, 'If rumors are true about how much time punk-rock racer Sage Sikora has spent at Klaus Franke's home on Santorini, it's no mystery how her perky bum landed in Emerald's second seat. Does Franke, a notorious womanizer, have a Formula 1 casting couch on his Greek isle getaway?'"

Fury wicks up my spine and spreads in a blanket of heat. I clutch the steering wheel hard. "Okay, that's *it*. The creep's gone too far this time." At a stoplight, I swivel and give Priya a determined look. "I'm calling Phaedra, and we're gonna sic legal on him." I stare back out at the rain, eyes narrowed. "Prepare to be humbled, you sexist London dickbag."

2

LONDON

ALEXANDER

The only thing better than waking up to a hand on your cock is when the hand belongs to someone with a pair of tits like these. Brigitte is leaning on an elbow, sheet draped over her hip, showcasing her bountiful charms in a way that would be sufficiently inspiring even if she weren't caressing me.

"Bonjour, mon preux chevalier," she greets in a sultry whisper.

"Well, hello to you too."

I sit up and reach for a water bottle on the bedside table, fortifying myself for another round. With a mischievous smile, she gathers a rope of her long, disheveled blond hair and trails it down my chest. I set the water aside and pull Brigitte close, rolling her beneath me.

My kisses are halfway down the path from her neck to one of those luscious pink nipples when my doorbell rings.

I ignore it, but when it rings again, Brigitte lifts her head. "Should you not…?"

"That's correct—I should *not*," I tell her, sliding my knee between her thighs.

My mobile chimes and the doorbell rings a third time.

"*Alexandaaaire*," Brigitte groans in frustration. "Allez! Make it stop…"

I sigh, leaning on an elbow and reaching for the mobile. "One moment, my dove—don't you dare move your delectable arse."

The line of text on my preview screen reads, Get up and open the door.

I slide a hand down my face. "Fuckin' hell. It's my mother."

Brigitte yelps, leaping from the bed and scrambling to gather her clothes. "It is Nefeli? Mon Dieu…" She struggles into her jeans, not bothering to put on knickers first, and yanks a pale blue jumper over her head.

I pull on a dressing gown and knot the sash. "Just stay in here and she'll never—" I fall silent as I hear the front door slam. "Scratch that. I forgot she has a key."

Combing my fingers through my hair, I hurry toward the sound of clicking high-heeled shoes, hoping to cut her off at the pass. Suddenly she's framed in the bedroom doorway, all five feet one inch of formidable terror, hands on her hips.

"Jesus wept," my mother says with disgust. "I thought you promised 'no more fishing off the company pier'? Bloody hell, we'll lose another good freelancer."

Brigitte looks near tears, clutching her wool coat and knee-high boots against herself. "My apologies, madame. Please—"

"Save your breath, love," my mother interrupts. "You're a talented photographer, and the magazine is lucky to have you.

Just…please don't quit when this turns into a disaster. There's a good girl—see you Monday." She waves in the general direction of the front door, and Brigitte rushes to leave without a backward glance.

As the front door slams, my mother turns on her heel and strides to my kitchen, opening and closing cupboards until she finds a box of PG Tips.

"I don't need any myself," I tell her.

"I'd not make you tea were you dying of thirst, so you're in luck." She splashes just a touch of water into the electric kettle—making it clear it's only for herself—then flicks it on. "You've got the magazine threatened with a lawsuit. *Again*, I might add."

"Oh? What now?"

Her icy look skewers me. "Wipe that smirk off your face. You've disgraced us with the blog I allowed you to link to the *Auto Racing Journal* website—consolation, mind you, because you pouted like a child over Natalia Evans getting the *ARJ Buzz* YouTube show."

"That?" I scoff. "It's all in good fun. Someone took offense?"

She straightens from digging in my fridge, milk carton in one hand. "*Good fun?* Are you thick? You said Emerald's new driver fucked her way into the job. Neither she nor Phaedra Morgan will take this lying down."

I pull a grape from the fruit bowl and pop it into my mouth. "Rumor has it Sage Sikora *did* take it lying down."

"They want me to fire you, and I've half a mind to do it."

My smile wilts. "You won't."

"No? Oh, *do* tell me more, Alekos." She taps her sternum.

"I had a Pulitzer before you could tie your shoes. Your father and I rescued a dozen magazines from the nineties print-media slump. What have *you* done? You're like a parody of a spoilt only child. You spend money and write when it suits you and noodle on the piano and chase women." She points at my bedroom, then the front door. "Specifically and unhelpfully, screwing your way through my best talent, after promising not to."

"Brigitte is freelance; I have no authority over her. And I haven't so much as winked at an intern in months."

She gives a sarcastic clap. "Congratulations on having cleared that low bar. Smartarsed thirty-one-year-old idler." The kettle light flicks on, and she flips the switch off before pouring hot water into a mug. "*My God* how you test my patience. When we get on that call with Emerald today, if they—"

"Steady on," I cut in, holding up a hand. "*What* call?"

"With Emerald's team principal." She pours milk into her tea, then turns her wrist to peer at her watch. "In three minutes. Why do you think I was hanging on your bell?"

I follow as she strides into the living room. "Because you wanted to ruin the lovely morning I was enjoying with a leggy Parisian?"

Pointing at my laptop on the coffee table, she makes an impatient hissing noise. "*Tsst!* Get that booted up—don't stand there gawping." She perches on the sofa edge.

I open the laptop and slide it toward her. Her fingers fly over the keyboard, switching to her account and logging in, then tapping a link before I can duck away to comb my hair and put on a shirt.

She waves me back, angling an imperious finger to the sofa. "Sit."

"I'm not dressed for the occasion."

"You look like the dog's dinner, and it's fitting."

"Stunning. Cheers." I settle beside her and adjust my dressing gown to close it more, then make another attempt to calm the disarray of my auburn hair.

A window opens on-screen to display a dour-looking Phaedra Morgan, Emerald F1's hot-tempered team principal.

"Ms. Morgan," my mother greets, all warmth. "How are you this morning?"

"Well as can be expected," Phaedra replies. "Sage'll join us any second."

My stomach twists. "Oh? She's weighing in?"

Phaedra lifts an eyebrow. "Considering she's the one you accused of sleeping her way to the top, *obviously* she'll be here."

I can't resist a small barb. "The *top*? Emerald? Perhaps sleeping her way to the middle..."

"Alekos!" my mother snaps. "Skáse!"

Another window opens: Sage Sikora, that pixyish beauty—rosebud lips, deep dimples, flashing honey-brown eyes, all framed with ice-blue hair. My stomach does another aerial trick, and I feel heat creep into my face like I'm an adolescent with his first crush.

"Hey, cats and kittens! Let's get this party started." She points at the screen. "You, sweetness," she says with heavy sarcasm that's clearly directed at me, "have a great future in the fast-food industry. But I'll personally break every one of your soft little rich-boy fingers if you go near a computer again."

"Are your soft little rich-girl fingers going to do the job?" I return, feigning boredom.

Her eyes narrow, and she rakes a tendril of hair away from her face, tucking it behind her ear to expose the peacock feather tattoo that runs up the side of her neck. Her pink bow of a mouth opens to throw a comment back when Phaedra speaks.

"Nefeli? I'll direct this at you, because your fuckwit son doesn't have the sense not to double down on his fantastic dipshittery. He's put your magazine at risk for a defamation suit."

"And I couldn't be more embarrassed," my mother says. "I understand exactly why you—"

I cut in, "I was reporting on rumors, stated in the form of *questions*."

"You're here to grovel," my mother snaps. "And you're doing a piss-poor job."

"I'm not the *groveling* type. Humility is for the people flying in coach."

Phaedra rolls her eyes, but to my surprise, Sage has a lopsided smile. She studies me with challenge, as if she's sussed out the rules to a game.

My mother's expression, however, is near murderous. Her nostrils flare. "You're fired."

"Oh, *stop*," I say with a chuckle. "I'm only taking the piss."

She turns back to the screen. "Ms. Morgan, he'll not trouble you further. We can print a retraction if that's your preference, though you may wish not to have more attention drawn to such an offensive rumor. He's lost admin control, and it won't be reinstated. I suppose we could even delete the blog entirely, if—"

"Hold on a bloody minute," I fume. "That's my intellectual property!"

Ignoring me, she continues. "If Emerald wishes to initiate a lawsuit, I encourage you to name Alexander personally. He neglected to get editorial approval before uploading that nonsense, and as of today, he's no longer an employee of *Auto Racing Journal*."

"Are you serious?" I demand.

Still addressing Phaedra and Sage, my mother says, "I wash my hands of this. My son is a fool. Better late than never that he learns from his mistakes, so feel free to handle this as you wish. He's all yours."

I give her a sardonic look. *"All yours?* Handing me over to Emerald in service like a Dickensian orphan? What does—"

"Yeah, okay...I'll take him," Sage cuts in.

Phaedra laughs. "Not a bad idea. Seeing as Mr. Laskaris is now *unemployed*, how's about a little internship at Emerald? No pay, of course, but"—she smirks—"loaded with opportunity for personal growth."

I offer a thin courtesy smile. "Not interested."

"Perfect," my mother deadpans. "When does he start?"

Sage winks at me. "Welcome to Emerald, honeybee. Looks like I'm your new boss."

3

PORTLAND, OREGON

SAGE

I know it pains my mom that Julian and I don't get along. We're only thirteen months apart; my mom had us practically back-to-back just before turning forty. Maybe it's us being so close in age, but Jules was my first and fiercest competitor, and that's made me who I am. My aggressive hates-to-lose personality is probably due to this lifelong dynamic. It's worked great for racing, so I wouldn't change it if I could.

Jules is way mellower than I am. And things didn't sour between us until eleven years ago. But I can't tell my parents why. I haven't told *anyone*, including Priya. She's been my best friend since we were toddlers and is the daughter of my dad's business partner. We grew up together. She's carried a torch for Julian since puberty, and I won't hurt her by telling her that Julian once let me almost die.

When I was fifteen, the two of us went hiking one day while our family was visiting Thailand. Jules was annoyed, because he'd wanted to go climbing instead. But because I was feeling under the weather, I insisted on hiking. So, we'd already started out the day grouchy, flipping each other a lot of shit.

My parents stayed at our rented bungalow in Tonsai Beach with friends. I had pain in my side that I figured was premenstrual twingy cramps or something, and it got worse during the hike. On our way back, it was so bad that I mentioned it to Jules, who was complaining about me slowing him down.

He gave me a ton of shit, saying it was just a stitch in my side and I needed to stretch and drink water and "stop whining." When I sat down to rest for a few minutes, he left me behind in disgust. My appendix ruptured, and I don't remember what happened before the hospital, but apparently I was lying unconscious just off the trail for hours, basically dying. My dad and brother came back to look for me when it was getting dark and I still hadn't returned.

I was taken by helicopter to a hospital and came close to not making it through the ordeal. The incision scar is pretty huge, bigger than what's typical. It was nearly five months before I could go back to karting.

Julian has never apologized.

I have no idea why I didn't rat him out for abandoning me. My parents were already so upset that I guess it seemed wrong to compound things by pointing fingers. Since they found me off the trail, Julian's story was that he *did* look for me right away but couldn't find me and figured I'd taken another route.

It's obviously bullshit, but I've let him get away with it for our parents' sake. Their marriage has always been rocky, so I try not to make the family even less stable. It's easier to keep my feelings to myself—something I'm already practiced at. Another by-product of growing up in a competitive sport. You can't let people in, because anyone could use your vulnerabilities to their advantage. Your image is your identity, as far as everyone is concerned, and...yeah, it makes you guarded.

It's been a great visit home because *Julian isn't here*. I can relax and have my mom all to myself. My "trustafarian" jerk of a brother is off climbing in Puerto Rico. Tomorrow, Priya and I are flying out to rejoin Emerald, so Mom's been in the kitchen all day, whipping up the family favorites. Priya and I are hanging out with her, sneaking bites of things and getting tipsy off White Russians while quoting *The Big Lebowski*.

When my mom cuts into an eggplant, I remind her that it's Julian who likes it, not me.

"Julian is going to be here in ten minutes or so," Mom says, focused on her knife flying across the cutting board.

My gut tenses. "Why didn't you tell me?"

Priya sets her cocktail down and touches her hair as if trying to remember how it looks. It's in two messy braids, and she's wearing cutoff sweats and a faded T-shirt. "*Oh my God*," she mutters. "Um...I need to...uh...I'll be back."

She dashes from the room—presumably to put on makeup, fix her hair, and change into something adorable-yet-effortless-looking. My mother and I exchange a knowing smirk.

Mom slices the eggplant with precision. "Those two," she says with an indulgent chuckle. "I wonder if they'll ever give it a shot? She's so sweet on him, and Julian couldn't hope for a more lovely girl."

"Why would you inflict that on Pri? I thought you liked her."

"Be nice."

"But I'm not 'nice.'" I reach for Priya's abandoned drink and pour it into my own before taking a gulp. "Pri's too stable for Jules—he always goes for the squirrely ones. Remember the fire dancer who put a snake in his bed when she thought he was cheating? Or that artist he brought to your anniversary party, who wore the bustier made of condom wrappers and lectured everyone on Marxism?"

Mom winces, then dumps the eggplant into a bowl of olive oil and herbs. "Exactly. Priya would be good for him."

I hide behind another sip of my drink, holding back my next snarky comment. The doorbell rings, and down the hall I hear the guest room door slam—Priya barricading herself until she gets her shit together.

"Can you grab that?" Mom asks. "My hands are all gloopy."

I gulp down the rest of the White Russian and smack the glass on the counter before taking my sweet time sauntering to the front door. When I open it, Julian is scowling, phone pressed to his ear.

"*Paz*," he says with a world-weary sigh. "*Paz, stop.* I can't talk right now. Can we finish this later? Christ almighty. I'll—" He cuts off and looks at the phone. "Great. Perfect." Finally acknowledging me standing there, he offers a feeble smile. "She hung up."

"Trouble in paradise?" I stand back to let him in, and when he walks through the doorway, he tries for a one-arm hug. I ward him off by raising one fist for a fist bump instead. "Yeah, *no*."

He barely touches my hand with the side of his, then adjusts his duffel bag on one broad shoulder and pockets his phone before raking his overly long hair out of his sorta Hemsworth Brother–ish face. "House smells great," he tells me as I close the door behind him.

"Definitely smells better than you."

He dumps his bag at my feet. "Why don't you make yourself useful and carry this?"

"Get bent. Carry your own shit."

My father's voice comes from the living room. "Stop squabbling, you two. Can we have a few minutes before the war kicks off?"

My brother goes in to greet Dad, and they walk together to the kitchen where my mom mops off her hands and flings her arms around her adored firstborn. I lean in the doorway on the other side of the living room, watching them. I know my bickering and distance with Jules doesn't help in a family with parents who are already frosty with each other.

Priya comes up behind me and rests her chin on my shoulder. "Julian's here already?" she says innocently.

"As if you wouldn't sense that guy like a shark smelling a nosebleed a mile off. Sounds like he and the most recent girlfriend are on the outs, so here's your chance, babes. Can't say much for your taste, though."

"That's ridiculous. I'm not his type at all."

"Yeah, well...that fuckup is definitely *your* type—'tall, dark, and disastrous.'" I reach back and pat her cheek. "Take my advice and steer clear. Remember when you didn't listen to me and got ringworm from that box full of stray kittens?"

"Oh my God, Sage. We were eleven years old."

"My point exactly. You still can't resist a cuddly catastrophe."

She hugs my shoulders, teasing, "That's why I put up with *you*."

It's two in the morning, but I can't sleep. There's so much on my mind.

I escaped the post-dinner chitchat tonight with the excuse that I need to sleep before a long day of travel tomorrow. But really I was getting too much in my head, worrying about the upcoming season.

Everyone thinks I'm confident all the time, but...the weight of being a woman in a position this visible, of being "an inspiration" to a new generation of girls in motorsport, it's *heavy*. Sometimes it feels like I'm not allowed to have needs.

Sick of tossing and turning, I get up and head for the kitchen to snag another one of the éclairs my mom made. The kitchen light is on. Julian stands near the sink with his back to me, shirtless, fiddling with something on the counter. He sniffles.

What the hell? Is he crying?

His head dips. Another sniff, followed by a tapping sound. He turns and spots me in the archway, his fingertip in his mouth...and suddenly I realize what he's doing.

"What the fuck are you putting up your nose, you degenerate?"

He wipes his hand off on his plaid pajama bottoms. "Just… medicine."

"*Bullshit.*" I cross the kitchen and snatch the orange pill bottle off the counter, but he grabs it back before I can read it. "Are those oxys?" I demand. "Fuck, Jules! *Still?*"

"It's for my back! Because of the surgery after my fall at Tahquitz."

"Oh, of course," I say acidly. "I'm sure the bottle says to crush 'em up and snort rails—that's the recommended method, right?"

He rakes a hand through his messy hair. "Can you crawl outta my ass? I just…sometimes I need it to kick in faster."

"Your surgery was two years ago. I was on that stuff after my appendix, and they don't give it to you for very long."

"In my case not long *enough*. But I'm dealing with it, and it's under control. This isn't a fucking crisis."

"You're 'dealing with it'? Like Uncle Russ did? Maybe go ask Mom how confident she is that you have it 'under control.' You remember how destroyed she was when he died."

"Jesus, Sage! Don't play that card. This isn't the same."

"It *is* the same, and that was her point when she talked to you about this last year when you were still asking for refills. 'An equal-opportunity ruiner of lives,' she said. We have a family history with this shit. You should know better."

He looks sad enough that I almost soften, but I know I should be stern. If anyone in this family can call Jules out on his bullshit, it's me; I'm not deterred by his puppyish charm.

We stare each other down. I beckon, nodding toward the bottle. "Hand it over."

"Fuck *no*," he says with a harsh little laugh. "This is none of your business."

I shove my hand closer. "I wanna see the date on the label."

He pockets the bottle. "Quit hassling me, all right? Fine—*you got me*. It's expired. I'm dealing with a lot, so I have to get creative. And I use the old bottle so I can travel with it."

He folds his arms across a tan torso littered with scars from various climbing accidents over the years. His jaw is hard. The glitter of his green eyes—like Mom's, not mine and Dad's—is inky-deep from his splayed pupils.

I cross my arms too, mirroring his stubbornness. "So, 'creative' means buying from some black-market lowlife with a pill press?"

"Don't be dramatic. What do you care anyway?"

"Because, dumbass…if you overdose on fake pills made of fentanyl and chalk, it'll *ruin our parents' lives*."

He looks down at his bare feet. "I…I use test strips," he mumbles. "For fentanyl."

"Gee, that makes me feel *so* much better about it." My fist shoots out and I punch him on the shoulder so fast that he doesn't have time to block it. "How much are you using? I have every right to be worried!"

"I'm not talking to you about this," he retorts, rubbing his shoulder. "You're just getting off on feeling superior. Rack up those points, Sage. Life is a zero-sum game to you. You don't even like me, so why bother acting concerned?"

We fall silent, and for a minute I watch his stupid feet on

the Italian tile floor. His left one is a funny shape because of the missing pinky toe. I hate to admit it to myself, but it really hurts to hear him say, *You don't even like me.*

There's a creak of footsteps behind me as someone walks into the kitchen, and I hear Priya gasp. I spin around and find her standing in the black Petzl T-shirt Julian was wearing when he showed up. Her mile-long legs are bare beneath, and she takes a quick step back through the archway, panicked eyes going from me to Julian.

"Oh, for fuck's sake," I growl, smoothing a hand over my face. "Really?" I glance at my brother, who's gnawing on his lower lip, studying Priya as if he's not sure whether he should invite her over and throw an arm around her in a show of solidarity or avoid her like poison oak.

It wasn't until this second that I realized just how much I'm *not* okay with the idea of them getting together. Doesn't fail-son Jules get enough already? I've always suspected he's my parents' favorite, even though I'm the achiever. *He needs me so much, and you're so competent*, my mom once said. I've never forgotten that. Why does being a fuckup make him special?

And now he gets Priya too? *My* best friend?

"Again," I tell her coldly, "I can't say much for your taste. And now he's apparently a drug addict—even better! What a catch."

She tugs the T-shirt hem down, but her pale blue panties are still showing. "He...he's...I mean, he said his back is hurting tonight. It's just medication." She looks at him. "Isn't it?"

I blow an impatient raspberry. "He may've thrown his back

out fucking you, but that ain't 'medication' in the bottle, honey-bee. It's street junk."

Her big eyes are all concern as she focuses on him. "Julian, what does she mean?"

"It means," I tell her, "that he's perfect for you now. You can't resist a stray in need. Time to get out a cardboard box and a blanket and nurse another one back to life."

Immediately I know I've pushed too far. Her eyes go wide—first shock, then pain—and she flattens her lips in the way she does when she's trying not to say something. I recognize that I'm in the wrong and hate myself for how I lash out instead of letting people see it when I'm feeling vulnerable. I open my mouth to take it all back, but the words are frozen in me.

Does Julian have a serious problem? If he does, and he and Priya are together, what will that do to her? Uncle Russ's girlfriend ended up circling the drain with him, caught in his downward spiral while trying to rescue him...

"Don't be mean," Priya says, her woundedness pivoting to anger. "What's wrong with you? That's not helping anyone, Sage."

At her change in tone, my remorse twists into reciprocal hostility.

"It's not my fucking job to help!" I snap. "People can only help themselves. Maybe you should consider that before signing on to babysit your new junkie boyfriend."

Oh shit...Why am I making it worse?

As I storm out of the kitchen, my heart hurts. I want to apologize, to tell them both that I'm just scared and I don't mean any of it. That Priya is a million times better person than I am. For an hour, I lie in bed and run through speeches and pleas and apologies in my head that I'm too confused and ashamed to deliver.

Finally, I get up, deciding to pack my suitcases and take an Uber to the airport before Priya and Jules wake. I'm too mortified to face them in the morning, knowing how I've fucked up. I'll see Priya on the plane, but…I'm not ready yet.

As I cram clothes into my suitcase, I try to convince myself this is all Julian's fault.

None of this would be happening if not for his recklessness, right? I know I should be understanding, like Mom was with her brother. But what did Mom's patience get her? Uncle Russ died. I'm not giving Jules a free pass on being a trainwreck. Haven't we all done that his entire life? Why does he get to be the favorite? Jetting all over the world rock climbing and flinging money around and getting laid, no real goals, no self-discipline…

The uncharitable thoughts play on repeat, mixed with spasms of regret that send me as far as my bedroom door to go apologize before I subdue the urge.

Heartsick and frustrated, I haul my baggage—literal and metaphoric—to the front door, once again the victim of my own stupid hotheadedness and pride.

When Priya arrives at the boarding area, her eyes look red. I'm not sure if it's because I'm an asshole or because she was sad having to say goodbye to my dumb brother. Probably both. We exchange one wary glance, and because the only empty seats in the room are singles, she sits far away and I get another half hour of feeling miserable while she ignores me.

Once on the plane, I sling my carry-on into the overhead compartment, sidestep into my seat, and pop my sunglasses back on. Minutes later, Priya wrestles her bag in beside mine. In lieu of a greeting, she tosses something onto my lap. I pull my glasses off and inspect it.

Shit. A Violet Crumble bar—my favorite, and a little hard to find. My guilt swells even more uncomfortably as Pri plunks down next to me. I'm never sure if this habit of hers—doing something nice for me when I've been a total shit—is a genuine olive branch or a strategy to make me feel worse. But it's not like I can call her out on it if it's the latter. What am I gonna say? *How dare you bring me candy after I acted like a monster?*

I prop my sunglasses on top of my head and give Pri a weak smile as I hold up the Violet Crumble. "Okay, now I *really* look like a dickhead."

"Even better," she says, avoiding my eyes. "Because it's not from me. Julian got it for you."

I mash one hand over my face, sighing. "Wow. Okay." I stare at the candy, then break it at the approximate middle before tearing the wrapper down the seam. "Want half?"

"I'm all right—no thanks."

I pinch the wrapper closed and set the candy aside. "You're *not* all right. And I really apologize, Pri. I was super shitty. It was a cheap shot for me to act like it's a character flaw that you're so fucking nice." My throat tightens, and I swallow. "I got punchy because I panicked when I caught Jules with the pills. Will you forgive me?"

She angles a side-eye my way, assessing me for sincerity. "Don't I always?"

There's an edge of bitterness to it that makes it clear this isn't a casual way of saying, *Yes, I forgive you.* She's gone straight to the heart of the problem, and my stomach twitches like the expectation of an undelivered punch.

"You *do* always—yeah. And maybe you shouldn't." My voice cracks at the end. Pri shoots another guarded look my way, and I push onward. "Look, I know that me being a disaster is, like, a feature not a bug for you, in a weird way." I offer a shrug, smiling. "Keeps you pretty busy, right? Always looking out for me, and for *everyone*. But…do you think people won't love you if you're not doing something for them?"

"Of course not! Jesus. I'm…I just like to help."

"I know, and I probably take that for granted." My hands tangle in my lap. "It's okay to tell me to fuck off sometimes. To stand up for yourself."

She lifts an eyebrow. "Uh-huh, sure. Worked great last night! I tried to push back and you stomped off and then went to the airport without me."

I fix Priya with a sober stare. "I left because I was embarrassed." My voice is a ragged whisper, absorbed by a perky announcement spilling through the intercom. "I know I'm reactive. But…like, it's my job—the aggressive reflex."

Her dark, soft eyebrows rumple. "I get it. But you can't do that with *people*. We're more complex than cars." She takes my hand and squeezes it. "You're not gonna lose me. But I worry that your stubbornness and hot-tempered pride is someday going to cost you."

I give her a wry look. "You mean like a partner? Fuck that."

"You think you don't care. But Julian has a point about you always needing to win. Relationships—whether it's partners, friends, or family—aren't about winning. If you screw up in a race, you analyze the mistakes and bring what you learned to the next one. But that's not always possible with people. Sometimes they don't give you another chance."

I sit with what she's said, focusing on the stream of passengers creeping up the aisle toward their seats. Priya lets my hand go.

I peek at her. "So…are you and Jules an actual thing?"

"I don't know yet."

"Because he really might have a problem. With the, uh, you know what."

She shakes her head, eyes closed. "He says he doesn't, and I believe him. And you're evading the issue."

With a frustrated sigh, I twist toward the window and push the shade up, staring out at the tarmac, the cloudy sky, a worker in a Day-Glo vest pushing an empty baggage cart. My head is noisy and my heart is heavy. After a minute, Priya taps me on the shoulder. I wriggle around in my seat to face her again.

"Hey," she says. "Can you do me a favor? Tell Julian you're sorry too?"

I roll my eyes. "Fine."

She waits. "As in…*now*." When I scowl, she adds, "This is me sticking up for myself, remember? You said I should."

I dig my phone out of my pocket. "Okay, technically you're sticking up for *him*, but whatever. If it'll make you happy."

"And because it's the right thing to do."

"Yeah, okay. That too."

I tap my contacts and scroll down to his number. Priya watches me like a teacher supervising detention. She notices that I have him listed as "Foolian" and makes an exasperated growling noise.

"Seriously, Sage?"

"What? It's funny! He probably has me listed in his phone as something way worse."

Her jaw shifts. "Change it. *Words mean things.*"

"Shit, all right, all right." My thumbs fly over the keyboard. "Done. Happy?"

"Happy enough."

I type, Hey, Jules. I apologize for losing my shit last night. I pause, considering a few things to add, something supportive or concerned or maybe funny so it can all blow over, but in the end, I just write, Thanks for the candy, then tap the send arrow and shove my phone back into my pocket.

A flight attendant pulls the first-class curtains closed and I remember that douche Alexander Laskaris making his lame quip about people who fly in coach.

It's the perfect icebreaker to change the subject with Pri.

"*Humility,*" I say in an exaggerated posh English accent, lifting one hand as if holding a teacup with my pinkie out, "*is for peasants.*"

Priya cracks up. "Oh God—*him*." She makes a face. "I almost forgot he existed. Did you have to remind me?"

I grab the Violet Crumble bar and offer a chunk. "Truce?" I ask.

"Truce." She takes the candy and delicately bites off a brittle corner. I gnaw at mine too, swiping at my shirt as flakes of honeycomb rain down.

"So, Laskaris is meeting us in Bahrain," I say around a mouthful. "Wanna help me figure out some stuff to torture him?"

My best friend's warm brown eyes light up. "You're on."

4

LONDON

ALEXANDER

My early upbringing was a battle between my mum and dad, and I'd be lying to claim that didn't have an impact. Nefeli and Konstantin Laskaris had very different views on parenting. Thus, I—sole progeny of two fantastically wealthy and stubborn people—lived before the age of thirteen in a tug-of-war between two child-rearing styles.

My father was stern and demanding. He installed tutors in our huge Lake District manor, like a Brontë sisters novel. I was practically a young prince in our village, where our palatial home on a hill loomed over the surrounding cottages. There was something feudal about it, which suited my father down to the ground.

Mother came from a fishing village a half hour from Athens. She'd been allowed to run wild and credits that freedom with having made her into the thinker and celebrated writer she became. She wanted me to have a similar childhood and encouraged my wandering and mischief.

So, from my father's camp: rigid lessons, endless piano practice, and dining so formal as to be a misery. From my mother's: tearing all over the village unsupervised, feral and scabby-kneed.

The end to my idyllic youth came when I was shipped off to a grand old school in London at thirteen. It's fair to say every one of my peers was better suited to that environment than my culture-shocked self.

On my second day, we were drafted into teams to play rugby. I'd done plenty of roughhousing, lake swimming, falling out of trees and such, but wasn't particularly good with team sports. I'd got tall early but had no weight behind it. I was a freckled, lanky kid with huge gray eyes, big feet, and a mockable air of superiority.

When we were being partitioned off for rugby, I made the mistake of protesting that I couldn't participate because if I injured my hands, I wouldn't be able to play piano. I was promptly labeled "Piano Twat." Booted into the game, I soon found myself under a heap of smelly, jeering boys, furious and sore. I turned my wrenched neck to find a hand extended to help me up. Above me stood the biggest, blackest kid I'd ever seen in my sheltered life.

He smiled a little wryly. "Piano Twat, meet Drum Twat. I'm Badrick Jones."

And that's how I met my best mate.

Badrick was born in Jamaica, though he moved to Birmingham when he was two. His family owns a Jamaican bank and a few other financial firms. He and I bonded over music, a mutual loathing for sports and school food, and our shared outsider status.

It took a few weeks for the whispers to catch up to me about Badrick being gay. But I saw no reason that should be relevant; he didn't want to *date* me. We listened to Thelonious Monk LPs, gorged on Monster Munch, and played Xbox. Two sides of the same coin.

He's the only friend who really knows me, having seen me through every stage of trying on identities over the past eighteen years. I suppose I needed to play the parts of many characters as a child—expectations of me were so disparate.

Badrick and I usually go for drinks at Swift, but tonight we're meeting at Satan's Whiskers. It's mid-March and rainy as hell. When I walk in, Bad waves an arm from where he's sat at the bar.

I sidle through the crowd and make my way to him. "You're early."

"Bruv. You're *late*." He signals the barman for a refill on his scotch and another for me. "I know why you said not Swift tonight. Figured it out."

"Oh? Do tell."

He gives me a side-eye, taking the final sip of his first scotch and shoving the glass aside. "Avoiding Emma. And don't give me 'Which Emma?'"

I point at the basket of chips near Bad's elbow. "Did you put vinegar on these?"

"Too feckin' cheap to order your own," he jokes, pushing the basket toward me.

Ah, Emma—a gorgeous bartender at Swift. It was months of hard graft to land her, but I don't mind playing a long game. I assumed her impenetrable aloofness was a guarantee we were on the same page about keeping it casual. But the very-much-penetrable Emma surprised me by bringing me pancakes and coffee in bed the morning after our first night together, then suggesting a trip to Tate Modern, followed by—I kid you not—*lunch with her parents.*

Something about her reaction to my lavish Chelsea flat indicated she was angling to upgrade immediately from "good time" to girlfriend. Over the two weeks that followed, she went from sweet to pouty to vicious, and…well, I had to let one of my favorite cocktail bars go, or risk getting shanked by a lemon zester the next time I went in.

"I thought a new venue might be invigorating," I tell Badrick.

"You couldn't keep it in your trousers and now our best bar is cashed."

"Rubbish. We *always* go to Swift. Time for a change." I give a nod of thanks to the bartender as he sets down our drinks, then lift my glass toward Badrick. "Chin-chin."

"Rattlesnakes and condoms," he toasts, hoisting his own glass.

I pluck a chip from the basket. "You know what my problem is?"

He snorts. "Where do I start?"

"I'm miserably attracted to unstable women. It's why I have a three-shag limit: I need them gone before they go off like an IED and make my life a hellscape."

Badrick laughs, choking on his swig of scotch. "*Hellscape?* You secretly live for the headache, mate."

"Says the man with a boyfriend who threw a rare six-thousand-dollar bonsai at him during an argument, the moody French git."

"Laurent's got a temper, but he's dead fit. You take the good with the bad." He picks up a chip glistening with vinegar and folds it into his mouth. "Speaking of powder kegs, when do you put your neck into the yoke with the sadistic little racing bird?"

"Oh, right." I lift one shoulder as if I've only just remembered Sage's existence. "I fly to Bahrain in…three, four days?"

"As if you ain't counting down the hours," Badrick says. "I wonder if she's figured out yet that you only took the piss on your blog to get her attention."

"It worked, didn't it?"

He makes another pass over the chips with a flick of the vinegar bottle. "Did you consider just being a nice bloke? Like, 'Oi, Sage! Fancy grabbing a pint with me?' That sort of thing."

"Everyone wants to know Sage Sikora. Her anger gave me a guaranteed 'in.' I stand by my strategy in this game."

He shakes his head, chuckling. "*Game*? Feckin' bellend, that's exactly your problem—always playing games. Good luck to you, then, if you're not ready to grow up yet. But you might end up with a healthy dose of humility—I have a feeling that woman gives as good as she gets."

5

BAHRAIN

ALEXANDER

I never should've made that joke during the video call about people who ride in coach. Not only did Emerald book me in coach but you'd think they'd also planted "ringers" in the adjacent seats.

On my left was a gentleman (if we may call him that) who immediately removed his shoes to fragrant effect. His carry-on was a vat of crisp cheese spheres he consumed during the flight, open-mouthed like a cow chewing his cud, when he wasn't slurping soda.

Occupying the right-hand seat was a woman holding a squalling infant who looked like a goblin and smelled like a dung heap. Midway between London and Bahrain, she changed the nappy of her homunculus *on her lap*. I protested and was ignored. When I summoned a flight attendant to complain, I was at least gratified that the woman was reprimanded for her actions, but regrettably she was wrist-deep in poo and couldn't change course.

When I finally shamble off the airplane, I duck straightaway into a men's room to assess the damage. I put my hair mostly to right, but there's nothing to be done for my rumpled suit, which looks like I've slept in it. It's charcoal plaid paired with a melon-orange necktie—one of my favorite ensembles, as the colors complement my gray eyes and auburn hair. I lift one arm and give the sleeve a sniff, hoping I don't smell like neon cheese, damp feet, and baby filth.

Shouldering my carry-on, I head back out into the throng of people and make my way toward the exits to claim a cab. A few yards after I've cleared the secure passenger area, I hear a gruff female American voice—dropped low in a parody of menace—say, "Excuse me, sir...I have a warrant for your arrest."

A pair of hands locks on to my forearm and I pivot toward the speaker. A short woman is grimacing fiercely at me, her perfect white teeth bared. Her eyes are concealed behind mirrored aviator glasses. A baseball cap with FUN POLICE emblazoned across the front hides her hair. She's wearing an oversize black field jacket with the collar popped, formfitting black leggings, and Doc Martens boots.

"I beg your pardon," I reply, pulling my arm free.

Sage Sikora whips off the sunglasses. "I thought I'd have to do something way worse to get you to *beg*." With a breezy sigh, she pockets the glasses, loops her arm through mine, and hauls me into motion toward the exits. "You're too easy, Sandy-boy."

"Miss Sage—*Salvia officinalis*, genus and species. Well met."

"*Miz*, thanks."

I angle a smirk her way. "Ooh, she diminutizes me to 'Sandy' but gets stroppy over 'miss'?"

"Watch it, pal. Don't make me put these on you." She withdraws a pair of pink plastic toy handcuffs from her pocket and dangles them from one finger.

A deliciously unwholesome image flickers through my head. "It won't be *that* easy to tame me, pet."

"I'm going to break you, not tame you."

"We'll see who gets broken." My words are aloof, but my heart is pounding. *God, she smells lovely, like warm gingerbread.* I want to pull her absurd hat off and bury my face in her aquamarine hair.

"*Wellllll*," she drawls, "place your bets on who wins, babycakes. I plan to make you suffer, and"—she wiggles her dark, perfectly arched eyebrows—"I can be very innovative."

We pass a family group apparently uniting after a long absence. A small boy and girl run into the arms of a father who kneels to catch them, raining kisses on their faces, then standing—children attached like starfish—to pull his wife into an embrace.

Sage watches with open admiration, continuing to gawk whilst walking backward, holding my arm. Her face is unguarded, sharing a small moment of joy with no fear of looking ridiculous. I wonder if I've ever felt such freedom to make an arse of myself, even as a child. I suppose it's an American thing.

She turns back around with a little hop and resumes towing me along, now singing some song in which she's threatening to use jiujitsu to kick people out of our way.

Suddenly loosing my arm without explanation, she dashes through the crowd, leaving me to stare after. Her impulsiveness is startling, but magnetic. She goes to a drinking fountain and turns her hat backward before bending to partake. I examine her lean legs, wishing the field coat were a bit shorter so I could see more. As she rotates my way again, I rearrange my infatuated expression into one of cool impatience.

"Man, look at you…" She does a froglike scowl that's meant to mimic my face. "You're uptight as fuck." She snags my arm again. "It's gonna be fun tormenting you."

We join the queue exiting into the burst of heat outside. As we reach a roadway to cross, going toward the car park, her hand slides down my arm to manacle my wrist and drag me past the line of cars waiting at a stop sign. She's almost holding my hand, and a prickle of warmth floods my torso. As we complete our crossing, I twist out of her clutches, unsettled, and swipe the sleeve of my jacket as if to remove wrinkles.

She pauses on the sidewalk, her gaze dropping to my gesture. I can't tell if she's amused or offended. She says no more for the remainder of the walk to her car, a silver Mercedes GT Coupe. Squeezing the key fob, she pops the boot and sweeps an arm at it, indicating for me to place my bag inside. When I close it, she's leaning against the roof, her heart-shaped face propped on one palm, watching me.

"Hey, question," she says.

"Yes?"

"Did you know the Latin for 'sage' off the top of your head, or did you look it up"—she grins before concluding—"because you kinda dig me?"

I place both hands on the car's roof. "You have a fantastically high opinion of yourself, pet. I knew the term because I'm very smart."

Ah, fuck…she's already got me dead to rights. I did look it up.

The hotel in which I've been installed is three miles from the Ritz-Carlton, where Sage and the rest of the Emerald team are staying. I am, however, expected to arrive at Ms. Sikora's suite by six o'clock in the morning on the first day.

When I asked for a car fare per diem, I was told to *rent a bicycle*. Left with either the option to walk or pay my own car fare, I chose the latter. It galls me to cover the expense myself, but I'm at least still rich and can scarcely be expected to wear out the leather on my Berlutis.

Sage's suite door is opened by a tall woman with skin the color of warm sandstone, clad in a saffron-bright silk robe. Unfortunately, there's not much more that's sunny about her—she responds to my winning smile with an eye roll and a flip of the door, leaving me to walk in and shut it behind myself. A long, dark braid trails down her back.

"Not a morning person?" I say with amusement.

She heads for the U-shaped sofa area and sits, then plucks up a tiny ceramic cup and takes a sip before donning a pair of tortoiseshell reading glasses and leaning toward an open laptop. "I'm not a *you* person," she replies. Flicking a hand toward the bar, she adds, "Espresso maker's over there if you need."

"I had tea already, thank you."

She shrugs, typing on the laptop without looking up. I go to the sitting area and settle on the love seat perpendicular to the woman. She's lovely, and by reputation, Sage is fluid in her dating preferences. I wonder if they're an item.

Throwing a glance at the closed bedroom door, I ask, "Are you…Ms. Sikora's girlfriend?"

She looks at me over the tops of her glasses. "No, doofus. I'm her best friend and PA, Priya."

"I assumed *I'd* be playing assistant."

"More like a gofer. You're whatever we feel like making you, *intern*. First assignment: Don't talk to me. I have *real* work to do." She nods toward the bedroom door. "Sage'll be out in a sec."

The bedroom door flies open as if on cue. Sage bounds into the room like an actor taking center stage in a musical—she's even singing, off-key and loud, wireless earbuds in her ears framed by a profusion of piercings. She's wearing neon tracksuit bottoms that swish as she walks. Her upper body is in a formfitting tank top, and the tracksuit jacket is draped over one forearm. My eyes follow the peacock feather tattoo that starts below her ear and trails down to disappear under the shirt's neckline.

She catches me staring (though "catches" isn't quite the word, considering how she courts attention) and does a dramatic twirl, throwing a mock-seductive look over one shoulder before putting on the jacket—sliding it side-to-side like a burlesque dancer with a feather boa—then zipping it. I lift an eyebrow, undeterred, my gaze dropping to her arse, obscured though it is by loose nylon fabric.

"Mornin', Sandy," she says, popping her earbuds out and zipping them into a pocket. "Ready to do my bidding like a good widdle boy?"

I pick a bit of imaginary lint off my cuff. "Tread carefully, Salvia officinalis."

She clucks her tongue, crossing to where I'm sitting and trailing a fingertip along my shoulders as she passes. "You take yourself way too seriously. It must be exhausting."

The scent of her hits me, clean and warm. She ducks into the fridge behind the bar, bobbing up with a bottle of mint-essence water.

Priya clears her throat. "So...little development with *Sports and Tortes*?" She darts a look from Sage to me, as if unsure whether she can speak freely.

Sage grips the water bottle hard, making it crunch. "What's that harpy posted about me?"

"It's not a new post; it's that she's about to nab a bazillion new followers. Y'know that hothead chef with the TV shows, Gavin Yates? He gave CJ Ardley a shout-out in a video and linked her blog to an Insta post of his because he loves her cakes."

"Half the internet 'loves her cakes,'" Sage says with a smirk. "They're always on display in bikini selfies."

"She can show off her boobs if she wants," Priya scolds. "That's not the issue."

"Why are you defending her?" Sage snaps. "Are you guys best friends now or something?"

A brief, awkward staredown follows, in which I note a surprising vulnerability in the typically prickly Sage. The ripple of anxiety on her brow is like water disturbed.

I'm used to seeing her at grands prix, in the paddock, and in press gatherings, where her hotshot energy is nothing short of preening. But here, in a less structured sphere of her life, it's as if she's not sure who to be away from racing. There's a nakedness in her essential nature, like a hermit crab dashing for the next shell.

It reminds me of myself a bit.

With a breezy chuckle, Sage concedes the battle of wills with Priya and plunks down on the love seat. "Okay, whatever. Let's give Sandy something to do. If *Sports and Tortes* is poised to skyrocket with this Gavin Yates plug, we've gotta put the pedal to the metal on making me look fun on social media. Regular posts, with viral potential. Maybe he can put a thing together."

"How's your photography game?" Priya asks me. "You seem like the kind of narcissist who's probably always taking selfies."

"I'm a journalist," I retort, ignoring the dig. "I daresay I can competently wield a camera."

Sage hums a laugh. "Ooh, you *daresay*, do you, fancy pants? And…you're not a journalist anymore," she adds with a wink. "Such a shame. Your blog *used to* be good. Like, a year ago, maybe."

I can't hide my surprise. "You read it? Before the, erm…" I'm a little embarrassed to refer to how I baited her, but I'd eat glass before admitting it.

She shrugs, one leg bouncing like a metronome ticking out allegro time. "Here and there. Before it turned into another gossipy shit-heap like *Sports and Tortes*, that is."

I confess that I do read CJ Ardley's blog. The woman is sassy and sharp, and her sultry selfies aren't without appeal. She has that north-of-forty aggressive sexuality that inspires the imaginations of hopeful schoolboys. And within every man, a hopeful schoolboy still resides.

Sage withdraws her mobile, prolonging a carefree sigh while typing something. "Anyway, I'm gonna make a shopping list for you. I want all this stuff by the end of the day." A wicked smile flickers across her expression. She pauses, gazing at the ceiling, pensive, then taps away with her thumbs again. "All righty, that should do 'er." She pokes the screen in a showy way, and my mobile chimes in my breast pocket.

I take it out and inspect the list:

- A large rubber duck
- Tap-dance shoes, women's US size 7
- Three real peacock feathers
- A string of Christmas lights (multicolor, not white)
- A vintage pulp-style detective novel
- Bag of potting soil
- A prop/joke knife (plastic, retracting blade, but realistic looking)
- A blue glitter keychain that says "I Heart Bahrain" (not a heart symbol, but the actual word "heart")
- Cervical balm (organic, fragrance-free) with applicator

By the time I've reached the end of the list, my eyebrows have practically migrated to the back of my head. "This is absurd. Where's the real list?"

She leans back on her hands, surveying me beneath low lids. "You're lookin' at it, honeybee."

"Bollocks. You're winding me up." I peruse the screen again. "A rubber duck."

"*Large* rubber duck," she clarifies.

"And where might I find such a thing?"

"Toy store's your best bet."

"Potting soil." I give her a brittle smile. "Are we a farmer now?"

"It's a critical part of a video concept I'm developing."

I glare at the list again. "The keychain design is quite specific."

"True fact." She does a little *rah-rah* fist pump. "I believe in you."

I look toward Priya in hopes of support, but she's stopped typing and is watching the interaction with amusement. "Have fun," she whispers with an evil smile.

"Oh, cheers." I lift my mobile in a sarcastic toast. Before tucking it into my pocket, I note the final item again. "And this…balm you mention."

"What about it?" Sage asks, one corner of her mouth lifted.

"This is, I presume…some stripe of…feminine product?"

"Yep."

"I've not…That is to say, I—" Clearing my throat, I press on. "I'm unclear on what this is. Or where I might procure it."

"Drugstore, obviously." Grinning, she adds, "Maybe you don't know your way around a woman's body as well as you think you do."

"I know what a cervix is," I deadpan.

"Congrats. Want a medal?" She takes a drink of her water. "Anyway, it's for cramps. But it can be hard to find. Kinda expensive, so they don't stock it right on the shelf. You have to *ask for it*. Like at the pharmacy counter."

"Ask for it?" I rotate toward Priya in appeal. "You might

have better luck with this sort of thing. Or at least more experience."

She lifts both hands. "Nope, busy. Enjoy your day."

"Think of it as an opportunity to explore the city," Sage tells me. A ringtone chimes in her pocket. "Shit, it's Dagna—she's gonna rip me a new one for being late." Backing toward the bedroom, Sage wiggles her fingers at me. "Later, Sandy. Happy hunting."

6

BAHRAIN

SAGE

Holy *balls*, this day is kicking my ass.

Dagna and the rest of my team "worked me like a rented mule," as my father charmingly puts it. Intense cardio, strength training (neck day...*I hate neck day*), reaction drills, tests with Doc Bartosz, mental-conditioning activities (I have a trainer who's specifically for playing speed rounds of the board game Go), two depressingly healthy meals (I hate sprouted mung bean burgers almost as much as I hate neck day), and four video events where—no pressure—I inspire the youth by representing All of Women in Motorsport (and try not to drop F-bombs).

I'm in my driver room in the paddock now, drinking a nasty kale smoothie in a foil pouch while I study the Go board, analyzing where I went wrong on the last round. My phone rings, and it's Dion from security.

I tap it open to speaker. "What's up, my dude?"

"Guy here named Alexander. A redheaded Brit. No pass, but he wants to see you."

I hear Alexander's voice, peevish in the background. "I'm not a sodding ginger, for fuck's sake. My hair is dark auburn."

Dion chuckles. "Forgive me, Your Majesty. You catch that, Ms. Sikora? His hair is *dark auburn*."

I roll my eyes. "Give him a guest lanyard. I'm in my driver room."

The last thing I hear before Dion hangs up is Alexander protesting, "A *temporary* pass? Do you know who I—"

A self-conscious impulse spurs me to turn in a slow circle, taking in my room, wondering what it'll look like through Alexander's eyes. It's messy, but that's how I like it. *I'm* messy. My driving style is about risk and possibility. It's hot and full of hunger, not cool and calculated.

My "relationships" are messy too, but awesomely so. Undisciplined, wild, brief. I don't stick with anyone long enough for emotionally ugly stuff to happen. I like fun, uninhibited people with larger-than-life style. Sexually adventurous sloppy loudmouths who throw themselves full throttle into a weekend of dancing and debauchery, satisfied to make memories rather than promises.

I pluck up a few articles of clothing draped like sweaty Spanish moss on a chair, hunting for an alternate place to toss them before deciding fuck it and setting them back down.

I finish the smoothie and jump-shot it into the corner trash can as my door flies open—no knock. I spin around with a bark of protest on my lips, which evaporates when I see the homicidal glare on Alexander's face. He's gripping the doorway with one hand, and from the other dangles a very large and heavy-looking shopping bag. He advances into the room—his once-pristine suit wrinkled, hair mussed—then calmly shuts the door. Near silence descends, aside from distant noises from the garage.

Alexander drops the bulging plastic bag at my feet. "It doesn't exist," he bites out. He takes another step, so close now that I can examine the freckles on his sculpture-perfect nose and cheekbones. I can smell his sweat, but weirdly in a good way. It's like a combination of ocean saltiness and slightly overdone buttered toast.

After Phaedra and I got off that call with Alexander and Nefeli last week, Phae said, *It's really a shame a guy that hot is such a garbage-monster. Hell of a face on him.* I pretended I couldn't see the appeal, but from six inches away, there's really no way to miss it.

"It. Doesn't. Fucking. *Exist*," he repeats. "Your 'lady needs.' Complete bollocks, dreamt up to make me look like an arsehole in asking for it at the shops."

Oh God…I'd almost forgotten adding that to the list. *Priceless*. My lips quirk in a smile I cover with one hand. A bubble of laughter escapes. "Um, April Fool's?"

"It's March," he snaps. "I asked half a dozen fucking chemists for your fictional remedy. Finally I concluded, 'Well, it must not be sold in this city,' and looked it up on my mobile, only to discover your little hoax."

"*Oops*," I whisper, biting my lip to keep from laughing.

He jabs an arm downward, pointing at the bag between our feet. "And I'm sure you can imagine the result of my asking shopkeepers where I might purchase a 'plastic retracting-blade knife with which to *pretend* to stab someone.' That went over marvelously."

I fiddle with the guest pass hanging at the center of his chest. "Did you find the 'I Heart Bahrain' keychain? It was important—"

"None of it's 'important'!" he cuts in.

The pupils of his gray eyes are beads of fury. He slowly moves a fingertip to poke the center of my chest. I could stop him, but I don't; it's exhilarating to see him lose his cool. Like when another driver is trying to overtake me and gets so frustrated that he makes a mistake.

Victory.

I wrap my hand around his prodding digit. "Watch who you're fingering, honeybee. It's not that kind of party."

As I hold him—*his hands are warm, fuck*—he presses into my sternum with surprising gentleness. I lower into the chair behind me, captured by the fixed beam of his glittering eyes.

He grips both arms of the chair, corralling me, and leans closer. "Hope you've enjoyed your prank, Salvia officinalis. Consider us even. I'll be on the next flight back to London."

A jet of adrenaline blooms in my chest, right under the spot where his finger was. "You can't leave yet. We have an agreement."

"I most assuredly can, and *am*." His hands tighten on the chair arms. "I won't be abused like this, not by you or anyone."

Through the fog of unwilling attraction, I remember why I can't stand this guy. The goal was to humiliate him, and he deserves far worse than my fairly innocent practical joke. *How dare he act like the injured party?*

"Abused? *You?*" I growl. "Jesus Christ, you wrote that I fucked someone to get the Emerald seat! And even before that, you came at me like I personally pissed in your cornflakes. Insulting me with your 'her talent is all in her pants' bullshit—"

"Oh, don't kick off. I said your *assets*. It was a pun."

"Flinging your old-timey insults," I go on, my voice rising, "like 'hoyden' and 'poppet,' as if your disrespect is excusable as long as you drag me in Shakespearean terms. You threw sand for months, and I finally threw back a handful. Consequences, babes." I lift a bare foot and lay it against his thigh, pushing him back so he lets go of the chair. "So if you want to avoid a defamation lawsuit, you'll pick up that bag and take it to my hotel room and quit crying. All I did was make you embarrassed in front of some store clerks. But *you*? You basically called me a no-talent slut on a world stage. *It fucking hurt me*, in case you're too dumb to realize that."

There's a flash of grief in his eyes, as if it's just occurred to him that my feelings *could* be hurt and regret is kicking in. His eyebrows draw together and his lips part as if to say something. Goddamn those lips—they're the kind I like, with that sort of tenderly angled upper lip like a Pre-Raphaelite painting.

I lean into my fury, unwilling to let this remain unsaid now that I've started. "My God, men are fucking ridiculous. You can't stand to be mocked by women—it's like the worst crime to emasculate you pack of insecure fuckwads. Meanwhile, you all can say any heinous shit you want, and if we get hurt, it's 'Don't be a humorless cunt. Can't you take a joke?' Well, I won't tolerate it. Fuck your double standard and fuck you,

Laskaris." I point at the center of my chest. "You taunt this bull, expect a fuckin' horn in the kidney."

I'm practically panting by the time I fall silent. He studies me for a long time, and I stare right back.

"For what it's worth," he says evenly, "'poppet' isn't an insult. It's an affectionate term."

"I know how to use a dictionary, asswipe. It's like a child, or a doll. Something *small*. Not a compliment."

Our staredown lingers another half minute.

He looks away first. "I suppose an apology is in order."

"You suppose right."

He reaches out as if for a handshake, and I pointedly ignore the gesture.

"I *am* sorry," he says quietly, hand dropping. "With your reputation—the mischief, the toughness, the saucy comebacks—I got carried away. My treatment of you was inexcusable."

"You're not forgiven. But…I'm glad you said it at least."

Another long silence stretches between us.

Finally, he picks up the shopping bag. "I did get the keychain, as it happens."

"You found one?"

He sinks an arm into the bag and fishes something out, then hands it over. "Not exactly. I had it made in a tourist trinket shop."

I flip it over it on my palm. Yep, blue glitter, with I HEART BAHRAIN in pink lettering. "Okay, points. That was resourceful."

The guy's a dick, but it's amusing to have him around.

"Are you really going back to London?" I fold my arms and give him a bored look, like I'm just curious but don't actually care.

"I might. But…if I didn't, what would you ask of me tomorrow?"

I spin the keychain around a fingertip, avoiding his eyes. *Spin, catch. Spin, catch.* "On your way over in the morning, I need you to pick me up a bag of pickle-flavored sunflower seeds. The kind in the shell. I'm craving them pretty bad, and Dagna won't let me have 'em."

His lips tilt in a skeptical way. "Pickle?"

"It exists! Feel free to look it up on your phone."

He takes a bracing breath and follows it with a grumpy exhale as if reluctant to say something.

"What?" I prod.

"My mobile was stolen today. I stopped for a bite in the old market district and was sitting at an outside table with a coffee and two tahina–chocolate chip biscuits. An unattended child loitering nearby was eyeing my plate with longing, so I offered him the second biscuit, and when he came over to collect it, he plucked my mobile off the table and sprinted into the crowd."

My jaw drops open. "Whoa. Mind…*blown*."

"You're shocked that I was pickpocketed?"

"I'm shocked that you shared a cookie with someone."

He laughs, and I'm pretty sure it's the first time I've heard it. *It's a nice sound, I gotta admit.*

"Surprise, surprise," he says, walking to the door. "See you in the morning, Salvia officinalis. I'll have your revolting pickle seeds."

My eyes remain on the doorway after he's exited, and… yeah, I'm confused by the guy. I mean, he's definitely a prick. Spoiled, pretentious. I'm not forgiving him for what he said in that blog post. I never give men a pass on shitty behavior. I'm not the type to look at a man and go, *But* why *is he acting like that? I need to understand him, fix him…*

Fuck that noise. People are responsible for fixing themselves. Not my circus, not my monkeys. I've never had a boyfriend or girlfriend, only hookups, and this is exactly why. I won't analyze people like they're the goddamned Rosetta Stone.

I don't care what makes Alexander Laskaris tick.

Still, he surprised me. Noticing that some random kid is staring hungrily at his cookies, then offering to share? Even *more* shocking is that he was reluctant to tell me about the incident. He seems like the type of entitled fuckchuckle who would've blamed me for his shit getting stolen, like, *I was running all over town for you and I got pickpocketed, so you owe me a new phone.* But I suspect he might not've mentioned it if I hadn't brought it up.

Wheeling around, I stalk back to the Go board and continue my strategy analysis. I place a fingertip on one of the Go stones and reposition it, and the slide of that cool stone against the board reminds me of when Alexander touched my chest and nudged me into the chair.

"He's not gonna win me over by pretending to be a Nice Guy," I mutter. "The rules don't change mid-race."

THE NEXT DAY

I'd already left for the paddock when Alexander arrived this morning, but when I get back in the early evening, my pickle-dust-coated sunflower seeds are on the coffee table. Perched on the corner of the bag like a hat is an origami-folded triangular pocket with a note:

> The requested item, Your Grace
>
> Respectfully, ~A
> P.S. New mobile, same number

I tear open the bag. Flopping onto the sofa, I crunch the seeds, depositing damp split shells into the origami pocket. I send a text to Alexander's new phone: "Your Grace"? Why don't I get something fancier like Your Eminence?

Immediately he replies. Your Eminence is for cardinals of the Catholic Church. I suppose I could upgrade you to Your Highness or Your Majesty. But you'll have to earn it.

"Oho!" I say aloud, sinking deeper into the cushions. "Very sassy."

I text back. Dude, you are on thin ice with me already. Your next question should be "How else may I do your bidding today?" Don't push your luck or I'll use you as a fuckin footstool.

A few minutes pass and I wonder if he's got his feathers ruffled, but then he says, I can be there in fifteen minutes if you need anything. Aren't I supposed to help you create a video?

I'd forgotten about that, but now I have to play it out, so I tell Alexander, Yeah let's shoot a post or two. Make it snappy, intern.

When I let him into the suite, it's been exactly fifteen minutes, but he's totally chill like he didn't hurry—bespoke teal suit and a plum shirt unbuttoned practically halfway to show off his chest, not a "dark auburn" hair out of place.

He saunters to the sofa and manspreads himself, one arm uncurled across the back. I spit a few sunflower shells pointedly into the paper envelope, eyeing him.

"Putting that to use, I see," he says, and the sly look on his face makes me wish I hadn't spat anything out in front of him.

I drop his repurposed note into the trash can. "Wouldn't've taken you for a craftsy guy."

"I've loads of hidden talents." He glances around the room. "Where's Priya?"

"Downstairs at the gym. So, about the video thing. Ideas?"

His eyebrows lift. "What happened to your purported 'concept'?"

I step onto the adjacent love seat and perch on the back so I can look down at him. "Yeah, there was no concept. I just wrote down random shit to keep you running around town all day."

A brief narrowing of his gray eyes makes me think I've won and he's going to throw a hissy fit, but he just chuckles. "Well played. But"—he points at me, and I feel it like a touch—"fool me once."

"*Psh!* You think I'd recycle the same prank? I have a hundred better ways to torture you."

"Seems you'd have far more pressing demands on your time, but make a meal of it."

It's annoying how this guy turns even my wins into losses. Now I look pathetic for putting this much energy into it. I slide down onto my back on the love seat and pull a throw pillow over my face and comically scream into it. When I fling the cushion aside and look at Alexander, his smile is surprisingly genuine rather than smug like I expected.

"Rough day, pet?"

"I'm fucking tired. And tomorrow's press day. I don't have the energy to 'be delightful on socials.' I shouldn't have dragged you over here. I guess just take a pic of me like this"—I flip him off with both hands and give a sarcastic open-mouthed grin—"and let's call it."

He gets to his feet, and when he leans forward, the partially unbuttoned shirt gaps open and I see more of his chest and I feel like some creeper ogling women on the subway.

Why does this shitbag have to be so cute? He could at least smell less delicious—that'd be helpful. But no. The complete wanker I thought I was going to put through the wringer is putting *me* through the wringer, with his smooth voice and big pretty hands and a scent that makes me want to bite his neck. *Hard*.

"Where's that sack of nonsense you had me purchase?" he asks.

I throw one arm over my eyes and flip a wave toward the bedroom. "Chair in the corner. Why?"

I hear him walk off, then the bag crinkling as he brings it back. It thumps down and he rifles through it, setting items onto the coffee table. "Plenty of possibility here," he says in a thinking way. "I don't suppose you can actually tap-dance?"

I blow a raspberry. "Yeah, no. I'm a fucking great dancer, but not with anything formal. I just like dancing in clubs."

More crinkling. Then, almost under his breath, "I'd like to see that."

I uncover my eyes. "What, me dancing?"

"Indeed." He takes one of the shiny black tap shoes from the box and holds it up. "Let's start with this."

"I already said I don't know how."

He takes his phone from the inside pocket of his suit jacket. "YouTube. There's a tutorial for everything. People would find it charming. Watching someone who's enormously skilled in one field show a relatable lack of skill in another is funny. You'd be sure to get plenty of views. Shall we?"

I sit up slowly, trying to look casual. "You think I'm *enormously skilled*? Like, as a driver?"

He breaks our gaze, tapping something into his phone. "Obviously so, Salvia officinalis."

"You said I was a no-talent gimmick who 'slept my way to the middle.'"

He sets his phone down with a sigh. "I never thought that." One side of his attractive mouth tightens. "I was courting your attention. Picking a fight was asinine, but…effective."

"Bullshit," I shoot back. "You're saying this because you want me to forgive you and call off the internship so you can go home and, like, do whatever you posh douchebags do with your time."

He pushes the pink shoebox across the table toward me. "Believe what you wish. In the meantime, I'll do the tasks required of me. Let's learn how to tap dance."

"All right," Alexander says, peering at his phone and rotating his free hand, directing me as the camera runs. "And again! Shuffle, brush, ball change, repeat."

I switch my weight to the other foot and fling my arms out and completely fuck up the simple move. With a screech of frustration, I go into a ridiculous stompy dance, chicken-flapping and spinning like a manic toddler who needs a nap. "Delete that one. Let's start over."

"I'll do no such thing. Your profound clumsiness is bewitching."

"Hey!"

He gives me a wink, and usually I find a wink cheesy but it's not bad on him.

"Did you claim you're a good dancer?" he taunts. "Because I'm skeptical."

"Get bent!" I say with a laugh. "I'm just not good with stuff that has rules. I'm a free spirit, babes. 'A rider at the gates of dawn, and I take no prisoners.'"

A shocked smile freezes on his face. "You know that show?"

I'm equally shocked that he recognizes my quote from *The Young Ones*. "Yeah, my brother and I watched my mom's DVDs of it constantly when we were teenagers." A little wave of sadness goes through me, remembering when Jules and I still got along, and even hung out and watched shows together. I push the feeling away and plant my hands on my hips. "Hold on, you and I aren't, like…*bonding* here. You're still a total fuckchuckle, even if you have good taste in old sitcoms."

He cradles his perfect jaw with a mock-pensive look. "Is that an upgrade, from 'posh douchebag' to 'fuckchuckle'? Be still, my heart."

"Yeah, don't count on it." I take my Emerald F1 hat off and Frisbee it at him, and he ducks. "Fine, go ahead and send that video to Pri and she can post it in the morning."

He inspects it, staring at his phone with a little smile that's almost tender. Finally he looks up. "Would you let me write the copy as well?"

"*Ha!* As if. You've done enough damage, writing shit about me." I hop on one foot, wrestling off one of the tight tap shoes.

"That's why I'd like to make it up to you. I can send it to Priya for approval first."

I wrench off the second shoe and underhand them toward the sofa. "I mean, go for it, but she doesn't have any obligation to use what you write, got it? I still don't trust you."

"Understandable."

I pull my hair out of its ponytail and can't help noticing that he watches me as I run my fingers through it. I scowl and pass him, trying not to notice his warm, spicy smell as I go to the sofa and flop down.

"Okay, you're off duty, Sandy. Hit the bricks." I almost thank him, then decide he doesn't deserve it yet.

He pockets his phone. "Anything I can bring you in the morning to make press day less trying?"

I close my eyes, feigning exhaustion, but to be honest I'm just trying not to look at his tailored trousers and wonder what's underneath that pricey fabric. What the hell is wrong with me? I can't wait for the Australian GP. There are some great clubs in Melbourne, and clearly I need to get laid.

"Sure. A jasmine tea with agave syrup." I open my eyes to peek his way, then close them again. "And if I'm not too wrecked tomorrow night, we can do some more videos. Deal?"

"As ever, I am your creature," he says with amusement. "Good night, Salvia."

I keep my eyes closed as he leaves, like a kid "hiding" from the monster under the bed.

The monster I'm hiding from, I realize with dismay, *is me. I think I might've hired this guy not as payback but because I want to fuck him senseless.*

7

BAHRAIN

THREE DAYS LATER

SAGE

I don't think anyone is above experiencing schadenfreude, so I take that into consideration when strangers are giddy about my failures. The flip side of having little girls lose their minds with joy when I sign their shirts and caps is having to deal with sexist assholes on social media telling me I should "pack up my Barbie Power Wheels and go home." Or having Maya Ardley's grudge-holding mom act like it was some sinister conspiracy that I just plain *outdrove* her daughter in testing with Harrier.

But despite being well-conditioned to endure shit-talk, the day I'm having today is hitting me right in my worst insecurities.

Not even making it into the top 15 out of 20 on my first qualifying session of the year? It isn't a good look. *Sports and Tortes* will definitely gloat. So many eyes are on me, judging whether Emerald were nuts to take a chance on me. And there's a clause in my three-year contract that says if I trail Cosmin, Emerald's other driver, by more than a hundred points at the end of the season, Emerald have the option to put someone else in my seat.

When I head out in Q1 today, the car is fighting me. I'm so far off the pace it's heartbreaking. In dialogue with my race engineer Imani about the details, we agree that we should revert to yesterday's setup. I come into the pit and they wheel my car backward into the garage to make some quick adjustments.

Okay, back out for my next attempt...

Things are feeling great until I lock it up in a corner, compromising my exit and losing time down the next straight, and creating a flat spot on the tyre so I'm getting a vibration. Into the pit again, with minutes left. I'm in the drop zone, not yet having banked a fast enough lap to advance to Q2.

Back out with fresh tyres, I'm on a hot lap.

This is the one.

"You're purple in sector 2, Sage," Imani tells me.

Fastest on track!

The moment expands around me. My heart bounds with a powerful rhythm like a sprinting predator closing in on prey that's inches from their jaws...

Oh, fucking *what*???

João Valle, my former teammate at Harrier, overcooks it and puts his car into the wall. As I pass the debris field, I know a red flag is coming. It's too close to the end for the session to be restarted, which means my gorgeous lap just went into the shitter, and I'm out.

Sure, Q1 got red-flagged because of João. But at the end of the day, critics will say it's my fault: I could've honed my setup better in practice yesterday, I could've avoided locking it up in that corner and needing to pit for fresh tyres.

Sadly, they won't be wrong.

It's nine p.m. when I get back to the suite, and I know I'm supposed to go to sleep immediately—tomorrow is race day, and everything will be in motion before dawn—but I'm too nervous. *My first grand prix with Emerald.*

I wish I weren't starting it from sixteenth on the grid.

The world is watching.

Judging.

This will be my tenth grand prix. I drove eight races for Harrier the year before last after João Valle got a penalty-points race ban, then broke his femur in a snowboarding accident like a dipshit. Last season I subbed in for Valle's teammate when he got an appendectomy (relatable!) and I scored a killer fourth place in quali. But this will be my first race as a non-reserve driver, and my first time driving in Bahrain.

I have a night-before-the-GP routine that worked pretty well for me during that eight-race stretch. First a light dinner—tonight a frittata with salmon and vegetables, along with quinoa salad. Low-impact workout with lots of flexibility stuff, followed by a massage. Next I'll go to my room and put on some music, read through the notes Imani sent me, play a few solitaire rounds of the card game SET, take a bath, and go to sleep.

That *was* my plan. But as I come into the suite, I hear Priya on the phone in her room and she sounds upset, so I sneak to the open doorway to eavesdrop.

"We should tell her, Julian," she says. "She needs to know, regardless of where you two are with each other right now."

Needs to know what?

"It's three weeks until the Australian GP," she goes on. "I don't want the stress of holding this in for that long. It shouldn't be a secret."

Details, please!

"No, honey…no no no. Don't get upset. Please? I won't tell her what happened to you. No, I *won't*. I wish I could hold you right now. Mount Arapiles is only three hours from Melbourne—I'll come to you there. We'll figure this out, don't worry."

Figure what out?

"Where were you when it happened?"

When what happened, dammit?

"Julian, *no*. Don't do anything nuts, all right? Just *wait*. I'm here for you."

What's he doing that's "nuts"? Dammit, I should just storm in and demand answers…

"Okay, but I've gotta go. Sage is gonna be back soon."

I hear a rustling sound and I'm pretty sure she's headed for the living room. I dash to the front door and slip out into the hallway, shutting the door silently behind me.

What the hell are they hiding?

Jules must be in some kind of trouble, and on a certain level it feels bad that he's telling her and not me. But that's stupid, right? Why would I expect he'd tell me *anything*? Pri is the rescuer, the nurturer. I'm the hothead who punched him on the arm rather than having a serious conversation with him when I caught him with the pills.

I kind of hate myself right now...

I wish I could stress-eat the sloppiest mile-high hamburger ever. Stacked with a greasy layer of onion rings. Enough melting cheese to constipate a flock of geese. A slab of chocolate cake on the side. And two fingers of bourbon, neat.

Fuck it.

I head for the elevators and go down to the lounge to break some rules.

━━━

The lounge's dress code says *casual* when I check the website, but the place is all dark paneling and luxurious upholstery and gilded tables and thick rugs. It looks like where rich Edwardian dandies would go to smoke their pipes and talk about…I don't know, shooting big game and colonizing someplace?

I take a chair. It's so swanky here that "casual" or not, my Damned MACHINE GUN ETIQUETTE T-shirt feels out of place. My blue hair is freshly dyed and pulled into a sweaty topknot. A guy in his fifties at a nearby table gives me that look recognizable as a combination of *What's wrong with youngsters nowadays?* and *Yeah, I would*, eyeing my neck tattoo and holding his lips in a way that's both prim and lascivious. *Ew.*

I flash a sarcastic toothy smile before turning to put in my order on Emerald's team account. I ask for a slider and a side of onion rings, chocolate cake, and a bourbon.

While waiting, I swipe open my phone and compose then delete texts to Priya.

Me: Sooooo...is there anything you'd like to tell me?

Me: Every time you lie, Priya Ramachandran, a hummingbird collides with a windmill and DIES

I growl in frustration and smack my phone face down on the table, too hard.

Self-conscious, I look up to see if anyone caught my little tantrum. My gaze lands across the room where there's a hot guy watching me, his hands paused over the keyboard of an open laptop. There's an Irish coffee mug beside it, half empty.

What the hell...?

Alexander raises his eyebrows, then closes his laptop and slides it into a leather messenger bag before shouldering it, standing, and plucking up his coffee. I study his approach. Cream-colored linen trousers and a matching vest, wine-red dress shirt beneath, rolled to the elbows. Gold necktie pulled loose, top two buttons undone, displaying that peek of chest.

He sinks into the wing chair opposite me.

"Why are you here?" I ask. "You have your own hotel."

"You mean that delightful accommodation where the sink water was half rust, and I woke this morning to find a spider the size of a steak-and-ale pie on my pillow? For some inexplicable reason, I gave it up and moved to a suite here. For which I'm paying."

"This place is booked during race week."

"I have my methods." He checks his Patek Philippe wristwatch, then slides the laptop out of his bag and opens it. After perusing something, brow stern, he snaps it shut again.

A flutter of paranoia goes through me, considering the miserable qualifying session I had. "What are you writing?" I fold my arms. "Is it about me?"

"It isn't, you vain girl," he says with a twinkle in his eye. "But why the hostility? You've liked the things I've written this week for the social media posts. I thought I was crawling back into your good graces, no?"

Alexander has created good content this week, it's true. Those props I had him buy have been put to surprisingly great use.

The tap-dance video was a hit—he was right about that. The next night we did a pic of me (fully dressed in my racing suit) sitting in the unfilled bathtub with that stupid rubber duck perched on my head. Then one of me peeking seductively over the top of a vintage sexy detective novel called *A Not-So-Nice Girl*. He even posed for a "revenge pic" Priya took last night, where I'm holding the prop knife to Alexander's throat and he's looking comically terrified.

He's been a little bit fun. But it's not like we're friends or anything.

"I wasn't writing just now at any rate," he assures me, re-rolling his left sleeve so it's more symmetric with the other.

"Lemme check." I beckon. "And no clicking anything away."

"Are you daft? You've no right to my laptop."

"Whatsa matter, Sandy? Afraid I'll see your porn tabs?"

He gives me a lofty look. "Contrary to your delusion that you own me, pet, I'm untrammeled by your authority."

"Don't blow smoke up my ass, Captain Thesaurus. What is it you don't want me to see? It's something time-pegged, if you can't resist checking it." With a squeak, I clasp my hands. "Oh my God…Are you on a dating site DMing with a girl? Lemme see."

"Absolutely not."

"Aww, c'mon," I coax. "I'll show you mine if you show me yours."

"Nothing good starts that way."

"*Everything* good starts that way."

His slate-dark eyes flick to his watch, and after pinning me with a long look of consideration, he cracks the laptop open. I jump up and dash around to his chair, hip-checking his knees to force him to make room as I perch on a corner.

On the screen is something called plumvinylauctions.com, and there's a picture of a boring-looking record with a plain white label. I reach for the track pad and Alexander gives the back of my hand the tiniest scolding pat before refreshing the page.

"Fuckin' A!" I exclaim as I zero in. "Twenty-three *thousand* dollars? For a record?"

"A very rare John Coltrane test pressing." He angles closer to the screen, long lashes dipping as he squints in disapproval. "Bugger all. Takahiro…*why*? Just let me bloody have it." His fingers fly across the keyboard as he ups his bid by another grand.

"Who's Takahiro?"

"A rival collector."

"It *soooo* tracks that you're one of those superior assholes who listen to jazz and collect rare vinyl. Could you get any snobbier?"

"Stunning. None taken." He leans toward the screen again, and with his movement is a waft of a smoky-ambery cologne. He refreshes the page. "Forty seconds 'til close. I've got him on the ropes."

I sit back to settle in for the end of the auction, leaning slightly on Alexander. "I dunno, dude. Jazz leaves me cold. It always sounds like Linus is about to explain the meaning of Christmas to Charlie Brown."

"Little savage," he says with an edge of affection.

"And the whole 'Ooh, vinyl just sounds better' thing—what horseshit! A bunch of hissing and popping isn't an improvement. Digital is way smoother and more efficient."

"Is a vibrator an 'improvement' over a partner?" he asks lightly.

I'm a brazen loudmouth, but I didn't expect the comment, so I feel my chest and neck heat in a blush of surprise. "Uh, what the fuck?"

His pretty lips tilt in a *gotcha* smirk. "Plastic is smoother, and a motor is efficient, wouldn't you say? A recording on vinyl is warmer and more real. Like human skin."

Our eye contact holds for a few seconds; then with a small gasp he shifts his eyes to the screen, leaning in with a serious look and submitting a bold final bid with a three-thousand-dollar jump. He seems to hold his breath, waiting, and upon next screen refresh, it's confirmed that "A£exandertheGr8" bagged a ridiculous piece of thirty-thousand-dollar plastic with four songs.

"Congrats, I guess?" I say. "You win at having more money than sense."

"Such a brat," he pronounces, rolling his eyes. "This is precisely why I didn't want you to look. I don't need the fuckin' grief."

A server appears with my food and bourbon. I dart to my chair, eyes wide, tracking the server's every move as items are placed on the table. Alexander taps away at his keyboard, presumably addressing some auction-finalizing details. After a moment he throws a glance at the food, which I'm staring at but not touching.

"Pre-race carb-loading?" he asks.

"I wish. I'm not actually allowed to have any of this. Have you eaten dinner yet?" I lift the top bun on the slider and pile on a few of the smaller onion rings. "I'm only taking a single bite and sip. Someone should eat the rest."

"*One bite?*" A ghost of an impish smile. "I'd not have credited you with that level of discipline, my little hedonist."

"Do you want my leftovers or not?" I pick up the slider. With the added onion rings, it's too tall to properly fit it into my mouth, but *fuck it*, why be dainty?

My eyes never leaving Alexander's, I indelicately cram the stack between my teeth and sink through layers of seasoned meat, fluffy bread, fried onions, and drippy sauce. Holy fuck, it's the best thing I've tasted since my mom's cooking when I was visiting home. An involuntary groan escapes me. My eyes close as I chew, setting the slider blindly onto the plate.

I keep them closed, meditating on the flavor and texture of this single precious bite as I work it around in my mouth. Too soon, it's over. I swallow, then open my eyes while grabbing my napkin to wipe the grease off my lips.

The look on Alexander's face says it all.

"I'd buy tickets to see that again," he murmurs, his tone playfully gritty.

"What a perv." I shove the plate an inch in his direction. "All yours, honeybee."

He puts his laptop into the leather satchel, then reaches for a knife and fork. With easy precision, he carves out a bite and pops it into his mouth, and…dammit, I absolutely *am* watching him do it, and he's enjoying every second of the attention. I snap out of it, plucking up the dessert fork and gathering the cake toward me.

I rotate my plate, inspecting the best bite since I only get one, then stab into the middle, freeing a chunk with a ribbon of gooey-looking ganache down the center. I lift it slowly, again trying to make this a full experience—admiring the look and smell.

Alexander cuts an onion ring in half and forks it up. "This is quite good, and I was hungrier than I thought. Thank you."

"No prob." I bring the small, moist wedge of chocolate perfection closer to my face. "Okay, no talking. Don't distract me—I'm almost there."

We both realize how it sounds and dissolve into laughter.

"Let no one say I impeded your pleasure, Salvia officinalis," he quips.

I insert the bite and smush cake against the roof of my mouth with my tongue so the ganache oozes out, then chew, leisurely.

He's still watching. And part of me is very into it.

"You have gorgeous lips," Alexander says, reaching across the table to break off a corner of the cake and put it into his mouth. He licks a frosting-smeared fingertip, quick and neat, but still sexy enough that I can't help staring.

Dammit, I don't want that to be as hot as it is.

I'm broadcasting signals like a horny SETI cruising for hot space alien action. My tongue darts out to touch a morsel of stray crumb on my upper lip.

Jesus, what am I doing? Flirting with this fuckwit just because he's pretty and I haven't gotten laid since January...

I break our blatant eyefuck and lift the tumbler of bourbon. "Well, here's mud in your eye, Sandy." I take a generous gulp. "I gotta get some sleep."

"Bereft at the loss of your company, pet."

"Oh, quit making fun of me."

A small frown mars his brow, then evaporates. "I assure you, I'm not."

Argh, why do I kinda want to keep hanging out with him?

My stomach sinks as I remember Priya's furtive conversation with my brother. I just know if I go back to the suite now and she's awake, I'm going to start an argument. I almost laugh as I think of how hilariously appalled she'd be if I went back to Alexander's room with him. She trusts him even less than I do. (Probably because she's not swayed by this weird hormonal thing that's happening to me, but whatever.)

I allow myself another tiny sip of the bourbon, then set it in front of Alexander. "Hey, wanna go to your room and do another video? Like, right now?"

I expect him to leer and say something cheeky, but his expression is…What *is* that? Gentle and sad and maybe a little hopeful. It passes, and he picks up the glass, tipping back the liquor in one smooth, open-throated shot, then fixing his gaze on mine.

Look at those damned eyes of his. I can only imagine the power they'd have if I *really* liked the guy. *Fuuuuuuck, he has me rattled…*

But then he gives me a slow smile, right back to his sly, flirty self.

"You're on, Salvi. Lead the way."

8

BAHRAIN

SAME NIGHT

ALEXANDER

Sage claims she's tired, but I see no evidence of that. On the way up to our floor, she bounces on her feet in the lift, hopscotch-leaps along the patterned hall carpeting on our floor, and does a martial-arts kick over the top of a rubbish bin, concluding in a spin and some thrown air punches. She's a bright little electron, and being in her atomic field is exhilarating.

Of course, I keep myself to a mild stroll, hands in my pockets, as if unaffected. We pass my room and turn down the next hall, headed for the VIP suites so Sage can retrieve the video props. She's doing an alternating sideways gallop, singing to herself, moved by her own internal music. She arrives at her door while I'm still half a hallway behind, and swiping her key card, holds up a finger to let me know she'll be right back.

I catch up and lean against the opposite wall, waiting. Seconds later, I hear her headed for the door again, in raised-voice conversation. The door is flung open and Sage bounds out, plastic sack slung over one shoulder like a burglar, with Priya trailing behind.

Priya glares at me, then at Sage. "You've got to be kidding. Surely you have better *taste*." The emphasis implies a callback to some previous conversation between the two.

Shoving the bag at me to carry, Sage pivots toward her friend and leans against my side. "Aww, you're gonna hurt his feelings."

"He doesn't *have* any," Priya snaps. "Aside from 'horny' and 'superior.'"

I offer a bland smile. "Don't mind me—I'm just holding the wall up."

She ignores this, and her expression goes from annoyed to plaintive as she stares at Sage. "You said on the plane that we're gonna *talk about stuff* rather than you throwing tantrums. You're obviously pissed off, but I can't fix it if you're fake with me."

Sage gives a dismissive snort. "Nothing to discuss, babes. If you need someone to keep you company that bad, I'm sure you can call Julian."

The name seems to hit Priya like a slap, and there's a moment of tense silence between the two; I feel like quite the gooseberry. Are they in competition over some man? An ex of Sage's, whom Priya is now dating? The bitterness is palpable.

"Is that what this is about?" Priya asks.

Grabbing my shirtsleeve at the bicep, Sage pulls me into motion. "I'll be back in a few hours!" she throws over her shoulder.

"Sage, this is stupid," Priya calls after us. "Tomorrow's the GP. You need to go to bed."

Spinning to walk backward, arm linked through mine, Sage

replies, "Who says that's *not* where I'm going?" As I'm dragged around the corner, I hear the suite door click shut. Once we're out of sight, Sage lets me go.

We proceed to the door of my room and I usher her through. Inside, she chews at her cheek with a faraway look. Brow knitted, she plants her hands on her hips and does a circuit of the modest room, dominated by one king-size bed.

"Salvi," I say, dropping the bag on a chair and following her to the window, "why are you winding up your friend? You seemed to imply to her that we're here for…other reasons."

She wrinkles her nose at me. "Just a li'l mischief, honeybee."

She looks back out the window, and the way the city lights below cast a glow on her face reminds me of childhood, holding a buttercup under someone's chin for its golden reflection. This woman affects me so oddly, I scarcely know what to make of it. From afar, it was just lust and curiosity. Now that I'm near her, it's stitched through with a bright thread of something that tugs at the heart of me. I'm both restless and relaxed, like the feeling of seeing London draw nearer out the window of a plane when I'm arriving home.

The words escape me before I can evaluate the emotion that spurs them. "I won't have sex with you as a practical joke, or because you're rebounding or feeling spiteful."

Her stunned laugh is almost a hiccup. "Well, that's mighty presumptuous! You're in no danger. I was just messing with Pri." After a pause in which mortification curdles in me, she asks, "But seriously, you wouldn't? Like, if I asked nice? I assumed you're kind of a slut."

I perch on the arm of a chair, keenly feeling the danger in

our proximity. "Not for the reasons I stated, no. Though possibly for others. I can't claim I don't fancy you."

"What kind of other reasons? *Love?*" She adds this last word with a disdainful sarcasm.

"Honest attraction would suffice. I'm far from impoverished sexually, where I'd leap at any offer, and no one likes the feeling of being a pawn in a war in which they have no stake."

"Huh." She folds her arms. "That's fair. But for realsies, I wasn't angling for the D." Her smile spreads wickedly. "Though I'll admit, the look on Pri's face was hilarious when I told her I was going to your room." She crosses to the props bag and peers inside, withdrawing the fairy lights. "What could we do with these?"

I take the box from her, opening it and unslotting the string from its confines. "Hmm. Let's light it up and think a bit." I find an outlet and plug the lights in. They're multicolored, the bulbs in the shape of stars, and flash in a steady rhythm.

"Ooh, disco lights," Sage says.

"Perfect. Let's get you dancing, then."

She cackles. "I'm not cramming my feet into those tap shoes again!"

"No, just…however you like." I hold the string out for Sage to take. "I'll put on music."

"Not your crappy jazz, though." She takes her mobile from a pocket. "Lemme pick."

She connects to my speaker and scrolls around, then finds the song she wants and kicks her shoes off before making a gazelle-like leap onto my bed. While jumping up and down, she ties the bottom of her T-shirt into a knot at her rib cage, showing off an arresting expanse of chiseled stomach. "Hand me the Christmas lights!" she calls out, breathless.

I pass the long string to her and she drapes it across her shoulders and arms, one forearm across her face like a vampire with a cape. I pluck up my mobile to record her performance.

She sings along, shimmying and twirling on the bed, her bare feet twisting eddies into the duvet. A hundred things crowd and push through my mind like commuters on a tube platform. I don't speak any of it aloud, not wanting to ruin the video (or look like a mug), but inside, I'm saying, *You're dazzling. I've never met anyone like you. I could watch you forever and not get bored. I want to unwrap you like a perpetual Christmas…*

As the song hits its finale, she belly flops onto the mattress and rolls herself into the fairy lights like spaghetti around a fork and wails out the final words along with the singer. The music ends and I can hear her heavy breathing. Tangled and giddy and glittering, she catches her breath, and her expression as she meets my eyes is almost shy. I stop recording and place my mobile on the table before going to the bed and reclining so we're parallel.

She tips her head sideways. "How was that?"

"Honestly lovely. You're…more like a weather event than a person sometimes. It's invigorating."

"Yeah? Thanks. I think." She wriggles out of the grip of the lights and shoves the string to the floor in a clatter of plastic. "That was fun."

"Agreed." We watch each other, our faces a foot apart.

She sits up, cross-legged. "Hey, make me some origami. You can do more than triangles, right? Like animals and stuff?"

"It's been years, pet. Triangles are easy." She looks

disappointed, so I add, "I might remember how to make a frog that jumps, but no guarantees."

"Great!" She clambers off the bed and goes to the desk, withdrawing a notepad with the hotel's logo across the top and tearing off a sheet.

I scoot back and we end up diagonal on the huge bed, facing each other. My stockinged feet rest on the night table and her legs swing behind her, ankles twining. I take the paper from her and first have to remove part of the rectangle to make a square. She watches as I run the folded bit across my tongue to make it tear easier. The usual crass comment I'd make under the circumstances retreats like a wallflower at a cotillion.

I fuss with the paper, finding my way, making errors and unfolding, starting again, gradually progressing.

She edges closer on her elbows. "Wait, shouldn't that bit fold the other way?" She takes the paper. "Like this. So it'll pop up." She hands it back.

"Perfect. Sharp eye." I continue defining a concertinaed frog limb. "We make a good team," I say lightly, not looking at her.

"Both talented with our hands."

Her tone is sly, and I slant a look up at her. "You're flirting."

"Little bit, sure."

No more is said until I complete the frog. Laying it on my flattened palm, I press down on the business end and it gives a feeble hop, falling to the duvet, on its back like a dead insect.

"Don't quit your day job," Sage teases.

"Tragically, I've no future as a world-renowned paper-folding artist."

Sage turns the frog over and prods it some more, her chin

resting on one hand. I inspect her pixyish face, the curve of her lips, the naked fringe of eyelashes, and can viscerally imagine kissing her. My hand in her pastel-blue tresses, cupping the warmth of her tattooed neck, leaning in. A pause in which the intimacy of eye contact from an inch away stops you with a playful push like magnets of the same pole, and you know that beyond this point, everything changes.

Her eyes, golden as the bourbon we shared an hour ago, lock with mine, and I see a flicker of invitation there. The unmistakable sign—her glance at my lips, then back up to see if I do the same—announces that a kiss is imminent.

Without warning, she scuttles backward off the bed, standing and stretching. "Send me that video, 'kay? I gotta hang it up and get some sleep. Tomorrow's kind of a big deal."

"It is."

She yanks the fairy lights from the socket and stuffs them into the bag, then pockets her mobile. "And, uh, you don't have to stay for the race. You should go back to London now."

I get to my feet. "You don't need me?"

"I thought you wanted to leave," she says, a bit peevish.

My eyes narrow. "Is this…" My words falter and I point at the bed. "Did something almost happen here, and now you're angry with me? Because I felt as if—"

"Nothing 'almost happened.' Jesus, you *wish*." She unties the knot in her shirt and swipes the wrinkles. "You know what? Skip Saudi too. Don't show up until Melbourne. It's… probably better."

"For whom?"

She rolls her eyes and turns away, grabbing the props bag.

"I'll call if I need anything before the Australian GP. But, y'know, I *won't*." She backs toward the door.

"You're punishing me and I'm unsure why."

Her expression darkens. "Got about a year for me to list off the reasons? We can start with your fucking blog."

So. Here we are, in a dance that feels like ten steps forward, nine back. "All right. I'd hoped we might move past that, but apparently not yet."

She twists the neck of the bag. "Look, you have your moments, and you're hot and all that, but I don't trust you. And I can't afford a distraction." She pulls a wry face. "I can get away with taking one sample bite of cake, one sip of booze. But I'm not, uh, not sampling *you*."

I follow her to the doorway and open it for her. "That's probably wise," I say, flashing a devilish smile despite the sting in my heart. "I don't think you could stop at one bite either."

LONDON

ALEXANDER

I've been home for over a week now but have felt a bit shit. I've spent my time playing my piano and day-drinking a case of 2009 Chateau Latour. Badrick is in France visiting Laurent's family, or I might've had a pint with him…though maybe not, since it would take roughly thirty seconds for him to diagnose my malady and give me no end of grief about it.

Salvia officinalis.

The deluge of her fierce, impulsive nature is like a mad cloudburst, and I submitted to the storm and opened my arms until I was soaked to the skin.

I can't count the number of times I've imagined caressing the strong curve of her tattooed neck, the ink peeking between my spread fingers. Walking her back against the nearest wall, our eyes locked. Bracing her in place and devouring that sweet, impertinent mouth of hers…

It's doing my head in, longing for Sage. I can't wait for the week of the Australian GP when I can see her again. I want to hear that taunting chuckle of hers, catch her scent as she dances past, oblivious and grand in her unselfconscious movements.

But part of me hopes she sends a message saying, Don't bother coming to Melbourne; I've had my sport of you and it's done, thus freeing me from my intractable lust. Maybe then I can return to the hunt with uncomplicated—and less venomous—prey.

I'm sitting at the piano, fueled on wine and depression as I lean into the angst of "River Flows in You," when my front door flies open. I don't even have to look; my mother is the only one with a key.

I close my eyes briefly, sighing, but don't miss a note. "Can I help you with something?" I ask the busy clatter of her high heels, which grows louder as she advances to the living room.

The noise muffles as she steps onto the Oushak rug. "What are you moping about?" she asks with her trademark hint of mockery. "You always play the Yiruma when you're moping."

I continue to the end of the measure, then drop my hands

discordantly to the keys. "No, when I'm feeling blue, I'm more likely to play Brubeck's 'The City Is Crying.'"

Never mind that I did *just play it…*

I lift the marmalade jar of red wine from its makeshift coaster—a takeaway menu from a nearby kebab shop—and polish off the last inch before lifting the bottle and finding it empty.

"Hmm." She comes to the piano. Flicking a red-taloned fingertip against the paper menu, she pulls a face. "Are you a student in a bedsit? Bloody hell." She waves an arm at the room. "Like a haunted attic in here. Litter everywhere"—in evidence she gestures at the menu, a stack of neatly folded laundry I've simply neglected to put away, and a pair of slippers on the floor—"and an empty bottle at noon. Drinking out of a jam jar? How very bohemian. Surely you're not taking unemployment so hard." She strides toward my window to throw back the drapes, inviting a feeble wash of rainy-day light.

"I'm rich. I've no need to be employed," I say, dancing an arpeggio up the keyboard.

"Good lord—" She cuts off and forces out a cough as if choked by dust. "At least get your maid in here to hoover and run a rag over things."

I stand to take the wine remnants to my open kitchen, setting the bottle in the bin and the jar in the sink. Shoving the wine-stained menu into a drawer, I lean against the counter and fold my arms. "Might I inquire as to the reason you're gracing me with your presence, Mother? Just here to take the piss?"

"No, here to take your art," she shoots back. "I want your Marguerite Horner. I've had my home office redone, and a little black-and-white dash of drama would be perfect between the south-facing windows. Where is it?" She plants both hands on her hips and scans the room, then takes off for my bedroom when she doesn't spot what she's looking for.

"You can't have that one," I protest, following at her heels. "I love it. If you're just trying to match a color scheme, can't you move your Robert Longo?"

"Already thought of that, dearheart. It's too big." She finds the Marguerite Horner and stretches to pluck it off the wall with the brisk efficiency of a bird divesting a branch of its berries. "This will do." Seeing my scowl, her own expression softens to a girlish pout. "You don't truly mind, do you, Alekos?"

"You'll wear me down anyway if I say no, so just have the damned thing." I push my unkempt hair off my forehead. "Why give me any thought, beyond how I might be of use?"

She squints with amusement, passing me into the hallway. "Whoever's made you melancholy, *don't* bring her to the gala tomorrow. I don't need you making a scene with some ill-mannered tart. We hardly need a repeat of what happened when you brought the last one to Glyndebourne."

My stomach roils with a combination of sudden anxiety and empty-stomach cabernet. "The gala's tomorrow?"

"*Tsk!* Of course you forgot. If you still had a PA, you'd have remembered. But you enrage the plain, sensible ones until they quit and fuck the pretty ones away."

"I lack an assistant because *you fired me.*"

She lifts a towel off the stack on my breakfast bar and wraps it around the artwork before reaching to grasp my chin and turn my head toward the window, inspecting my stubble-shadowed face. "Sort yourself out before tomorrow. You look like a drifter."

"Surely you know better than to use terms like that, even *at your age*."

She gives a crooked smile and pats my cheek. "Nice try, love. But you'll need sharper tools to wound me." She adjusts the painting in her arms before rotating on one stilettoed heel and heading for the foyer. "Go to Guerlain and get a facial, for God's sake," she calls over her shoulder. "This will be the first time we've allowed so-called influencers at the publishing gala, and I need you in top form, seeing as you're comfortable moving in that sphere."

She dips her knees to reach the door knob, then descends my front walk with her sprightly steps clacking away, dying out as she ducks into a black Bentley Mulsanne held open by her long-suffering driver, Ismail. I give him a polite nod, and he nods back.

After closing my door, I peer at myself in the oval mirror beside the coatrack. I'm ghastly—a week of drink has done me no favors. I look like a child who's smeared on Halloween makeup to appear as a cartoonish approximation of an old man. I try to brighten things with a smile, but it's conspicuously half-hearted.

Possibly, I admit to myself, *because the* other *half is currently in Jeddah with Sage.*

~~~~~

"I'd like a Macallan, please," I say to the woman behind the bar. "And...?" My voice rises, stopping her as she reaches for the visible bottle of twelve-year.

She looks over her shoulder, stern and silent.

"Not that one," I specify. "I know there's a bottle of Macallan 30 hiding back there—Mother wouldn't settle for anything else." Seeing the skeptical downturn of the woman's lips, I shoot a winning smile at her, smoothing a hand down my necktie. "Alexander Laskaris, pet. I'm approved for the good stuff. Now, do let me whet my parched nepo-baby whistle."

Remaining wordless is one of her only weapons of revenge, and she wields it deftly. She levels a jigger with miserly precision and tips it into a glass—not a drop more than an ounce and a half—then slides it across the bar top.

I lift it and inhale the heady scent before taking a sip. Pulling a £50 note from an inside pocket, I drop it into her tip jar—a Lalique "Bacchantes" vase—as compensation for having to put up with me. I'm an annoying prat, but at least a self-aware one.

My mother wouldn't suffer a DJ for this event, despite the recommendation by both myself and her assistant, Inez, that the annual gala drag itself into the modern age. A band plays at one end of the huge room, doing classical-sounding covers of current pop songs. Older guests won't recognize the tunes (does the world need a cello-and-harp version of "Unholy"?); younger ones no doubt view it as corny.

I'm the heir to Laskaris Publications and will one day be at the helm of a global enterprise of—at current count—twenty-three magazines and newspapers. My father assumes I will perform adequately in this role owing to the possession of a Y chromosome and the family name. My mother is more realistic and has been, for the past decade, fortifying the business with an army of people who can field the tricky bits. She's like the grim head of a medieval army, readying the castle for impending siege.

Both parents have asked me never to sell the business. I wish I could promise that, but I'm realistic about how media is evolving. If things look unprofitable when the somber day comes that I must steer Laskaris Publications, I will leap straight off like it's a gut-shot horse, lest I be pinned beneath its fall.

Badrick has asserted—and I concede he's not wrong—that part of the reason for me being an incompetence-feigning wastrel is to annihilate my parents' confidence in me enough that they sell the business. I do live in fear of the eventual responsibility.

When I was at university, there was a time when my mother hoped I might marry the daughter of our company's CFO and cement a union that would ensure a stable future for the Laskaris legacy. And I did fancy Leyla—we dated for three months. But the last time she directly spoke to me was when she stopped her car on the side of the road during a holiday in Cornwall and directed me to get the hell out, then threw my mobile out the window before screeching off.

At twenty, I already had a well-established pattern with women—lamentably so.

I move to one side of the bar and pull another woodsy-gingery sip of the scotch while my focus drifts across the crowd. I'm not insensible of my duty to chat up this year's newest attendees and make them feel welcome and all that rubbish, but it would be easier if they were more interesting. To say this isn't the worst party I've attended lately is actually an insult; the *truly* bad parties are far more amusing.

A slim form sidles up next to me in a floral cloud of Miss Dior. I angle my gaze to take in the dress and legs first: textured bronze silk cut well above the knees, perfect calves, and a pair of those dreadful chain-link heels that have for some bewildering reason become fashionable.

"I've been looking forward to cornering you," the woman drawls, low and smoky.

Her accent is American, and for a fraction of a second my heart jolts with the thought that it could be Sage. But of course that's impossible—the Saudi Arabian Grand Prix is tomorrow, and this voice clearly belongs to an older woman.

As I connect with her eyes, I estimate she's midforties. Nicely turned out. Willowy figure with a spill of cleavage disproportionate enough that it's surely surgeon gifted. Her face is familiar: sharp cheekbones, aquiline nose, coffee-dark eyes adorned with fake lashes. The one flaw in an otherwise lovely composition is filler-enhanced lips that have been taken too far.

Ah! The woman who dislikes Sage Sikora far more than I ever pretended to. An overcompensating sport-mum with an axe to grind and a brand-new celebrity ally in global gastronomic tyrant Gavin Yates.

She smiles and extends a hand, palm down as if I'm meant to kiss it. I slide my fingers beneath hers and hold just long enough to give some doubt as to my intentions. We watch each other for a few beats, both reading the signals.

"What a bad boy," she tuts. "Pretending you don't know

who I am." Her eyes narrow with mischief. "Don't think I haven't noticed you 'liking' my Seychelles bikini photos, or the naked ones from the mud baths in Muğla, Turkey."

I give a small hum, as if only just recognizing her. "CJ Ardley, from *Sports and Tortes*. I hardly recognized you with so many clothes on. Well met."

"Oh, don't be naughty," she says, "or I'll have to turn you over my knee." She smirks from behind the slender glass she lifts to those inflatable life-raft collagen lips. Touching her tongue to a bead of champagne, she surveys me. "My friends call me CeeCee."

"Always a risk to introduce oneself that way. Setting up for an unkind dig."

"Oh?" she returns, fully at ease. "Go ahead. I want to see that pretty mouth of yours say something a little mean."

"As you insist: We're *not* friends."

"But we could be." She leans in, enveloping me in a gust of sugary perfume, peppermint, and champagne. "We have interests in common, after all. At least one." She reaches to adjust my necktie in an obvious ploy to make contact. "Correction: *two* common interests. I know your reputation. One of them we should talk about tonight, and the other…" Her crimson-glossed smile spreads. "Well, we can negotiate *that* as it…comes up."

For her invitation to be any clearer, it'd have to be accompanied by aircraft-marshalling wands, illuminating the runway to her hotel room. I'm not drunk enough to take the bait, though I confess to being curious. But I have a vexing case of Salvia officinalis "love indigestion," if not outright love*sickness*, endlessly replaying every moment Sage and I spent together making those silly videos. I'm not typically one to dream of specific women, but I do dream of her. My longing to see her in Melbourne is adolescent in its degree of melancholy.

CJ plucks the glass of scotch from my hand and sashays toward an empty table. "Shake a leg, handsome. Come sit for a spell." She toys with the pendant of her necklace, sliding it side to side along the chain as we settle across from each other. Leaning in with a conspiratorial wink, she begins, "Sooooo, a little bird told me that you got your fangs pulled by Emerald and are workin' for them to avoid a libel lawsuit."

I rotate my highball glass on the linen tablecloth. "And who might I thank for gifting you with this morsel of gossip?"

"Oh, hon…you know I won't tell you that. But if you think I'm here to gloat, you can stuff that egg right back up the chicken. I ask because you're in a unique position to gather intel from the Emerald camp, and I'm offering to be your gal on the *out*side. Pass me fertile dirt over the wall and I'll plant something that takes root and grows." She tips back the rest of her champagne, watching me. "You've probably noticed that my following has taken off like gangbusters since Gav Yates invited me into his circle. I'm a big ol' damned deal. A new fork in the road has opened to me." She winks again. "Might be fun to have some company on it."

I tip my head as if I'm bored. "You have an inaccurate view of my situation."

"Do I?" When she folds her arms on the table, a bulge of tanned cleavage rises. "So, you're not working closely with the team's newest acquisition, the little smart aleck you've called a dozen insulting names on your blog? Well, then." She sits back. "Silly me. I thought you were champing at the bit to take down Sage Sikora. I don't like her either, and I think you and I'd make a great team, Al."

Indignation and protectiveness spread within me, fast and dark as a summer storm, until I'm hit by the lightning-strike realization that CJ's assumption isn't unwarranted. I was horrible to Sage. People's belief that I want to "take her down" is, in fact, my fault.

Perhaps now I'm also the one best positioned to shield her from harm.

I need to put CJ Ardley at ease so she'll tell me more about her plan...

"I've been critical of Emerald's pocket-rocket driver, yes." I flirt my eyes up, searing into my companion's with careful intensity. "And you're not mistaken: I do have liberal access to the lady in question. But I'd be a fool not to have reservations about you—a woman with such an obvious *personal* motive. You blame Sage for your daughter Maya's unsuccessful move from F3 to F1. Perhaps you believe that when Maya lost out on the seat with Harrier, it was the 'final straw' that made her quit racing."

"That's a *fact*, not what I 'believe.' Game over, thanks to that tattooed brat."

In the interest of keeping her on the line, I hold back the mention of what has long been common knowledge in sporting circles: Maya Ardley did not love racing. Her mother bullied her into sticking with it long after her passion had waned.

Seeing the simmering vengefulness on CJ's face now, it

becomes clear to me: Sage's fiercest opponent isn't anyone on track. It's this fashionable and connected "wronged" mum. Suddenly, CJ Ardley looks less like a petty gossip and more like a cast member of *The Real Housewives of Dante's Ninth Circle*. She'll go after Sage whether I'm along for the ride or not.

I can't let that happen.

I drop a hand over hers. "She *is* a brat, isn't she?" I offer conspiratorially. "But you"—I move my thumb in a seductive sweep—"are a very...wicked...girl."

She freezes, and the anti-Sage fury melts from her expression, softening the lines of her angry mouth into a silky pout. "I've been described that way."

CJ Ardley is exactly the kind of woman for whom it's foreplay to label her a girl. Everything in her is perpetually straining toward a youthful recklessness she's afraid she's left behind. If I play this right, she'll spill her secrets. I have to know what she's planning for Sage so I can influence the trajectory.

"If you really think you could do something clever with information I give you, I'm sold. But? You'll need to trust me and be willing to...take direction."

Her smile is slow. "I don't mind having you on top, honey, as long as you know what to do once you get there."

"Good." I take my mobile from my jacket and swipe it open to Contacts, then slide it toward her. "Your number, pet."

9

MELBOURNE

ONE WEEK LATER

SAGE

If I could get away with it, my pre-race ritual would be the same as seventies F1 driver James Hunt: drink and party for a week, have sex with a gorgeous woman immediately before the race, then anxiety-vomit before getting into the car.

I'm certainly suffering a lot of anxiety this week.

My first two races with Emerald were garbage. In Bahrain, I qualified like shit but had made it up to twelfth place when João Valle tried going three-wide into a corner and caused a collision bad enough for a red flag, and me retiring my damaged car.

During the last race—Saudi Arabia—my poor performance was all on me. No one to blame. I let personal shit get into my head and got a terrible start, then earned a penalty for speeding in the pit lane. It was all downhill from there, fuckup after fuckup, tumbling like dominoes. I finished in thirteenth, *five* places below where I qualified.

I got into Melbourne on Sunday. And I really was gonna be a good girl this week and eat right and sleep well and all that, but then Priya was acting weird after a phone call Sunday night (obviously with Julian) and told me she was taking off to "explore hiking spots" and wouldn't be back until sometime today. I got mad and sulky because she was so clearly lying to me after being all like, "Ooh, we have to be so real and communicative with each other," and…yeah, my unfortunate self-destructive impulses had a moment.

I dressed up in about three square inches of fabric and went dancing at Cherry Bar last night, knocked back four extra-dirty martinis, and brought a stunner named Ruby to my suite. This morning I sent an early text to Dagna with the made-up excuse that I'd be a couple hours late to my workout because I've been "stricken by questionable tacos."

Ruby and I woke up horny, and I'll probably never see her again, so…make hay (and roll in it) while the sun shines, right?

I'm walking around the living room naked an hour later, perusing the room service menu on my phone, when there's a knock at the door that must be Priya. Before she left, I snatched her key card from her hand and told her not to bother coming back (obviously bullshit, but I get dramatic when I'm mad), so she's locked out.

Staring at my phone, I call out to Ruby, "Should we order Bloody Marys?" as I fling the door wide.

"Oh my. That's a turn up for the books," a smooth male voice says. "Good morning."

I drop my phone just before my eyes meet Alexander's, and I would've slammed the door if not for the jolt of pain as the phone's corner smashes my pinky toe.

I hit the floor like a stone—bare ass freezing on the tile—and cradle my foot, yelling, "Fuuuuuuuuck!"

Ruby rushes out of the bedroom and across to me, shirtless.

Could this get any worse?

I must have said it out loud, because Alexander replies, "From where I'm standing, the question would be, 'Could it get any *better*?' Here, pet—let me past and I'll get you some ice."

He starts to step over me and I punch at his shin. He retreats and I manage to get the door shut from my awkward position half blocking its swing arc. It's not lost on me that with the leg-contortion necessary to this operation, he's seen enough of my lady garden to draw a map of it.

"Who was that?" Ruby asks, helping me up. Her long braids sway tantalizingly across a mesmerizing pair of cinnamon-brown tits. "Did you order him from room service?"

"Hardly. Can you grab me one of those robes from the bathroom, then let him in?" I hobble to the sofa and flop down, inspecting the damage to my foot.

Ruby places my phone on the coffee table and breezes off, then comes back and drapes a robe around me. I wriggle into it as she goes to open the door, tucking her shirt in.

"Are you all right?" Alexander asks, coming down the two steps into the sunken living room and sitting on the opposite sofa.

"Never better," I grumble, prodding the toe. "What the hell are you doing here already?"

"You requested my presence last night, did you not?"

"It's twenty hours from London. Did you teleport?" I turn sideways and yank the thick white terry cloth over my knees.

"I was in Wellington, pet. Art auction at Dunbar Sloane. Four-hour flight. I did mention it when you called, but you sounded fuckin' trollied, so it's no surprise you don't remember."

I angle a hostile glare at him, wishing I had a good comeback, but...he's not wrong. I vaguely recall shouting into my phone over the pulsing music in the club, dizzy on rebellion and top-shelf gin. It comes to me with a solar flare of mortification that I may have said, *Get that sweet ass of yours to Melbourne, asap*, and followed it with a wolf howl.

It's a great-looking ass, but the last thing his ego needs is for someone to tell him.

"Whatever. How'd you get to my door, though? They're not supposed to let just anyone wander the halls."

He stretches both arms across the top of the sofa, displaying himself. "I'm *not* 'just anyone.' Also"—he tips a sideways nod at the foyer—"my room's at the other end of the hall. The magazine had a reservation for Natalia months ago, before her maternity leave." He points at my foot. "Shall I get that ice? You're quite tetchy. This isn't the reception for which I'd hoped, especially considering what greeted me at your door."

Behind me, I hear Ruby chuckle as she walks to the sofa and leans over the back to plant a kiss on my cheek. She's gotten dressed, even wearing the cute hat I commented on when we met—a yellow pencil-brim ranger. "I'm heading out, Francesca," she tells me. "Had a blast."

"No breakfast?" Catching her dimpled chin between my thumb and forefinger, I turn her for a lingering kiss on the mouth.

She half straightens, smiling, then closes in for another. "No thanks, darl. But hit me up next time you're around."

I give one of her braids a friendly tug. "Will do."

We both know I won't, but that's what you say, isn't it?

As always, when I hear the door shut, I'm flooded with a sense of relief that she's gone. It's not that I don't like people, and I'm certainly not ashamed of one-night stands. But knowing no more will be asked of me, beyond what I already gave, is always comforting.

Alexander sighs with the indulgent tone you'd use on a misbehaving child. "*Francesca?*"

"Like you've never given a fake name to a hookup."

"Believe it or not, I haven't—I'm far too vain. I want full credit for my performance."

I can't help laughing. Tucking my legs under the robe, I twist to face him. "That tracks."

He gets up and saunters to the bar, opening the mini-fridge's freezer. "Now, about that ice. I'll need a flannel from the en suite to wrap it…" He points at the bedroom.

"Ha! Nice try. You just wanna see the bed I wrecked with Ruby."

"Clever girl. Guilty as charged."

"I don't need ice anyway. It's fine."

He returns to the sofa, sitting beside me and gesturing for me to put my foot on his lap. "Allow me to inspect."

After a few seconds' hesitation, I comply. He scrutinizes the toe, gingerly bending it, then squeezing and giving it a little twist.

"Pain?" he asks.

"Yeah, duh." The way one of his hands is cupping my heel

makes me think of how someone cradles the back of your head before closing in for a kiss. He's surprisingly gentle. "Your hands are warmer than I expected."

He looks up from my foot with a sly smile. "I don't require batteries, love. I am, believe it or not, human."

I know he's calling back to our conversation in the lounge in Sakhir, when he referenced sex toys versus human partners. A blush flares at the memory, and I hope it's not visible.

Okay, calm the fuck down. Stop picturing yourself planting a stiletto-heeled foot against Alexander's bare chest, giving him a shove, ordering him to undo the buckle on the ankle strap with those white teeth of his...

Oh my God, I haven't showered yet—do I smell like sex?

On the pretense of locating a strand of hair clinging to my face, I touch my nose and check out my theory.

Uh, yeah. My hands smell like a mermaid petting zoo.

He presses his fist into the arch of my foot and massages, and an involuntary groan escapes me. I burrow deeper into the cushions and close my eyes. I know I should pull away, but my feet are really sensitive and I decide to let myself enjoy it for a minute.

"Pleasant?" he asks.

I shrug, eyes still closed. "Sure, I guess."

"As your intern, I live to serve," he says with amusement. I open my eyes to look at him, and he asks, "Did your squabble with Priya blow over?"

I adjust the robe to cover me where it's fallen away from my legs. "We made up, but then I got pissed off again a few nights back. Long story."

"I have time." His thumbs spread along the ball of my foot deliciously.

"It's...yeah, no. Just personal shit. I don't wanna talk about it. Let's just say on the road to better communication, there are some potholes." I wait a beat, deciding whether to reveal the next part. "I did kinda tell her I fucked you, though."

His probing thumbs freeze. "A lie counts as 'better communication'?"

"Oh, shut up. I never said I was perfect. But I'm trying."

He resumes massaging. "And the sex—how was I? Any good?"

The side-eye he's giving me makes my heart race, so I close my eyes again and offer an A-okay sign with my fingers. "Five stars."

"I'll add your rating to my CV."

"Though it would've been *way* more funny to tell her you were hung like a hamster."

His laugh is a smooth rumble. "Are we certain that's an insult? Proportionally speaking, domestic rodents might be massive."

I click my tongue and point at him. "True. Add 'Google proportionality of rodent genitals' to your to-do list, intern."

"Never a dull moment in your employ."

He kneads my heel and works the thumb of his other hand along the base of my toes and *fuck* it's nice. It's confusing how relaxed I am around him. Is it because I don't give a shit what he thinks of me? I spend a lot of time feeling "onstage" in this sport, so it's a relief not to be performing. Even socially it can be a problem, because I have a wild reputation. But sometimes the sassy armor gets heavy.

"Y'know," I begin, "I should be all kinds of uptight and defensive with you, but for some weird-ass reason, I'm kinda the opposite. It doesn't make any sense."

"Maybe I smell right," he says, adjusting his massage stroke in a way that makes me go practically boneless. "Some people have an inexplicable soporific effect. It's chemical, and immune to logic. Pheromones."

"Hmm. Maybe."

"Or I reckon it could be that you don't give a toss about my opinions."

My eyes fly open, hearing him echo what I was just thinking. I'm about to say something when my phone chimes on the table.

Alexander glances at the screen. "Ah. Priya. Shall your 'intern' take the call for you?"

I fold my arms. "Let it go to voicemail."

"As you command, pet." His tone—playful, but a little cautious—makes me wonder if he likes the idea of me bossing him around. I open one eye and he's watching my face.

The phone rings again, and it takes a few seconds for Alexander to break eye contact. Finally his gaze angles toward my phone. His eyebrows lift.

"Ah, the mysterious Julian. Bit of a love triangle?"

I struggle upright, trying not to flash my crotch in the too-big bathrobe. "You sound jealous. But Jules is my brother, dumbass. Do your research. I thought you were a journalist?"

A text from Priya appears on-screen: Pick up, Sage

The ringing stops for a few seconds before starting in again, and I hand the phone to Alexander. "Here, make yourself useful. Tell her you just fucked me into a state of exhaustion and I can't come to the phone."

"Most assuredly not. I know better than to get into the middle of your catfight."

"Wow, '*catfight*'? So condescending…"

"But I'll take a message." He taps the call open, on speaker. "Sage Sikora's phone, Alexander speaking. How might I help you?"

There's a long pause. "What the hell?" Priya says. "You're back? I thought we got rid of you. Where's Sage? Put her on."

"She's indisposed. Oh, Salvi, my sweet plum tart? Do you want to get out of that delectable wreckage of a bed and take this?" He gives me a wink, having conceded to play along a little.

I crack up silently, then hold out my hand for the phone, which Alexander lays on my palm. It takes me a second to get my shit together as it catches up to me that he used the Salvia officinalis nickname again. *Dammit, why does that make me feel kind of melty?*

I clear my throat. "Hey, Pri. What's up?"

"Why are you still hanging out with that creep?" she demands.

"I dunno—why are you hanging out with my brother? Don't think I don't know that's where you've been the last few nights."

"I never said I wasn't."

"You told me you were hiking!" I snap.

"We *were* going to go hiking. But—" She breaks off and I hear the murmuring of another voice that's definitely Jules.

"Okay, look," she continues, "he can explain. We need to talk with you. Can we meet up?"

I wait, letting her dangle a bit. "I don't have time. I have to get to the paddock. I'm super late for my workout."

Julian speaks up in the background. "Ten minutes, Sage. I have to tell you something."

I meet Alexander's eyes and am surprised by the genuine sympathy there.

"Uh, sure," I tell Pri and Jules. "I'll meet you guys downstairs in a half hour."

"Okay," Pri says. "But we should come up, because—"

"No, I have to leave. I'll be passing through the lobby in thirty minutes on my way to work," I interrupt. "Show up or don't."

I end the call and shut off the phone before dropping it into the robe's pocket. "I need to take a shower and get outta here," I tell Alexander. "You can go. But I might need something later tonight. I'll text you."

"All right." He looks disappointed.

"Sorry about the drunk-dial last night."

"No need to apologize. I'm flattered that you thought of me."

Dude, if you had any idea how often I've thought of you in the past few weeks, it'd be pretty embarrassing...

His brows lift in a speculative way. "May I give you a ride to the paddock? I have a hire car this time. Didn't need you telling me to 'rent a bicycle' like in Sakhir..."

"Ha! Oh God, I did say that, didn't I?"

"Indeed. Little brat."

I fiddle with the bathrobe tie, considering his offer. I kinda do want to hang out with him longer. But I can't risk him knowing anything about what's going on with Julian. I want to believe him that he was just messing with me on his blog, but part of me still doesn't trust him.

"Sure, you can drive me," I say. "And I'll introduce you to Jules, but then you have to fuck off and go get the car and wait for me outside. I'll make it fast—it's probably just some stupid thing where he needs to 'confess' that he's dating Pri and get my blessing or whatever."

"Entirely fair."

He goes to sit on the sofa and I head for the en suite, wondering if Alexander is an even bigger risk to me than I take behind the wheel going 200 mph.

10

MELBOURNE

ALEXANDER

When Sage goes to the bedroom to shower and dress, she neglects to close the door. This doesn't particularly surprise me. One could call her an exhibitionist, the way she invites attention.

The shower water turns off. She's singing an old Gary Numan song, her voice dropping low and sooty as she delivers the words *We are not romantics*…A minute later, she leaps onto the bed and springs across, hopping down on the other side to hunt for something on the floor.

I'm mesmerized, as always, by her combination of innocent unselfconsciousness and raw sexiness. She's only partially dressed. When she drops to all fours near the bedside table and sweeps one seeking hand across the rug, pale blue satin tightens across her muscular bum. She's bobbing along to her own singing, and the motion looks for all the fuckin' world like an invitation. I recross my legs, adjusting for the enthusiasm of my suddenly half-rigid cock.

"Lovely knickers," I call out. "Are they French?"

I'm surprised at myself for alerting her to the view I'm getting. Normally I'd just enjoy it, but for one thing, I need to sort out this inconvenient erection before we can leave, and for another…well, somehow it feels wrong.

Who am I?

"Nah, they were like three bucks," she calls back, continuing to hunt for the elusive item on the floor, not fussed that I can see her. Finally she pops up, standing on her knees and holding aloft an earring. "Aha! There you are."

She tips her head to one side, affixing the bauble as she rises to her feet. I can't help marveling at her strength. Every muscle is cut hard as granite, and she seems impervious to gravity. Going from kneeling to standing, she doesn't lean, doesn't touch the floor, there's not even a catch of breath.

I spend loads of time at the gym, but getting to my feet from the floor takes more effort than what Sage employs. The woman moves through space with the effortless three-axis physicality of a seal in water.

She rotates to face me as she adjusts the dangling earring. "What?" she says with amusement, planting both hands on her hips. "You've already seen way more than this."

The way she's flaunting herself is pure challenge. To my surprise, I kept my eyes mostly averted earlier when she opened the door naked—I was more concerned with whether she'd broken her foot, and it all happened so quickly. Now I accept her apparent offer to look my fill.

My gaze rakes every plane and sinuous arch. She's compact, powerful, elegant, her posture proud, shoulders back. Like a statue of an athlete in ancient Greece. An uncharitable viewer might call her flat-chested, with curves little bigger than the bottom of a Jaffa Cake, but she's every bit as sweet.

She's more inked than I assumed, with a detailed underwater scene of a kraken exploring a shipwreck wrapped around her right side. There appears to be a scar hiding amidst the seaweed, but it may just be a trick of the light. Her left thigh has a spot-on reproduction of an old Art Deco–era racing poster: MONACO, 8 AOUT 1937.

I must look half-witted, because she laughs. "Whatsa matter, Sandy? Never seen a real live woman before? And I thought you were such a swordsman."

I lift my chin. "You're provoking me."

She closes the distance to the doorway and lifts her arms to hold it, her body a suggestive letter Y. "If I were provoking you, you'd know." With an impish wrinkle of her nose, she turns and darts out of sight.

It takes a minute of focused breathing to calm the effect her words have on my, erm…lap. She's singing again, now Elvis Costello's "Alison." Her voice is off-key, breaking with that hint of raspiness I love on the high notes. I could listen to her all day.

"Hey, could you do this?" she calls out from around the corner.

Whatever it is, the answer is yes, I want to say. Instead, I take my time crossing the room, then lean in the doorway.

"You summoned, O seraph?" I say dryly.

She's in front of a tall mirror, her hair pulled into a messy bundle that makes her look *more* postcoital than when she opened the door of the suite. Her jeans are all but painted on, and she's wearing a tight T-shirt that reads ENCHANTED FOREST, OREGON. The shirt's neck is cut off wide and ragged, displaying the pale blue straps of her lacy bra.

"I can't get the clasp done on this thing," she mumbles, fiddling with a necklace, hands behind her head. "Can I borrow your, uh, fine motor skills?"

Drawing up behind her, I take the chain ends from her fingertips and have the clasp done in a second, but take longer to fuss with it just to be near her, breathing in the warmth of her neck. My eyes follow the tiny stepping stones of her vertebrae, and there's a tugging in my chest—and below—as I imagine pressing my lips there, feeling the peachy softness of her skin.

"You know what'd be hilarious?" Sage poses. "You should stay here with me tonight to piss Priya off." She meets my eyes in the mirror with a glimmer of mischief. "We can make sex noises and freak her out. Get super theatrical about it."

I rest my hands on her shoulders. "Are you so practiced at feigning your pleasure?" I tease.

"*Pff!* I'm not polite enough to fake it. If a guy's doing a shitty job, I just say so." She moves away to get her shoes, and my hands feel empty. She sits on the bed and laces up her trainers. "Also, I don't *have* to fake—I'm highly orgasmic, and I've got a prominent clitoris."

Were I taking a drink of anything, it would have launched through my sinuses. I cough and laugh at the same time. "You're alarmingly candid."

"Ain't I?"

"But again I'd remind you that I want no part of you

winding up the best friend, who—by every indication—wants what's best for you and is distressed by your...communication issues."

"*Psh!* Why do you care? She doesn't even like you, dude."

"She has every justification. I was a complete tosser."

Sage rolls her eyes. "It'd be funny! Just a joke. I thought maybe you were game to mess with her head a little, after the way you answered my phone. But never mind."

As she tries to sidle past me into the living room, I put an arm out and stop her. She remains pressed against my forearm, as if stepping back would be a win that she refuses to give me. She turns slowly, her jaw hard, and meets my eyes.

"*What*," she says, her tone flat.

The scent of her is driving me mad. I lean closer. "If I spend the night in your bed," I growl, "it won't be 'just a joke.' You're bold as brass on the track. Have the courage to proposition me because *you want me as much as I want you*—don't hide your true intentions behind immature pranks."

Her golden eyes narrow, and as we study each other for a long beat of silence, the ENCHANTED on her shirt rises and falls.

"You think I want you?" she asks, not quite managing the haughtiness she's trying for.

"Yes."

Another half minute passes as each of us refuses to look away first. Finally she hums out a dismissive laugh. "Yeah, maybe. But..." She chucks me beneath the chin in the same patronizing way I've done to women a hundred times myself. "You want me more."

When the lift opens, Sage and I each hold one side of the door and gesture for the other to precede.

"Ladies first," she drawls, pointing for me to step in. "God knows *I'm* not a lady."

"Such a brat. Fine, you win."

She chuckles, following me into the mirrored enclosure. "I *looooove* to win."

She plucks at her aqua hair, fluffing it up and away from her eyes as she checks the reflection of her teeth. Turning around light as a ballerina's pirouette, she claps her hands once, pinning me with a look of determination.

"So here's the dealio, Sandy-boy. Julian is my older brother, and a dipshit deadbeat. He comes off all charming"—she rolls her eyes—"and everybody loves him; he's a goddamned delight, *ugh*. But don't buy into it. You're on *my* team, got it? No becoming best buds with him after a handshake."

I don't think Sage realizes how much she's told me about herself with this caveat. I can view the mechanics of not only her relationship with the ne'er-do-well brother but also Sage's fears, through a layer of self-control stretched so paper-thin as to be translucent.

Her posture betrays her feelings; she doesn't seem to know what to do with her shoulders, which adjust like the antennae of a threatened insect. I want to embrace her, to tuck her head under my chin and hide her from everything.

It's in this moment that I feel the most guilty for what I wrote about her on my blog. She appeared so impervious to hurt that it seemed a harmless way to engage her. Reaching out with compliments would've been futile. I'd have been just another trivial fanboy.

But if I infuriated her? Becoming her enemy gave me a *place*, a status.

Badrick was right—I should have used a different strategy. Not because I think my redemption in Sage's esteem is now impossible (though it might be with the frosty Priya, who clearly loathes me), but because in the space of weeks, I've come to care for Sage so much that I'm overwhelmed with defensive rage at anyone who might hurt her surprisingly tender feelings.

The current chief threat is malignant blogger CJ Ardley, whom I've kept at bay over the past week. I told the woman to lie low and not to mention Sage in her posts, because I'm "working on something sensational," which I'll soon share with her.

I'm pondering the right time to speak with Sage about my role as double agent. Given her mischievous nature, she may find it entertaining to collaborate on providing misleading details to feed to her nemesis. But another side of me is concerned about bringing it up.

Sage has mentioned more than once that she doesn't trust me, so I don't have complete confidence that when I reveal my phony "allegiance" with CJ, Sage will believe I'm on her side. What if it shuts the door to a growing friendship? There might be no more hanging out, no more small shared confidences and glimpses of vulnerability.

Should I wait until we're closer and she knows me better before saying anything? I have the situation well under control for the time being...

Folding her arms in almost a parody of childlike disgruntlement, Sage concludes, "I don't want you and Jules bonding over 'idle rich-boy shit' like how cool it is to sit in a hot springs in Iceland and watch the northern lights with a supermodel on your lap. Or whatever."

I cross the elevator and lean beside her, draping an arm around her shoulders, which to my surprise relax under my touch. "I won't be so easily enraptured by Julian's glamour. I'll fight your corner, pet."

I dare to plant a light kiss at the crown of her pastel blue hair, and she jerks her head away with a scowl. "Hey, watch where you put those lips."

"So shy," I tease, "despite the intimate familiarity you told Priya we've shared."

"Haha."

"I confess to curiosity about the story you spun." I step back and lean against the wall. "Just what was our fictional tryst like?"

She snorts a laugh. "Man, you're so narcissistic. Of course you're dying to know the details of something that didn't even happen, and how it reflected on you."

"Guilty," I reply, holding my hands up.

She pushes her lips into a thinking moue. "I said that when we went to your room to make that Christmas light video, I basically attacked you. *Rrraawwwrrr!*" She forms her hands into claws and lunges at me, grabbing my pecs. "Then we fucked like a hundred times, and—"

"I'm rather energetic in your fantasies, aren't I?"

"I had to keep it believable."

"A hundred times is believable?"

"Okay, exaggeration. Maybe I said *four*. I'd rather do it four times at fifteen minutes each than once for an hour. Get on, get off, reboot, go again. That's my style."

"Duly noted."

The smile we exchange is all cautious mischief. I reach for a coil of Sage's hair that's escaped its confines atop her head and smooth it behind one of her abundantly studded ears.

"Sometimes I wonder if I dreamt you," I say before I can think better of it.

Her eyes widen, amused. "Uh-oh. Not just a narcissist, but…what's that called—solipsism? You're the only thing that exists, and I'm, like, your hallucination?"

"Frustratingly defiant hallucination, you." I sink my hands into my pockets. "Let's test your hypothesis. I'll imagine you're kissing me, and we'll see if it happens."

"Dream on."

"I'm trying! Yet my lips remain tragically unkissed."

The elevator stops at a lower floor and two women from Team Easton get inside, dressed in their white work shirts with sponsor patches and lime-green trim. One glances at the other silently as the doors shut, and a look of agreement passes between them.

"Not to be disloyal," the taller woman says to Sage, "but we're both *huge* fans. I hope you kick ass on Sunday."

As I watch Sage chat with her admirers for the rest of the trip down to the lobby, I'm impressed by how fluidly she adapts in social scenarios. She has that driver's talent for making complex things look easy—her manner smooth, her timing impeccable.

Longing drags through me like a plow stabbing at hard ground. I want to know her…to *really* know her. The heart of Sage Sikora, with all its blind alleys, a place where I suspect I could lose myself.

Or maybe find myself.

11

MELBOURNE

SAGE

Standing in the lobby, Priya's wearing the sweater I gave her for her birthday. There's a shiver of grief in my chest as my body has the impulse to do what I'd normally do: make dinosaur noises while running up and hopping on her, piggyback. Then we'd hug and she'd laugh and scold, and I'd drop some inside-joke quote from one of our favorite sketch comedy shows like *That Mitchell and Webb Look* and she'd automatically fire back her part of the exchange.

But she's got her arm looped through Julian's, and they're looking out the big front window and talking, turned away. My posture stiffens. I take Alexander's arm and yank him closer before Pri and Jules see us.

Something tender is in Alexander's expression, looking down at me. I can't help wondering what he's thinking any time he lets that cool upper-class mask slip. He's usually like someone who has an opinion about polo ponies, but occasionally something very real is there, and it sends an achy thump through my chest that's not entirely unpleasant.

I'm annoyed by him, yeah; the guy's an arrogant prick. But I'm also kind of fascinated. He keeps surprising me. I'm not sure if it's just the obvious physical attraction or if there's more, an X factor that isn't typically mixed into my "lust cocktail." A dash of enigma, a sprinkle of exciting aggression, a pinch of relatability.

Maybe I'm the narcissist. Does he remind me of myself?

Nah. It's just hormones. If I was going to catch feelings for anyone, it wouldn't be Alexander Laskaris.

I peek up at him again.

Alexander's face is handsome, but it's also interesting. For one thing, he has freckles, which I'm sure he hates, but I can reluctantly admit (at least to myself) that they're adorable. The other thing he probably sees as some hideous flaw is the scar across his right eyebrow. It cuts it into one-third/two-thirds segments and is angled like a backslash. I wanna ask him how he got it, but he'd probably make up some bullshit.

Ugh, okay…stop gawking. What's wrong with me?

As we walk up to Pri and Jules, I greet them with, "Well well well, if it isn't—"

I'm about to throw out one of my usual mocking nicknames for my brother like *Dildo McFuckup* or *Useless von Loserton*, but when he turns around, his face is beat to hell and the snark evaporates on my tongue. I jerk to a stop and my arm in Alexander's goes rigid. He slides a hand over mine in a quick caress of support.

"What the fuck happened to you?" I ask Jules.

The chagrined look he gives me is lopsided from the damage. His left eye is swelled almost shut, there are cuts and scrapes on his left cheek, and his lower lip is split badly enough that there are stitches poking out like little whiskers.

Priya glares at Alexander, then me. "Can we not do this here? And with *that guy* sitting in?" Her voice drops. *"Didn't you read my texts?"* she whisper-yells.

I fish the phone from my pocket and turn it on, and three messages come though.

> **Priya:** NO! not downstairs. we shd come up to the room or u come here. julian looks rough
>
> **Priya:** ffs is ur phone turned off ???
>
> **Priya:** this is not the time to be stubborn. your brother needs u

Jules slips an arm around Priya and this is when I notice that his right hand is in a partial cast, two fingers encased in plaster that rings his wrist to stabilize it.

"Hey, sis," he says to me. His jaw is stiff from injury, and his wreckage of a face frames a pair of melancholy green eyes, one of which has a bloodshot firework burst at the outside corner.

I scan the lobby, checking if any fans or journalists have caught sight of us. My heart is pounding hard and my throat is tight. "Hi, yourself. Meet me upstairs, okay?" Without waiting for an answer, I pivot and stride toward the elevators, towing Alexander by the hand.

An old couple tries to board with us and I ask them, "Hey, could you guys wait for the next one? We're gonna have sex in here."

They're shocked silent, taking a step back as I drag Alexander aboard. His reflexive laughter dies away as the doors close and he takes a thorough look at me. He plants his feet in a solid, tree-trunk-like stance before me and cups my face. "Salvi, pet..."

I have to pretend my teary eyes are purely from anger, because no way am I admitting I'm sad and scared for that fuckwit brother of mine—not mere minutes after I gave Alexander a whole song and dance about how Julian shouldn't receive sympathy or friendship from anyone.

"I'm fine." I push his hands away. "Just annoyed that now I'm gonna look like a bitch if I don't feel sorry for the fuckin' prodigal son."

Alexander retreats, leaning against the opposite wall. For a minute, an awkward silence reigns. "I suspect it's more than that," he remarks in a tone of studied casualness.

"Stay in your lane, Sandy," I fire back. "Christ on a fish stick, you're the least qualified therapist on the planet."

My nose is prickling again with the threat of tears, and I feign a sneeze to hide it, giving myself an excuse to sniffle. I straighten and rub my face. The elevator opens at our floor, and Alexander holds out an arm, waving me through.

As I pass into the hallway, he says, "It's a good thing you refuse to fake orgasms, because you'd be terrible at it. That was the worst phony sneeze I've ever witnessed."

Back in the suite, Alexander heads for the little bar/kitchenette area, instinctively giving me space.

"Mind if I make tea?" he asks. "Do you want any, or a coffee?"

I cram the askew sofa cushions back into place and pluck some clothes off the floor, tossing them through the bedroom door. "Nah, I'm good."

My suite is more wrecked than usual due to Priya's absence. She keeps things in order, because she knows what to touch and what to leave alone. I generally don't allow housekeeping into my room midstay because they've been known to take souvenirs, and that creeps me out even if it's nothing valuable, like used makeup sponges.

I hear the mini-fridge open. "Only oat milk? Ah, sod it," Alexander mutters. With a sigh he sits on one of the sofas. "Are you certain you want me to stay? I was going to quietly take my leave, but you were holding my hand with the ferocity of a tornado victim."

I can't help a weak laugh. "Yeah, sorry about that. I wasn't thinking too clearly."

"I can go," he assures me, pointing toward the door. "This is obviously a family matter."

"Maybe? Fuck, I don't know." I pace toward the window, then back. "I'm not sure what's going on, but…like, if you stay, you'll keep it under your hat, right?"

"The soul of discretion." His brow crumples and he fusses with one cuff of his shirt. "I'd like to prove that I can be a good friend to you, if you'll allow it."

I feel the sting of tears fogging my eyes, and I'm not sure if it's because I'm a little moved by his words or just scared and frustrated about Jules. Probably all of the above. My legs tense to turn away, but I make myself stand firm, watching him until he meets my stare.

"Okay, but here's the deal, Sandy: If you're messing with me, I won't forgive you, and my payback won't be harmless practical jokes. You don't want to be my enemy—believe me."

He looks so dumbstruck by my possibly-out-of-left-field hostility that I feel kind of bad. He gets up and crosses to where I am. His hands go to my shoulders; then he seems to reconsider touching me and instead adjusts the stretched-out neck of my T-shirt so it covers my bra strap.

"Few would call me a serious person," he says, "but I couldn't be more in earnest when I vow that I will never hurt you. To be honest, I'd fuckin' dismantle anyone else who dared to do so. I'm…growing quite fond of you, Salvi."

In the tense silence that follows the declaration, I hear voices in the hall, then a knock.

I take a step back, murmuring, "Uh, here they are."

"Of course." He steps back too.

Was I sort of wishing he'd hug me?

My face heats up and I turn away and stride to the door, opening it for Pri and Jules, waving them in. As I walk behind them, I can tell from Julian's posture that he's really hurting, and it freaks me out because this is a guy who I've seen take falls that'd wreck other people and just laugh it off.

Priya's holding his non-broken hand. That cramp of sorrow grips me again, and it makes me feel selfish but I can't help it. Jules always wins at being the most likeable, the most coddled by my parents. Now I guess he wins the "most broken" title with Pri too. *I need her*, and I've been nothing but a total bitch for days, and...this is the result.

Jesus, no wonder I need a fucking hug.

I glance at Alexander, who's taken a spot on the love seat. He gives me an encouraging smile and pats the cushion next to himself and for a second I feel better.

Julian lowers onto the couch, wincing. Priya hovers over him like a mother hen, waiting for him to get situated before she joins him. Another dart of jealousy jabs my chest.

If I don't fix this, I'm going to lose her.

Even before Pri's PA status was official and paid by Emerald, she's been with me. For over two years now, since I got the reserve driver gig with Harrier. She's been *my* mother hen—keeping track of the schedule; reminding me when and what to eat; nagging me about sleep and vitamins; picking up after my messy, careless ass; reading and bottom-lining my emails; covering for me when I do something stupid. The "gap year" she took from grad school turned into a much longer hiatus when she opted to stay with me and be my right-hand gal.

I can go back to university anytime, she assured me. *But I can hardly let you travel all over the world alone, can I?*

It's a common misconception that "nice people" are either less tough or less smart than assholes. Make no mistake: Priya is a badass, and practically a genius. Her steady kindness is a superpower. She reads voraciously (mostly nonfiction), speaks three languages, and isn't afraid to go in swinging when she sees injustice or cruelty.

But that dutiful compassion isn't just her superpower, it's

also been her consistent Achilles' heel. Watching her with Jules right now, I know I once again have been careless with her. I was unfair and surly and pushed her away. *What's my damned problem that I always do this?* Just like with my parents, any love going to my brother feels like less for me, and I took that out on Priya.

I'm on the outside of this situation with Jules because I chose to be here.

It's fucking lonely.

Even looking like four miles of bad road, Julian sends a winning look Alexander's way, half standing and reaching across the table for a handshake. "I'm Julian. Nice to meet you. Wish it were under better circumstances."

"Alexander Laskaris." He glances at me, then back at my brother. "I'm more than willing to take my leave if you'd prefer privacy."

Priya mutters, "*Yes*, thanks," but at the same time Jules says, "If Sage wants you here for this conversation, there must be some reason. I'm going to trust that she trusts you."

"No!" Priya snaps, exasperated. She glares at me. "Obviously he needs to go. He's not family just because you saw him without his pants. Can't you set him outside the door now that you're done with him? Maybe the hotel has a pickup service, like with the laundry."

I can't help laughing, and for a second I'm relieved because I think Pri's giving me a "you're forgiven" in, joking around, but the look on her face strangles the laughter right out of me. She's pissed, and it'll take more than humor to thaw her.

My brother slides his cast-bearing hand beneath Priya's, and

I know it's partly in a comforting way, but I suspect it's also a reminder to her of his wounded status, so she'll back off. I've seen this strategy from him a million times. Jules can be massively passive-aggressive.

"Pri, baby...we talked about this last night and I told you I'm ready to be honest. You said I don't have any reason to be ashamed."

"This isn't about shame," she insists. "It's discretion."

He holds up both hands like a scale balancing. "Discretion, secrets..." He shrugs, and I want to smack him, because *for fuck's sake, there's a difference.* I try to catch Priya's eye so I can show her that I'm on her side with this one, but she won't look at me, and my heart sinks.

"So, this"—Julian points at his battered face, addressing Alexander and me—"happened night before last, because I got robbed while I was trying to buy pills."

Well, shit. So much for discretion.

The image of Julian getting the crap beat out of him flashes in my mind, and I have a full-body wave of wanting to tear whoever it was apart for hurting my brother. But I don't let my guard down, because *he brought this on himself, didn't he?* What the hell was he thinking, buying dope off some rando in a foreign country? I'm sure it means he didn't even report it.

Jules tells Alexander, "I'm, y'know, hooked on them. Physically dependent."

Alexander just nods.

I wave vaguely toward Julian's eyes. "Docs must've given you the good shit when you went to the ER. You look high as balls."

He's both hurt and mad, and shoots back, "Nice, Sage. Once again, *you win*. More points for the champion. You're right—I did take the prescription they offered. Because in addition to this awesome makeover, I have a cracked rib and two broken fingers from when I was stomped, trying to keep them from stealing Dad's watch, because *you gave it to him*."

"The Carrera Tourbillon?" I blurt out. "What the fuck were you doing with it?" Ugh, that's the exact wrong thing to say, and I know it immediately.

Priya's hands dive into her thick, dark hair in frustration. "Why are you so awful?!" she wails at me.

I fold my arms. "All right all right *all right*, I'm fucking sorry." After a pause, I force the question out. "Are you, uh, okay and stuff?" I ask Jules.

"Never better, thanks," he deadpans. "And I had the watch because Dad lent it to me at the airport when he dropped me off. I'd left mine at the house."

Of course he did. Once again, my parents leapt to fix things for the Favorite Child.

I give an impatient sigh. "Okay, whatever. I can get Dad a new watch."

"You know what you can't buy, Sage?" Priya jumps in. "*A new brother.* Maybe think about that for five damned seconds."

Normally I'd hit back with a cutting comment about the type of new brother I'd buy if I could, but I'm not eager to make things worse. Both Pri and Jules look really upset, and...I don't know why I should care, but I also don't want to show my worst self to Alexander.

Julian holds up his non-cast hand, claiming the floor.

"Look, I'm in love with Priya. I have been for a couple years. It was a problem with me and Paz—it's why we broke up. I'm sure you think Priya's a moron for taking a chance on me, but I'm gonna try to deserve her. Which brings me to the other issue."

He glances at Pri, who gives a smile like a mom ushering her kid into a classroom for the first day of kindergarten.

"I'm doing rehab," Jules continues. "A place in Switzerland. I fly out tomorrow. I'm going to fix this, Sage. I wasn't crazy about the shit you said in February, but you were right. I've let this go on too long. I need help."

Alexander has at some point put an arm around me without me noticing, and he rubs a thumb along my upper arm in a silent message of support. The ball's in my court, but it feels like that ball is stuffed with silver nitride and will explode on contact.

I take a slow breath. "You really don't think you can just, y'know, *stop*? On your own?"

Julian looks at the ceiling with a self-mocking chuckle. "I've tried, believe me. Been junk-sick dozens of times. Though it's always when I can't get any, not really because I *decide* to quit. Every time, during the worst of it—days three and four of withdrawal—I tell myself, *This is an opportunity. I won't start again.* But once it's available?" He lifts his hands, helpless. "Yeah, I buy more."

Priya speaks up, "It's a medical problem, Sage. This isn't 'a habit,' like biting your nails. He needs support. Not just rehab, but…*you*. Family."

"Family?" I echo. "So you've told Mom and Dad? I assume

they're bankrolling it. Fuck, your ritzy Swiss treatment spa is gonna cost a mint."

He avoids my eyes when he says, "I'll tell them the details when I'm clean. There's no need to worry Mom. Please don't say anything to them."

The way he's picking at the edge of his cast makes me think I'm not getting the full story there. *And why did he only mention Mom?*

"If you haven't told Mom and Dad, what about the money?" I ask.

"I've got it handled," he says evenly.

"What does that mean?" My eyes narrow. "I know for a fact you've blown through most of your dough. Mom and Dad were talking a couple months ago about bailing you outta that startup with your friend what's-his-nuts. So how are—" I notice the deer-like innocence on Priya's face. "Hold the fucking phone. Is *she* paying? Because if she's using her grad school money, I'll strangle you both."

"I'm helping a little," she tells me.

"No," I retort. "*Hell* no. Pri, for fuck's sake—"

"It's my choice! And for this to really stick, he'll need to stay three months. The failure rate on short-term rehab is astronomical."

"You're not blowing your college fund, Pri. *I'll* pay, got it? Just give me the info and I'll send enough to cover it." I point at Julian. "But I'm not giving money to you directly."

"Sage, no. You don't have to do that," he says.

I suspect this is exactly where we were headed all along, and he guided us right here. He never intended to take Pri's money.

But I'm too tired and upset and self-conscious to call him out on it. Also, it makes Pri happy to think she was going to save him, so I'm letting her keep that, even if—once again—it was more of Julian Sikora's trademark passive-aggressive crap.

"No shit I don't have to do it," I retort. "But I'm going to, so shut up." My phone sings out with Dagna's text tone, "Physical," and I pick it up from the coffee table.

> **Dagna:** I've sent a car for you. It's outside the hotel now. Be here in ten minutes or I'm making you start with 100 clamshell side planks.

"Oh, fuckbuckets," I mutter. "It's Daggy, and she's loaded for bear. I gotta jam." I pop to my feet and point at Priya. "Your key card's on the table beside your bed. And *you*..." I point at Julian. "Don't fuck up this rehab thing. Otherwise *I'll* deliver your next beatdown."

He pushes to his feet with stiff effort and holds his arms open. After a pause, I meet him halfway around the table and accept a hug.

"Thanks, sis. I won't make you regret it. And I'm going to pay you back."

I shrug. "Like I care about the money, dumbass."

Priya pipes up, "Julian's staying here tonight. I'll take him to the airport for Switzerland in the morning."

"Whatever. Fine." I stuff my phone into my pocket.

Alexander stands. "Shall we?"

"No need for a ride after all. There's a car waiting, apparently."

He looks a little bummed. "Right. I'll walk you out, at any rate."

I give Pri and Jules a wave and head out the door with Alexander. Weirdly, after the emotionally depleting scene I just had to deal with, I kinda wish I could crawl into bed next to Alexander. Like, not even in a sex way. Just order room service junk food and watch bad TV and keep having him near, hiding in a cocoon of blankets with his nice smell and his voice wrapped around me like a smooth satin bow that's tying me together.

I think I'm glad he stayed.

I hope I don't end up regretting it.

I peek at him as we wait for the elevator to arrive. "So, uh...I don't suppose you'd be game for a sleepover tonight?" I ask.

He plants one hand on the wall above my shoulder, casual and sexy as hell. Oh God, those damned smoky-gray eyes of his...

"What are you asking of me, Salvia officinalis?"

"I haven't decided yet. But I guess I want you around. Maybe just to talk. Maybe so you can read me a bedtime story and rock me to sleep. Fuck, I don't know. Do you want a detailed schedule or something?"

He presses those delicious lips together, hiding a smile. "Happy to play it by ear, pet. I'll be there. Wouldn't miss it."

12

MELBOURNE

ALEXANDER

It feels disloyal to like Sage's brother, but he's an affable bloke and we get on immediately. After Sage left, I was prepared to go back to my own suite, but Julian invited me to dine with him and salty Priya, who glared daggers at me throughout a leisurely brunch.

After plates have been cleared, Julian and I are sipping cold brew sangrias and chatting about music (a show he saw in Berlin; I know the singer, though I don't mention it's because I've slept with her) when he turns his wrist to check the watch that's no longer there. With a resigned sigh, he digs his mobile from a pocket.

"Good thing I'm ambidextrous," he says with a tired smile, laying the mobile beside his plate.

"Are you?"

"Yeah, from climbing. Gotta be equally strong with both hands." He reaches to run a thumb across Priya's knuckles, where she's cradling a mug of oat milk chai. "Hey, uh...is it about time? Pretty close, right?"

She shoots a suspicious glance at me before replying to Julian. "A little early. Can you wait forty minutes? Thirty?"

"I'd rather not," he says with a sheepish smile.

She scrunches her lips in thought in a similar way to Sage, and I wonder if one of them acquired the mannerism from the other.

"I don't have them with me. I'll have to go up to the room." She pushes her chair back.

Julian's brow contracts, tugging at the scabbed area near his eyebrow. "Is that safe, leaving them there? They could get swiped by the cleaning staff. You should keep 'em on you just in case." He must realize how panicked he sounds. With a sigh of laughter, he relaxes into his chair and picks up his drink. "Sorry. I'm sure it's fine."

She stands and pauses beside him, squeezing his upper arm, then heads for the lobby. After she's gone, he sends a nervous side-eye my way.

Setting down his glass and toying with it, he says, "It's grown into every part of my consciousness, like fucking poison ivy." A wry sniff of laughter escapes him. "The other day I put a hand into my pocket and there was a little hole in the seam, and my first thought was, 'A pill could fall out of that.' Doesn't even make sense, because I never keep them loose in my pockets, ever. But this, uh"—his voice goes tight and he clears his throat—"this *problem* has bled into every corner of my life. It's ruined everything."

He gives the glass a push and it sloshes a dark stain onto the table linen.

"But even knowing that," he continues, "I don't wanna let it go. I'm counting down the hours 'til I get on that flight like I'm headed for a firing squad. And I wish Pri wasn't playing nurse so I could take enough of the fucking things to feel it." He scratches gingerly at the back of his head, where there must be another wound. "There's nothing as disappointing as having to use junk for actual *pain*. What a waste."

I'm not sure what to say. Everything that goes through my head seems trite and insincere. Finally I settle on, "You're not the first to have done this. Take comfort in following a well-marked trail."

He touches his tongue to the reddish-brown line of the split lip. "Yeah, a lot of the trail markers are dead bodies." His eyes meet mine, and I try not to focus on the web of red in the corner of one. "There's a few hundred on Everest, you know. And a bunch on K2—I lost a toe there." He presses his fingertip against the spreading coffee stain. "They're just part of it now—the bodies. Part of the natural landscape."

"She won't let that happen," I assure him. "You're not going to fail."

His expression brightens. "Yeah, Pri is amazing."

"I've no doubt. But I meant Sage."

Julian scoffs. "Are you kidding? Not to shit-talk your girlfriend, but—"

"We're not, erm…involved," I can't help confessing.

He rolls his eyes with a weary smile. "Ah. So you've joined the lonely ranks of people who've had to say that."

"Oh?"

He flicks a cautious glance at me like he's revealed too much, then shrugs. "I mean, good luck to you. You seem cool. But Sage wears 'em out and leaves 'em behind like Pirellis at a pit stop. One guy, friend of mine, he hooked up with her and the next time she saw him she didn't remember him. Said, 'He cut his hair—how was I supposed to recognize him?' Guy looked so wounded you'd'a thought he took a kick to the nuts."

"I can imagine that would be a blow to one's ego."

"And the girl who was her publicist at Harrier? They had a fling and when Sage tossed her aside, the girl quit her job entirely. Moved back to Italy, boom. Heartbreak city."

My stomach tenses, and I'm not sure why I'm worried. I've never had a problem keeping things casual, and for that matter, I've no clue if Sage has designs on me or is just bored.

"Anyway," Julian continues, "as for Sage looking out for my welfare or whatever, to be honest she'd be happiest if I OD'd or took a header off Annapurna. She hates me."

I confine myself to a lift of the eyebrows. "I don't have siblings, but it's my understanding that they do bicker. Sage is spirited. But surely she loves you."

"You can love people and hate them too. We've always been competitive, and at some point in our teens she just"—he makes an explosion gesture with his hands—"the gloves came off. It was around the time she almost died from a ruptured appendix."

In my breast pocket, my mobile vibrates. I take it out to see a text from the contact I've labeled "Rosé All Day"—CJ Ardley. The preview reads, Someone just posted a pic of you and Julian Sikora together. Are you getting me some nice dirt, hon?

My pulse quickens, and I try not to look conspicuous as I

scan the room for anyone who might be paying an inordinate amount of attention to us. No one seems to be gawking. As I focus on the doorway to the kitchen—food service workers are notorious gossips; I get a lot of good material from them—another message buzzes. I swipe it open.

> **Rosé All Day:** The boy looks like he caught the business end of someone's fist. Call me as soon as you can and give me the details. Juicy stuff!

I repocket the mobile. "Must deal with this; my apologies. The bill is paid. It was—"

"I invited *you*," Julian says in a tone of friendly offense. "You shoulda let me get the check."

"Next time." I pluck the serviette off my lap and lay it on the table.

"You coming back to the room tonight after Sage is off work?"

"I will, yes." Before taking my leave, I consider telling Julian not to swallow the pills Priya brings downstairs at the table, since someone is clearly watching him. But he's injured, which is at least an adequate excuse.

With a chummy handshake and some parting pleasantries, I take my leave, hurrying to head up to my room and call Ms. Ardley. Crossing the lobby, I see Priya exiting a lift. She spots me as well, and her expression goes dour and purposeful. She beelines toward me.

"I'm wise to your game," she says.

"And what game is that?"

"I don't know what it *is* yet—just that you're playing one.

Sage may've warmed up to you…" She gives me a lip-curled once-over. "For *boringly obvious* reasons. But I'm immune."

"Not damaged enough for your taste?" I reply blandly. I immediately feel horrible for having said it, but I couldn't resist repaying Priya's jab with one of my own.

"Oh, perfect," she snaps. "Showing your true colors. Consider yourself warned: I've got my eye on you. Even if you don't slip up, the countdown's begun. Sage'll toss you aside like a condom wrapper by race day."

She gives me a pointedly wide berth as she passes me to head into the dining room.

As I exit the lift minutes later at my floor, another text comes through. There's an attached screenshot from social media, two somewhat grainy pics showing Priya handing Julian something out of an orange prescription bottle, and the visible elation on his face as he swallows it. The observation angle does appear to be from the kitchen, as predicted.

Rosé All Day: Oh, honey, is that boy a pill popper? Spill the tea!

Fuckin' hell. I absolutely should've warned Julian. I stride to my room, hitting the callback button on CJ's contact as the door closes behind me.

"Hiya, handsome," she drawls. "It's about time; I was ready to give up on you."

"I arrived in Melbourne only hours ago, pet."

"And got straight to work! What've you got for me? Gimme the scoop."

"Ah, yes. Hate to disappoint you, but he's not a 'pill popper.' It's antibiotics. He took a fall while climbing. I'm afraid there's nothing 'juicy' to relate."

Her sigh gusts over the line. "Well, you musta gotten something I can use. Did he give up any fun tidbits? Embarrassing childhood anecdotes, family skeletons?"

"Be patient," I tell her smoothly. "I've got a long game at work, but you must say *nothing*. Not a whisper. If Sage sees you shitposting, baiting her, she'll become guarded. Stay under her radar until I get what you need. I'm earning her confidence, getting closer."

"Ooh, *how* close? You're gonna make me jealous."

"Come now—it's purely strategic. A girl like her is no substitute for a *woman*."

"That so? You'd better not be blowing smoke up my skirt, Al."

I drop my voice, sultry. "Don't you dare tease me with visions of what's up your skirt."

"Honey, I'm no tease. Ready to find out?"

"Careful who you taunt, love. You'll end up against the wall in more ways than one."

She chuckles darkly. "Let's discuss this a little *deeper* when you're back in London. I'll hop across the pond and we can make a night of it. Now, back to work, tiger. Go get me something good."

13

MELBOURNE

ALEXANDER

When Sage comes in at nine p.m., Julian and I are playing chess. I wish I were kicking his arse, looking like a genius, but we're matched in skill. As points go, we're even. But the look on Sage's face as she strolls over and folds her arms—gazing at the board, then me, with disapproval—makes me feel I could lose more than the match.

"Ain't this a pretty picture," she says with sarcasm.

I ignore her sour tone and offer a smile. "How was your day, my seraph?"

She doesn't reply, watching Julian as he studies the board. I can't tell if he's ignoring her or lost in thought. Priya appears just inside the doorway of the small second bedroom, looking out and sizing us up.

She balances one foot on the opposite calf in a yoga-like pose. "Hey, Sage."

"Oh, hey," Sage responds. Her tone is light, but more

embarrassed than aloof, like she wants to say more but is afraid to. She plucks my king off the board and tickles my earlobe with it. "Gonna take a shower. You should join me, honeybee."

Julian looks up from the board with a scowl. "Hey, put that down."

Sage backs away with a lazy smile and underhand-tosses the piece to him, forcing him to catch it against his chest. "Just gave you a win. You're welcome." She saunters toward the primary bedroom, and I can't resist watching that round little arse of hers. She throws a bit of extra hip sway into it as if she knows. "You coming, Sandy-boy?"

"At your command." I tip a helpless shrug at Julian as I rise and follow Sage to the bedroom.

The moment I'm through the doorway, she grabs me by the front of my shirt and yanks it open, sending a stray button flying. She pauses to look out into the living room as if remembering other people are here, then swings the door shut.

Smoothing a hand down my gaping shirtfront, she winces. "Sorry 'bout that. I'll buy you a new one." With an exhausted sigh, she goes and flops down at the foot of the bed.

"No need, pet. I've plenty more." I sink my hands into my pockets and watch her stiff posture. "But…a suggestion?"

She looks up, expression flat and defensive.

"Rather than putting on a ridiculous show"—I nod sideways toward the closed bedroom door—"and announcing a communal shower on which you most certainly don't plan to deliver, why don't you go talk to Priya and clear the air? The tension is—"

"*Urrrggghhh*," she moans, flopping back onto the bed and throwing her arms wide. "Not now, for fuck's sake. I'm tired, okay?

I'll bury the hatchet tomorrow. Right now I just want, uh..." She peeks at me, then drops her head again, sighing. "Like, no stress."

"I wonder if you're not making things harder for yourself unnecessarily."

"I wonder if I asked your opinion," she returns, sitting up. She pries off her still-tied shoes and flings them toward an untidy pile of clothing in a corner.

The level of wreckage in this bedroom is as if Sage has been squatting here for weeks: clothing, shoes, books and magazines, food wrappers, empty cups, styling tools and products, and—inexplicably—a dented papier-mâché bust of Saint Nicholas, wearing a pair of Sage's sunglasses.

I open a hand at it, changing the subject so Sage doesn't get stroppy and ask me to leave. "Story there?"

"Saw it in the trash outside a vintage store. They were just throwing it away!" She stands and heads for the en suite. "I gotta rinse off, honeybee. Make yourself at home."

While she's off-key belting out Violent Femmes' "Blister in the Sun" under the spray, I indulge in a bit of snooping. The magazines—battered copies of *Startling Stories* and *Weird Tales*—were clearly bought at whatever vintage shop was discarding the alarming St. Nick. There's a half-finished newspaper sudoku puzzle. Protein bar wrappers and empty alkaline water bottles. *So* many rumpled clothes.

Hanging off a wardrobe pull is a red satin brassiere, which I pick up to check the measurement. As I'm grasping the tag between my fingers, Sage's voice pipes up behind me.

"Thirty-six double-A, babes. Small boobs, but a sizable rib cage." She thumps a fist against her chest. "Strong as an ox."

Her hair is piled on top of her head, secured with a clip shaped like a slice of lemon, and she's wearing a white cotton camisole and men's boxers that read THE FAMILY JEWELS amidst a pattern of silver-glitter gems. The shirt fabric is so thin that for a moment I can't tear my eyes from the tea-rose outline of her areolae and nipples.

She does a slow catwalk toward me, shoulders held regally. Her scrubbed skin is faintly pink. She stops inches away, and a tempting whiff of piquant, soapy warmth hits me.

"I had a fun idea just now in the shower," she tells me.

"You may not want to know where my mind went when you said that," I tease.

"Oooorrrrrrr...that may be *exactly* where I wanted it to go." She runs a finger along my shirt placket where the button is missing. Glancing at my eyes to gauge my response, she shifts the fingertip to my skin, tracing down my sternum. "This is a nice chest you're always showing off with your disco-level unbuttoning habits."

"Saucy girl. 'Disco' indeed."

I move my left hand to her hair, open the jaws of the hair clip, and drop it. Sage's eyes go wide, and her breath catches.

"Is this allowed?" I comb my fingers through her steam-dampened tresses. "I'm not sure what you want tonight." I brush my knuckles along her tattooed neck and her eyes drop closed. "Pleasure? Or just to take the piss with Priya and make her think there's something between us?"

She sways a little on her feet and grasps the front of my shirt. "I don't know."

"Don't know what you want?"

She fixes me in the beam of those coppery eyes. "Don't know if there's something between us." She pushes my suit jacket off and steps close, pressing against me. Those delectable nipples of hers prod my torso, and desire rolls through me. My body is electric with the urge to pick her up and carry her to the bed, and my cock goes into high alert with a potent sensation like a good, strong stretch.

"I think maybe what I want," she tells me, "is for people two floors in either direction to be envious of the time we're having." She lifts her arms and drapes them over my shoulders, caressing the hair at the nape of my neck.

"Disingenuous theatrics. You're playing a dangerous game, sweet Salvi, teasing me if you've no intention of following through." I don't like how the words sound like a threat, but I'm too self-conscious to qualify it and admit that what I mean is *You're playing a dangerous game with my heart*.

Fortunately, she laughs, then affects a wide-eyed pout. "Who says I won't fuck you senseless?"

I grab her narrow hips and pull her against me. "You're a brat."

She looks pleasantly startled. "Goddamn, Sandy. Just what are you packing down there?" She takes a half step back, her hungry gaze raking me. "So, back to my idea in the shower." She angles toward me and whispers, "I want to give you a lap dance." Whatever my face does makes her laugh. "What, have you never had one? Don't tell me you're one of those boys who's uptight about strip clubs."

"I'm…No, it's not that. I'm just surprised. Though maybe I shouldn't be. You did say, back in the airport in Bahrain, that you plan to torture me."

She gives a mock-indignant scowl. "You think I'm going to be *that* terrible at it?"

"On the contrary, I think you've found the way to break me, as promised."

"Hmm, maybe so. But more than anything I want to show off how good a dancer I am, after weeks of you teasing me about being graceless just 'cause I can't tap dance." She drops her voice, parodying me in an accent so Northern that it'd dull the edge of a pocketknife. "'*Clumsy as a fuckin' buffalo, you*'—I believe that's how you put it."

I can't suppress my laugh. "I don't sound like that!"

She taps the tip of my nose, singsonging, "You do when you let your guard down…"

"Fuckin' hell."

"See?" She points at me, grinning.

Seized by a wave of ease with her, I grasp the hem of her shirt. "I like you, Salvi. I do feel unguarded when I'm with you." I move one thumb to caress the taut curve of her waist. "I hope you feel similarly. Whatever we're to be. Friends, or…"

I'm not sure what "more than friends" might be, so I leave it there. Julian warned me that Sage's lovers have a short shelf life. The thought makes me sad, and I wonder if I should tap the brakes on where we're headed.

The deed done, I may find myself on the next flight out of Melbourne. Would it be better if we stay in a holding pattern of perpetual sexual tension, like television shows that drag out an attraction between its lead actors for years, knowing that consummation will kill the series?

Her hands creep up the back of my shirt. "I don't need to

know if we're gonna 'be' anything. I like uncertainty. Risk. Living in the moment." Her short nails curl against my spine. "Would I do my job as well as I do if I couldn't roll with surprises? Now..." She prods me backward toward the wing chair and shoves my solar plexus. I collapse onto the padded velvet seat. "Sit, and stay." She bends at the waist, whispering, "*Good boy*. Time for you to get a treat."

Fuck—my will all but goes liquid after she says it. My heart hammers and all I can do is grip the chair arms, in a figurative sweat of anticipation for what she'll get up to next, the delicious bossy thing.

"I'm in your hands, *mistress*," I tell her.

She studies me a moment longer, then goes to her bedside table and powers on a Bluetooth speaker before picking up her phone and scrolling. A familiar bass-heavy pop song starts up, and Sage wanders back my way.

"Gimme your shirt," she commands with a smirk.

Our eyes are locked on each other as I undo my cuffs and remaining front buttons, sliding out of the shirt and handing it to her.

She presses it to her face. "You do smell nice, I'll give you that."

Turning away, she glides to the bed, where she sets my shirt down before whipping off her own and flinging it over her shoulder. It lands near my foot, and I resist the impulse to pick it up. The strong, defined lines of her back muscles are fucking poetry, and I'm assailed by the image of licking a path along their angular curves.

She puts on my shirt and spins toward me before fastening

one middle button, then reaches beneath the hem—hanging halfway down her lean thighs—and grabs the fabric of the boxer shorts, tugging them off and kicking them to one side. With the motion, the bottom of the shirt parts, and I get a flash of that pretty mound with its sable line of trimmed pubic hair.

"You're a delicious sight," I can't help murmuring.

"You look nice too, sitting there shirtless with an erection," she returns playfully. She goes to an open suitcase and fishes out a pair of sheer black organza knickers, stepping into them and sliding them up her legs. "Might be my favorite way I've seen you. You should be like that all the time."

I hum a small laugh. "Not for polite company, pet."

She heads toward me, each step picking up more of a dancing sway, impelled by the music. "It's a good thing I'm not *polite*, then." She smacks her hands down on top of mine where they rest on the chair's arms. "Don't move these, got it? No touchy-touchy. Look only."

"Understood."

As Kesha catapults into the song's chorus, belting out, "*I'm a motherfucking woman...!*" Sage throws one leg up and plants her small foot on my knee. Her inked arms shoot over her head, opening the shirt like a theater curtain, and her hips rotate, smooth and provocative. I scarcely know where to rest my starved gaze as it tours her body.

Her foot is warm where it braces on my knee. The pale highway of her leg, mapped with its bright tattoos, leads me to the gyration of her pelvis. I spot the appendectomy scar, which is unusually long, compared to others I've seen. My right hand tightens on the chair arm as I suppress the desire to run a fingertip along the irregular ridge of flesh.

I think she notices my attention there, because she slides her foot off my knee and shifts to straddle my legs. She wriggles against me, sinuous, her expression intense with erotic promise. The lushness of that taut bum and flexed legs rubbing my thighs is overwhelming. I grip the chair harder and meet the challenge in her leonine eyes.

"You'll be the death of me," I manage.

"Awww…" She rises and backs off me, but I mourn the loss of her for only a moment. Undoing the button, she pitches the shirt away before turning and settling over my lap arse-first. "But what a great way to go, ain't it?" she concludes.

All I can do is emit a helpless groan as she rides my lap. The knickers are cut high—not quite a thong but exposing most of those stunning round cheeks. She moves front to back, sliding along me with the obscured heat of her barely covered pussy. Every few passes, she backs up just enough to settle briefly on the aching pole of my tormented cock.

I've been a pathetically horny bastard all my life, but I can honestly say I've never been driven by a need this visceral. I feel like I could fuck both of us into a pile of sentient jelly, given the chance. Sage is the only thing that exists right now, and my desire circles her like she's the sole landing spot in a vast ocean. There's nowhere else to go, nothing other than this fiery woman, the rasp of fabric along my tense thighs, the tilt of her sweet hips, the music drowning us in its heady pounding.

My focus moves up the arroyo of her spine, fascinated by

the muscles rolling beneath her inked skin. Her arms are high, hands dancing around each other like candle flames. Soft, damp aqua waves swing along her shoulder blades, and there's nothing I want more—nothing I've *ever* wanted more—than to gather her hair in one fist and bend her over the bed, jerk down those filmy knickers, and give her arse a good smack before I sink my cock into the paradise I suspect is sultry-wet.

She rises and moves a few feet away, executing a graceful twirl to face me, running her hands over her torso. Seeing her touch skating over the hard nipples is agony. I want to taste every part of her. To lick and nip those rosy peaks, to devour her mouth and savor the vibration of her moan as our tongues join. I want to weave my fingers with hers, kiss my way down her body, and feel her hands flex and twist in a delicious anguish of arousal as I flick and tease and suck her engorged clit, pulling back to flirt along her labia until she thrusts against my face, begging me to put my mouth back on her clit and let her come.

My jaw tight, nostrils flared with tension, I grit out, "What would it take, Salvi? Name it. I'd fucking burn the world to have you."

"Oh yeah?" Her voice is high and airy, teasing me.

"Five floors of this hotel can know how hard I am for you, how I'll make you feral, shuddering and pleading for more until you're hoarse. Let's take this where we really want it to go. One night—anything and everything you crave. I'm your eager fuckin' servant."

She stalks back my way and straddles my lap again, assessing my face for a long minute. "Don't…you dare…move…"

she finally whispers. Cupping my jaw, she places a featherlight kiss on my right cheek.

The self-control necessary to keep my head immobile is humbling. To *not* turn and capture her mouth, my hands diving into her hair and squeezing fistfuls…I'm not sure how I exert the discipline. But I'm too afraid this heavenly battle of wills could be called off with any false move, sending her into a mischievous leap to her feet, chuckling over my pain as she walks away and tells me to sleep in the chair.

She reaches between us and opens my trousers, and I arch to help her in the task as my tragically aching cock is freed into her grip.

"This," she says just above a whisper, so close to my lips that I can feel the flutter of her words, "is a nice girthy dick you've got."

She slowly strokes it to the base, then back up to the tip, twisting her wrist to smear me with the silky beads of moisture she's wrung out. A shiver drags through me.

"Can you be a good boy and let me fuck you?" she murmurs. "No touching me, no kissing. Just let me get myself off on this big pretty dick with noooo thought of your own pleasure."

For a moment I can barely speak, my throat is so tight. I swallow hard. "Watching you come *would* be my own pleasure," I almost gasp. "A fucking privilege. Take whatever you like."

Her smile is a Cheshire cat curl. She rises and goes to her suitcase, withdrawing a string of Magnum condoms and—oh, bloody hell, *yesssss*—the pink handcuffs she had in her pocket when she collected me from the airport. She tears one condom packet off the strip and drops the rest on the bedside table before coming back to me.

"Stand up and get your pants off, then turn around," she directs. To free up both hands, she licks the wrapped condom and sticks it to her chest, just below a collarbone. I hardly know how to react, whether to laugh or groan—the gesture is both silly and unbearably hot.

I comply, and she puts the cuffs around my wrists behind my back before rotating me and shoving me onto the wing chair. Climbing aboard my lap again, clad only in those black knickers, she rises tall on her knees and folds the condom into one hand before thrusting a pink nipple toward my face. "Show me what you can do with this," she commands.

My eyes close as I brush my lips across the hard, warm peak. The scent of her skin is paradise—citrussy and sugary. There's a golden muskiness rising between us, where she's lightly cocking her hips, rubbing her divine pussy against the iron battering ram of my cock. I lick a slow circuit around her areola, then tease the nipple in gentle passes with the flat of my tongue. She leans closer with a tiny, whimpering sigh, and I draw the delicious bud into my mouth and give a bit of suction while flirting the tip of my tongue on the underside.

She releases a shivery groan, and her hands go to my shoulders, digging in with her short, unpainted nails. "Nice, nice..." she breathes. "Fucking *nice*." Her eyes are closed, and without opening them she tears open the condom and sweeps it down over my throbbing length. "Okay, waitwaitwait," she half whispers, pulling her nipple from my mouth. "I don't wanna come too fast. I'm so turned on. Fuck, why do I want you so much?"

"I can't touch, but may I look my fill?" I ask.

"Hell yes, honeybee. Watch me fuck this big dick of yours."

I look down between us, and Sage pulls her knickers to one side, tilting her hips up and using two fingers to spread herself, showing off the generous mauve berry of her clit. Just as she told me earlier, it most certainly *is* deliciously prominent. My mouth all but waters, imagining licking and sucking it, leisurely and soft, with just enough pressure to make her beg for more, grabbing my hair and pulling me against her, writhing with need.

"You like?" she taunts, passing a fingertip side to side across the swollen bud.

My gaze lifts to her face. "I like *all* of you, Salvi. That sweet morsel is just the newest addition to the list."

Her laugh is low. Tugging her knickers farther to one side, she aligns with the head of my cock and rotates her hips in a slow circuit. She sinks onto me an inch, then retreats.

"Dreadful girl," I manage, my voice tight.

"You'll wait and love it." She slides down again, deeper, contracting to give me a squeeze before rising. "I am one hundred percent going to make you suffer for being awful to me on your stupid fucking blog—I warned you." Another inch-deep plunge, pulsing her muscles. "You're going to watch me come hard, and you're going to need to do it too—more than you need your next damned breath—and I…am not…going…*to let you.*"

She punctuates her last few words with increasingly deep envelopments of my straining cock. Lifting off again, she grabs me in one hand and uses me to stroke that stunning clit of hers. Her pupils are wide black pools ringed in gold, her lips are parted, and her head is tilted to showcase the flaming peacock feather tattoo on her neck. Disheveled pastel hair drapes over the opposite breast, the nipple peeking through.

With a sudden cry, she sinks down on me, hard and full. Eyes closed, she grabs one of my shoulders and puts the other hand on my throat, stroking the column, following the lines of my tendons with her thumb and forefinger. She grinds harder into my lap, and I feel the slick heat of her arousal paint my thighs.

I hold my lower body rigid, fighting the need to move with her as she begins to arch on me. Her thighs flex and her tight, wet little cunt wrings me as she rules my cock with increasing ferocity. Behind my back, my wrists turn and my fingers tangle. I grab the edge of the cushion where it meets the chair back as I'm assaulted by waves of perfect fucking bliss.

She's half gasping, half laughing for pure pleasure, her wicked angel face a gorgeous sight. I watch as signs of impending climax flit across her expression. There's nothing pained or contrived, just a natural combination of gasping breath and happiness.

Her eyes fly open and she looks at me almost as if remembering I'm still there, and for a moment I'm slightly hurt, until an authentic smile radiates from her. She slows her movement and leans closer to me, rising to fuck mostly the tip of my cock as she aligns her tattooed left breast with my mouth.

"Do what you were doing before, Sandy," she pants. "I'm almost there. I want you to lick my tit as I come…"

I apply myself with enthusiasm to the job, and she tips her pelvis so her clit rubs against my cock with her small, measured thrusts. She grips my shoulder with one hand, the other tangled in my hair. Unmistakably, I feel the tremors of her impending climax. A low, tight growling in her throat rises to a sensational wail, and she wrings my hair so hard that my scalp burns.

"Fuck! Yessssssss!" she shouts with an exhausted laugh, pulling her breast away from my mouth. The twitching of her pussy lingers, and she sighs in exultant relief, leaning her head against my bare, sweat-dewed shoulder. She stays that way for a minute as her breathing slows, and I realize it's the closest thing to tender she's ever been with me. My eyes close, savoring it.

I'm still miserably hard, but as warned, she climbs off me. Looking down at my lap, she says, "Uh, don't move 'til I get you a towel. I squirted. Stay right there." She dashes to the en suite, and the sight of her knickers askew—one arse cheek fully exposed—and her inner thighs bathed in glistening wetness is almost enough to send me over the edge without so much as a touch.

She trots back and crams the towel into my lap. "I end up paying for more goddamned hotel chairs that way," she confesses. "Here, lean forward and I'll, um, unshackle you."

She releases one wrist and I bring my arms around to my front, rubbing at a red, dented spot. I breathe slowly and evenly, willing my cock to relax and accept that nothing more is forthcoming, but the sight and scent of a freshly fucked Sage is a powerful aphrodisiac.

"I'll just, erm, excuse myself for a shower," I tell her, planning to take matters into my own hands.

"Yeah, I messed you up pretty good," she says with a mildly embarrassed chuckle, nodding toward the towel.

My eyebrows lift. "Oh, no worries there. I'd gladly be covered in you like a fuckin' double-glazed Chelsea bun."

Sage cracks up, resting a hip against the chair arm.

"I merely need a few minutes to…gather my wits," I conclude.

"Ohhhhhh, right. Okay, that's fair. You're allowed." She picks up her camisole and puts it back on. "By the way," she says with a hint of something like uncharacteristic shyness, "I don't always do that." She points to the towel again. "Y'know, *that*. The squirting. Just sometimes, when, uh…I have a lot of energy. And—" She scrunches her mouth as if debating whether to say more. "Like, if I feel comfortable. When I can totally let go."

Between this revelation and the fact that she called me Sandy just before she came, I'm assailed by a tender feeling that prickles behind my eyes. I stand, rubbing my face with the non-towel-holding hand and clearing my throat.

"Glad I could help," I say, my voice gruff with emotion.

She ducks her head, then turns away to go to her mobile. "Yeah, thanks. It was fun." She taps her screen. "I'll order grub. Kinda hungry after that." Without turning around, she waves toward the en suite, dismissing me. "Save me some hot water. I need to rinse off again."

I collect my trousers from the floor in front of the chair and go to the shower.

I can't help wondering, *Is she feeling something too? What have we done?*

14

MELBOURNE

SAGE

Shoving some books and a set of over-ear headphones off the bedside table onto the floor, I stack plates, then drop the napkins on top. "Just to be clear," I tell Alexander, "this never happened."

"The sex?" He leans back against a pile of pillows and casually puts his hands behind his head. "I reckon people could tell, pet. You're quite vocal."

The combination of low-lidded side-eye he's giving me, that naughty smirk, and the bulging definition of his arms and shoulders in that pose...*Aaauuuggghhh*, it's making me wet, but there's no way I'm copping to it. The bedsheet is wrapped low on his hips, showing off his gorgeous gym-punished torso. *Fucking nice.*

"I was talking about the food," I clarify. "Dagna would destroy me."

I give my greasy fingertips a final wipe on the napkin pile, then swivel to face him and wrap my arms around my raised knees. I'm back in the boxers and tank top, but Alexander is naked and totally at ease with that fact. His hair's freshly washed, damp-darkened auburn waves falling all cute over his forehead, giving off red glints. As I peruse the freckles on his nose and cheeks and the scar cutting across his eyebrow, my heart does a weird floppy thing.

Stop it, I snap at myself. *Post-orgasm oxytocin is a horrible drug. Worse than LSD probably, for causing delusions…*

Except that usually doesn't happen to me. The "love drug" normally just makes me feel friendly, or keyed up for another round. Right now, something else is happening, and whatever it is must be making me look worried. Alexander seems to notice, because suddenly he's mirroring whatever I'm doing with my dumb betraying face.

He opens one arm at his side in invitation. "Come here, Salvi. Give us a cuddle, then."

"*Hmph.* Whatever." I scoot next to him and allow the embrace.

He sort of nuzzles my hair, and I'm afraid he's going to kiss my head.

"No kissing," I remind him.

"I've been warned," he assures me.

I've got a mellowish playlist going quietly on the speaker, stuff that's as chill as I can stand—some nineties shoegaze like Lush and My Bloody Valentine. It's after eleven o'clock and I should be sleeping, but I feel antsy as hell. I wrestle the covers around to get my legs under them, but also partly to dislodge the sheet covering Alexander's goods. I catch a glimpse before smoothing the duvet over us both. Dicks are mostly just stupid-looking unless they're erect, but...*hmm*, I dunno—his is pretty nice even just sitting there.

"So," he says with some amusement, "you riding my manacled self to victory is, as you'd say, 'no biggie,' but a plate of chips and gravy is an unspeakable sin?"

"Pretty much. Only because of my job though—food guilt is lame, in general." I draw up my knees again, hugging them. "I don't have shame about sex. If I wanna fuck someone, and I'm safe about it, why the hell not? Like I have to spend X number of dates making small talk before I've earned it? *Psh!* I don't have time for the 'getting to know each other' bullshit."

"Fair point." He idly caresses my upper arm with his thumb.

"I mean, you can have a meal with someone, and that's social, but also servicing the body, right? My point: *So's sex.* Can't it be like sharing a meal? Fucking someone is basically a fancy handshake."

"Well, damned fine to have met you," he says, picking up my hand and offering a shake.

"You too, Sandy-boy." I want to keep holding his hand, but I don't *want to* want to hold it, so I let go and stretch across the bed to switch off the light on the bedside table as an excuse. When I sit back, he adjusts against me, and we both slide down on the pillows, reclining. I roll onto my side and throw one leg over his.

It's super dark, but with a splash of Indigo light from the speaker behind me illuminating the angles of his face. I look my fill, knowing he probably can't see me doing it.

After a long pause, he says, "*We* could get to know each other."

My heartbeat trips. "We already had sex," I say, a little defensive.

His laugh is a dark rumble I feel through his bare chest, which I've laid a hand on without being aware of it. "And who says we can't do the 'getting to know each other bullshit'—as you so charmingly put it—*afterwards*?"

I'm quiet for a long time, grappling with what to say. At a certain point I consider pretending I'm asleep, but if my sneeze in the elevator didn't fool him, a fake snore probably won't either. Finally I decide to be honest and nip this thing in the bud before it gets awkward.

"You're a good time," I tell him, "but I can't take you seriously."

"Have you ever taken a partner seriously?" he counters. When I don't reply, he continues. "Ah. *No.* That's why you choose people like me, isn't it?"

He sounds kind of world-weary when he says it, and I realize that the assessment, for him, is more a depressing revelation about himself than a judgment on me. I feel bad for him, not gonna lie. And just a teeny tiny bit I also feel bad for *myself*. So I do what I always do and create a diversion before it gets uncomfortable.

The hand I have on his chest slides lower. I cup my fingers lightly over his very nice dick and feel it rouse. "Are you tired?" I ask innocently.

He rolls me beneath himself, the motion smooth and natural. "Do I feel tired?" he asks, an inch from my lips.

I laugh. "Uh, no. My car goes from zero to sixty in two-point-two seconds, but I think your response time is even faster."

"I'm inspired." His hips settle closer to me.

I wriggle out of my clothes and draw up a knee to give him better access. One side of his face has a pale lavender glow from the speaker, and I know mine does too. Both of us half revealed, half hiding.

Sappy shit isn't usually my gig, but I can't resist cupping his jawline with both hands. "You're awfully pretty."

"Likewise."

"Why would you even want to 'get to know' me? We're doing this either way, right?"

"*Are* we doing this?"

I sprawl out an arm for one of the remaining condoms on the bedside table. "Hell yeah, I'm game for it." I tuck it under the pillow behind my head, and my hand rejoins the other in touching Alexander's face. I run a thumb over his lower lip.

He moves his head to playfully trap my thumb between his teeth for a moment, and I pull back, then give one of his nipples a pinch. There's a sharp intake of breath as he sucks in a small gasp through his nose. We both make a friendly noise, not quite a laugh. I move my free hand to the back of his neck, ruffling the hair at his nape.

"I want to know you better," he tells me quietly, "because I'm dead keen and not afraid to admit it." He moves his cheek to touch mine, but doesn't kiss me, then pulls back and focuses on my eyes. "I'm growing inordinately fond of you, Salvia officinalis."

The feeling in my chest goes all elastic and tingly. "Thanks," I say as offhandedly as possible. "You're kinda okay too."

His head drops to my shoulder for a few seconds, and I'm

not sure if he's laughing at me. He pops back up and slides his cheek against mine again, gradually approaching my lips.

My shoulders stiffen. "Not gonna kiss you," I assert again.

"I'm well aware." He sounds a bit pained. "May I ask why?"

"Because you want me to."

"I do. Very much." His chin nuzzles my cheek. "But I don't think that's why you won't."

"Oh, horseshit. I said I was going to torture you, babes."

"And you are. Properly doing my fuckin' head in."

I don't want to hear whatever he's going to say next—I *can't*. This is suddenly a lot. Either we need to get down to business or one of us is sleeping on that goddamned chair. I reach under the pillow and whip out the condom, ripping it open with my teeth and jamming a hand between us to get it onto him.

"Stop being all emo and just fuck me, will you?"

He lifts up so I can reach him better, and in case he decides to try some slow, sensitive lovemaking crap, I kick the covers away with one foot so we're not tangled by them and wrap my legs around him, tilting my pelvis to get him inside me, pushing his lower back with one of my feet so he'll get the message. He leans into me, pinning me to the mattress with one deep thrust and staying there, moving his hips in a fantastic grinding way that rubs my clit.

"That's it," I whisper. "Perfect. Fuck, you're a great fit…"

He pulls back, nearly all the way out, and with a frustrated whimper I dig my fingers into his muscular ass to draw him close. He thrusts into me again and again, teasing and sliding once we're joined hard, then pulling back so I arch and pant, desperate to feel every inch of him.

"Yes, yes…fuck yessssss…this is…yes, *please*…" The words spill out of me.

He leans his weight against me fully, sliding his hands up my arms to grasp my wrists, and the momentary feeling of being gloriously crushed under him is amazing. When he starts moving again, I buck against him in a fever of need, loving how seamlessly we fit together, how intuitively he responds. I don't know how he knows me so well without knowing me, but *damn*…the guy is paying attention, playing my body with quiet command.

Usually I'd be herding myself toward a quick climax, but weirdly I just want to keep doing this. His vocalizations are subtle—tense breaths and fragments of groans—and the sound of it is something I could listen to on repeat. He smells incredible too, a bloom of sweat rising on his skin and supercharging the base scent I already love.

I arch up and almost kiss him, not even thinking, just obeying the hunger in my body. At the last second I realize I'm doing it and twist my arms from his grasp, sitting half up. "Here, let me, uh…" I grab a pillow and flip face down with it under my hips. "Fuck me this way."

Rather than falling right back on top of me, he palms my ankles and caresses up my legs with teasing slowness. When he gets to my ass, I cock my hips, asking for it. He kneads my ass cheeks, then rubs between my legs in long, slippery passes with his full hand. His fingers settle on my clit.

"Fuckin' hell. You're aching to go off, aren't you?" I widen my legs, practically desperate, and he gives the area a pat with his fingertips. "Are you going to let *me* finish too this time?"

"Yes, anything…" I clench my ass and rub my clit against the pillow, looking for relief. "Just fuck me now—*hard*."

"Saucy girl, ordering me about." He cradles my ass in his hands and squeezes again.

I wriggle side to side on the pillow with a helpless moan. "I know. You should probably give my ass a few smacks for it."

"Should I?" A stinging swat follows close on the heels of his words. My welcoming yelp trails off to a whimper.

"Again, please," I direct in a gasp, shoving a hand beneath myself. "Keep doing that while I come. You can have yours after—" As I'm saying it, his hand arcs down again, and the sweet sting sends me into overdrive. I cup myself with one hand, thrusting against my slippery fingers, my panting mixed with nonsensical pleading as he smacks my ass. The delicious moment creeps closer until I finally thunder over the edge with a scream. My legs tense, knees shaking, and my pussy clenches in waves, clamoring to have him back inside me.

Either he knows, or he's following the dictates of his own need. He covers me with the taut, angular warmth of his body and docks into me with that exquisite dick. My legs are wobbly with aftershocks, but I prop onto my knees higher so I can back up to meet his strokes. The pillow is mashed between my legs in a way that makes me rub against it, and before long I'm headed up the peak again, my breath gusting as much in surprise as lust.

After a few minutes, his own panting twists into a strangled groan as he comes, releasing with a sound like, *Ah!* as if he's discovered something amazing. His tousled head falls to my shoulder, and his breathing as it struggles to catch up to itself is almost like weary laughter.

Something about it makes me really…fucking…*happy*. I'm listening to him, enjoying the sound, and I've pretty much forgotten that I was about to finish again until he winds his arms around me and rolls onto his back, taking me with him.

I'm lying on him like he's a pool raft or something, his dick still inside me, and to my surprise, he reaches one hand and settles it over my clit, then puts the other on my nipple. With gentle precision, he rubs me in both places at once.

My head is leaning back on his shoulder, and he says, "Come for me again like the fucking marvel you are. That's it, sweetness…follow it…"

I relax and focus on his hands, the rise and fall of his breathing beneath me, his scent, the vibration of his voice as he coaxes me again toward ecstasy. My legs tremor and my quick breaths transform into a shriek as another climax steamrolls through me. His touch goes whisper-light, then drops away. He smooths both hands down my shoulders and arms, then brings them up to cross over my chest, giving me a sort of backward hug.

After a few minutes of recovery, I ease off him and roll onto my face, completely spent. I feel him get up and go into the bathroom, then come back and get into bed, pulling the duvet over us both.

"That was fuckin' rad," I mumble with my cheek smushed against the mattress, barely coherent. "Where'd you learn the last bit?"

He chuckles, passing a hand down my back in a slow caress and punctuating it with a gentle pat on my ass. "I don't know," he admits.

"Well…" I lift one limp arm and manage to make a weak A-okay gesture, which he may or may not be able to see in this light. "My compliments, either way."

As I drift off, he nestles closer. The last thing I'm aware of is his lips delivering a lingering kiss to my shoulder.

I pretend to be asleep and let him do it.

I generally have girls sleep over after sex, because it doesn't feel safe to send them out alone at night. But guys? Nope. Total mood kill, the realness of sleep. The idea of some fuckwit snoring and mumbling and farting beside me, thrashing around and disturbing my rest…no thanks. Call yourself a cab and get the hell out, pal.

Alexander *does* disturb my rest, but not in the way I worried about. For one thing, the guy is so silent when he sleeps that it's eerie. I literally put a hand near his mouth to make sure he was breathing at one point. He sleeps on his side with both hands tucked under his face, like an illustration of a Victorian child waiting for Christmas morning. He should be holding a candy cane like Cindy-Lou Who.

I find myself thinking, as I watch him, *That'd be hilarious— I'm totally gonna sneak a candy cane into his clasped hands some time and get a pic of it…*and then I remember that there's no fucking way I'm ever letting the guy sleep next to me again. As soon as the sun comes up, this pretty idiot's gotta hit the bricks.

I did get a couple hours of "power sleep"—I have the same sleep trainer as Cosmin, my teammate, and that shit works—but about an hour before my alarm's set to go off, I wake up and spend the whole damned time staring at Alexander. I apparently have such a debilitating case of the dick-stupids that I even find myself wondering what he's dreaming.

Have I lost my mind?

Forcing myself to turn away, I grab my phone and toggle the alarm off before it can make a noise, then slide out of bed. I brush my teeth and step into the boxers and tank top I flung off last night, then gingerly open the bedroom door to go to the living room and make coffee.

Priya walks out of her room as I'm struggling with the machine.

"Lemme do it," she says impatiently. She's wearing yoga pants and another of Jules's shirts—it has a pic of the album cover of Pixies' *Doolittle*, because my brother may be a dipshit, but he at least has great taste in old indie music.

Her hair is in two sleep-fuzzed braids, and she looks tired and sad. She applies herself silently to the task of making espresso, and I hop onto the bar and watch her do it. I know I have to apologize. You'd think I'd be used to it, since it's a part of our established routine, but these days it actually feels a little *worse* every time, like picking at a healing scab so the scar keeps getting bigger. As I watch her fussing with the espresso machine, my heart aches.

She turns around and hands me the tiny espresso cup, and she hasn't made one for herself, which is an unspoken sign that she's ready to forgive me. It hits me again—as it does often—that she should've picked a better best friend, not a sarcastic bitch who doesn't enjoy the things she does, like old black-and-white romantic movies and cooking that has more than two steps and reading dry science books and doing crafts that require patience. Things I unfairly make fun of her for, because secretly I wish I was less cynical and sweary and impatient.

"Thanks," I mumble, taking a small sip. I look down at the caramelly surface. "I'm sorry for being shitty. I'm glad Jules is going clean, and I'm glad he has you. You're good for him, and to be honest I was fuckin' jealous."

"I know," she says simply. There's no sense of victory, no hidden *I told you so*.

I take another sip. She's still waiting for something. I glance over my shoulder at the closed bedroom door. "So, about *that*. I had to get it out of my system—the guy's hot, if a total prick, and I wanted to torture him a little. But full disclosure: part of why it happened was to piss you off, since you can't stand him."

"Very silly, considering that the reason I dislike him is for what he did to *you*."

My throat gets tight. "I hate that we're fighting."

She comes over and hugs me. "We're not anymore. Thank you for the apology."

I set the espresso cup aside and hug her back, hard.

When she pulls away, she glances toward my room. "Be, um, *nice* when you kick him to the curb, all right? He's a jerk, but probably doesn't deserve being a prop in some stupid fight."

"Oh, he got plenty out of it. Now he can go back to collecting art and rare vinyl and second-tier aristocracy chicks with names like 'Beatrice Hughes-Cavendish.'"

"Did you actually let him sleep over? You never do that!"

"Who says we slept?" I give a comical wink.

"Are you"—she lowers her voice—"*feeling something for him?*"

"Fuck *no*. I ain't built for it. I can barely tolerate the guy." I swing one leg restlessly, peeking at Priya. "But, uh, you and Jules, huh? Looks like you really love him, I guess. Just…not more than you love *me*, right?" I prod her with my bare foot. I'm trying to be light and jokey about it, but there's so much insecurity behind it that my heart cramps.

"Sage." She looks at me soberly. "You know it's not the same."

I blow a small raspberry. "That's the kind of bullshit parents say."

"And parents mean it too."

I roll my eyes, uncomfortable with how serious this is getting. "Yeah, well. You're way too good for the guy."

"Not true. He's a wonderful person. He's having problems right now—and I didn't realize the extent of it until last month—but it doesn't diminish who he is. Julian has a good heart. He wants to get better, but he can't do it alone."

"Mmm." I'm thinking again about what happened in Thailand, recommitting to not saying anything to Pri. Is it right to hold a grudge forever, considering that he was an adolescent when it happened? Incomplete brain development, high impulsivity…maybe I'm being too hard on him.

Do I need *to stay mad for some reason?*

"So, um," Priya begins, avoiding my eyes. "If the pills were a problem for him over a year ago, why didn't you say anything to me?"

I almost blurt out a lie. Then I decide she deserves better even if it makes me look like a complete shit. "Because I know how you are, 'patron saint of lost causes,' and I was afraid it'd make you invested in him, and…I wanted you to myself."

My God, it sounds even worse than I thought. So selfish. My conscience points out critically, *Maybe you and Julian both abandoned each other.*

"That's why I got so mad at you guys that night at my parents' house," I confess, feeling like it's now or never to say all of it. "I was scared for Jules and threatened by you two being a thing." I poke her with my foot again, smiling, needing to lighten the mood. "So much for you claiming all these years that you're 'not Julian's type,' eh?"

"*Psh!* I still don't believe I *am*. He's mister adventure sports, and the most adventurous thing I do is try out a really complicated recipe."

"You're doing something very adventurous: taking a chance on love. Helluva lot braver than me. I'd take a fifty-g crash over that romance crap *any* day." I point a thumb over my shoulder. "He was fun but…y'know, it's probably time for that pickup service you joked about last night."

My bedroom door opens, and Priya and I both swivel to look. Alexander leans in the doorway, sleep-tousled and shirtless and hot as a midrace tyre. My stomach drops, because next comes the moment when I have to tell him we're done. But what I really want is to crawl between the sheets with him and order room service and talk for hours, watch him have tea and read *The Guardian* or whatever fancy-pants bullshit he does with his mornings. I'm not ready for him to leave, but his expiration date was up hours ago.

"Morning, Salvi," he says with a sleepy smile. "I'd take one of those if it's no trouble." He points at my teeny cup on the counter, then nods sideways toward the en suite, indicating that he's going to shower.

The door closes. Pri and I look at each other. I feel heat in my face, and hurry to the compact chrome machine, prodding it. "How do you work this fuckin' thing?"

"I'll do it. Here, let me." She starts it up, and while it's purring out a glossy rope of espresso, she gives me a sidelong look. "What's 'salvi'?"

I shrug. "Just a dumb joke. *Salvia officinalis*. It's Latin for 'sage.'"

"Okay, that's honestly cute. Points."

"It *is* kinda cute, right?"

"He, uh, looks more like a regular person without a shirt."

I chuckle. "Took off his rich-boy chain mail." I gnaw at my lower lip. "He was, like, really nice last night. Surprisingly warmhearted and real with me. I kinda almost believe him that the blog stuff was a prank that got outta hand. He's maybe a decent guy. I think."

She flicks a smile my way. "Maybe you bring out the best in him."

"Wanna know something funny? He kinda brings out the good in me too. I didn't realize how dumb and immature I was being with you until some stuff he said made me see it through an outsider's eyes."

"Huh."

"And I'm a little impressed that even though he's been trying to get into my pants—like, you'd think he'd just agree with anything I say—he's stuck up for you multiple times."

She slow-turns, all amused bewilderment. "No way."

"Yes way. A hundred percent."

There's a long pause before she gives another, "Huh." She hands me the steaming shot. "There. Now go have coffee with the guy you 'barely tolerate,' who definitely didn't give you an adorable nickname."

I take both cups and head for the bedroom, gearing up for what feels like it might be the first heartbreak of my life.

15

MELBOURNE

ALEXANDER

Any good journalist is an inveterate eavesdropper, and I'm no exception. I overheard Sage telling Priya that she'd prefer to slam her car into a wall than love someone. Normally, for me, hearing that would be a relief.

But as Badrick would say, "Life's motorway is paved with irony." Today I wake in the sublimely wrecked bed of a woman I want to follow around with the doggedness of an electoral register canvasser running after someone with a clipboard… only to find that I'm about to be tossed aside like one of Sage's helmet visor tear-offs.

I'm basking in the assault of three showerheads when I hear the bedroom door close. I turn my face into the spray and massage with both hands. There's a small click on the marble counter.

"Brought your espresso," Sage tells me neutrally. "Pri made it."

"Thanks, pet. Out in a mo."

I wipe my eyes and look over my shoulder at her. She's perched on the countertop, bare legs swinging, ankles tangling and unwinding. I can't read her face—the set of that petal mouth is a half-smile, but her eyes are cautious.

"Unless you'd care to join me?" I add.

She necks the espresso in her own cup and hops off the counter, picking up her toothbrush. "No time, babes. Gotta be at the paddock in point-zipshit minutes."

She proceeds to clean her teeth, all the while bobbing her knees and humming what sounds to be the melody to Belle and Sebastian's "Step into My Office, Baby." She spits in the washbasin and rinses, and an image comes to mind of what I'd like to see her doing with that lovely mouth. She leans to wipe her face on a crumpled towel—the en suite is as much a tip as the bedroom—then turns my way with a pirouette that makes her foot squeak on the tile floor.

"How was the record?" she asks.

I lift an eyebrow. "Did we set a record last night? Certainly felt like it." Shutting the water off, I pluck a folded towel from the nearby stack.

"No, uh…the internet auction thing. In Bahrain. You spent like thirty grand on some record with four songs. Were they worth it?"

"Absolutely." I pull the towel over my head and scrub at my hair to dry it off. "But it wasn't the best thing to happen to me that night." Uncovering myself, I meet her eye. "That would be the moment you came and sat beside me on the same chair. Or possibly when I ate cake off a fork that had been in your mouth."

She pokes her tongue out. "Quit trying to charm me. You know you don't mean it."

"I do mean it. I suspect it's more the case that *you* don't."

Her brow furrows and she turns away, grabbing a hairbrush and yanking it through her aqua tresses. "Don't make this weird just to amuse yourself. I'm not into dating, and neither are you. I heard from Natalia Evans that around the *ARJ* offices you brag about having a 'three-shag limit.'" She drops the brush with a clatter and twists her hair on top of her head, trapping the haystack mess in an elastic band.

I wrap the towel around my waist and secure it, then walk over and stand behind Sage. Her arms lower slowly from her head as we watch each other in the mirror. I skim my hands over her shoulders, and the desire to kiss the nape of her exposed neck is intense. It doesn't escape me that her nipples tighten into rosy pebbles as my touch explores her.

"Two out of three, so we're owed another round." One of my hands roams to the base of her throat and settles there in a reverent V, framing her, and the other glides down to breach the waist of the boxer shorts she's wearing.

Obviously I crave her. For nearly two years now—since she was a reserve driver for Harrier—I've savored every sip of news about her, gone alert as a hawk at any sighting of her around the paddock. But atypically to my experience, the consummation last night has only made me want her more.

A womanizing friend of mine in New York once joked that immediately after sex, "a woman should turn into a six-pack and a pizza," and at the time I agreed. But right now, touching this diminutive, inked goddess, I never want to let her go.

She sags back against me, and her golden eyes close. "You're awful."

"Too true." My fingertips follow the path of her trimmed line of pubic hair, and she emits a pleased-sounding sigh as I circle her clit.

"Sandy..."

"Yes, my seraph?" I dip two fingers inside her, dragging their slickness back up to aid my caresses.

"You're gonna make me late."

"I'm going to make you come."

She cocks her arse back against me and groans in frustrated pleasure. I move my lips along the curve of her neck, lifting her thin shirt and stroking one of her nipples.

"You won't let me kiss that stubborn mouth," I murmur, "but perhaps I could kiss you here?" My fingers spread to glide along both sides of her swelling clit. "I want to bring you to the edge while you pant and beg and grind against my face." I sink into her heat again. "Fingers right...*here*"—I go in deep and brush the border of her G-spot—"as I lap up your sweetness and send you mad."

Her knees sag, and she turns in my arms, looking up at me from a foot below. "Okay, listen," she whispers. "I'm not, uh... we're not seeing each other again this week, got it?"

My heart sinks. "All right."

"But—change of plans—it's a solid 'maybe' for a date the week of the GP in Imola. I still want to fuck you. You're, uh, entertaining."

"A ringing endorsement," I tease.

She takes a step back and delivers a playful punch to my

abs. "You don't need my endorsement. Your name and that smile probably get you everything you want already."

I move an escaped coil of pastel-blue hair off her shoulder. "You like my smile?"

She inspects my face, her plump lower lip snagged between her teeth in thought. "Yeah, you're okay. Where, um, did you get the scar that fucked up your eyebrow?"

"Fighting a dragon." I tap her chin with a fingertip and turn away, headed for the bedroom so she'll follow me.

Sage vaults onto the bed as I gather my clothes and starts to jump on it like a trampoline, arms over her head. Stretching high, she grazes the ceiling with her fingers and loud-whispers, "Got it!" before dropping into a seated pose. I'm once again charmed by her unrestrained physicality.

"So you're not gonna tell me?" she asks, pointing at my face. "I'll bet it was some pissed off husband who found you in bed with his wife."

"You've a fertile imagination," I say, stepping into my trousers. "But it was nothing of the sort. Deliver on that date in two weeks and perhaps you can coax the story out of me."

She flops onto her stomach and props her chin on a palm. "Yeah, maybe. There are some great nightclubs in Ravenna though, sooooo…I might be too busy to hang out with you."

"My family has a small villa in Ravenna. I wonder where you'd have more fun?"

"Ooh, big talk," she taunts.

I hold her eyes with a wicked smile as I zip my fly. "I assure you, I can back it up."

As I sit in the chair that still faintly radiates the scent of sex, then lean to put on my socks and shoes, Sage watches me with the detachment one has for a muted television at the gym. I stand and take up my shirt, sliding it on, and Sage bounds off the bed.

"Here, lemme fix that," she says nonspecifically, going to her suitcase and digging about. She locates some small item and comes over to me. When she clasps it between her teeth to free both hands to fasten my shirt, I see that it's a tiny round metal pin, the decorative type one puts on a jacket. She pops it open and uses it as one would a nappy pin, skewering it through the part of my placket with the missing button. I look down. It's red on black, the *DK* symbol of the punk band Dead Kennedys. "There ya go," she says with a pat to my chest. "All better."

I chuckle. "That's a look, isn't it? But needs must. If you happen to know where my fallen button has gone, I'll take it—my tailor can put it back on."

"Jesus Christ, *you have a tailor*." She circles the DK pin with a fingertip. "I know where it is, but I'm keeping it. A souvenir."

A wave of unexpected tenderness goes through me. I settle my hands on her hips. "Bloody hell, I want to kiss you, Salvi."

"I know…" Her tone is cautious.

"Forehead?" I suggest.

There's a beat of deliberation, and her nostrils flare. "Sure, I guess."

I take my time with it, letting my lips rest.

"I'm not making any promises about Italy," she warns.

"Understood." I draw back enough to look at her.

She toys with the hem of my untucked shirt. My hands

smooth up her back. I'm afraid if I let go, I'll never get to touch her again. She's the fulfillment of everything I've not known I was moving toward my entire feckless life. My anticipatory dread of letting go now is like a child with a string tied around a tooth that's about to be pulled.

"I like this truce between us, Salvia officinalis," I say, doing my best to keep it light.

"As much as you liked the battle?"

One of my hands cradles the side of her jaw. "Far, *far* more." I touch her lower lip with my thumb, aching for the kiss I can't have. "You're the one who was driving to win, darling. Meanwhile, I was madly waving a red flag on the sidelines, hoping to slow you down enough to notice me."

Her brow furrows.

I can't believe I said it aloud. *Fuck, I've mugged myself.*

Backing out of my arms, she smirks. "You're a pile of red flags, all right." She goes to her suitcase and starts pulling items out. "You're still making me late and I didn't even get laid. Shove off, sailor. Text me your address in Ravenna." Hopping to her feet clutching an armful of clothing, she heads for the bathroom without a backward glance. "See yourself out," she calls.

I shrug my jacket on, throwing one last glance through the doorway into the en suite, where Sage is shucking her clothes and tossing them over her shoulder onto the floor, shimmying her way into the shower whilst singing PJ Harvey's "Dress."

The girl is perpetually in motion. Her mind, body, and spirit are restless, striving, stretching to grasp the next thing.

My God, how I long to be one of them.

When I exit into the living room, Priya is behind the bar faffing with the espresso machine. I realize I didn't take even a sip of mine and left the cup to join the other detritus in Sage's room. But it gives me an opening for something to say.

"Thank you for the espresso," I tell her.

"Tip jar's on the counter," she deadpans.

I cross to the bar and lean, watching her make a latte, foaming up a pitcher of oat milk. "I don't typically carry cash, so my tip will have to be 'never buy a Rothschild's orchid.' Bloody expensive and devilishly hard to keep alive."

She shoots a bland look at me over her shoulder. "Wow. Useful. I'll keep that in mind."

For a minute, the only sound is the whoosh of the steam wand, punctuated with metallic spoon tapping.

I clear my throat. "Is Julian awake? I'd like to say goodbye."

"Yes." She pours the foamy oat milk into a wide cup, crafting the shape of a heart. "Now go sit down and get out of my hair."

As if on cue, Julian comes out of the smaller bedroom, wearing only gray tracksuit bottoms, his hair damp from the shower. "Hey, man," he greets. "Good to see you. Wanna finish that chess game?"

Priya walks our way as Julian collapses onto the sofa across from mine. The look she sends me as she hands him his latte warns that the only acceptable answer is no if I want to keep my organs intact.

"Must dash, sorry," I tell him. "But if you're in London, ring me and we'll grab a pint."

With a regretful smile, he puts his feet on the coffee table—I can't help noticing the missing toe—and reclines into the cushions. "Probably have to be a ginger ale for me at that point. I'm guessing I won't get to drink anymore if I do this right."

Priya leans over the back of the sofa and kisses his cheek. "You won't even miss it," she assures him. As she's straightening, he captures one of her braids playfully and draws her back down for a kiss on the mouth.

"As long as I don't have to miss *you*."

Her look is intense. "Never ever," she assures him. After another kiss, she stands. "I'm gonna get ready so we can head to the airport. We'll get breakfast on the way." She fixes me with a wary look, one hand on her hip. "Everything I said yesterday stands. If you hurt anyone I love, I will *ruin you*, got it?"

A startled laugh erupts from Julian. He tips his head back to look at her. "Jesus...*ouch*."

"Heard, Chef," I tell her, holding out both palms with what I hope is an earnest smile. "I don't blame you for saying it. I have a great respect for your protectiveness of Sage, and...I won't abuse your trust, or hers, should I succeed in earning it."

Her eyes narrow. "*Hmph.* Did you practice that in the mirror first?"

Julian reaches for her hand. "Give the guy a break, baby. He's trying."

She points at me. "I don't trust him. He's got a hundred Sages, a hundred Julians. I've got one of each. If you mess with them," she directs at me, "*I'm coming for you.*" She backs away, then pivots and stalks to her room, slamming the door.

Julian winces. "She's on edge because of the rehab thing. In 'mama bear' mode. It's not personal."

"It's very much personal, but not unwarranted." I glance at the closed bedroom door. "I hope to change her opinion of me in time."

He sips the latte. "You make it sound long-term—'in time.' You planning on sticking around?" He nods toward Sage's room, behind me. "You guys a bigger thing than it seems like?"

Faintly I can hear Sage in the shower, her voice loud as she howls the chorus of the PJ Harvey song. I can't help smiling.

"That's my aim." After a pause, I venture to confess more. Something about Julian is, as Sage mentioned, irresistibly winning. He's an open book, and makes people feel interesting and important, without it seeming false. "I know I've a reputation as a libertine, but…" I rake one hand through my hair, sighing. "I fancy that girl in the most debilitating way."

He bobs a slow nod, looking into his cup, then angles a glance up at me. "Pri told me the shit you said about Sage on your blog. If I didn't like you, and if I wasn't already a fuckin' disaster"—he lifts his broken hand—"I'd probably have to knock you out for it."

"You'd have every right. I was categorically an arsehole. That I taunted her to catch her attention is no excuse—it only makes me sound like a child as well as a complete twat."

His face goes stern, and I get a chill, seeing the side of him that's not easygoing.

"Not just childish and shitty, but unprofessional, man. Implying that she fucked her way into the Emerald seat?" He shakes his head. "Her whole life she's worked to get where she is. She's a role model. I've never known a harder worker, with that kind of focus."

He points toward the sound of her singing in the next room.

"Don't let that fool you—the squirrelly façade. She may be a year younger, but I've always looked up to her. It's easy to feel…*inadequate*…having a talented sister." Taking another sip of coffee, he hides a smile. "Not that I'd give her the satisfaction of telling her that."

There's a soaring lift of pride in my chest, the way one feels when someone they treasure is praised. But the wings of the sensation are clipped by sorrow as I acknowledge that Sage isn't "mine" in any sense and may never reciprocate my emotions.

"I can't apologize enough for the asinine things I said."

Julian lifts a shoulder. "I hope you mean you apologized to *her*. I think you're a cool guy, but you'd better not be playing some long con on Sage, digging up dirt or trying to strike a deathblow by making her fall for you and then hurting her." He pauses for effect. "You and I understand each other?"

"Crystal clear. And again, I in no way fault you for believing the warning necessary."

A chill creeps over me at his mention of "digging up dirt." I've given little thought to CJ Ardley's asinine revenge plot since arriving in Melbourne. Like any besotted lover, I lost myself in the object of my affection and saw nothing but her.

I wonder if I should go back into the bedroom and tell Sage about it now. There's a *thud* as she jumps on or off something. It's followed by a mock-operatic peal of song and a cackle of laughter, then animated talking, as if she's answered a phone call and is reassuring the person on the other end. I know she's running late—I oughtn't bother her, marring her focus by giving her something to worry about. I still feel confident I can manage it myself.

I can tell her when we see each other in Italy if it seems necessary.

Julian walks me to the door, giving me one of those back-slapping half-hugs in parting, with promises all around that we'll get together after he's completed his program.

I go back to my smaller suite at the far end of the hall. After walking in, I stand for a few minutes, examining it. Shipshape and Bristol fashion, with the faint citrus smell of cleaning products. Everything at right angles. With a pang, I feel the lack of not only Sage's scent, but also her chaos. *Where are the tangles of clothing, the empty cups, the salvaged papier-mâché Saint Nicholas?*

I sit on the foot of the bed and tap open Contacts on my mobile. Straightening with resolve, I spend the next ten minutes weeding out and deleting any women—aside from Sage—who aren't relatives or business connections. I keep CJ Ardley's number, but change the name to "Alfred, Accountant."

I've been away from Sage for mere minutes, and already it seems an eternity.

I get up and collect my unpacked suitcase so I can check out. There's little point being in Melbourne if I can't see her. Suddenly I want very much to be home, to think and play my piano and count down the days until Italy.

16

MELBOURNE

SAGE

If it's a relief that he's gone, why do I feel kind of awful? I have to focus for the rest of this week. Guest-dick services are not needed.

As Pri and I are walking to the elevator the next morning so I can go to the press meeting, we pass Alexander's room, and there's a gray-haired French-speaking couple standing in front of it with their bags, having some sort of simultaneous bicker-fest as the husband opens the door.

I slow my walk and strain to peek inside as we pass. The room is pristine, and unless he's got a kinky thing for three-somes with elderly French people, it looks like Alexander's gone.

"He checked out," Priya tells me.

"What? Who?"

She rolls her eyes, holding the elevator door for me. "Quit it. Your dumb boy toy." She prods the button for the lobby. "I saw him leaving when Julian and I were catching a cab to the airport for…you know."

At the mention, her face goes all haunted. I hold back my quip, instead slipping my hand into hers and giving an encouraging squeeze. "Now's the part where you can *stop* worrying, babes. Jules is in a nice place, working through his shit. Probably already in a flotation tank with soothing affirmations and whale songs being piped in or whatever the fuck they do."

I definitely feel better knowing my brother is somewhere safe. He'd fuckin' better be, at €17,000 a week. I considered only pre-paying for one month, and they could ask me for more if he's still there after that point, but I didn't want to do anything that might demonstrate a lack of faith in him. So, the full twelve weeks it is—€204,000. Priya cried, but I shrugged it off, saying, *What else am I gonna do with money, buy a new vibrator? I don't need anything.*

This morning I looked up books on addiction and how to support someone struggling with it, and Priya's gonna go to a bookstore here in Melbourne and get as many of them as she can find for me. A lot of my assumptions about the issue are clouded by emotion, and I'd like to be useful in some way other than the money, so I plan to read up while Jules is doing his program.

Today's a busy day. In addition to the press bullshit and hours of training, I have a meeting at the paddock with Phaedra and my race engineer and a team of strategists (including a guy who didn't want me on the team—chief strategist Erich, kind of a sexist dickwad) and our new technical director, Basil Rowley, who's a fucking wizard.

I'm always stoked to talk with him, because part of how Emerald lured him away from Coraggio was...well, hiring *me*. He's such a rockstar engineer that everybody wanted the guy, and Allonby has way more money than Emerald because they're the current constructor's champs, plus they have rich sponsors out the wazoo. But Basil Rowley has four daughters, has worked in F1 since the 1980s, and is into the idea of getting a woman onto the podium. He's my champion, my favorite egghead nerd. The guy loves the challenge of designing a car around a woman driver, fine-tuning all the minuscule details necessary to the construction and setup to make the playing field as level as possible.

I've tailored my body to do this job, starting from well before puberty. Even though I'm short as hell, I'd take on any woman athlete in a test of strength with confidence. The g-forces of braking and cornering in F1 are insane. Your average Jane or Joe can handle about 8 kg of lateral push, and I can take *five times that*, piece of cake. But there are still some things that can't be influenced by a driver's physical conditioning alone, and that's where Basil's magic comes in.

It's gonna be a full day. And this evening is my favorite part, because I'm doing an event with a group of girls from Emerald's Jump Start program for disadvantaged youth. I have to say, when the criticism and condescension and misogynist shade finally builds up enough to penetrate my armor, spending time doing mentoring and seeing young women inspired... that repairs the armor and polishes it to a sassy shine.

Phaedra catches up to me as I'm heading for the garage after the meeting.

"Hey, Sage? Quick word…" She points toward the hallway leading to her office and peels off, and I follow. Inside, she shuts the door and sits on the edge of her desk. "I wanted to apologize for that shit from Erich. Holy shitbiscuits, I've warned the guy, but he—"

"It's fine," I dismiss with a tired chuckle. "I can give as good as I get. Fuck him."

Phaedra draws in a long breath. "Well, I'm still following through on the consequences and fining him every time he says shit like that." She rubs her forehead. "The guy's good at his job, but I can find someone just as good who isn't a piece of shit." She plucks up a bottled water and strangles the cap off, shooting a smirk at me. "You really did dish it back at him today. Fucking poetry."

The tense exchange was when Erich said the group should address the question of "whether Miss Sikora's performance might be impacted by her womanly cycle." I asked him to clarify, and he said, *We should track your menses in anticipation of increased hormonal impulsivity and emotion. Perhaps Dr. Brunner can report to us about that.*

Phaedra's hand closed around her coffee mug as if preparing to fastball it at him. Basil gave an embarrassed laugh, shaking his head. My race engineer, Imani, got a look on her face like she'd stepped in something. I sweetly told Erich, *If hormones play into it, are your strategizing abilities impaired by the fact that you probably haven't gotten it up without pharmaceuticals since 2005? Maybe your wife can report to us on how often you manage a poke.*

So much is riding on this next grand prix. Two poor

showings in a row might be excusable, especially since one was unavoidable. But three would look like a pattern, and my figurative "stock" would dip. This race has to be a banger.

In the evening, after the Jump Start event, Priya and I are walking out when I hear an enthusiastic, "Sage!" from the crowd of fans and press folk. I know that musical voice, and I freeze to swivel around.

Before I find the source, Priya's phone jangles and her face falls. "Oh God, what's…?"

I see my brother's name and a selfie of the two of them on the screen. Priya's staring at it, and again I hear another call of "*Sage!*" from nearby.

"Why is Jules calling you?" I demand in a near-growl. "He's not supposed to have his phone while he's in there."

"I'll…I don't know why! Jesus, quit scowling. I'll handle it." She flaps an arm to wave me away and scurries off several yards to answer.

As I'm staring after her—wondering why my idiot brother is making calls rather than having someone put heated rocks on his chakras or whatever—someone loops an arm through mine and I turn to see Maya Ardley, all smiles.

We've known each other forever from karting, then raced together in F3, both eventually testing for Harrier as a potential reserve driver. When I got the seat, Maya was so thrilled for me that I could tell it was partly relief. Since then we've kept up with each other as casual friends but haven't hung out as much as either of us would like.

Even though Maya and I aren't sporting rivals anymore, her mom, CJ, has kept up an imagined feud, blaming me for her daughter not "making it." But if you ask me—and surely if you ask Maya herself—she *did* make it. She moved to Australia with her boyfriend, professional surfer Tau Murray, and is enjoying a quiet life out of the limelight.

I throw my arms around her and we both do a little foot-dance hugging thing. I pull back and size her up. She looks great. Her blond hair is grown out long and she's got a glowing tan. There are sun freckles across the slightly crooked nose Maya wouldn't let her mom bully her into changing with surgery.

"Oh my fucking gaaaawwwd," I enthuse. "You're here, girl!"

"Couldn't resist coming into town for the GP!" She points over her shoulder with a thumb, indicating a vague *elsewhere*. "Me and Tau are living on his family's ranch now," she tells me. "It's beautiful." Her face looks positively dreamy, as if she's reflecting on her gorgeous six-foot-four boyfriend, a hot Jason Momoa type with even more tats than me.

"Where's your boy?" I glance around to find him.

"Tau's off at the Cape Town Surf Pro competition; it's just me this weekend. And…" She puts one hand up to slide a section of hair behind her ear, making a dramatic face to show that she's displaying her left hand, where a honkin' big diamond is perched.

"Oh, fuck *me*!" I cry, grabbing her fingers and inspecting the ring. "You're engaged?"

"*Married.* Last month! A little spontaneous thing on the beach."

I drag her into another quick hug. "I'm soooo stoked for you guys."

Just then, Priya appears beside us.

I wave an arm toward Maya. "Hey, Pri, remember Maya?"

"Hi, yes! It's been a few years though." They do a warm handshake. Pri's phone buzzes, and she holds up an apologetic finger. "Sorry—Julian again." She backs away to open the call.

Maya looks after Priya, who's talking in urgent tones to Jules.

"Julian your brother?" she asks lightly.

He and Maya dated briefly in their teens, so I hope she won't feel weird toward Pri.

"Uh, yeah. They have a thing going."

Maya's smile is genuine, and I can't help noticing she's playing with her new wedding ring when she says, "Well, good for them. She's always seemed really nice. I hope they're happy. Julian's a great guy."

There's a pause, and I'm a little uncomfortable, so I change the subject and ask, "Heyyyy...how's 'Karting Momzilla' doing?" We both called Maya's mom that back in the day, so I hope she still has a sense of humor about it.

"Oh, fine," Maya says with an eye roll. "Our relationship is mostly phone based these days. Don't know if you heard, but she's shooting her shot with that gross TV chef Gavin Yates, hoping to become his Wife Number Six. Anything to keep the upward trajectory on the social ladder."

"Ha! Well, if that's her current fixation, babes, it's at least keeping her off my jock. She hasn't shit all over me on her blog lately. Hallelujah."

Priya comes back and has that *I need to tell you something* look. Maya must see it, because she gives my arm a squeeze and says, "I won't keep you. But Tau and I'll be at Silverstone this year! We can all get together there."

"For sure! Let's totally hang out."

After goodbye hugs and before I have to go do the rest of my fuckin' job and be charming for reporters, I lean toward Priya and ask discreetly, "What the hell was the Jules thing about?"

She presses her lips together in her fretful way.

"*What?*" I urge.

"Don't flip out or anything, because it's taken care of, but… Julian isn't at the treatment center yet."

My jaw goes hard. "That fuckwit did a runner when he got off the plane in Switzerland?"

"He wasn't ready. He got scared."

I can feel that I'm doing a rage face, so I try to dial it back in case the journalists are taking pics. "I'll scare him with *my entire foot up his ass* if he doesn't get to that overpriced 'happy haven' five fucking minutes ago."

"He's going, he's going!" Priya loud-whispers, glancing at the people nearest us to make sure we aren't overheard. "I talked him off the ledge. And besides, it was for a good reason: He said he didn't want to show up at the place high. He wanted it to wear off first."

I give her a sardonic look. "Pri, I love you, but don't be dense. Do you know what he actually meant? *He didn't want them to confiscate the rest of his pain pills when he checked in.* He's going on a bender so they don't 'go to waste.' It's junkie behavior—not something noble."

Her big brown Disney princess eyes fill with tears. "Don't you think I know that?"

"Oh shit...no crying," I plead. "You know it breaks my heart when you're for-realsies upset. I'm sorry I got bitchy." I give her a hug. "I'm sure Jules is fine, and I'm glad he called you so you could keep him on track."

She takes a coffee shop napkin from the messenger bag she uses to haul my crap around, and it makes me feel awful, reflecting that she's carrying Julian, carrying *me*, carrying everyone but herself. She pats her cheeks with the creased paper napkin, trying not to fuck up her makeup.

"At least he doesn't have enough to overdose, right?" she asks anxiously.

"Definitely not. He's got maybe a dozen pills left? His tolerance is huge, so that's nothing." I put a comforting arm around Priya and start us on a slow walk toward the waiting reporters. "Buck up, pumpkin. We can't have the press seeing you all sad panda."

I don't tell her the concern that's really gnawing at me: Jules might hit the streets looking for *more*.

Hog-tying my fears and kicking them into a room I haven't opened much since childhood—a room where Julian and I are still carefree kids, flipping each other low-stakes shit and watching *The Young Ones* together—I put on my press face and throw both hands into the air.

"Hey, cats and kittens!" I call out to the waiting group. "Let's talk Jump Start."

Grand prix circuits that use public roads typically have shitty track surface, but Albert Park is pretty smooth. It's a fast, friendly track. Not to brag or anything (okay, 100 percent to brag) but I'm known not only for being a risk-taking, late-braking driver but also for having great tyre management. So I'm feeling euphoric about my prospects here.

The first two free practice sessions validate my confidence. During the meeting later, I float a few bold race-day strategies based on my observations, and when Erich is (predictably) a douchenozzle about it, I'm gratified that Phaedra, Imani, golden boy Basil Rowley, *and* my teammate Cosmin all back me up. I think it's the first moment when I really feel like Emerald is home.

On Saturday in FP3, we make our eleventh-hour adjustments, dialing everything in tight for the quali sessions that follow. I sail through Q1, then squeak by Q2 by seven thousandths of a fucking second. In Q3, my closest rival is Owen Byrne from Team Easton, and he cocks it up at turn 9. We end up qualifying neck and neck with me in fifth and Owen in sixth. Then…a stroke of luck when Anders Olsson, who's fourth on the grid, gets a three-place penalty for impeding. Suddenly Owen and I are bumped up.

I'm flying high and can't wait for the race tomorrow.

Some of the best racing advice I've gotten has been from my mom and dad, and it wasn't even *about* racing. My dad, for instance, has always said, "Don't stand in the way of someone who's determined to shoot himself in the nuts." It's his way of pointing out that with rivals—in sports, business, life in general—sometimes all you have to do is stand back and let the other guy be his own worst enemy. And my mother, working in the male-dominated field of physics, advised that I shouldn't be above taking advantage of the fact that "women scare the hell out of men." She said that although women exist under the curse of a fear of being hurt physically by men, *their big fear is being humiliated by us.*

"When you're pursuing the same goal as a man," she told me, "know that they're easily rattled into mistakes by the anxiety of potentially being 'shown up by a girl.' *Use it.*"

The complete package, for a top driver, is a combination of technical skill, conditioning, focus, observantness, adaptability, and creative problem-solving. It's surprisingly mental.

In my first two races this season, I either fucked up or carelessly got tangled in other drivers' fuckups. Today at the Australian GP…no mistakes, no mercy.

I'm so focused at the start of the race that I feel like an arrowhead—organic, cold, smooth, sharp enough to cut in all the right places. The first eight laps are golden. I don't lose position, but Owen Byrne drops back one, overtaken by Akio Ono.

I'm pushing my soft tyres as long as I can before I have to pit so I can keep my lead on Byrne and Ono. Meanwhile, Imani tells me that Byrne has been fighting so recklessly to regain the place he lost—which he does, but at a steep cost—that he's hammered his mediums. There's a chance he'll have to box on the earlier side of the 14 to 20 lap range.

When I'm called to box on lap 13, I insist I should wait. I can feel the degradation big time by lap 14. Then Byrne dives into the pit early. His undercut could've blown up in my face if not for a fortuitous occurrence: a tangle between Ortiz and a rookie driver from a back-field team results in a yellow flag.

My pit crew have been waiting, so they're on point when I come in, and I claim the advantage of the faster pit stop inherent to yellow flag conditions. *Fuck yes.*

Imani is normally matter-of-fact over the radio, but she sounds downright celebratory about the way I get a leg up on Byrne. I can't resist a cheeky comment: "Tell him I'm coming for his girlfriend next." (His partner, Brooklyn Katz, is hot as hell. I kinda have a harmless little crush on her.)

For most of the race I'm hunting the frontrunners, looking for any opportunity to advance. But in the final six laps, I switch to playing for Emerald and not just myself. Cosmin's hold on P2 is heavily threatened by Drew Powell, ahead of me in third. I take my mom's advice and rattle Powell, all over his fucking gearbox, toying with him and forcing him to focus on fighting me off rather than overtaking Cosmin.

Fourth place is still delicious—I'll take the 12 points. With Cosmin's P2, it gives Emerald 30 total. For the first time this season, I feel like I've earned my keep. The post-race press briefing is a mob scene, reporters all over me. I'm hyperaware that everything I say is *a quote* (and could possibly become a meme). That's sports in the era of social media.

Phaedra is inspiring, talking up the fact that this is the first time in history that points have been earned by the combination of a woman driver with a woman race engineer, on a team with a woman owner/team principal.

Byrne hears about my "coming for your girlfriend" sass and offers charismatic return fire, saying I couldn't handle Brook if I tried, and the press of course eats it up. Everyone loves a rivalry, and the fact that it includes something sexy is a bonus.

Gorgeous day all around.

The icing on the day's cake is the floral arrangement in my suite when I finally get back, exhausted, near midnight: a riot of jagged purple thistle, black roses, some plant that looks kinda like alien eyeballs, and…*well well well*, stalks of good ol' *Salvia officinalis*.

I open the tiny card speared on a spike of thistle:

> *You're a force of fucking nature, Salvi. Congrats on a stunning race. Don't break my haggard excuse for a heart by denying me your company in Ravenna.*
>
> *~Cheers, your Sandy*

He also sent Priya an orchid, which she told me with a grumpy smile is "kind of an inside joke," and…I'm glad they have one. He's really trying to win her over, and it's sweet.

As intense at the grand prix was, I think my pulse is drumming harder now as I hold the card against my lips.

"Your Sandy"…

I still won't let myself deliver a kiss, not even to a silly scrap of cardboard.

But maybe in Italy I'll finally test out those pretty lips of his.

17

LONDON

ALEXANDER

In my adult life (such as it is), I've suffered occasional spasms of feeling like "a better man" under the influence of a woman. It's always temporary, leaving me weak and wrung out, like food poisoning, to recuperate slowly and rebound to being the scoundrel I was before my affliction.

I know the signs. My replies to texts and emails are more prompt and less sarcastic. I'm already a generous tipper, but during a Better Man phase, it becomes borderline extravagant, a festival of "paying it forward" and spontaneous acts of largesse. For a brief time, I eat healthier, floss more thoroughly, and dust off the hardbound classics on my bookshelves.

It's performative—I recognize that—but not for the benefit of the other person. I'm playacting for myself, like a bored, lonely child in an attic with a box full of loose clothing, trying on disguises before a dusty mirror.

I've often been accused of being a chameleon, altering

myself right down to the vocal mannerisms and accent to fit in. Many women have criticized this tendency in me as being manipulative, and I reckon that tracks with my image, so I never dispute it. But the truth is, I don't quite know who I am when I'm by myself, without the reference point of who I am to another person.

Something is different this time.

After returning to London, I hole up in my flat, hermit-like. I'm afraid that if I go out, I'll fall into doing what I usually do in one of these phases, like buying the ingredients for smoothies and salads, or dropping £100 notes into charity collection boxes. If I did so, it would mean that *this*—the perplexing thing I'm feeling for Sage—isn't new or meaningful but merely the latest iteration of the same old game.

So for several days, I just sit with the bewildering emotions, and neither try to distract myself from nor capitalize upon them. I work on a few piano pieces (Coltrane's "Giant Steps," which is complex but not insurmountable, and Prokofiev's Piano Concerto No. 2, which is strictly for masochists). I let myself survive off pistachio gelato and red wine and stupidly dear cheeses and sourdough from Little Bread Pedlar. I fall asleep reading airport suspense-thrillers whilst vulgar reality TV shows play on mute in the background.

Several times I open my laptop and try to write an intro for a glowing article about Sage, something to annul the terrible things I once posted on my blog. But everything comes out wrong. It's too slick, or trite, or downright fucking mawkish.

Trying to do her justice affords me ample opportunity to reflect on what the bloody hell it *is* about this woman that's knocked me for six. She undeniably makes me feel some type of way.

With other women, it was easy to view their "on paper" assets. But I find I can't define Sage as a list. Not to say such a list wouldn't be long; it absolutely is. She's talented, beautiful, spirited, sexually voracious, and possesses a wicked sense of humor.

But what I love about Salvi—*oh God…am I truly thinking that word:* love?—is a hundred small, subtle things. The way she's always singing (and poorly). Her cackling laugh that's not unlike waterfowl being violated. The perforated trails of a half-dozen earring holes in each lobe, placed unevenly in a way that suggests she might have impulsively done some of them herself. The set of her lips when she's thinking. The thick, raised seam of scar tissue where her appendix was removed. The way her hotel rooms are chaotic records of everything she's done since walking through the doors, surfaces littered with her story.

Ultimately, the fucking enigma of her. I want to spend years exploring it, unearthing her details with the care and reverence of an archaeologist at a Bronze Age settlement.

It feels an apt metaphor. I don't know what's buried down there…not with either of us. Her mystery, my emotions. Who I *am*, for that matter. It's humbling that for the first time in my life, I want to know. Enough so that I'm ready to get my hands dirty with the excavation.

A week before the GP at Imola, I get a message from my mother asking me to come see her at the *Auto Racing Journal* offices. When I arrive, our front desk receptionist, Callum, barely looks up, he's so riveted to whatever's on his computer screen. His hands are clasped under his chin, and his adoring gaze is straight out of a cartoon.

"Och, the little angel...did you ever see the like!" he coos.

I pause at the desk, clearing my throat. Callum gives me a flicker of a glance, then focuses again on his screen. I scan the room and note that everyone is similarly rapt, staring at their computers.

"She yawned!" I hear a high voice that's unmistakably my coworker Gillian, coming both from across the room and from Callum's computer screen. "That is *too* adorable."

Stepping to the side of the reception desk, I peer to see what the fuss is about. On the screen, familiar faces from around the office appear in a grid flanking a box in which my former coworker Natalia Evans appears, holding a new-looking infant swaddled in a pink blanket.

"Ah," I say. "Did that happen already?"

Callum makes a shooing motion with his hand.

"Lovely to see you too," I tell him blandly. "Oi, Evans!" I direct at Natalia, leaning down into the camera's frame. "Congrats on the bundle of joy. What's its name?"

"Hi, Alex. *Her* name is Leonie."

"Right, then. Well done." I give her a little parting salute, keenly feeling Callum's desire to get rid of me. As I start to stand, Natalia speaks up again.

"Sorry I didn't send you an invite for the call," she says. "But I figured you, uh, weren't back from purgatory."

"Not fussed," I dismiss with a shrug. "Another time."

In one of the little squares, I see Brigitte—the leggy Parisian who was in my bed the morning I was cast into servitude with Emerald—lift a hand and address me. "Ohhhh, tête de noeud," she says in a long-suffering way, stretching those lovely French vowels, "come to my desk and you can sit in. That ees okay, Natalia?" she checks.

"Sure, fine."

I look up and see Brigitte stand and beckon from a desk near the break room. She's apparently been enticed into a staff position with the magazine—my mother must have offered a fortune to get exclusive rights to Brigitte's formidable talent. There's a nameplate on the desk announcing her new title: BRIGITTE MICHAUD, CHIEF PHOTOGRAPHER.

I grab a chair from a break room table and set it beside hers, close enough to see the screen but not impose myself or catch the triggering fruity-powdery scent of Lancôme Trésor.

She gives me a businesslike nod. "Allo, Alexandaire."

Normally I'd launch into flirting, but I just nod back with a smile I hope doesn't look too stiff. "Nice to see you, pet. You're looking well."

She rolls her jewel-bright eyes. "And you look like shit."

"Oh, cheers."

A slight smile cracks her façade. "I am joking. But you do look sad around the eyes." She twists back to face her laptop and unmutes herself.

The group call goes on, and I listen politely. Natalia looks appropriately blissful, though with an undercurrent of exhaustion. When discussion veers into maintenance matters such as nappies and spit-up, I give a cordial wave and excuse myself.

Before heading to my mother's office, I pop into my own. It's silent and has the stagnant air of a storage room. I wander to the desk and pick up a favorite pen I left behind, pocketing it and staring out the window at the gray spring afternoon.

I wonder what Sage is doing right now. Is she in Italy yet? It's an hour later in Imola. I glance at my watch. Just gone two o'clock here. Is she in a meeting? Working out? Attending one of her many obligatory publicity-boosting events?

Does she think of me during the day?

A voice snaps me from my reverie. "Alekos, come give your mother a kiss. I'm in a dreadful hurry."

I pivot and cross to her, depositing a peck on her rouged cheek.

"Walk with me." She strides off, leaving me to trail behind. In the open office area, it sounds like the call with Natalia is winding down.

I sweep a hand toward someone's computer screen as we pass. "You didn't catch any of that? Evans's new bambino?"

"Spoke with her yesterday," she tells me. "But I was on a call with Spain during this."

It's amusing how she phrases it as "a call with Spain," as if the entire country is a single entity, presumably one that was grateful for the attention of Nefeli Laskaris.

My parents, bless them, are the most self-congratulatory people I've ever known. Admittedly, they're both frightfully smart. But it's no wonder I turned out to be such an arsehole, coming from two such as my mum and dad.

My mother goes into the glass cube that is her office, and when I pass her through the doorway, she sweeps a look out at everyone saying their goodbyes to Natalia. Closing the door, she says, "Cute little thing, Nat's baby. She'll be a stunner, with that mother and Klaus Franke for a dad." She ducks behind her desk and proceeds to dig in a drawer for something.

"Do my ears deceive me, or is the frosty Empress Laskaris sounding a bit sentimental?" I settle into a chair. "I hope you're not waiting for a grandchild. I don't plan to have any until I'm an inappropriately ancient and rich ninety-year-old marrying a twentysomething supermodel."

She gives up on whatever item she was hunting and slams the drawer. "Sentimental my arse. I'd sell your baby teeth for a tenner."

"There's the mother I know."

She checks her little wristwatch. "I'm on the horn with Lucia in Milan in seven minutes. Enough chitchat—on to business."

"Yes. Well, if you called me in for an update on my so-called internship with Emerald, you'll be pleased to know I've redeemed myself with Salv—erm, *Sage*." I clear my throat. "Miss Sikora, that is."

I make the mistake of angling my eyes away after my verbal stumble. I can feel Mother's laser focus cut into me even as I continue, trying to keep my tone even and adjusting a cuff link that hasn't a thing wrong with it.

"I hope you'll consider my penance served," I go on, "and allow me to…erm…" Finally I acknowledge the Grinch-like smirk that's overtaken my mother's features. "*What?*" I snap.

"You're sleeping with her."

I scoff. "Obviously not. She despises me."

"Of course she does. But I'm not wrong, am I?"

I don't know why I bother engaging in staredowns with

Nefeli Laskaris. I've never won, not once. I take an audible, long-suffering breath through my nose. "That has no bearing on whether I get my job back." Seized by a sudden worry that it *might*, I rather timidly add, "Does it?"

She taps her keyboard and shouts at her *ARJ* assistant, Rhys, "Tea, darling! Why am I staring at this empty cup like a beggar?" Directing her focus back at me, she says, "You're not going to work here, Alekos."

I straighten in my chair. "Why not? Because of Sage?"

"No. I have something better for you—not that you deserve it. The more fool me. I coddle you indecently." She shoves her empty teacup to the edge of her desk. "And it's nothing to do with Sage Sikora. Christ, I'm just relieved to hear you haven't entangled yourself romantically with that stick-insect American who writes the sport-mum blog. *Eeuugghh*, the woman is so—"

"Steady on," I interject. "The...do you mean CJ Ardley? Why on earth would you think I was involved with her?"

"Oh, stop it this instant—you with the same manufactured indignation you'd wear when 'falsely accused' of stealing biscuits from the kitchen as a child. A hustler from the cradle." She chuckles in a disparaging way. "Murmurs got back to me the night of the publishing gala. You *canoodling* with that classless mare."

Rhys enters, setting down a fresh cup of tea and whisking away the empty. He gives me a sympathetic nod as he passes. I'm hardly well liked around the office, but working so closely with my mother, Rhys knows how trying she can be. The door closes quietly behind him, and I renew my refutation.

"Ms. Ardley cornered me for a bit of conversation," I insist, "but it went no further."

"Relieved to hear it, love." She picks up her tea and sips, shooting a sly look at me over the golden rim of Spode Stafford White. "At any rate, the editor of the jazz section of *Caterwaul* is retiring this summer, and…well, frankly it can't happen soon enough. He's an old bore, and the section is dull as ditchwater. I'd like you to step in, shake things up."

I'm honestly surprised. I made my pitch to work for one of our music magazines a decade ago but got stuck with *ARJ*. "Me?" I manage.

"Your heart was never in racing. I said as much to Kon years back, but your father has his own mind about things." She pulls a wry face. "He saw music as rather soft—despite having been the one who was militant about your piano lessons—and hoped to point you at something…hmm, *grittier*, in adulthood?" She sits back. "So. Enjoy a few more months of being a skiver. Provided you don't disgrace yourself again, you're gainfully employed in August. Does that suit?"

"Yes! I'm chuffed. Great news."

A chirp from Mother's laptop draws her attention, and she taps at the keyboard. "I need to take that call. Why don't you poke around in the back issues of *Caterwaul* and send me a report about what's shit in the jazz section? End of the month?"

"Good as done." I stand and button my jacket.

"Lovely." She skewers me with a look over the tops of her glasses. "As to the issue with Sage, at least now we'll avoid a libel suit—however you achieved it."

"Erm, glad to have been of service." I take a step toward the door.

"Not to be one of those tedious old marrieds who must

offer 'wisdom,' but if you care for the girl…do work on this one a bit. You two might be a good match. She's fierce. She doesn't bloody need you, and that's exactly what *you* need." Before I can muster a reply, she taps open her call and starts chattering in Italian.

As I leave the *ARJ* offices and head downstairs, I'm overtaken by anxiety. It's as if my mother saying all this somehow increases the chances of a miserable irony wherein I get my hopes up and Sage has already moved on.

I pull my mobile out in the lift and stare at it, wondering what message I could send her that would sound suitably casual. I keep staring as I wander through the lobby, nearly colliding with a tall ginger beauty who glares silently at my apology in such a way that I have to assume I slept with her at some point, and things didn't end well.

After getting into my car, I spend another minute strategizing a message, finally typing, I've landed on my feet—new job starting in August. Thank you for not suing me. Am I approved to see you in Ravenna?

I'm gratified to note that she's activated read receipts for our texts—not the case before. The *Read 14:13* pops up immediately, and I cautiously smile, both eagerly anticipating and dreading her response, which could be a brush-off.

After what feels like an eternity of studying three blinking dots, a reply:

Salvia officinalis: You're approved for more than seeing me, honeybee. Ci vediamo in Italia.

18

RAVENNA, ITALY

ONE WEEK LATER

ALEXANDER

The last time I eagerly anticipated the sound of an arriving car was when I was ten years old, the year the Xbox was released. My father had gone to America for a business trip and couldn't be home for Christmas, and to make up for it, he was bringing home an Xbox. It was newly available in the States, but not slated to make it over here for several more months.

I spent that rainy day in a fever of anticipation, prowling back and forth to the windows looking out on the drive leading up to our big house on the hill, my ear trained for his Lamborghini Diablo (he was "in the throes of a midlife crisis" at the time, as my mother put it).

Tonight is much the same—I'm pausing even at the hum of insects, determining whether it's an approaching engine. I arrived at the villa in Ravenna yesterday and immediately sent for the occasional housekeeper, Cinzia, who does for us. The landscaping is kept up even when no one is staying here, so the outside looks tidy—pink sandstone paths swept, seasonal blooms and trees in order, fountain clear and musical. The interior is aired, spick-and-span, all surfaces shining.

When Sage's sporty little Mercedes—one of the Emerald vehicles that upper team members have at their disposal—roars into the circular drive, I can't help glancing nervously down at myself, checking to see if I look both attractive and sufficiently casual. I check my hair in the mirror in the foyer, then adjust the cuffs of my linen shirt, rolled to the elbows. Opening the front door, I go down the path to meet Sage, who's pulling an army-green duffel bag and a tailor's garment bag from the boot of the car. She looks up at me as she slings them over her shoulders, and her genuine smile makes my heart trip.

"Hey, Sandy-boy!" she calls out, coming around the car. She's wearing a simple black halter dress that ties behind her neck, hair upswept and pinned atop her head, baring the sculpted column of that gorgeous, tattooed neck. Even in wedge sandals that add several inches, she's petite, nose-height relative to me.

I'm struck with sudden anxiety over the greeting. I'm likely still not allowed to kiss her. Perhaps a one-arm hug? If I obeyed the dictate of impulse, I'd pull her into a fierce embrace and kiss her breathless. But as she draws up beside me, my body is pulled in so many directions at once that I make a complete prat of myself.

My arms do something hesitant and graceless that concludes in sweeping Sage's head toward myself in the crook of my elbow and *almost* kissing her forehead, then fearing it wouldn't go well and laying my cheek briefly against her pile of aqua hair instead. She laughs, looking up at me from inches away.

"I've really fucked you up with the no-kissing thing, haven't I?" she teases.

"Hopelessly." I reach for the duffel bag, the heavier of the two items, and she twists away with a sly smile before handing me the garment bag.

"Take this one," she tells me. "It's technically yours."

"Really? Hmm, I'm intrigued."

"You may not say that once you see it."

"What is it, vinyl trousers and a ball gag? Sequined gown and cha-cha heels?" I joke. "Full of mischief, you."

I keep an arm around her as we go up the path and into the house. The skin of my forearm feels electric from touching her warm, bare shoulders. As stilted as the greeting embrace was, walking like this seems natural. When we get inside, I point toward an arched hallway leading off to the left.

"Bedrooms are there. You've your pick, of course." I don't want to assume, so I had all three guest rooms made up with fresh linens and floral arrangements. An assortment of pricey toiletries and thick towels are in every en suite.

She tilts a sardonic look at me. "Obviously I'm sleeping in *your* room, dumbass."

I lead her to the open doorway of the first and largest room. "In that case, this happens to be the 'primary dumbass chamber.' Make yourself at home, pet."

She saunters in and drops her bag on the floor before turning a full circle, inspecting. "This is swanky."

"Thank you." I half close the door and hang the garment bag on the back. "May I open this?"

"You can change into it for dinner. I made us reservations at a nice trattoria."

"Oh? There *is* food here, if you prefer to stay in. Our girl Cinzia made a baked pasta dish and left it in the fridge this morning."

Sage takes a short backward flying leap onto the bed, giving a few extra bounces for good measure. "*Our girl*?" she echoes, amused. "What century are you from?" She puts her hands between her knees and leans forward in a Marilyn Monroe posture. "If she's our girl," she says, sotto voce, "she'd better be hot as hell."

Despite Sage's bisexuality, nothing like this has occurred to me before now, and it must show on my face.

She laughs, leaning back. "Aww, did I unlock something there, Sandy? I don't suppose you're good at sharing."

I rest both hands in my pockets and lift one eyebrow. "I'm not. Though it's a nice mental picture, to be fair."

She pulls the pins from her hair, tossing them carelessly behind her to tick on the tile floor. Lifting one foot, she directs, "Take my shoes off, lovely boy."

I walk over slowly, our eyes locked. Sage rolls her ankle in an enticing circle. I cradle the heel of her foot and work the silver buckle open. The shoe drops, heavy, and I run both hands up her calf. When my fingers dip into the hollow at the back of her knee, Sage's eyes flutter closed.

"I suspect," I tell her quietly, "that you and I are going to have a *very* good time getting to know more about one another."

I turn my wrist and massage two knuckles into the soft, slightly damp valley behind her knee and note the way she sucks in a breath. Removing her other shoe, I grasp her behind both knees and pull her to the edge of the bed, legs on either side of my chest. My hands glide up her thighs. When I reach her hips, I realize she's not wearing knickers. My eyebrows lift as if I'm scandalized, and Sage grins.

"Italy is so hot," she says with a pout.

"*You're* so hot." One of my hands migrates to skim over her appendix scar and go to her belly button, circling it with my thumb, then slowly dropping until I reach the downy strip of hair adorning her mound. "How hungry are you for dinner?" I follow the soft line lower. "I'd love to taste you as an appetizer."

"Impatient boy," she croons, putting two fingers over my lips. "I actually am starving. And our reservation's in forty-five minutes."

She scoots back and executes a windmill move with her legs to disengage, rolling onto her stomach and sliding off the high mattress, flashing the curve of her bare arse as her dress rides up. Dancing away, she goes to the duffel bag and bends pointedly low to yank it open.

I shake my head. "Merciless."

She stands with a crumpled handful of pearl-gray fabric in one hand. "I'm gonna rinse off." As she walks into the en suite, she calls back, "You can open the bag now! Put it on."

She leaves the door open and peels the dress off, then does something I've never seen anyone do in my life: steps into the shower before turning it on, then starts the water. She shrieks, then laughs, as the cold water hits her. Once it's adjusted to her satisfaction, she breaks into her bold, off-key singing.

It feels oddly like home—I'm so happy to hear it again. She's bawling out the Pogues' "A Pair of Brown Eyes," injecting it with an affected drunken drawl. I lean through the doorway, savoring the din of her complete lack of inhibition (or sense of pitch). Her arms shoot over her head and she dances, hips bobbing side to side, rotating in the spray of water.

I go to the garment bag and pull the zipper down.

"Bloody Nora," I mutter, my expression falling. Returning to the bathroom doorway, I ask, "Salvi, darling…you cannot be serious with that suit."

She peeks around the edge of the frosted glass divider, her body fetchingly covered in suds. I try not to gawk, but those tiny rose-petal tits dripping handfuls of white foam…dear God. *Give me strength.*

"A hundred percent. And I put a lot of work into thinking about it, not to mention paying my tailor in Korea and having it overnight-shipped here." She disappears behind the glass wall, then ducks back to add, "Oh, and there's cologne in the pocket. You gotta wear that too."

I pause, wrestling with how I might plead my case and escape the mischievous humiliation Sage has engineered. "It's a very, erm…*thorough* prank—I'll give you that. Point taken. But I'm not wearing that getup in public."

She peeks out again. "Dude. Remember in Melbourne you said something about how you'd 'burn the world' to have me? Consider this the final payback. You're a vain guy, right?"

"I can scarcely deny it."

"All right. So are you willing to feel as embarrassed as I was when you wrote that shit about me? This is pretty fucking mild, comparatively—walking around for a few hours in an ugly suit."

"It's more than 'ugly,' pet. It's aggressively clownish."

"Yeah, I know." She turns away and resumes washing. "The day you made that blog post, I was literally throwing Skee balls at a clown-face target and pretending it was you. This closes the circle. No complaining."

I look over at the unzipped garment bag, which appears to be disgorging a poorly digested meal of colorful patterns. "If I do this, we're even?" I ask.

"Yes. The slate is clean."

With a sigh of defeat, I return to the garment bag. Fishing out a brown-glass bottle of sample-size cologne, I inspect it: something called "Chaps." I twist the top open and sniff, then recoil. "There are fuckin' limits," I growl, capping the abomination and dropping it back into the pocket.

Minutes later, Sage comes into the bedroom as I'm suiting up in the absurd outfit. She's wearing a dress of thin gray T-shirt material inflicted with deliberate horizontal slashes, the fabric laddered and exposing much of her tempting pale skin. It's sleeveless, with rhinestone-spangled straps, and clings to her, dotted with dark water stains as if she put it on without toweling off first.

She brushes my hands aside to button the shirt. "You're gonna wear the tie too, right?"

"Ghastly as this is, I'll wear it until you take it off me."

It's worth noting that none of the six pieces of the

ensemble—trousers, shirt, necktie, vest, jacket, and socks—matches. The trousers have a pattern of pink iced doughnuts. The shirt, though adult size, is something a child would wear, littered in a cartoon cowboy motif: horses, lassos, boots, Stetson hats. The vest has flying saucers and green space aliens. The necktie is decorated with Christmas ornaments and reads CHECK OUT MY BALLS. The jacket's pattern is an assortment of sandwiches. The socks are bright yellow and adorned with fishing flies.

She gives my chest a pat after rigging me out in this visual headache, then leans in, standing on her toes, to sniff my neck. "You're not wearing the cologne." She reaches into the garment bag pocket to retrieve it.

"I draw the fuckin' line at dousing myself in that 'cowboy disinfectant.' It'd bring me out in a rash."

Her lovely toffee-gold eyes widen into pools of melodramatic despair. "Sandy, you *have to* wear it!" She opens the cap and thrusts it toward my face.

"Such a brat," I gripe. "Determined to make me look a pillock and smell like a 1980s honky-tonk bar shat itself."

I take the bottle from her hand and dab on the smallest possible quantity. When I go to the en suite washbasin and scrub my hands to remove the residual cologne from my fingertips, Sage draws up behind me and wraps her arms around my torso, peeking at my reflection. I turn and pull her into my arms, and having her pressed against me like this, the world could end in a barrage of meteors and I'd go out happy. Everything feels so right that I'm simultaneously euphoric and terrified, not knowing how long I have before it's all over.

Her upturned face has the look of an invitation to a kiss, but I'm afraid to risk it. The dance floor is always moving beneath her—her rules, whims, focus, manic actions, the whirl of her thoughts…all of it unpredictable.

The thought intrudes: my mother's counsel to "work on this one." Inside, I'm all in. But I know it's too soon to state aloud what I'm feeling.

My brain arrives at a safe compromise. "You know," I begin, stroking a thumb up and down Sage's spine, "I was fuckin' lost from the moment you grabbed my arm in the Bahrain airport."

She wrinkles her pert nose. "Yeah, I could tell."

"Oh? What gave me away?"

"You seemed…relieved. I don't know if it's because I was or *wasn't* what you expected, but I saw the tension drain out of you, and I thought, 'Fuck, is he actually kinda into me?'" She puts one of her bare feet on top of mine, and the simple intimacy of it thrills me to the marrow—there's something so fundamentally human about it.

I toy with a tendril of her hair, damp at the tip from the shower. "I very much was. And remain so. And as to the future…" I wrap her curl of hair around my fingertip. "I'm no seer, but the way I feel when I'm with you—"

She covers my mouth with one hand and presses her bee-stung lips together as if embarrassed, then steps back out of my arms. "Don't go getting all serious on me, Sandy. As the saying goes, 'I'm here for a *good* time, not for a *long* time.'"

My heart drops like a sinkhole, but I force a smile. "As if anything could entice a bounder like yours truly into 'getting all serious.'"

"Good. Let's hit the road. I don't wanna be late for our reservation." She grabs my necktie and tows me into the bedroom, then heads for the hallway. "And FYI, you're still hot as a three-dollar pistol, even dressed like a fucking clown."

The restaurant is one I've passed often, but at which I've not dined. I'm hoping that inside we'll be seated at an intimate corner table, dark enough to camouflage me. But surely this mischievous minx won't let me off so easily. She parks nearly half a kilometer from the restaurant, claiming (with a naughty glint in her eye) that she "wants to window-shop" and that it has nothing to do with furthering my mortification by making me stroll through town.

A sheepish demeanor, I realize, will only make it worse, so I take her arm and saunter along as if I'm in the know about a new fashion trend. This strategy works until my false confidence is punctured by a small child pointing and laughing, crowing out, *"Che scemo!"*

My relief, walking into the restaurant, evaporates as I lock eyes with the woman at the hostess station—a buxom beauty with a jet-black pixie cut. Nicoletta and I had a dalliance last year that she clearly doesn't recall as fondly as I do, considering her caustic glare. I'm not sure whether the buffoonish suit makes me more despicable to her or less so.

As I'm mentally scrambling for the least awkward course of action, Nicoletta's catlike gaze shifts to Sage and her eyes light up. She smacks her hands together and cries out with joy, and I have a moment of panic wondering whether Sage and I have slept with the same woman. My confusion lingers as the two launch into chatting in Italian. I had no idea Sage spoke it. I stand dumbly, trying to catch a few easy words, a courtesy smile frozen on my face.

Finally Nicoletta comes around the lectern and elbows me aside to get a selfie with Sage, who then signs a menu for her. They continue bantering gaily as we're led to our table, which is, to my dismay, bang in the middle of the back patio, displaying me to all.

I pull out Sage's chair for her and then sit. "Do you and Nic— Erm, do you and the hostess know each other?" I ask, draping the linen serviette across my lap.

Sage smirks. "No, she just recognized me and she's a racing fan. But apparently *you* know her."

A small sigh escapes me. "No point denying it. And luckily she was starstruck by you, or I might've got a Biro to the eye socket."

I thank the young man who comes to deposit menus and pour chilled glasses of sparkling water for us; then Sage thanks him as well, but better, in Italian.

"I'd no clue you spoke the language," I tell her.

She pulls a breadstick from an upright metal basket and crunches it. "Surprise!" she says, chewing. "I also speak decent Spanish, a little French, and a smidge of half-assed Polish— enough to keep my grandma happy. How 'bout you?"

"I regret to report that I've little skill with languages. I've retained some schoolboy-proficiency French. Chiefly pertaining to business or seduction."

"That's so on-brand for you. Wow." She twiddles the breadstick like a cigar, eyeing me with humor.

I suffer a spasm of insecurity that the more Sage knows me, the more likely she is to be unimpressed. I'm wealthy, a stylish dresser, well read, and good at playing the piano. But is that enough for a dazzling spitfire like this woman?

We fall into easy conversation that moves from foreign languages to our respective travels—the most underrated and unusual destinations—and when the server shows up, we realize we've not even looked at the menu.

"What's captivating you, Sandy-boy?" Sage asks me, doing a quick scan of the items listed on the cream-colored page.

You.

Everything about you.

The flash of your eyeteeth when you laugh. The way one of your ears sticks out a tiny bit more than the other. The sultry gold of your irises, like sunrise shining through a ribbon of treacle. The high arches in your feet. Your American accent, the tone lazy and warm and elastic, like palm trees nodding on a California beach...

I give a helpless chuckle and turn my menu face down. "No clue, pet. Shall you order for us?"

Her eyebrows go up. "You'd trust me? Sure I won't set you up with something weird?"

"You said this wretched suit evens the score; I've no fear of being pranked. Also..." I reach across the table and take her fingers in my hand. She almost pulls away, then settles, and her expression softens. "I *do* trust you," I tell her. "Unreservedly."

Her shoulders relax as if she's letting out a held breath, and her smile is a window opening. "Shucks. Don't go gettin' all corny on me..."

As she grasps the menu again and gazes down at it, I spot a brush of color fanning over her cheekbones. She orders starters and two pasta dishes to share, and I can't help noticing that her Italian is a little halting now, as if her mind is half elsewhere. To my surprise, she reaches for my hand again after the server walks away and props her chin on one palm.

"This is fun," she says, almost shy. "You don't seem to mind the suit too much…"

I regard my sleeve. "I'd nearly forgot I was wearing it. Good company will do that."

"You make it look sexy. Or else everyone here is too polite to stare." Her eyes narrow. "Maybe I took you to the wrong spot, eh? I should've dragged you to a club."

"I'm afraid dancing goes in the same column as foreign languages for me."

"You suck at it?" she says with a kind of euphoria, sitting up straight. "Holy balls, Sandy. All that shit you flipped me about being clumsy, and you can't even dance?"

"Not vertically," I quip, unable to restrain a wink.

She rolls her eyes and snort-laughs. "Okay, what *are* you skilled at, aside from the obvious?"

"Ah, *the obvious*? You think I'm good at…"

"Yes, writing and origami," she teases. "Oh, and you know about rare jazz, I guess. What else?"

I brush my thumb across her knuckles, pleased that she's still letting me hold her hand. "I play piano well. I started when I was three and still work on it quite a lot, so one might say I'm a dab hand."

"Will you play for me when we get back from dinner?"

"Certainly." I give her a slow smile. "I more than owe you a reciprocal performance after you demonstrated your dancing prowess in Melbourne."

For a half minute we watch each other, our eyes telegraphing memories of that night. Oddly, the recollection affects me as a blooming warmth in my chest more than in my lap. I want to see her again like that, raw and boundless as she was with me, everything about her new as spring. The heat of her breath, the unrestrained pressure of her fingers, the crackling hints of emotion in her voice. The fulfillment of holding *all* of her, being engaged with her tip to toes, from the disarray of her stormy hair to her small feet as they flexed with arousal.

She pulls her head back, eyes startled as the intensity of the moment appears to rattle her. Those honey-dark eyes widen.

I let her hand go before she feels the need to withdraw and turn the subject to lighter things—books and movies. As starters arrive and we dig into bruschetta, I confess that I typically tell people my favorite films are *Lawrence of Arabia*, *The Godfather Part II*, and *Seven Samurai*, but in reality they're *Monty Python and the Holy Grail*, *What We Do in the Shadows*, and *Groundhog Day*.

Next, sharing a plate of stuffed squash blossoms, we have a good-natured debate over whether Hemingway was a genius or a bullying drunk bastard (a bit of both, we end up agreeing), and whether Margaret Atwood is more brilliant as a poet or a novelist (again, both—who could choose?).

As we're eating communally off two plates of pasta, Sage falls quiet, holding my eyes for a long moment with a bewildered-yet-heated look that takes my breath away.

I set my fork down. "Salvi, pet. What is it?"

She shakes her head. "Shit, I don't know. I kinda dig you, Sandy." She jabs at a chunk of olive on one of the plates. "I mean, I feel calm around you. Usually my brain is going a million miles an hour, but, uh…" She shrugs. "You slow me down. In a good way."

A squall of emotions grips me, temporarily paralyzing my ability to respond. I'm flattered, grateful, humbled by the trust she's put in me, the man who mere months ago antagonized her in a boorish campaign to draw her attention. I want to tell her she's both nothing like I expected and a thousand times more complex and fascinating than I'd imagined, and that I like her *more* for that fact. I want to confess that I've never had a strong sense of myself, but I feel like I know exactly who I am when I'm with her. She's the North Star, the equator, the prime meridian. She's a universal constant, like the speed of light or the value of pi.

Instead, I artlessly manage, "Thank you. I'm pleased to hear it."

Fuckin' hell, could I be more tiresomely British?

She hums a laugh. "Yeah, well. I'm surprised by you, not gonna lie. I had you pegged for a useless nepo-baby douche, but…you're funny and smart, and you *ask questions*. It's depressing how many guys don't. You're interested in what I think, not just what I do."

"Your every detail, as I discover them," I tell her, turning her hand palm-up and smoothing along her lifeline with both thumbs, gently kneading, "is more bewitching to me than the last. You're a treasure house I could explore forever."

She closes her hand over my thumbs. "Oh, bullshit. Now you're just making fun of me."

I capture her gaze, and I must look quite serious, the way the smile fades from her lips. Her eyes widen.

"I'm gravely earnest, Salvi. If I've said too much…well, there's no taking it back. Cards on the table. I've never known anyone like you and I won't bother pretending I'm not besotted."

She chews at her lower lip, then breaks the tension with a breezy laugh, releasing my hand to pick up her water glass. I'm sure I've cocked things up irreparably by coming on too strong and she's either going to take the piss or pretend I didn't say it. But after a sip of water and the slow, pensive chewing of an ice cube, she meets my eyes.

"I must be a tiny bit smitten too, because…that fucking suit would scare away any sane person, but it isn't slowing me down. Let's go back to your place and make out."

19

RAVENNA, ITALY

SAGE

I manage to make it through the drive back to the villa without pawing him too much, but only because the car is too small to comfortably fuck in. But the second we walk through the door, my hands are on the buttons of the ridiculous vest and shirt, clawing them open as I push him against the wall of the foyer. He's watching my lips; I know he's dying to kiss me, and the power trip of keeping that from him is delicious. I whip his unknotted tie off and he flashes a knee-weakening smile and picks me up, walking into the living room.

He lays me down on a huge, buttery-soft leather sofa, balancing on one knee between my legs while he pulls off the jacket and vest, then sinks to lie half on me. He slides a hand up my side, dragging my dress over my hip; then an almost pained expression overtakes him and he drops his head, stroking his cheek against one of my nipples.

"You'll forgive me for begging..." he begins.

"Are you kidding? I *love* making men beg."

His laugh is sultry. "Permission to kiss you everywhere from the neck down, if those tempting lips are firmly off-limits."

My clit sends out a tremor at the thought of Alexander's mouth there.

"Deal. And as long as we're doing the sex boundaries talk, here are my basics: I don't swallow, nothing goes in my ass, the term 'Daddy' skeeves me out, and I don't use specific safe words because no means just that. Got it?"

"Clear as a bell." He presses a kiss to my nipple through the fabric of my dress, then gives it a bite with those pretty teeth.

"And, uh...about condoms. Like, how slutty are you? I'm on Depo, and STI testing is part of my regular thing with my Emerald doc. It's been ages since I was with a guy before you, for that matter. Almost a year."

He looks up from my chest, and the way his auburn hair tumbles over his freckled forehead is beyond cute. "You've not? Why?"

Suddenly I feel a little bashful about it. I give a faint shrug. "Just didn't run across any guys I was into enough to bother."

His slow smile is strangely tender, like I've hit him in the feels. He traces a fingertip along one of the slashes in my dress fabric, then hooks it and draws it aside to expose my breast before encircling my areola with small, featherlight kisses. "I'm honored, Salvi."

"Oh, shut up," I say with amusement. "It's not like you've been knighted or some shit."

He hums a laugh against my skin, and heat surges down my legs. Jesus Christ, what *is* it about him? I don't think I've ever been this in-general turned on by someone, and…for fuck's sake, the guy is lying on top of me wearing clothes that make him look like a cross between a doughnut fairy and Woody from *Toy Story*.

"I'd take this over knighthood any day," he says, skimming a hand along my hip. "And as for my 'sluttiness,' the last woman in my bed was…well, the morning you and Phaedra Morgan called me to threaten a lawsuit. And Brigitte was firm on the requirement of clear test results before there was any, erm, *frolicking*."

His curled palm fits so perfectly into the dip of my waist that it's like he was engineered for me. *Dammit, I need to hold myself together…*

"That said," he continues, "I've no problem with condoms. But…" He rolls onto his back and pulls me on top of him, then slides my dress up to bare my ass, his big hands caressing. "The thought of having you with nothing between us makes me fuckin' sweat."

His dick is hard as a park bench under me, and when I adjust one leg to feel him better, he gives a sort of sighing groan. It's a full-on auditory aphrodisiac—it sounds so much like what I heard the last time we fucked.

"That *is* pretty tempting," I tell him, shifting my hips to grind against him. "Let's play it by ear." Saying it reminds me that I was going to have him play piano, and as hot as I am for him right now, it's irresistible to make him wait a little longer and work for it.

I nod sideways toward where a beautiful piano stands near the windows. It's a reddish-brown wood the same color as Alexander's hair, with a velvet padded bench.

"Hey, you owe me a performance."

He squeezes my ass in a nice bossy way that sends electricity through me. "Delighted."

I laugh. "Not that. Okay, not *just* that. The piano. You said you'd play for me."

"What might you like to hear?"

You. Just like this. But closer, even closer…

I love the vibration of his low, quiet voice where our chests are pressed together. His roaming hands spread little shock waves of lust through me. When I peek at his face, I'm just about done in by those gray eyes, all dilated-pupil-dark and full of erotic promise, framed by gorgeous rust-brown lashes. His lips are magnetic—I could fall against them so fucking easily.

"Surprise me," I tell him, resting my own too-hungry lips against his jawline.

He sits up, pivoting to put his feet on the floor with me on his lap. "Upon one condition, my little brat." Combing a hand into the back of my hair, he pulls my head close and says into my ear, "I am not…wearing…this outfit."

"Fine, you win." I jump up and push his open shirt off his shoulders—*holy fuck, this guy has a great chest*—and coax him to his feet so I can undo the pink doughnut pants. Underneath he's wearing fancy boxer briefs that are cut great and say FLEUR DU MAL on the waistband. Kicking aside the silly trousers, he takes my hand and walks to the piano, then lifts me by the waist and sets me on it.

"I feel like a torch singer." I recline on my elbows and swing my hair melodramatically. *"Come on and cryyyyyyyy me a river…"* I belt out.

Alexander drops his big, pretty hands to the piano and does one of those arpeggio things up and down the keyboard. His fingers glide, dancing over each other, smooth and effortless.

My eyebrows jump. "Damn, you actually know what you're doing!"

"In this, at least. Hmm, what shall I play?" His lips scrunch to one side in thought. "Ah! That night in Bahrain you said… what was it? That jazz 'sounds like Linus is explaining the meaning of Christmas to Charlie Brown'?"

With that, he launches into—*oh my God, are you kidding me?*—that Charlie Brown Christmas song, the thing they all dance to. My mouth drops open and I lean with both hands gripping the edge of the piano, watching his fingers leap over the keys like it's nothing. He's a combination of totally relaxed and alert. His eyes are soft, almost reverent, but fully engaged, like he's reminiscing with an old friend.

The lamplight glimmers on his freckled shoulders, and for possibly the first time in my life I have the feeling of seeing *all of someone*, in a way that sex and even racing has never done. Maybe it's because in this moment he seems more unguarded than he's ever been around me, or maybe it's just because watching a man do something well is hot as shit. But it's wrecking me.

He's *let me in*, and more than anything in the world I want to stay here.

This is the exact moment I fall for the guy.

For the next few minutes, I'm a thing I rarely am—*speechless*. Even though it's a bouncy, happy tune, I feel misty, like the first time I heard Leonard Cohen's "One of Us Cannot Be Wrong," or Bruce Springsteen's "The River."

When Alexander comes to the end, he reaches up and taps the tip of my nose affectionately. I must look blown away, because his brows crumple in a self-conscious way, and he asks, "Is that adequate?"

"Wow." I shake my head. "Just…thank you."

He drops his head and his fingers trill out a scrap of melody. His hidden smile is boyish. "You're quite welcome."

"Play something sad."

He looks up, surprised. "Has a song ever made you cry?"

"*Psh!* Of course not," I lie. "I'm fuckin' nails."

"So you tell everyone." He plinks out a grumpy-sounding collection of notes at the very bottom of the piano's keyboard, lifting a skeptical eyebrow at me. "I, for one, don't buy it."

"Oh, aren't you just the smartest boy in the room," I deadpan.

"I'm the *only* boy in the room."

"My point exactly."

For long seconds, we watch each other. He breaks eye contact first, and there's a struggle in me, because I'm glad I won the staredown, but…I kinda wish I hadn't. Maybe if I'd looked away first, it would've given him a clue to what I'm feeling, without my having to say it.

In a race, it's one thing to lose *an advantage to an opponent, and another thing to surrender it voluntarily.*

Without preface, he starts a slow song. It's hesitant and

melancholy, then picks up pace into a twinkle of notes that sound optimistic before they slow down again and get all angsty. I sit with the rise and fall of the melody—it seems to exist outside of time.

Too soon, it's over. He peeks at me.

"That's beautiful," I almost whisper. "It *is* sad, but also kind of, uh, hopeful."

A hint of pain flits across his expression, then he gives me an easy smile. "Well. We live in hope, don't we?"

There are so many questions I want to ask, but I can't let myself. I sit up, fiddling with a coil of my hair, flicking it with a fingertip.

"What song was that?" I ask, casual.

"It's called 'River Flows in You.'" He takes a slow breath, then clears his throat lightly. "I played it a lot after I left Sakhir. Because…it sounds like sorrow and hope."

Oh God oh shit oh dear. I'm lost…

He stands abruptly, and the *squonk* of the bench sliding back startles me. Our gazes fix on each other. I remember all the things we talked about over dinner, hundreds of details we shared, each like a pebble in that fable about the crow and the pitcher of water. We dropped them into a place seemingly inaccessible, raising our level higher and higher until it became… well, whatever this is. Something we can reach, something to quench a long thirst we've both had.

"Hey, Sandy," I manage.

"Hey, Salvi." He sidesteps to where I'm sitting and positions himself between my thighs. His hands comb through my hair. His dark-pewter eyes are intense, but I see how he's fighting to appear aloof. With a defeated moan, he lowers his face to the curve of my neck. His breath is warm and alive, and when I grip his hair in both hands, I feel more than hear his small gasp.

"Don't go," he says.

Cautiously, I echo the words. "Don't go?"

He shakes his head against my neck, like a child waking from a dream.

"I'm staying all night."

"That's not what I mean." His words touch my skin as gently as snow.

I pull back, and the expression on his face is just this side of despair, like he fears he's said too much. I nibble at the inside of my cheek, deliberating. "I really, *really* want to kiss you," I admit.

He strokes one curled knuckle under my chin. "I know why you'd deny me, but why would you deny yourself?"

Guiding my head up, he leans to brush my lower lip with a touch of his upper. The sensation gives me goose bumps in the best way. I dig my fingers into his shoulders and switch the angle of my head to meet him again. The second kiss is longer, but still tentative for us both. The third is a passing slide, lips still closed, like we're charting a blueprint of each other and don't want to miss a single line.

I pull back an inch. "This is actually a great idea."

"Brilliant," he murmurs. His smoky gray eyes flick from one of mine to the other; then he closes the distance between us. My mouth softens, and when his tongue touches mine, I whimper like a stupid kid who's never been kissed before. I weave my hands into his hair and go in deeper, testing and teasing him, searching, tasting the forbidden mouth that I've been dying for so long to kiss.

When we pause, I whisper, "Fuck, I'm glad you're good at this…" and he chuckles, giving my lower lip a bite, then soothing the spot with a tender lick before closing in again.

I can't tell if we stay like this for a minute or an hour, exploring each other in a way that's both desultory and half starved, but finally he lifts me and heads toward the bedroom. I'm raking his hair, lost in the skill of his mouth, our kisses ranging from restrained, taunting nibbles to deep plunges like we're mining for our own damned souls somewhere down there.

He carries me into the hallway, where we bump the wall in the middle of a particularly intense kiss. He pushes me against the cool stucco and when I unwind my legs from his waist to put them on the floor, he makes a small, pained noise and murmurs, *"Stay…"* against my mouth, lifting me so we don't break the momentum.

After another minute, he pulls back and studies me. The velvet light on him is so goddamned pretty, he's like a Dutch Golden Age painting. I resist the urge to say one of my usual cavalier, horny things. I study him right back. Every freckle, the curve of his nostrils, the glint of light in his left eye, the white scar on the opposite eyebrow.

I trace my forefinger over the smooth, pale interruption. "Looks like a Morse code letter A," I whisper. *"Dit, dah…"*

He kisses me, a ghost of a skim across my lips. "The beginning of a message. You'll have to stick around to decipher the rest."

Our mouths find each other again, and he moves us into the bedroom. What's left of our clothes are peeled off and tossed, and we tumble onto the mattress in an urgent tangle, hands everywhere, as if we're afraid that anything not being touched might disappear.

Rising over me on his beautifully corded arms, Alexander murmurs, "My bed will never look right again without you in it."

There are a dozen clever replies on my tongue, but for some reason it feels like eleven too many. Right now I want *one* thing to say, and the right person to say it to, but…fuck, seriously? What the hell is happening to me? It's almost intimidating to look at him, I'm feeling so much.

"That," I tell him, pinching one of his nipples in an irreverent way, "is very corny."

"But true." He moves a knee to part my thighs and begins a leisurely trip down my body, his lips visiting every plane and curve.

It feels amazing, like he's painting dabs of pleasure-static all over me. My body is taut with anticipation, and he responds so naturally to my subtlest cues—a muscle tensing, a slight intake of breath—elevating me to a state of longing I can barely stand.

"Why are you making me wait?" I groan.

"Why are you making me rush?" he serves back, amused.

When he kisses his way down the sensitive valley between my leg and mons, I nudge him with my thigh and start to sit up and scoot back. "Not to be discouraging, but you probably won't get me off like that. Don't, uh, be bummed if we can't hit the mark."

Sex-wise, there's not much that's as annoying as a guy who decides it's his life's work to make you come from oral even though he's mediocre at it, and then seems hurt when it doesn't happen. Usually only girls do it right, probably because they understand the landscape better.

No matter how much direction I give guys, they always go too hard—I get oversensitive fast, and it scares away the arousal and replaces it with irritation. And what is it with the consistent problem that if, by some miracle, it starts to get good and you're vocal about it, they think it's a great time to switch things up? *Take a fucking clue, gentlemen, and stay on task.*

With a chuckle, Alexander scoops both hands under my ass and pulls me close. "More process than goal here." He brushes his lips across my small trail of pubic hair in a teasing way. "Every square fuckin' inch of you is heaven, and I want to taste it all."

He gentles his thumb over my clit, then kisses it, and… it's just the first light touch of his lips there, but *oh my God*, it's better than what I fantasized, because it's *real*. My thighs relax, but I'm practically holding my breath, willing him to do it again. Normally I'd be barking commands right now—I'm not shy about what I want. But the uncertainty is part of the excitement. I want to see what he's going to do. So far, every way he's touched me and kissed me has felt right.

His ministrations are soft, languorous, and have effortlessly perfect pacing. He seems to understand to keep his touch so light that sometimes I'm more feeling the heat of his breath. When something is exactly right and I arch and push against him, he's there with more. Two of his fingers flirt at my pussy and I didn't even realize I was aching to feel him inside, but I open my legs wider and tilt my hips and he slides in.

Holy fuck, I will never look at long "piano fingers" the same.

The delicious whisper-light rasp of his tongue is killing me, and I don't know if I've babbled some encouraging directions or he's just paying attention, but…the nerves aren't always perfectly the same in me from day to day, and tonight I'm feeling best a little high up on the left side of my clit and *he fucking finds the spot*, and better yet he sticks with it like a goddamned champion of both intuition and patience.

My hips are rising and falling with my gasps that are increasingly close to sobs, and before I know it, I'm wringing the sheets. But then as climax rumbles onto the scene and stampedes over me, I just want to be *closer, closer, closer*, and my arms shoot over my head so I brace my palms on the headboard and push against him like I never want him anywhere else. My shocked scream fractures into laughter and I cover my face with both hands, but not as if I'm hiding—it's more like I want to hold this joy so it can't leave.

After the last tremors rattle through me and I settle, he moves up beside me, laying one big hand gently on my lower belly. I lift my head and his arm tucks beneath it. I can feel him hard against my hip, and I both want to fuck him stupid and to sleep for about ten hours, I'm so blissfully wrung out.

I side-eye peek at him. "I'm pleasantly surprised that you're talented at more than piano."

He kisses my shoulder, smiling. "Thank you, love."

My heart clenches at the word, and I remind myself that it's just a casual Briticism and people call complete strangers "love" at the grocery store in England and it doesn't mean anything. Also, I have zero interest in being *in-love* loved. But for some idiotic reason I want to cry, and...it's both in a happy and sad way.

I am losing my shit big-time. Hormones, right?

A wave of paranoia that he'll see this on my face makes me turn away. I roll onto my side, then scoot back to stay pressed against him. I place my hand on top of the one he has lying open on the bed. When his fingers close around mine, they're a bit sticky, and it turns me on because I think of where they just were. His dick is temptingly settled between my ass cheeks. I trail my fingernails up his forearm and adjust my hips so he's right at the gate.

He gathers me back against his chest. "*Salvi*," he whispers simply.

I clasp one of his hands—the one I just came all over—and playfully bite the tip of his forefinger. He curls it and enters my mouth a knuckle deep and I sweep him with my tongue, tasting myself. When I suck a little, he groans and tilts his hips to slide that fantastic dick of his into me. As he begins his slow thrusts, I rock sinuously back against him.

Goddamn, this guy has the best sex soundtrack I've ever heard, and that's something you can't engineer—it's either right or it isn't. Some guys are businesslike-silent when they fuck (not great, but at least it isn't distracting), and most are stupid sounding. Like, it's a monologue of the type of dirty talk that porn taught them, and they're rattling off a litany of *You love it, dontcha, baby?* and other such horseshit that never feels rhetorical enough to ignore.

But fuuuuuuuck, Alexander is pure erotic music. I can hear every change in what he's feeling with his catch of breath, his small groans that are a natural surrender to pleasure, his occasional dominant growl. He doesn't talk much, but when he does, it's like hearing words spoken in my own language after years of speaking something else.

I raise one leg and hook it back over his, and as I reach to touch myself, his hand is there too. Sometimes when that happens with a guy, I'll shove his hand away so I can do what I need, and other times I cede and just let him fumble around. But I thread my fingers into Alexander's and move his hand how I want, so we're both touching me. Maybe it's like how he can focus on both the left and right sides of a piano keyboard at once, but he has absolutely no trouble caressing me softly, even while he's clearly getting close to his own climax.

My ankle flexes around his leg and I move my hips in time with what he seems to need, and that fucking auditory witchcraft of the way he sounds boosts me higher as his helpless and slightly shocked groan breaks. I can feel him jerk inside of me, and his fragmented release of breath is a little like the way I tend to laugh when I come—something I've always felt self-conscious about, like people might not understand that I'm just happy.

Knowing he's happy too does something unexpected, and yeah, definitely this is a new thing for me—I'm so...*here*. A flicker of impending orgasm blooms on my horizon and I let go of his leg with my ankle and tense both thighs and push his hand against me, grinding my pussy into his palm as another peak hits, harder than expected for a second round.

As we both come down, the two cadences of our breathing play off each other and I listen to us and think *syncopation*, and I wonder if I should confess to Alexander that when he left Bahrain, the day after he bought that stupid record, I looked up a bunch of jazz stuff because I was curious about it, and…well, curious about *him*.

I try to fight the sleep that's creeping over me. The last time we had sex I was all, *Thanks, dude*, and rolled off him and was out like a light, so it seems like I should try to do the polite chitchat thing. But he pulls my hair away from my neck in this nicely tired and lazy way and kisses the curve of my shoulder, then nuzzles against me and *falls asleep first*, still half inside me, which for some reason makes me really blissed out.

As I follow him into unconsciousness, I can't help thinking, *Maybe we're sort of a good match.*

20

RAVENNA, ITALY

ALEXANDER

For years, it was my preference to send women off with a friendly pat on the bum after sex—*ta-ra, thanks for the memories*—and that was obviously not nice. Then came a night when I was twenty-four and a woman named Rose screamed at me in my foyer, "It's still muggy even if you pay for the cab, you feckin' tosser!" before slamming out my door, and the angry tears in her eyes made me feel like a world-class arsehole.

Since then, having women sleep over if it's their preference has been, to my mind, part of the deal. But this is the first time I've been delighted with it.

When I wake just after 5:00, Sage is lightly snoring. I prop on an elbow and watch her in the faint light. She sleeps on her stomach, arms and legs sprawled, face unglamorously mashed against the pillow, and I've never seen anything more lovely.

After we'd slept for a few hours last night, I was pleasantly roused by Sage's mouth on me. I assumed the sex would be one of those drowsy, quick things people do with minimal words, but we ended up making love for an hour or better (contrary to her previously stated preference for speed and repetition). She still won't kiss me when my cock is in her, and I'm not sure how to feel about that, but I acknowledge that she makes the rules.

After about ten minutes of meditating on her adorable snore, wondering what she might be dreaming when the fingers of her left hand twitch in a sequence that appears deliberate, I quietly rise, put on a dressing gown, and go to the kitchen. I take the kettle from the hob and fill it, then set it on a burner, remembering the moment last night when I realized I was not merely enamored, but—for the first time in my life—*in love*.

Sage mentioned her parents' "weird relationship that's sorta 'open' but actually my mom just turns a blind eye to a shitload of cheating." With a cynical flip of one hand, she concluded, "Anyway, who cares? At least it was enough to discourage me from ever being a romantic."

As multiple realizations assailed me, my heart stumbled back and forth like someone walking the deck of a ship in a gale. *I want to be the one to make her believe in love* came first. Then a heartbeat later I was crushed by the acknowledgment that I am the wrong person, hopelessly unqualified. Another beat and I thought, *What "qualification" does one need other than a genuinely selfless, actionable desire for the other's happiness, whatever the cost?* I want the world for Sage. I would do anything to ensure her happiness, comfort, safety.

After a lifetime of feeling like any personal detail about a woman—even as insignificant as knowing her birthday or preferred coffee drink—is an imposition, a nasty little hook that might be set into me...I'm greedy to know everything about my sweet Salvia officinalis.

As I wait for the water to boil, I pick up my mobile from the counter to peruse my messages, and my stomach drops to see two from "Alfred, Accountant"—the contact name I made up for CJ Ardley. I swipe the thread open.

> **Alfred, Accountant:** I'm finding it a little suspect, hun, that you still don't have gossip to pass along, especially considering you and shortcake are apparently having a slumber party in Italy.
>
> **Alfred, Accountant:** If you're jerking my chain, be warned that I bite.

Fuckin' hell.

Fake contact name or not, the meaning of that message would be clear if Sage were to see it. I stare out the back window into the garden for a long minute, my heart pounding, and finally dash off a reply.

> **Me:** Playing a long game takes patience and subtlety. I believe you said you'd allow me to "be on top"? Don't question my methods or the deal is off.
>
> **Me:** Or do you think I couldn't find another recipient for the riches I mine?

Once sent, I delete the exchange, sick at heart over my deception. Oddly enough, I feel bad not only for hiding things from Sage but also for lying to CJ and using a blustering, imperious tone that reminds me unpleasantly of my father. I should've had the courage to tell Ms. Ardley, that night at the gala, *Sage is my friend and I won't help you to make a fool of her.*

Clear and simple, no games.

My God, Badrick is right—I'm such a fucking child sometimes.

I finish making the tea, then go to the bedroom and climb under the covers, sipping and thinking as the sky outside stains along the edge with hints of dawn.

What happens now? She doesn't "do" attachments. Is this the template, going forward: I fight for each moment with her, perpetually carrying the anxiety that it's our last? How long until she finds someone else, or simply tires of me?

She emits a small groan, then her left hand slides across the bed as if she's trying to place where she is. With a deep intake of breath, she rolls onto her back and drags the tousled blue hair out of her face. Looking over at me, she smiles, and my relief is almost palpable.

"Morning, sweetness." I set my tea aside and lean toward her. "Kiss?"

"At your own risk, pal," she says in an amused, sleepy mutter. "I just woke up."

In deference to her reticence, I brush her closed lips lightly, then deliver a longer kiss to her warm forehead. Retrieving the mostly full tea mug, I offer it to her. "You can have this. Or I'll make fresh if you like."

"Yeah, I'd take a sip or two."

She struggles upright and the sheets fall away, exposing her torso. It comes to me again that yes, I must be feeling something very new, because rather than ogling her pert breasts, I find myself looking at the impressions the tangled sheets have made on her skin. I have that sense of wonder at the small living details of her. Those dented lines might as well be the intricacies of origami, the way they captivate me.

I hand her the tea and she drinks a few gulps, then takes one more just before handing it back, swishing it in her mouth in her uninhibited way before swallowing. When she leans to kiss me again, there's a warmth and familiarity to it that makes me hopeful. I go in for another, then she deepens it, and when I pull her on top of me, she makes a tiny despairing moan against my lips and asks, "What time is it?"

"Just gone half five."

"Fuuuuuuuuck…" Her forehead drops to my shoulder and she whooshes a sigh against my skin. "It's a forty-minute drive to the paddock. I gotta shower and get on the road."

My hands drift down her spine. "Come back tonight?"

"Can't. The rest of the week is fuckin' nuts." She sits up, straddling me, and I noticeably respond. Feeling it through my dressing gown, she wriggles her hips. "Don't suppose you wanna go to Barcelona in a month? We could hook up there…"

I don't let it show how the term "hook up" affects me with its sudden revert to distance.

She pivots and hops off the bed, shimmy-dancing toward the en suite, singing Gorillaz "Clint Eastwood" in a slow, sooty drawl. When she turns on the water the same way she did last night—step in, twist the tap, scream, laugh—I'm flooded with the gratifying sense that this is now a thing I know about Sage, a routine detail of her. It's like being given a prize.

After a few minutes, I follow her into the en suite, where I go to the washbasin and began to shave. Her singing drops to humming, and I hear the squelch of shampoo suds as she washes her hair.

I examine myself in the mirror, stripes of clean skin showing through the foam. "You know," I find myself saying before thinking it through, "I've never told a woman 'I love you.'"

Fuck...what have I done?

Sage falls silent. I hope it's because she's not heard me, but she peers around the frosted glass panel with a nervous amusement. "Well, don't start now. I'm not *that* good in bed."

She disappears again, and I return to scraping the line of my jaw, fretting over what I've said.

A minute later, she speaks up. "You mean not in a romantic sense, right? But you tell your mom and stuff? Because guys who are dicks to their moms are total walking red flags."

I'm struck by two things: first, a dart of hope that she's talking about "red flags," since that denotes the possibility of examining my suitability for partnership; and second, whether I should lie, or try to explain why I haven't said those words to my mother either.

I run my razor through a stream of water. "I'm British, darling."

Her skeptical snort turns into a cough as if she's got water up her nose. She leans to look at me again. "Oh, like, 'Keep calm, and don't bother telling Mum you love her'?"

"She knows, Salvi. Fuck's sake."

When I turn to make eye contact directly rather than through the mirror, Sage is scowling.

"So that's a no?" she presses. "Because, I mean, I haven't ever told someone I've had sex with 'I love you' either, but...I definitely say it to my family."

"Nefeli Laskaris is not sentimental. Just last week she joked about selling my baby teeth."

"Okay, so she's a smartass like you," Sage says a bit coldly.

I narrow my eyes. "She'd find it mawkish and embarrassing if I told her directly that I love her. Again, in my defense, *she bloody knows*."

Sage's only reply is an irritated growl, and she steps under the shower spray again.

A horrible sense that this conversation is about to go off the rails makes me feel like the ground is shaking under my feet. I'm about to redirect things and ask Sage if she'd like for me to make her some toast before she leaves, when instead I utterly shoot myself in the foot by saying, "Do you tell Julian you love him? Because he told me in Melbourne that you hate him."

I see her freeze for a moment behind the glass divider, then turn the water off with a smack. Stepping into the shower doorway, she fixes me with a baleful look and swipes a towel off its peg.

In a mocking imitation of me, she repeats my words. "In my defense, *he bloody knows*." She strides into the bedroom.

I towel my face off, imperfectly shaved, and follow. "Salvi."

She ignores me, pawing through the chaos of her clothes until she finds a pair of jeans and steps into them. "Don't talk to me. I'm annoyed at you."

"I see that." Rubbing my face, I add, "Can we not?" I open my arms in invitation for a hug, and after a pause she receives it woodenly.

"It's hitting below the belt to bring Jules into it," she mutters against my chest.

"I don't know what I was thinking." I kiss the damp top of her head, and she softens in my arms. "How is he? Have you got word of his progress?"

"I don't wanna talk about it."

I'm stung; it feels like the intimacy I thought we'd achieved might be one-sided. But I don't dare push her, or I've no hope of seeing her in Barcelona next month.

"We needn't, then." I give Sage another kiss on the head, and as she draws away and dips to grab a T-shirt and pull it on, she looks distant. She's already somewhere else, a *hundred* elsewheres. She's at the paddock in a meeting, she's in her car, she's talking with the press, she's worrying about Julian. It's humbling to know I'm the least relevant of her concerns.

Gathering her things over the next few minutes, Sage reinstalls her carefree mask, cracking wise as if we didn't very nearly quarrel. But I can tell there's something fragile beneath it. I wish I could pull her back into bed and reset this all in the way we both know best.

When she grabs her mobile, the screen is crowded with messages. She focuses on them in a pointed way, as if needing me to understand that my usefulness has expired.

She declines an espresso, then toast. I offer to box up some of the baked pasta Cinzia made so Sage can have it later, and when she consents, I can't be certain it isn't out of pity. As I pack up the lunch—*my God, when have I ever packed a lunch for anyone?*—I discreetly check my expression in the reflection of the microwave door to ensure I look appropriately detached and neither lovesick nor panicky.

Soon, the moment arrives when I walk her to the foyer. On the living room floor, just within my peripheral vision, I catch a smudge of pink—the absurd doughnut trousers. Last night seems a hundred years ago.

She opens the door and when I pull her close, she grips the back of my dressing gown with both hands. I cradle the side of her neck with the burning peacock feather tattoo and touch her chin, tipping her up for a kiss that turns into a half dozen. Finally she steps back, shouldering her duffel bag and taking the container of pasta off the credenza.

"It's been real," she says with a crooked smile that's a little sad.

"Very much so." I lean in the doorway, trying to appear unbothered. "See you in Spain."

"Maybe," she says. Just as the ambivalence of the word is killing me, she winks. "*Probably*. But don't go counting on it."

I put a hand on my chest, comically. "Dagger to the heart, that."

And then she's gone with a backward wave, and I'm left to overthink the past twelve hours, wondering how I'll live without her if she's forgotten me next month.

21

RAVENNA, ITALY

SAGE

I make it three miles before my stupid fucking tears make driving unsafe and I have to pull over. I'm overwhelmed. When Sandy mentioned telling a woman he loves her…shit, the last time I was that scared was when I had a big crash at Interlagos in the wet and got T-boned. The second before contact, it was like I could feel myself being fatally crushed, and…well, the L-word thing wasn't much different, even though Alexander wasn't technically declaring it.

I still don't know why he said that. Was it a warning: *I'm incapable of love, so don't hold your breath*? Was it an overture for a dialogue about our respective hopes for whatever the fuck we're doing? Or was he test-driving how those words feel? Because this has gotten serious whether we wanted it to or not.

And worst of all, I think I actually *might* want it.

I turn off the engine and start doing breathing exercises. The car's top is down, and above me a huge laurel tree is shrugging in the breeze, making shadow patterns on me, and I focus on that because I have to stop thinking about turning around and going back to the villa. There are screechy bugs trilling off in the distance, so I switch to concentrating on that as I take five more measured breaths.

Oh, fuck it...

Snatching my phone from the console, I tap the top of my text thread with Alexander and call him. It rings four times and I get nervous and almost hang up, but then there he is.

"Salvi? Are you all right?"

It's all warm and nice in my chest, because for one thing I'm hearing his voice, and for another, he's obviously concerned, and...the *continuity* of that fact is pleasing. I don't hang out with sex partners enough for them to have an investment in what I'm doing from one moment to the next, once we're not in bed anymore. But something here feels comfortingly unbroken, real, like there's a string tied between us. I have to swallow hard before I can speak.

"Yeah, there's no crisis," I tell him. "Like, not with the car or anything." The lump in my throat strangles me and tears leak out along with a sort of emotion-hiccup.

"Oh, pet," he says quietly.

Through the phone I hear a noise I recognize, the plink of a single piano key, and it makes my heart ache even more, because *I know that sound*, and things about Sandy are getting familiar and that both elates and terrifies me.

"Are you crying?" he asks.

"Of course not," I snap.

He chuckles, and I love the sound in my ear. "No, because you're 'nails,' wasn't it?"

I sniffle, reaching for the glove box to see if I can find tissue. There's a cocktail napkin from some Italian bar, and I swipe at my nose with it before realizing there's a girl's phone number on the back. Who the hell writes their number down anymore? I hope it wasn't important to whoever used this car last. This time it wasn't me.

Thinking about it makes me realize that I don't want to meet people in bars anymore. I just want to lie in bed with Alexander and talk and have sex.

Goddammit, I fucking like him so much...

"Sandy," I start tentatively, "I'm sorry I was bitchy about Julian this morning, and it's not true that I don't want to talk to you about it. I majorly do. But I'm not good at talking to people I sleep with. I mean, most of the reason I stick to hookups is so I don't have to talk. It's like, 'I don't speak Greek, and you don't speak English, so let's just get down to business,' y'know?"

After a pause, he sighs. "I do know. All too well."

I'm not sure if he means me or himself, but I press on. Now that I've started, I need to say it all, or I might never be brave enough again.

I take a controlled breath. "As for how Jules is doing, I don't know because we aren't allowed to talk with him, and…I was relieved about that, because *it means I don't have to*. I think I'm a big coward that way. But also I'm really trying to understand what he's going through. I got some books and I'm learning a lot. Truth is, the day he was supposed to go in, he went AWOL and had a junk bender in some Swiss hotel room. I'm worried."

"Fuckin' hell."

My throat cramps, and I tip my head up to look at the tree. "And I *haven't* told Jules I love him, no. Which I do. But…I also hate him, because he let me almost die once and I can't forgive him." I pinch my nose with the napkin again. There's a long enough silence that I look at the phone. "Um, Sandy? Don't be disappointed in me. I know it sounds shitty—"

"It's not that. I just wish I could hold you right now. You can't be that far away. Could you come back? And tell me more about this?"

"No," I say miserably. "I have to go to work."

"Understood." He sighs again. "I very much want to see you though." He does a little throat-clear. "There *is* another race before Spain. I could come to Miami. A plane ride is a plane ride, and…frankly, the thought of not seeing you for a month has me wretched."

Now *I* go quiet, because I don't know if I can say the next part.

"Salvi, love?"

"I…I need a month. Because I'm feeling sort of, um, *too attached*."

I can hear the smile in his voice. "Truly?"

"Yeah, but don't get all pleased with yourself. I don't know how this is even happening. You're, uh…you're way less of a dick than I thought, I guess."

"Damning with faint praise, but cheers," he returns, amused.

I roll my eyes. "Why aren't you just an asshole? It'd make things so much easier if you were still the 'yourself' I thought you were months ago."

In a sort of pensive tone, he says, "I'm unsure if I even know the 'myself' I thought I was months ago." His next words are lower, and I strain to hear them over the insect-shrieking noise. "I find I'm a person I like a lot better when I'm with you."

It's so similar to what I thought about myself last night, while we were talking at the restaurant, that I'm stunned. To stop from confessing it, I switch to teasing him.

"You know, your douchebaggery is so legendary that Cosmin does a hilarious impression of you. He told me about one time before he and Phae were official and you tried to give him advice about women, and you were all, 'Let her see you with some hotties! Make her jealous! Chicks dig it!'" I laugh at the bad, confused mashup of accents I'm trying for—a Romanian guy trying to sound like a British guy trying to sound like an American frat boy. "He told me he threatened to give you a beatdown."

Alexander laughs, and it sounds like both relief and embarrassment. "Guilty as charged. I was trying to impress him and ended up looking like a twat. Which...well, historically it's a thing I do far too often, and I'm not proud of that. It's not who I want to be."

For a half minute, we're silent, just being with each other. I swear, if he coaxed me a little, I'd point this fucking car east again...

"You really prefer to wait until Barcelona?" he asks softly.

No! I don't even want to wait until tomorrow.

"Yeah, definitely. Sorry." My eyes sting, and I rub them with a thumb and forefinger.

"I'll be counting down the days." After a pause, he adds, "And as long as we're making confessions...erm, regarding what I mentioned when you were in the shower...I may never have said those words to a woman—not *yet*—but I absolutely have thought them of late."

My heart hammers, and I put my hand on my chest, wondering if I'll be able to feel it right through my sternum like a cartoon. I force a carefree laugh. "Clear air, smooth track. Let's just not fuck it up." I start the car's engine and rev it loud to drown out the wobble in my voice when I say goodbye, then whip back onto the road in a spray of dust and gravel.

MIAMI

Home race is always a big deal, not only because you want to do well, but also the added pressure is you want specifically to *not suck*. There have been so many drivers who completely stink up the track at their home race, and the media are rarely kind about it.

Florida is just about as far as you can get from my actual home and stay on the same landmass, but it's still a home race. Definitely couldn't have Sandy tagging along, making me all scatterbrained and puppy-lovey. Also my mom is coming to stay with me and Priya in my suite, and I'm super stoked to hang out.

The morning she's scheduled to arrive, early in the race week, she sends a message that makes me nervous: Your dad isn't coming along and I have something we need to talk about.

Um, fuck.

I didn't expect my dad to come to Miami, because he's usually too busy with work. The fact that my mom explicitly mentioned it, along with the vague "something we need to talk about," doesn't bode well. And it must be serious—a thing she's afraid I'd find out anyway if she didn't deliver the news—because otherwise she knows not to stress me out before a race.

Pri goes to pick Mom up because I'm in a bunch of back-to-back training sessions, then a team meeting, and won't be able to see her until early evening. When I open the door of the suite, I smell her presence right away, but it's nice, not one of those lady perfumes like a sickening fog of flowers. Mom uses this berry-scented hand lotion, and her normal person smell is a little like bread baking, so there's that too, and I'm tired and sore but I relax immediately, before I even have the door closed.

"Sagey!" she cries out, hurrying out of the main bedroom on the left. She looks energetic, and that's great because now I know the bomb she's going to drop on me can't be that she's sick. She has a new haircut with highlights in it, and it takes about ten years off her. She's also toned-looking in a top that bares her shoulders and arms, like she's actively been at the gym and not just taking her usual walks.

She hugs me, and Pri comes in, and we're all chattering, talking half over each other, happy as hell. Pri orders room service, and she knows what I'm allowed to eat during race week, so that's a big help. Mom and I go to the sofas near the huge windows that look out on the beach and she opens her straw carry-on and starts pulling presents out. She always brings presents, like I'm a little kid.

There's a pair of socks with kittens on them that say THIS GIRL TAKES NO SHIT. There's a Toblerone bar, which she apologizes for since she knows I can't have sugar this week. And there's a book, a PostSecret collection, which is a fun nostalgia trip because I used to read that blog all the time when I was younger, and she remembers.

There's nothing quite like a mom to hold all your details sacred.

Over dinner I ask her what the big news is, and she waves it off, saying, "Oh, we have plenty of time for that." We're having fun, *Pride and Prejudice* is playing in the background and personally I'm not nuts about sappy romance, but it's a fave for Mom and Pri, and I concede that a young Colin Firth looks hot in a wet shirt.

Mom offers to sleep next to Pri so she doesn't "disturb my rest," but I know she's probably not gonna tell me the news until we're sitting quietly in the dark, so I ask her to bunk in my room. The bed is huge, so I tell Pri she should stay too and we'll do a girlie sleepover.

Once we're all settled under the sheets, me in the middle, Mom says, "Sagey, don't be mad at me, but I'm divorcing your father."

I blow out a relieved breath. "Oh my God, is that all? You had me worried as fuck. And frankly, it's about time."

"Is it because of the cheating?" Pri asks, and I flop an arm to give her a smack, which she responds to with an indignant, "Ow! Jesus!" before smacking me right back.

Mom chuckles. "The cheating didn't help. But that wasn't the breaking point. And I'm concerned about tainting your view of your father, so don't be too hard on him, but..." She sighs. "I'm disappointed with how he's handled Julian's...*problem*. And things came to a crossroads where our differences are now irreconcilable."

Pri and I are both frozen at the mention of Jules. It's silent for a half minute.

Finally Mom says, "I *do* know, girls. About his opiate dependence. There's no shame in it. I just want to help. But your father's been spending recklessly for years, Sage. And I don't fault him entirely for that, aside from the fact that so much of it has been spent on other women."

"Wait," I interrupt, "are you guys broke?" I think back to all the art pieces that were gone last time I was at home, and how Mom said she'd sold them because she wanted to "declutter."

"'Broke' is too strong. But eighty percent of the assets we had five years ago are gone."

I cover my face with both hands. "Fuuuuuuuuck..."

"Honey, it's not a big deal. But your brother has depleted his trust fund with travel and...well, his illness. So he asked us a month ago if we could pay for this treatment center, a place in Switzerland, very expensive but excellent success record. I said of course, but because of our financial situation, we'd have to downsize the house to fund it, which—"

"Mom! I grew up there!" I protest. "Why didn't you just ask me to help?"

"I'm guessing you *have* helped. Right?"

There's a pause where I make a kind of noncommittal grumbling noise.

"Last I heard from your brother," Mom goes on, "he told me he'd found 'a place that would take him' and would be out of contact for a while. Then when Priya picked me up today she said Julian is 'climbing in Switzerland,' and…I can put two and two together, girls."

"Sorry for lying," Priya mumbles.

Mom reaches across me and gives Pri a pat. "It was sweet of you to protect him, honey. And me too." She turns her head my way. "Sage?"

"Yeah, I paid for it," I admit. "It's fine—no big."

She reaches to squeeze my hand. "You're a good sister." Her voice is rough with emotion.

"I'm not, really. And everything's taken care of, so *please* don't sell the house."

There's a huff of bitter laughter. "Oh, we didn't. Your father told Julian we'd do no such thing. That it was his fault he'd 'made poor choices,' which not only isn't fair but is also very 'pot calling the kettle black.'" She folds her arms with stubborn resolve. "That was it. I told Matthew, 'For God's sake, I've put up with enough, you can give me this,' and he wouldn't budge, so the day your brother got on a flight for Melbourne, I went to a divorce lawyer."

I rub my face with a long groan. "Why is Dad such a dick?"

"He just doesn't understand this issue. But he was a good father while you kids were growing up. I think he'll come around, but that doesn't mean I have to stick with the marriage.

I've been unhappy for more than a decade. It's not like I have limitless time—I'm in my mid-sixties. I'd like to...you know, maybe date and whatnot. See what's still out there for me."

Priya reaches across me for Mom's hand. "Good on you."

"Agreed," I add, squeezing their clasped hands. "But I thought Jules didn't tell you guys. I asked him point-blank, and he was like, 'I don't wanna worry Mom.'"

"Oh, Sagey," she says in a tone of indulgent amusement, "he didn't want to worry *you*. Can't you see that? Julian thinks the world of you, and I'm sure he figured if he told you what happened, you'd be angry with your father. He was protecting you."

"*Psh!* 'Protecting'? He does *not* think the world of me. I know it hurts your feelings that we're not all nice to each other like *The Waltons* or something, but...yeah. No."

Mom is quiet for a long time. Then she rolls on her side toward me and props on one elbow. "I don't want to make you feel bad, honey, but your brother carries so much guilt since you got sick in Thailand. He's never forgiven himself, even though he did everything he could."

We've never, *ever* talked about this, so I'm taken aback, and instantly so pissed about her defending him that I almost launch into a *He left me to die* rant, but instead I just sputter, "Everything he could?"

"My God, yes. He and that young man he talked to on the trail—a boy from Germany—they went back and hunted all over. Checked other routes and asked everyone they met up with, and...nothing. So when he rushed to get your father and tell him what'd happened and they went back to search again, a lot of time had been lost. It was your father who thought of looking *off* the trails, in case, well, you know. He thought you might've been attacked. Then they found you unconscious, and good lord, honey—your brother has never stopped berating himself, 'If I hadn't walked away, if I hadn't wasted time looking in the wrong places…'"

My body is flooded with a cold, numb prickling, I'm so stunned. I can barely breathe.

Julian came back for me right away?

I've always assumed he fucked off without a backward glance, and no one gave two shits until he showed up without me, and it was *my parents* who'd insisted on going back to look.

"I can't tell you how often I've told him to talk to you about it," my mom goes on. "Or even a therapist! But he's too ashamed."

The cold shock breaks in me, my heart is hammering, and with a keening sound I don't even recognize as being made by *me* for a few seconds, I roll onto my stomach, sobbing as eleven fucking years of anger dies and is sluiced away by *the worst fucking grief*. I've wasted nearly half my life hating Julian, looking down on him, being resentful and competitive and just plain fucking *mean*, and it was for nothing.

And both Mom and Pri are there for me, confused as fuck but comforting anyway, hugging me as I weep my stupid heart out. I can't tell them why it hurts so bad—I hate myself too much. I think of all the times I was horrible to Jules, and meanwhile he was moaning to Mom about how he'd never get over the guilt of almost killing me.

What if we'd been close, that night in the kitchen months ago? What if I'd been a good sister, and when I saw him putting that shit up his nose, I'd first yelled at him—because, yeah, obviously I'd be mad—but then I'd hugged him and begged him to stop hurting himself? If I'd been understanding and supportive and compassionate and *real*? Instead I made fun of him, shamed him, and when I paid for his rehab, acted grouchy about it.

With all the reading I've been doing on addiction and recovery, I understand it so much better now. I'd been convinced of all these unfair and straight-up inaccurate things, like that Julian just didn't have the "grit and determination" to get his shit together. Learning about the psychology of addiction and the medical reality of his physical dependence, I was finally able to see that success or failure in recovery isn't about "willpower," or what type of person you are. The primary difference is that *those who succeed have a support system.*

I couldn't win races based purely on willpower or mental toughness. There's an entire team of people devoted to making my success possible. Julian needs that too. And just like being shamed for making errors during a race wouldn't help me to do better next time, I can't use that approach with my brother's illness.

I'd accepted this, but there was one little part of me still resenting it—being a scorekeeper, playing a zero-sum game, just like he pointed out—because I thought he hadn't made any effort for *me* when I'd needed his help.

It's like the last wall crumbles, and I'm relieved, but also so, *so* sad for everything we've lost, all the time wasted.

Fuck, and I also made him and Priya miserable about being in love.

I am the literal worst sister on the planet.

I want to call him right now, but I can't; they took his phone when he checked in.

After I've drained myself crying, I go to the bathroom and rinse my swollen eyes with icy-cold water, then come back to bed, get between Mom and Pri again, and tell them, "On Sunday I'm getting my first fucking podium, and I'm doing it for Jules."

Rockstar technical director Basil Rowley's youngest daughter is almost exactly my age—her birthday is the day after mine—and I think that's part of why he has a special fondness for me. According to said daughter, Iris (we even both have plant names), he tried to get her into racing when she was little, but it turned out swimming was her thing…like, she's done the English Channel, for fuck's sake. Anyway, we've become friends this year, and she's here for the GP.

Early on race day, I'm in my driver's room when Iris taps on the door and peeks in.

"Should I have texted first?" she asks, coming in and closing the door, leaning back on it. From one hand dangles her ever-present water bottle, covered in stickers.

"Hey, babes!" I go and hug her. "It's fine. But I have to do reflex drills in like five minutes. Nice to see you—I didn't know if you'd make it."

Iris is a foot taller than me and looks just like Basil

(fortunately without the mustache). She has strong, angular features, and her accent makes her sound like a pirate. She's super fun—one of my favorite new people.

"Pressure's high, eh?" she asks, crossing to a chair that's draped in cast-off clothes and plunking down on the wrinkled mess. "You'd think Taylor Swift were at the paddock, the way fans and press are circling, all for you."

"Oh, bullshit," I protest with a laugh. "There's always a ton of that at races. It's not me specifically."

"Nah, it's you. *So* many women with signs, every one of 'em pulling for Emerald." She pops the straw on her water bottle and sips, smiling at me. "To say nothin' of all the lads who fancy you. I saw two of 'em wearing shirts with your face and 'Marry me, Sage.'"

"Jesus Christ," I scoff.

"Speaking of boys, who's your one in Ravenna?" she asks, pronouncing it adorably as *Ravenner*.

I freeze in the middle of adjusting the laces on one shoe, glancing up. "What? Who?"

"You tell me." She gnaws at the silicone straw with a taunting look.

I focus on my shoelace again, buying time, then finally sit up primly straight. "What did you hear, and where, exactly?"

Iris shrugs. "Thought you'da heard the goss already. From the blond slag with the Turkey teeth who writes the sport blog. No specifics, but said you've a new fella and he distracted you so much in Italy that your drive was pants."

"Oh, CJ Ardley can get fucked. I got four points for Emerald at Imola."

She squints. "Yeah, but you qualified in sixth, so the eighth-place finish was..." Trailing off, she leaves the rest painfully implied.

Truth is, I *was* majorly in my head at the last GP because of all that emotional drama with Sandy. I'm glad we have a month off from each other.

Today I'm feeling a crisp, blue-sky-to-the-horizon's-edge clarity, despite the shock of finding out about Jules from Mom a few days back. I'm full of inspiration. But the news that Maya's mother is shitposting about me again isn't exactly great. And unfortunately, she always stays on the other side of the line where I could sic Emerald's legal team on her.

"Aw, don't believe everything you read," I tell Iris with a flap of one hand. Shoe adjusted, I stand and jump up and down in place a few times, checking the fit. "Everyone can watch my fuckin' dust. This is my first home race since I got a seat, and I'm not accepting less than P3."

⛝

A few factors in the third qualifying session set me back farther than I was hoping for—seventh—but I'm trying to see it as a challenge. I came into turn 13 a second after Mateo Ortiz hit the wall in Q3 and it had just started raining, so the slick conditions plus debris on the track slowed me down. But my car's setup is beautifully balanced today and I'm gonna fight like hell to advance.

The straight from pole to turn 1 isn't long on this track, and there's always a fucking free-for-all leading into it. But this section is one of my secret weapons down the road. It's a DRS zone, and on another lap I might be set up for a pass.

At lights out, I stay clear of the chaos, then make my first pass at T11. Climbing into P6 on the first lap gives me confidence. Everything else falls away and it's just me and the car, one body, working together to devour the track.

On the third lap, after the uphill twisty bits in turns 12 to 15, we exit T16 into one of my favorite spots—the nearly mile-long straight where I'll be flying at over 200 mph before hard-braking T17. Ahead of me, avoiding a tussle between Drew Powell and Cosmin causes Akio Ono to drop back. I stay on his ass around the tight turn and into the DRS detection zone, then pass him at turn 1 as the fourth lap starts.

I opted to start the race on hard tyres because of my position farther back. Every driver in front of me started on mediums, and the race will be a one-stopper for most. My passes thus far on the harder tyres have owed to two things: the gorgeous car Basil Rowley has put under my ass, and my pushy, risk-embracing, late-braking driving style.

My tyre management is solid, and the track's surface temp is taking a toll on everyone. As the race progresses and the frontrunners start boxing for new rubber, I build up distance while I can. For one lap I'm even in the lead, and lemme just say...Alexander is a great lay, but leading a grand prix will always be better than sex.

My pit window is between laps 35 and 41, and I push it as late as I can. I'm all but limping at lap 40. My best chance is staying in that clearer air as long as possible. Just as I'm starting lap 41, there's a dustup between Anders Olsson and one of the rookies, and I'm blessed by the Yellow Flag Goddess and get a sweet deal on my pit stop. I gain three seconds before even exiting the pit lane.

I retain P4 with sixteen laps to go. Owen Byrne is in P3 right now, six seconds ahead of me, which feels like an eternity. But my mediums are faster than his hards, and Team Easton have been having trouble this season with their Energy Recovery System overheating. It's cost him positions twice already this year.

For the next dozen laps, I work my way up until I'm right on Owen's gearbox. His car is strong, and he's just not making any damned mistakes.

Until lap 54.

After the balls-out speed of the sector 3 straight, we roar into turn 17, where a combination of my late braking and Owen going too wide gives me an opportunity. I cut past like an Iron Chef showing off flawless knife skills. Cosmin and Drew are too far ahead for me to get higher than P3, but my podium is a sure thing as long as I don't fuck up.

Which I don't. I polish that scorching, rubbered-in track with the glide of a surfer, wasting no movement, no breath, existing in the natural space created by driver, car, and hot ground. When I cross the finish line, Imani lets out a giddy laugh.

"Fifth race...podium, baby!" she says.

"Told you I would," I shoot back, elated. "Jules, if you're watching, this one's for you."

It's not until an hour later when a journalist asks me who "Jules" is that I realize I probably shouldn't have drawn attention to him. Someone might get curious enough to dig around, wondering what's going on with my brother.

I decide I'm being paranoid, and just allow myself to enjoy the day. The press is predictably going apeshit over what they're now calling Formula 1's Leading Lady. Of course, the first time a journalist brings it up, I have to sass. "I'm no lady… What's the fun in that?"

It's a great fucking weekend.

I can't wait for Spain.

22

BARCELONA, SPAIN

ALEXANDER

Even with nearly a month to plan, it was still devilishly hard to find anyplace with a vacancy in Barcelona the week of the Grand Prix. But I found out about a friend of a friend who lives in the city and isn't a racing fan—an artist with a studio flat in the El Born neighborhood—who was willing to shove off for the week and let me stay there.

The expense was immoderate; I had to pay ten thousand euros, plus buy her a round-trip plane ticket to Thailand and put her up at a luxury spa in Phuket. But when I arrive the night before Sage is to join me, I conclude that it's well worth it. The place is charming, bohemian, and has a great view. High ceilings, rustic beams, cream-colored brick walls, and—as one might expect of an artist—fantastic paintings and sculptures.

On the kitchen island is a bottle of Vega Sicilia with a note saying *Enjoy your stay*. I pick it up to examine it and find it's quite a good year and must have set her back €400 to €500 (which I suppose she can afford, given how I was gouged on the price, but it was kind nonetheless). On impulse, I take photos of the wine, the view off the balcony, a particularly nice salon-style collection of paintings on one wall, and the bed, then send them to Sage.

It's midmorning where she is, six hours earlier, so I don't expect her to respond. But minutes later, she calls.

"Hey, Sandy-boy. Love the pics. Is that where we're staying?"

"If you'll do me the honor." I sprawl onto a thick chenille sofa and toe my shoes off before putting my feet up. "Shall I collect you at the airport?"

"Nah, I have to go straight to a meeting. Then I'll drop Pri off at the motor home and come over."

"Congratulations again on the podium finish," I tell her, plumping the collection of pillows behind my head and leaning back. "You took my breath away. A stunning drive."

"Aw, thanks."

"And it was very touching that you dedicated it to Julian."

"We'll see if that bites me on the ass," she says wryly. "But, uh…I have stuff to tell you about that, when I get there. The thing I mentioned about the big grudge, and how Jules almost let me die? Yeah, turns out I was full of shit."

"I look forward to hearing the details," I say lightly.

Sage can be emotionally defensive enough that it nearly qualifies as combative, so I'm careful to give her space. Her tone has a combination of sulkiness and comic self-deprecation

I already recognize in her, one that tells me the upcoming revelation is a sore subject. Best to move the topic along so she doesn't get mired in regret or embarrassment.

"Speaking of family relationships," I begin, shifting the focus to my own shortcomings and offering her the opportunity to take the piss, "you may be happy to learn that in my last telephone conversation with my mother, I told her I love her."

This turns out to be the right approach. Sage gasps in a stagey way, then demands, "Oh my gaaawwwwd, do tell."

"Before signing off, I said, 'Just so you know, Mother, I love you.' There was an unnervingly long pause, and her reply was, 'Why on earth would you say that? What have you done? You must be feeling guilty about something.'"

Sage cackles, and the unbridled sound of her less-than-dainty laugh warms my heart. I don't know how I can stand to wait nearly thirty hours to see her again.

"Holy fuckbuckets, your mom is hilarious. Did she at least say it back?"

"Not in so many words. First she scolded, 'Don't scare me like that—I assumed you must be in a ditch covered in glass shards, to get all soppy.' Then after wrestling with a reply, she offered a terse 'Obviously you know I do too.' Couldn't quite manage the word itself."

"Well, there ya go. You guys are all set for another twenty years."

"At least."

In my mind, this was going to be a great place to tell Sage how I feel about her, insulated by the safety of five thousand miles' distance. But I change my mind, because…what if I scare her away from coming here at all? Saying it to her in person may be terrifying, but at least it has the advantage that she won't be able to disappear.

Instead, I tell her, "I plan to fuck you on or against every surface of this flat."

Her hum of approval turns into a low chuckle. "Take your vitamins, honeybee. I'm holding you to it."

I try not to loiter near the windows the next evening when Sage messages me that she's leaving the paddock and headed my way, but I can't help it. After twenty minutes of pacing (slowly enough to reassure myself that it doesn't count as pacing), I go to sit on the balcony overlooking the cobbled street, then open a copy of Elizabeth Bowen's *The Death of the Heart*, because apparently I'm a lovelorn adolescent who wants to look clever for a girl by reading an angsty classic on a Spanish balcony at sunset.

I warned Sage that parking is horrid here, so she arrives by cab, and when I spot it coming up the narrow lane, I consider standing in a regal way and waving in greeting from the balcony, then decide, *fuck it* and hurry downstairs. I nearly lock myself out in my rush, and by the time I exit the building's front door, Sage already has her bag hauled out of the cab's boot and is striding my way.

She's in a babydoll dress featuring layers of sheer black lace from the chest down, with a little zip-up bustier bodice that's a pattern of fake-blood-splattered newsprint. Her combat boots round out the look perfectly, but all I can think is how feckin' long it'll take to unlace them and get them off. Her aqua hair is piled in charming disarray on her head, and now sports streaks of emerald green, which she added after the podium finish. Her lips are plump pink and made for kissing.

"Salvi...my God, you're a fuckin' sight for sore eyes."

She stops about five yards from me and sets down her rucksack. "Wanna catch me? It'll be like a movie." She opens her arms, prompting me.

I laugh. "Absolutely."

She makes a run at me and leaps, and like a muppet I take a half step back at the impact, catch my heel on a cobblestone, and fall on my arse hard, straight into a planter of flowers flanking one side of the walk. Sage hoots with laughter, snaps a petunia off its stem, and tucks it behind my ear.

"I missed you, would you believe it?" she says, kissing my cheek as I struggle to right us. "Are you okay?"

"Better than I've been in a month."

I lift her and she winds her legs around me, refusing to get down as I pick my way along the path over to where her bag sits, leaning to grab the strap and hoist it. I carry Sage into the building's foyer, ignoring the old woman who's screeching at me in Spanish out a window, probably about destroying the flowers.

As I tramp up the steps to the flat, Sage is aggressively kissing my neck, and I have to concentrate on my footing to make sure I don't kill us both.

"Hope you're not tired," she tells me as I shoulder us through the ajar door. "I haven't gotten laid in a month and I'm dyyyyyyying."

I shut the door with my foot and push Sage against the

back of it, flinging the rucksack aside. Her hands dig into my hair, wrestling my face into position for her to assault with a deep kiss that leaves us both breathless. One of her hands dives between us to work at the button of my trousers, and between the two of us we get them pushed down so we're separated only by a layer of cotton on me and the sheerest silk on her.

One of my arms supports her, the other is planted against the rough, artfully crazed paint of the door. Sage's mouth is agile, hungry, striving against mine. She pauses and pulls back to meet my eyes, both of us gasping. Cocking her hips so she rubs against me, she lifts an eyebrow.

"What's going on with the half-mast here?" she teases.

I give a mild, rueful laugh. "Would you believe I'm nervous?"

Her gaze is curiously tender, and she touches my face. "For real? That's kind of adorable. You're sure it's not that you've used up all your energy fucking a parade of hot Spanish girls?" She wears her trademark smirk, but I spot the vulnerability hiding beneath it.

I step out of the tangle of my trousers and carry her to the bed, a low, pillow-littered futon behind a folding screen that's collaged with antique book pages. Laying her down, I pull my shirt off and kneel by her feet, unlacing her boots and dropping them onto the hardwood floor.

"I've not been with anyone else." Gliding my hands up her legs, I catch the edges of her knickers and pull them off. "And apparently you've not either? A month, you said?" I recline on my side next to her, caressing the thigh of one of her drawn-up legs, trying to appear casual.

"Yeah." Her expression is shy, and she moves her focus to

pulling the zipper down on the front of her dress. "I think I might wanna go steady with you. Is that super lame? You said you're not into sharing, so I figured you aren't an open-relationship guy. But six weeks is too soon, right? Probably weird?" She opens the top of the dress and wriggles out of it, then disentangles the clip from her hair and tosses it.

"Fuck, Salvi…" I pull her on top of me as I roll onto my back. "Not too soon. Or maybe it is—I don't know the rules to these things. But at any rate, I feel the same."

"Wow, holy shit. Okay…" She takes a deep breath and exhales in a nervous titter. "Looks like we're doing this."

My hands slide up and down the firm, smooth length of her as far as I can reach, and I'm hopelessly ensnared in the electric copper of her eyes. I catch the back of her head and coax her to my mouth, brushing her lower lip with mine. "We are. But on one condition." My free hand spreads at her lower back and gently presses her close against me. "I want the right to kiss you whilst we make love. Not just before or after."

Her eyes go a bit wide. She drops her forehead against my shoulder. "Is that what we're doing—making love?" she asks, muffled against my collarbone.

"*I've* been. All along," I tell her quietly. "Even the first night when you had me in those ridiculous pink plastic handcuffs and were essentially hate-fucking me."

She wriggles up a few inches to whisper in my ear, "I had a total thing for you already."

"Is that so?"

She pulls back, smiling as she paints one finger along my lower lip. "Yeah."

After what looks like a thinking pause—a small wrinkle of something almost worried crossing her brow—she angles over my mouth, kissing me hard. The warm darts of her nipples are firm against my chest, her chiseled body is perfection beneath my eagerly roaming hands, and her hair falls down to enclose us in a seafoam-tinted curtain illuminated by the bedside lamp.

I'm drunk on her, lost in her scent, her touch, the warm taste of her mouth, the small groaning sighs and whimpers she emits as I stroke her back and cup her firm cheeks. My once-hesitant cock is like granite now, and Sage shifts to push my boxers down just enough to impale herself on me, still pressed close against my chest, our mouths locked in hot combat.

Her hips undulate, fucking me with enough slow subtlety to drive me mad when I want to pound into her hard. But God...I *love* her control over me in this moment, the way she chooses our pace. It reminds me of that racing quote that says one should drive "just fast enough to win." Sage is going at it with a perfect balance of urgency and leisure, sinking again and again onto my cock merely by tilting her hips. I can feel how she's rubbing her swollen clit against me, and see the results in the taut ecstasy on her face any time we pause in our fevered kisses.

With her knees on either side of my thighs, she speeds up, thrusting shamelessly against me, nails dug into my shoulders. Her upper body has enough clearance from my chest that she can rub her nipples on my skin as she nears her peak. Her eyes squeeze shut and her neck arches, and there it is, that telltale shocked hitch in her breathing before she comes with a scream, bearing down against me hard, crushing us together.

The feeling of her sweet arse tensing as she grinds rhythmically is possibly the hottest thing I've ever felt. I didn't even know how close I was myself—I was so lost in watching her take her pleasure—but the sensation of her muscles clenching under my palms catapults me into a climax so devastating that it hits me like a plunge into water, both suffocating and exhilarating.

Her sweat-damp head droops down to rest on the crook of my shoulder. As we pant against each other, catching our breath, I move one leg and realize Sage has gushed all over me and we're both soaked.

She hums a tired laugh. "Probably shoulda put down a towel."

I give her a pat on the bum and turn my head to kiss her hair. "I'll buy our host a new bed. Let's go ahead and ruin this one."

Sage nestles into me like I'm a soft pile of leaves in a small animal's den. "I've never kissed someone while I was fucking them before," she confesses in a sleepy voice. "It's actually pretty rad." As I'm trying to determine how to reply to this revelation—my heart swelling in a pleasantly painful way—she adds, "I don't think I'd do it with anyone else though. It's just a you thing, Sandy."

Whatever was still intact of my heart breaks beautifully. I can barely get the words out when I gruffly reply, "I'm... beyond flattered. Thank you, love."

For several minutes, I pet Sage in long strokes, feeling her body gradually relax against me. One of her hands twitches, accompanied by a cute little snort sound, and I realize she's actually drifted off lying on top of me. I wait a few more minutes to make sure she's fully asleep, then edge onto my side, depositing her on the bed and stretching to pull the duvet diagonally over her as far as it'll reach.

I sit up and shut off the lamp, then roll Sage's way, watching her face in the light from the balcony doors, which are still open. Hopefully the neighbors didn't get *too* much of a theatrical soundtrack, but to be honest, I'm beyond caring. Looking at this lovely creature, serene and unglamorously real in sleep, is everything I could want.

I move a curl of hair off her face and lean in to kiss her right eyebrow. "I fuckin' love you, Salvi," I say just above a whisper to her unconscious self.

As I'm reaching for my pillow, I'm stunned when she replies in a drowsy mumble, "I love you too."

I freeze, propped on an elbow, one hand clutching the pillow, and watch her. Did she say it in her sleep? I can't tell. And if so, does that make it invalid? Or does it mean she's revealed something of her secret, guarded heart?

Sinking onto the pillow, I decide that whichever it is…I'll still take it.

*****

"Oh, fuck. We probably really *did* wreck this woman's bed," Sage says, laughing.

I struggle up from an unexpectedly deep sleep to find Sage on her knees, scowling down at the sheets in the wan presunrise light. She stands on the futon and hops down, then heads across the room in full, gloriously naked view of the windows and ducks into the small bathroom. I hear her habitual sequence: shower water, screech, laugh.

I get up and pull on my boxers, then follow her in. The little room is outfitted in retro décor, right down to the walls tiled in 1970s mirror squares marbled in gold. My bladder is insistent, but I'm gripped by a wave of self-consciousness and lean on the counter, waiting.

Sage soaps herself in the most bewitching way, and the only thing preventing me from joining her in the glass shower cubicle is the fact that I have to piss rather miserably. I think she senses it, because she waves a hand at the loo. "Are you, uh… Should I turn around so you can pee? You look nervous."

I didn't expect to be uneasy about such a simple thing, but as it comes to it, I've never had a degree of familiarity with any woman that extends to this issue. "It's ridiculous, I know."

She smiles indulgently before turning away and continuing her enthusiastic lathering. "Guess it's on-brand for you though. You're not uptight about sex—thank God—but, like…I noticed you don't have social media, aside from the blog itself. You seem private about some things."

"The blog is still inactive." I shuck my boxers and step up to relieve myself. "I wanted to talk with you about that, in fact. I'd love to do an article on you, a complimentary one, to make up for…well, all the complete shite I posted before."

"Huh. Maybe?" She sidesteps into the shower spray, and I'm touched at the way she's giving me privacy rather than mocking me as I half expected. "But I dunno, Sand. I think I like just being, uh, whatever this is with us. More than being 'interviewer and subject' or whatever. I always feel kinda guarded with journalists. I don't want to be like that with you."

My heart does a small skip at her reveal—that she specifically wants to nurture trust with me. I do my best to keep a casual tone when I say, "That's fair." I push down the flush handle and it apparently depletes the cold water instantly, based on Sage's shriek. "Oh bugger, I'm sorry," I tell her, stepping into the shower with her. "Here, misery loves company. I'll take it." I duck into the scorching spray, and Sage passes the soap to me. As I work up handfuls of suds, the water returns to a bearable temperature. We swap places, and I wash while Sage rinses off.

"So yeah, why don't you have any accounts?" she asks. "Or do you, but they're all secret?"

I can't help my smile. "You checked?"

"Yeah, obviously. I wanted to see, like, your normal life. Friends and stuff. Do you have pics?" A flicker of alarm passes her face. "Wait, do you have *friends*?"

I chuckle. "I do. And plenty of photos on my mobile. But I don't post them anywhere." We switch places again. "This may sound dramatic, but I was kidnapped briefly as a child, and I've been leery of social media since. The type that announces where you are, what you're doing, and with whom. I don't—"

"Whoa whoa *whoa*," Sage interrupts with a laugh, holding up one hand. "You can't just drop an 'I got kidnapped once.' What the fuck? How old were you?"

I wet my hair, then examine the shampoo options. "Nine years old. We were traveling—my family. It was surprisingly *un*traumatic. It was obvious my parents had money, I was wandering unsupervised, three men herded me into a van, my parents were informed, money was exchanged. I was back before supper, entirely unharmed." I squeeze a dollop of something coconut-scented into my palm and wash my hair. "I wasn't even frightened after the first five minutes. They gave me candy and a stack of comic books to pass the time. But I'm cautious now about pointlessly announcing my whereabouts or publicly volunteering who my friends are."

"Wow. That's...not what I expected. I figured you don't have social media so you can avoid women you've fucked."

I rinse my hair and wipe the sudsy water from my eyes, then give Sage a wink. "Just a fringe benefit, pet."

"Oh my God, you suck," she says with a laugh, stepping out of the shower and grabbing a towel. "Can *I* look at pics of your friends? Do you have, like, a bestie?"

"Of course. Badrick Jones is my best mate, since forever. And yes, you can look. My mobile's on the kitchen counter."

The instant I say it, I wish I hadn't. What if CJ has sent a message badgering me again about "getting dirt"? But if I call out to Sage now, retracting my offer, it sends up an obvious flag.

I scramble to finish rinsing myself and shut the water off, listening for any word from Sage that might indicate a problem. Snatching a towel off the rack, I whip it around my hips and exit the bathroom, nearly colliding with Sage as she wanders back in.

She looks up from the mobile's screen and turns it around. "This guy? That's Bardrick?"

"Badrick, yes." I watch as Sage swipes through pics from a party at Bad's new digs, when he moved in with Laurent. I'm glad it wasn't one where I took a date.

She smiles at the progression of pics. "He's got a boyfriend?"

"Fiancé. Laurent. He's French, and a bit of a tosser, but Badrick adores him."

"Huh. Gotta admit, at one time I'da thought you were the type of guy who'd be too insecure to have a gay best friend."

I chuckle. "Again, my seraph, thank you ever so much for the left-handed compliment. But who Badrick dates is the least relevant factor. The truth is, he's always been cooler, smarter, and more talented than me—he's a brilliant jazz drummer—and I'm lucky he's put up with me for eighteen years."

She narrows her eyes at me with a speculative smile. "Y'know, you're way less awful than people assume. Glad I finally met the real you." Setting my mobile aside, she folds the towel she has draped over her naked shoulders and places it on the counter, then hops up to sit on it, bobbing her eyebrows playfully and reaching for me. "We should take advantage of all these mirrors. Whaddya think?"

In thirty-one years that most would already classify as shamefully privileged, I find that this week in Barcelona is the happiest of my life. Sage returns to me every evening, full of chatter and lust and the mosaic of tiny details that make her who she is. My sweet Salvia officinalis, my dream-I-didn't-know-I-had, my *future*.

We can barely get through a meal for how abundantly the talk spills out of us, making up for years that no longer seem merely "before" the other person, but more "*without*"...as if we knew each other, were already conjoined at the soul, but cruel circumstance had kept us apart.

And so the week stretches out, generous and surprising and electric. We eat, sleep, go for walks, good-naturedly disagree only to make it up with epic sex. We half watch, half make love to the backdrop of several movies. We organically develop a repertoire of inside jokes and phrases instilled with private significance. One night she sings me the entirety of a parody version of "American Pie" featuring the plot of a *Star Wars* film in her touchingly off-key voice, and I relish every minute. (By the end, I'm singing along to the choruses.)

She tells me about the decade-long misguided feud with Julian. Her parents' troubles and impending divorce. Her friendships and frustrations. The month at age fourteen when she nearly gave up racing because she decided she wanted to be a blacksmith.

I tell her about my bizarre family dynamics. The perennial adolescent unpopularity that clung to me until I grew into my rangy limbs and got decent-looking and went to university. My loss of virginity to an older girl—a singer in a club—during a family trip to Portugal, and how it engendered a lifelong debilitating attachment to fado music.

Then, on Friday night, a seemingly unparalleled blessing is dispensed when the *one fucking thing* that was still a nagging source of dread washes away with a single text exchange.

As I await Sage's late arrival after a busy day at the paddock, including Free Practice sessions, the thought intrudes with a jet of anxiety that CJ Ardley is still awaiting my intel. I pluck up my mobile and send her a message.

> Will have something impressive for you soon but need more time.

To my surprise, a reply is typed and sent immediately:

> No need, hunny bunny. I have my sights set elsewhere. You're off the hook.

Fuckin' hell, I could dance. After sending back a small, Thx, good luck to you, I delete the text thread and her contact, tossing my mobile onto the sofa, tension draining out of me as I rub my face and laugh for plain joy.

She's moved on. Bloody marvelous! I suppose she found another "nemesis" on whom to fixate—maybe a rival for the affections of Gavin Yates, with whom she appears to have successfully cooked up a romance, if the gossip sites are to be trusted.

I no longer need suffer the guilt of never mentioning this to Sage. It took care of itself.

I feel as if I've been freed from the jaws of a steel trap.

How did Sage put it? *Clear air, smooth track.*

Our future starts in earnest tonight.

23

BARCELONA, SPAIN

SAGE

When I come through the door, Alexander is there, barefoot and scrumptiously shirtless. He sweeps me into his arms and spins me around before I have time to warn him not to, and it isn't until he leans me against the wall and kisses me and I sort of hold my breath and whimper that he realizes I'm in pain.

"Salvi..." He deposits me gingerly on the floor, pulling back. "Are you all right?"

"Uh, not a hundred percent. More like...sixty?"

An old back muscle injury (from that crash in São Paulo) has chosen the worst possible time—with quali tomorrow and the grand prix the day after—to flare up. I downplayed it to Dagna, got a massage and a little acupuncture from Himari, did a soak...but there's a spot in my back that's still spasming, contracting like the legs of a dead spider.

"My back's kinda fucky," I explain as I shed my clothes and drop them on the floor en route to the bed, then sink down, flat on my stomach.

"Are you well enough to race?" Alexander asks.

I lift my head and glare at him, and the awkward position makes the tight spot in my back twinge hard. "Of course I can fucking race," I snap. "Jesus, don't even say that."

He looks wounded, and I feel bad for being defensive. But I *am* defensive on this issue. I'm the "engine" of my car as much as the literal engine is, and it doesn't work right unless I'm in top form. The driver's body is the most complex piece of machinery in the car. If I have so much as a fucking hangnail, all I can think is, *Will this affect how my fingers feel in my gloves on race day?* It's a constant worry.

I soften my expression and hold out a hand for him. "Sorry, I just need to be careful. It'll probs be fine tomorrow. C'mere…"

Alexander reclines carefully beside me, trying not to jostle the bed. "What can I do for you, love? Have you eaten?"

"Yeah, I'm good." I breathe out a contented sigh as his palm settles warmly between my shoulder blades. "That's nice. I like your hands on me."

He trails a fingertip down my spine. "It's a lucky thing you didn't break my 'soft little rich-boy fingers' as you threatened during that first video call."

I can't resist a cackle of laughter, opening my eyes. He's smiling, and fuck, I drink in everything about the sight of him. It seems crazy now that I wanted to kick his ass a few months ago. A twist of his rust-dark hair tumbles over the freckles on his forehead; the muscles in the arm he's leaning on are sexily tense, showing off his nice ropy tendons and veins; and his thickly lashed gray eyes are tender and *all mine* and dammit…I'm actually in love.

I must be, because I'm perpetually in a half-witted state where my brain convinces me that every element of his existence is a newly minted thing, never before seen on a human. Like Greek gods sat around doling out Alexander's Alexanderness. *Yes, other mortals may look cute when they sleep*, Zeus would say, *but behold! I bring you cuteness unsurpassed. You shall swoon at the power of his wink, tremble at the aural sorcery of his voice. Even the shape of his toes will seem faultless, wondrous…*

The strip of sore muscle twitches as Alexander's hand glides over it, and I suck in my breath. "Okay, so I have an idea," I tell him. "In the inside pocket of my duffel bag is a vibrator. Could you put it on my back? It'll be like those ladies back in the day, y'know, the ads for 'facial massagers' with some perky housewife rubbing a dildo against her cheek, as if she wasn't gonna buzz one out with the thing."

He laughs, his hand gliding down to my bare ass and giving me a gentle pat. "Is this a test of my ability to stay on task and not make it into something lewd?"

He gets up and crosses to my bag, where I hear him rummaging around, and I have to think for a few panicked seconds whether there's anything in there I *don't* want him to see. But at this point I'm past the secretive phase. My universe has changed from 2D to 3D in the space of a month. There's just so much *more* of everything. I can move, emotionally, in every direction, and I wonder how I ever lived without this.

I'm caught in a paradox, wanting time to freeze so we can

spend longer together and wanting it to be years from now so I can see if it lasted, whether this is the real thing.

I hear the hum of the vibrator turning on, then off. "Isn't this charming," he says, coming back and lying down beside me. "Like a little pink egg."

He turns it on again and rolls it along the middle left side of my back, and I'm impressed by how he pays attention. I haven't specifically pointed out where my back is fucked, but he still zeroed in on it exactly. I sink into the futon, boneless. He leans down and presses small kisses along my spine, and reflexively I part my legs.

"None of that, minx," Alexander mock-scolds. "Much as I'm tempted. You need to heal."

"Orgasm is *very* healing," I mumble with amusement, my face smushed against the pillows.

He chuckles. "In that case, I'm applying this to the wrong area."

I roll carefully onto my back. "Looks like you'd best get to work, then."

"For my sins," he teases, the scarred eyebrow lifting.

Setting the little plastic egg aside, he kisses me, deep and slow and intoxicating, one hand roaming featherlight over my body—gliding down my neck and shoulder, teasing a nipple, trailing a knuckle down to my belly button. When he dips lower, I tilt my hips up in encouragement.

He pulls back from my lips with a wicked smile, then puts two fingers into my mouth. "Suck."

I work his beautiful fingers, nibbling, sucking, and sweeping my tongue around them. When he pulls them out, he holds my gaze as his hand moves, fingertips wet and warm, between my legs. I open wider. He kneels beside my thighs and caresses the furrows at both sides of my clit with two slippery fingers. We've learned so much about each other's bodies; I love the fact that he's responded to my sometimes painfully high level of clitoral sensitivity by finding dozens of indirect ways to touch me.

For years I've been used to getting off fast, but he's made it an art to slow me down, so when I do come it's an all-encompassing storm that I practically feel to the tips of my hair. The way he teases me, his instinct for pulling back and building me up higher until I'm losing my mind…fuck, it's wrecked me for life. How could it be this good with anyone else?

For long, delectable minutes, his fingers explore, drifting, sinking inside my aching pussy to extract my slickness and spread it everywhere with his masterful touch as I moan encouragement, my hips churning slowly.

"Sandy, please," I breathe. "I want you inside me. Very seriously needing your dick right now."

He withdraws his hand and I groan in frustration. When I open my eyes, he's looking at my pussy so lovingly that I almost feel teary.

He drags one finger lightly over my clit. I'm close enough to the edge that I think if I brought my legs together and tensed my thighs, I'd come. "Fuckin' beautiful, that," he murmurs. "Like a little red strawberry."

"*Please?*" I whisper.

He places a hand over mine on my belly and stretches out beside me, coming up to kiss my lips. "We oughtn't risk it."

Another kiss, deeper. "But if I weren't afraid of breaking your gorgeous self, I'd nail you to the bed with my cock."

I lift my head to meet his next kiss, but he pulls back with a sly half-smile, watching me, then leisurely closing in again.

"I could fill your lovely cunt so many times," he says near my lips, his voice a quiet growl, "that your eyes would fog up like steam on a fuckin' mirror." He gives my lower lip a bite.

I can feel him hard against my hip, and I slide a hand from beneath his to touch him. "You want it too."

He moves his head to my breast and licks my right nipple. "Mmm-hmm. Alas."

"Sandyyyyyy," I plead. "Look, I've got an idea…" I turn perpendicular to him on the bed and drape my legs over his hip as he's on his side facing me, scooting closer until I can feel him against my soaked pussy. "This way? I promise, I'll hardly move."

"I'd say, 'You win,' but…" He aligns himself with me and stretches me nicely as he goes in deep with a satisfied groan like he's waited for this his whole life. "Fuck—we *both* do."

My breath shudders out. I'm so happy and relieved, I don't even care that our angle makes a weird squashing sound because I'm so wet. His hips start to roll, sweet and easy, and I focus on the feeling of him stroking me inside, watching the slow rapture of his expression. I'm both scared and excited that he's studying my face just as attentively.

We're too far away to kiss in this position, and to my surprise I find that I miss it. I sprawl an arm toward him, and he takes my hand and kisses the palm, his eyes closing briefly. Releasing me, he reaches for the vibrator and flicks it on.

"No no no," I manage, a little breathless. "It's too much right now."

"I know—I want to try something..."

He sets the vibrating egg on my mons, just above my clit, and I spread my legs a bit, giving him access. Holding the toy between his two middle fingers, he settles the pad of his palm over me so I can feel the vibration through his hand.

"Close your eyes, beautiful," he tells me. "Don't think about anything but this. Relax completely. Let it take you."

Usually during sex I'm moving in some way, even if I'm just getting oral. My muscles will be taut, I'll thrust my hips, grab the sheets, play with my nipples...*something*. But this time, I try the same technique I use when I do my sleep exercises, thinking my way down my body, letting every muscle go slack, consciously releasing tension.

I'm blissfully aware of Alexander moving inside me, his nice long girth stroking me, the warmth and faint vibration of his hand cupping the front of me, the captivating sound of him that always gets me hot as hell.

As turned on as I am, it's interesting to find that this process is taking me a while—lifted gradually to the peak, not chasing it—without the assist of my hands and movements. I'm a little self-conscious about looking so lifeless, eyes closed, every muscle lax, existing only in two places: my mind, and the golden glow of arousal below my waist.

"You're radiant, like a breathtaking painting," Alexander tells me, his tone hypnotic. "My cock was made for you. The way your sweet pink cunt takes me is fucking poetry."

His thrusts are leisurely, and I stay cradled in my silence, observing with fascination as climax approaches. It's as vast and as soundless as the bloom of a sunrise. I relax my hands, my shoulders, my thighs, just breathing and *feeling*, single-mindedly fixed on the sensations.

As the orgasm cracks open in a flood of bliss, it's like I'm reading the fine print on my own pleasure for the first time, able to read what it's saying. I breathe through it, watching where it goes, fascinated to map its trajectory, the small hidden corners of me that it illuminates.

My involuntary moan floats out, and as the wave crests, I'm rattled by a shudder I don't try to control. I'm liquid everywhere—not only have I flooded the bed, but my eyes run with tears that leave me surprised and slightly embarrassed. A small hiccupping sob betrays me.

Alexander's voice is tight as he grasps my thigh with one hand and says, "Sage, *fuck*…I love you…" and pushes deep into me, staying there, grinding against me as he's annihilated by his own climax. His crushing fingers divot the Monaco Grand Prix tattoo on my thigh and his face is like a saint in spiritual ecstasy and I suddenly know exactly what he meant about me looking like a painting.

When he opens his eyes and sees me watching him, he smiles, exhausted and beautiful. There's a wrinkle of fear marring how happy I am, because I'd give anything to never stop feeling this way, and nothing should have that kind of power over me.

He pulls himself up on one elbow and moves to my side and gathers me close, tugging the duvet over us so we're hidden, at least for now, from whatever's going to fuck this up.

The next evening, I'm riding high in every way. Quali went great and I'm starting the race tomorrow in fourth. My back, oddly enough, hasn't given me any trouble since the *transcendent* sex last night. My mom sent me pics of the cute apartment she just got in the Pearl District, and she seems distinctly *un*heartbroken by the upcoming divorce. Julian sent a snail-mail letter to Priya and me, and he told us he got his thirty-day clean-and-sober chip.

And finally?

Yeah, *Alexander Demetrius Sebastian Konstantin Laskaris*, he of the many middle names (lots of uncles, apparently), has laid siege to my stony little heart.

Because I'm not superstitious, I don't worry that the abundance of joy is setting me up for a fall. No malicious Fates are rubbing their hands together with manic, fly-like glee as they engineer my comeuppance. But I *am* aware of the unfortunate fact that the faster you're driving when you overcook a turn, the harder the impact is.

Which is why my stomach flops when Priya calls me instead of texting—always a bad sign. I'm just exiting Phaedra's office after talking with her and Basil when the phone rings.

"Hey, Pri. What's up? I'm kinda in a hurry."

There's a pause before she replies. "Are you…Is everything okay?"

"What, my back? Yeah, it's fine. I didn't—"

"No, I mean, uh…Okay, you need to come to the motor home. Like, now."

I stop in the middle of the narrow white hallway between

meeting rooms. "What's going on? Is Jules all right? My mom?" I swallow hard, my mouth suddenly dry. *"Grandma Lena?"*

"It's nothing like that," she tells me. "But you need to come talk to me. There's something I have to show you."

I prod myself into motion again, headed for the glass exit doors with the Emerald logo. "Oh, fuckin' hell," I say, realizing as the words leave me that I sound a little like Alexander. "It can't wait? Tomorrow's the GP and I don't wanna get upset over trivial bullshit."

"*Sage.*" Her tone is bleak. "I've been fretting for an hour for exactly that reason. I wouldn't bother you, but I don't want you to hear about this first when some reporter asks." My stomach plunges straight to the basement at her next words. "And you probably won't want to stay with Alexander tonight once you've heard it."

When I climb through the doorway of the motor home minutes later, she's sitting at the banquette with her laptop open on the table and rotates it to face me.

The door shuts behind me with a pneumatic hiss. I slap down a hand beside the laptop and lean to take in the page of CJ Ardley's *Sports and Tortes* on the screen. Down the right-hand side are publicity photos of me and of Julian, and below that, a candid one of Jules with Alexander in what must be the dining room of our Melbourne hotel. The headline reads, "Shocking Secret of Formula 1's Leading Lady! Junkie Brother She Hides in Luxury Loony Bin."

My heart is pounding hard and my back is suddenly such a tangle of pain that I can barely get a breath. I click rapidly through a slideshow: unflattering paparazzi pics of Jules and me, the front of his treatment facility in Switzerland, old photos of us as kids that CJ must've had to dig deep to find online.

I slide into the seat across from Priya, who's quietly crying. Pulling the laptop around, I start reading the article. It launches with mocking references to celebrities with family skeletons in the closet, sarcastically congratulating me for joining their ranks.

"This is fucking evil," I growl, shooting a glance at Pri over the laptop screen. "Did you tell Reece and Phaedra yet?"

"Sent them links right after I called you. But, Sage…"

I'm already reading again, now the part about Jules being in rehab and how much the place costs and whether I'll go bankrupt taking care of him.

"What's the bit you mentioned about Sandy though?" I ask her distractedly as my eyes track down the page. "There's this pic from Melbourne, yeah, but that doesn't mean he was *responsible* for it. There are a lot of ways she could've found this stuff out, right?"

"Sage," she repeats, "um, keep reading. Then I need to show you something else."

Finally I get to the part she must be talking about:

> After a decade-long rift originating when Sage nearly died of a ruptured appendix during a family trip to Thailand—an incident that apparently owed to Julian's negligence (Was he already on drugs then, in his teens? One can't help but speculate…)—the siblings have buried the hatchet enough for Sage to pay a king's ransom to dry out her ne'er-do-well brother.

> But one couldn't be called a cynic for suspecting that the most likely reason is *discretion*, not love. Such bad timing to have a self-destructive sibling circling the drain during Sage's debut year at Emerald! If anything, Julian Sikora's posh private rehab is an investment in maintaining his famous sister's carefree image.

My hands are shaking so hard that I lay them flat on the table. My eyes meet Priya's teary ones. "How would she know this?" I manage in a near whisper. "No one does. I didn't even tell *you*, Pri. I mean, you knew about my appendix obviously, but not Jules's role in what happened. We didn't talk about that until Miami, when my mom brought it up."

She reaches for the laptop and spins it toward herself, clicking something. "So, I googled their names together, just in case, and I found this. But please believe me: *I didn't want to be right*. Despite all the things I said, and how suspicious I was of Alexander at the start."

She turns the computer back toward me. There's a new tab open, pics on the *HELLO!* magazine website—a publishing gala in London about a week before the Australian GP. CJ Ardley sits at a table with Alexander, his hand covering hers, eyes full of flirty mischief.

"You didn't tell me the details of what happened in Thailand, no," Priya says solemnly. "But did you tell *him*?"

༺༻

I have a strict system I follow the night before a race, and this sure as shit ain't it. And no matter my training, conditioning, and pro level of control…no mental exercises will help me break up with a guy I'm in love with and then go back to my pre-race routine.

On my way up the steps to the apartment, I coach myself to concentrate on the anger so I can avoid crying. Have you ever noticed that F1 drivers don't blink a lot? That gets surprisingly fucked up if your eyes are irritated because you've had a crying jag. And in a sport where thousandths of a second make the difference, I can't afford to start at any disadvantage.

When I open the door, I can smell Alexander. I didn't expect immediate pain, but knowing that breathing in his scent won't be followed by kisses, arms entangled, his lips on my neck, his voice an inch from my ear…it's killing me.

He straightens from where he's leaning into the refrigerator, then swings it shut and makes his way toward me with a smile that fades by a half-dozen steps. He freezes, feet bare on the honey-blond hardwood.

"Salvi, what is it? Has something happened?" When I don't reply, he continues. "I saw you qualified fourth. Well done, pet."

Normally this would be when he'd pull me into a hug, but he's eyeing me cautiously. I'm not silent for the sake of drama. I just can't get any words out. I thought I had it sussed, what I'd say, but it collapses into scraps of sentences that dash around in my head like unruly children.

He tries again. "Is it your back?"

"No."

For shit's sake, one word and already my voice cracks. *How will I do this?* Not trusting myself with more, I unsling my bag and fish my phone out, then search the article. I set the phone on the kitchen island. Alexander peers at it. I watch his face for the reaction.

He takes in the headline, then murmurs, "What have I done?" before resting one hand over his mouth.

His words, confirming what I didn't want to believe, hit me like a midrace collision. I manage a flinty smile. "Oh, you've done plenty, babes."

"Fuckin' hell, that's not what I...I didn't...It...it truly *isn't* what you think," he stammers.

He's panicked enough that for a half second I almost buy it. But no one else knew these details. It had to be him, unless I'm willing to entertain the absurd idea that my mother or Priya conspired with my fucking enemy.

"Not what I think?" I jab a finger at the phone. "Take a nice close look, dickhead, and try selling me that. Who else knew this, about Thailand, and Jules abandoning me?" My eyes blur with incipient tears and I fan the anger to burn them away. "I told *you*. And days later, this happens."

He grabs my phone and scans the article, pacing toward the balcony and closing the open doors, probably in case I scream at him. He scrolls to the end as he slowly walks back my way, then sets the phone down.

"I don't know how she got this information, but it wasn't from me, on my honor."

"Your honor is obviously shit, Alexander. Priya was right about you."

He shakes his head as if struggling to focus. "It could've been someone from the treatment facility."

I snort. "The fact that Jules is *there* maybe. But not the specific personal shit."

"The personal bits too—yes! He might've revealed something in a counseling session. Anyone looking to sell such information would need only search your name to find this woman with a history of slagging you off."

My smile is harsh. "In the six weeks you've set up this... this *long con* with me, you couldn't construct a better excuse?" I angle stiffly toward him, my voice rising. "You just fucking said, 'What have I done?'! And I've seen pictures of you and that plastic surgery disaster all touchy-feely at the publishing gala! Don't bother with denials." I stomp toward the bathroom to collect my things.

"Sage, please! Let me explain what I meant."

"Yeah? Go ahead and have fun shitting out more lies in the next two minutes. You're wasting your breath."

He stands in the bathroom doorway, gripping the jamb in a martyr's pose as his words tumble out in a fevered rush. "She did ask me to 'get dirt' on you when I spoke with her at the gala. It was my intention to tell you about it when I arrived in Melbourne."

"Yeah? And *why didn't you*?"

His head drops, and when he looks back up, his hair is hanging in that way I've come to love, but instead of softening me toward him, it just enrages me. My attraction to him is what fucked me from lights-out, and he knew it, and he *used it*.

The night in Bahrain when he bought the vinyl record and we shared food and made the Christmas lights video, he saw that I'd warmed up to him. Once he clocked my weakness, he must've run straight to CJ Ardley and hatched a plan to tear me apart for getting him fired.

And I fucking fell for it. His sad gray eyes and floppy hair and cute boyish freckles…it's all been part of the swindle.

The sex? The "I love you"? All these nights talking for hours, sharing our fears and insecurities and favorite things?

Sharing our secrets…

Holy shit, I'm a moron.

What could be a better revenge than fucking me over while he fucks me literally?

I zip up my toiletries bag and barrel toward him, ducking under his arm to exit.

"You'll think it bollocks," he continues, following close on my heels, "but I didn't want to worry you. I feared it might make you more guarded if I told you what she'd asked of me. I know that's selfish. But I felt confident I could manage the situation myself and keep her from posting about you by promising some big payoff if she waited—"

"And then you obviously fucking gave her one!" I viciously throw the bag I'm holding toward the open top of my duffel bag, but it bounces off and rolls away.

"I *didn't*. I was keeping her contained, protecting you!"

"That's bullshit and you fucking know it, Sandy."

Hearing my stupid betraying mouth say his nickname startles the tears out of me quick as a slap. To hide it, I kneel and grab my toiletries kit and cram it into my bag, avoiding his eyes.

He drops to his knees beside me with a *clunk* that sounds like it hurts.

"I was afraid to say anything. I didn't want to upset the

balance of...whatever this is between us." He puts both hands over his face and slides them off, and it shocks me to see from the red of his eyes that he's near tears too. "*I was playing her.*"

"You're a fucking liar and I hate you for making me trust you," I seethe. The pain that spills through my chest when I say it is overwhelming, and the muscle in my back is a knife twisting. I yank the zipper on my duffel bag and the tab breaks off and I'm so pissed that I half snarl, half scream.

"It's true!" Alexander insists. "Then last night she told me she'd—how did she put it?—set her sights elsewhere. I assumed she meant she wasn't targeting *you* anymore, but it's clear now she meant she'd found another source." He scrambles to his feet. "I'll show you the message."

I pluck at the broken zipper, both relieved and infuriated by the delay. Part of me is dying for him to produce something that'll change my mind. I want to fall into his arms and we can kiss and laugh with relief and everything will be fine...

From the bedside table Alexander groans and says, "Fuck me, I deleted it."

"That's convenient," I snap.

I get the zipper closed and push to my feet, and the pain in my back is so sharp I can scarcely stand straight. Alexander tosses his phone onto the bed and hurries over.

"You must believe me," he begs.

My tears are hot, poisonous, and I know I look awful. My nose is running and without giving a shit I lift the neck of my shirt and wipe it. I'm beyond caring, fully wrecked.

How did I get suckered by some posh fuckboy? I gave him my secrets; I gave him myself.

"Would *you* believe you, Alexander?" I ask bitterly.

His head drops back, looking toward the ceiling, and a small animal moan escapes him. He meets my eyes again. "I suppose I wouldn't, no. Given the evidence, and my history. I know it looks bad."

I study his face. Finally, in a miserable, almost childlike voice, I say, "You straight up jobbed me for revenge. This whole time—everything we've talked about—you've just been hunting for scraps you could use to break me."

"Never. Never *ever*, Salvi."

His dark eyes are like river rocks viewed underwater, glossy with tears that are probably fake, and I want to fucking slap him for it. Because even though I suspect he's full of shit and this was a scam and *he fucking won*...part of me wishes I believed it. I could've fallen asleep in his arms and had a great race tomorrow. Instead, I'm going to suck, and after that, I'll go back to screwing hot strangers and playing the Spitfire Sage role, the irrepressible agent of chaos.

I shoulder my duffel bag and he takes a step toward me, cupping my elbow. I windmill my arm away from him and feel the muscle in my back tear. Prickling numbness shoots down my arm.

"Please don't do this," he implores, clearly struggling to keep his voice level.

"*You* did it, Sand. Not me."

He dashes the heel of one hand against his face, wiping away tears, and I remind myself that spoiled, malignant liars are very good at this shit. It's a performance. It always was, and the sooner I accept it, the sooner I can get back to being *myself*.

I head for the door, and he follows.

"Once your…your anger wanes," he falters, "can we discuss this? We can't just *end things*."

I wheel back toward him, furious. *"Once my anger wanes?* Please ram that condescending bullshit directly up your ass, Laskaris. I won't give you time to fine-tune your setup with a better lie. Congrats on the payback for me getting you fired. Take your fucking W and choke on it."

I flip the door open hard and it smacks the wall. A framed black-and-white photograph of a pigeon smacks the floor, level as a guillotine, and I hear the glass crack like river ice.

He braces himself in the doorway as I start down the steps. "If I'd been hiding something, conspiring with that woman," he tells me in a rush, "would I have volunteered my mobile to you—the photos of Badrick? I was in another room when you looked. I'd not've risked that with something to hide."

I pause, one hand gripping the iron railing hard, then keep going.

Fuck, I want to believe him so much…

When I reach the bottom step, his words float after me, and he sounds wrecked. "I'm *not* giving up. This is real."

My shoes bark with my abrupt stop. I turn, yanking the iron railing in my frustration, and it rings with a metallic echo like fake thunder on a stage. He moves to the top of the steps and grasps it too, and it strikes me that we're connected now, like a completed circuit.

Exhausted, I tell him, "If you ended up accidentally feeling something during this fucking hustle, this emotional shakedown—if you're capable of being 'real,' which I doubt, since everything about you is tailored to fit the audience and always has been—*I don't care*. I have nothing else to give. You got what you wanted and played the game well, honeybee." I hop off the bottom step, onto the lobby tile. "And as for you 'not giving up'?" I call over my shoulder. "It isn't your choice."

At the paddock, in the darkness of the motor home's bedroom, Priya's voice is quiet over the background of night-bird song from the white noise sleep machine.

"I know you said you don't want to talk about it—"

"And I *don't*."

She pauses, then sighs. "Right. But you're not sleeping, and Dagna's gonna be in here barking at us like a drill sergeant in five hours and it's already after midnight, so technically it's race day and..." She rolls on her side toward me. "Maybe talking about it a teeny smidge would give you some comfort."

I roll to face her, mashing and punching my pillow until it's right, then settling. "He said he didn't do it, which is a total lie. I told him we're done, and meant it. End of story. Good night." I close my eyes, shutting out the blue-green shimmer the sleep machine is projecting onto the ceiling, then open them again after a few seconds. "And if you want to help, you'll let me switch this to 'autumn rainstorm.' The bird one isn't relaxing. Hearing a bunch of fuckin' owls and loons makes me feel like I'm in a haunted house."

"Okay, but the rainstorm one has those cracks of thunder and it wakes me back up."

I sigh. "Frog pond?"

"Frogs are funny. Funny isn't conducive to sleep. How about 'mountain stream'?"

"That trickling just makes me need to pee."

Priya laughs, and I smile automatically because the sound of her laugh is actually the best "noise machine"—I feel so at home. I reach for her hand and we clasp.

"Well," she says with amusement, "we can't do 'grandfather clock,' because ever since that time you said it makes you think of your own mortality, it creeps me out. How 'bout 'breeze in the branches'?"

"That works. Done."

She rolls away to change the noise machine and then comes back and takes my hand again and I just love her so fucking much.

"You know you're perfect, right?" I tell her.

"And you're perfectly imperfect," she returns.

It's something we've said since we were teenagers, and my shoulders relax into the mashed pillow and for a few seconds my heart doesn't hurt, but then the pain comes right back. I can see Alexander's red eyes, his shock and grief and the way there was a hopeless silence after I told him, *You're wasting your breath.* How bad I wanted him to say something—anything—that would make it all right.

As if she can hear my thoughts, Priya asks, "So, what was his defense when he denied it? How'd he explain the pic of him with CJ Ardley?"

"He claimed he was playing along with her. That she wanted him to get incriminating gossip from me, and he told her he would, but only to protect me. And he said he *isn't* the only person who could've known the stuff about Thailand, because Jules might've said something in a therapy session and an employee or another patient sold CJ those details."

She squeezes my fingers. "I actually thought the same thing after you left. It's not impossible that some unethical A-hole who works there tips off the tabloids about famous patients. And since Julian sent *us* a letter, another patient could've sent the info to someone on the outside." Her thumb moves restlessly on my knuckles. "Maybe consider that."

"Jesus, Pri. Why would you make this harder for me by defending him?" I groan. "I thought you couldn't stand the guy. Aren't you glad I'm dumping him? Or has falling in love with Jules made you all mushy?"

"I've *always* been mushy. And yeah, I haven't been a fan of Alexander. But this is like being on a jury, right? Maybe the defendant is a jerk, but you still have to admit it if there's a possible alternate explanation. Reasonable doubt."

I make an impatient growling noise. "You're just confusing me."

"It's worth talking to him once you cool off. The guy seemed to be—"

"Oh, fuck me…*you too*? He was all, 'Once your anger wanes, we must talk,'" I deliver in a mockingly posh accent, "and it's just so patronizing."

"You know I'm not like that. Don't be unfair." Priya's tone is impressively stern, and I've gotta admit I like the way she's been sticking up for herself. "But I know you, Sage. We talked about exactly this issue on the flight to Bahrain—the fact that someday your stubbornness and hotheadedness might trash a good relationship, and—"

"*Tsk!* Oh, and *this* is the 'good relationship' you were afraid I'd fuck up? Alexander fucking Laskaris, the shit-talking playboy? Yeah, okay."

"Look, I hated the things he was writing about you, and I hated him for writing them. But I also thought it was possible, the explanation he gave you that the blog trash talk was just a clumsy bid to draw your attention. You know why I found it believable? Because *you do that kind of stuff all the time yourself,* taunting and pranking and hiding your feelings and intentions behind a bunch of sassy schoolyard mischief."

I sit up on an elbow. "Pri!"

"Am I wrong?"

There's a long pause, and I know my next line, because we use this *Big Lebowski* quote all the time to de-escalate when we're on the verge of bickering. "You're not wrong, Walter—you're just an asshole," I supply, collapsing back onto the pillow.

She hums a little chuckle. "Anyway, as far as my perspective goes, I'll just say this: Julian is proof that someone can screw up and still be fundamentally good. And seen from the outside, with no context, plenty of people would assume *you're* a total jerk, but because I know you, I understand that a lot of your behavior is insecurity. Alexander might be—"

"What? I'm like the least insecure human on the planet!"

"That's your disguise, but I know the real you. And all the things you've told me about Alexander in the past month, he seems to have the same defenses, but *a good heart*. I've had a few hours to think about it, *really* think about it, and…he made you happy, Sage. Don't walk away from this based on an assumption that might be wrong. You need more information first."

"I won't talk with him again," I snap. "*Ever*."

"You'd rather be alone than risk being wrong?"

"I'm not alone, honeybee. You know what lives in my heart? Carbon fiber, steel, engine grease, E10 fuel, asphalt, rubber, and *speed*. Not some cotton-candy love bullshit." There's a minute of silence as I listen to the sighing and tapping of recorded forest breeze. "Also he'd never forget that when I confronted him, I said, 'I hate you.' Men don't forgive that. It's too much of an ego punch. I called him a liar and said I hate him."

"Okay, but—"

"And remember how you told me, when we talked about all this on the flight to Bahrain, 'Sometimes they don't give you another chance'? This would definitely be one of those times."

"Hmm. Did he say it back?"

"No! He just gave me a look like I'd incinerated his soul." My chest drums out an arrhythmic ache at the memory. His soft, perfect lips, parted in disbelief. His smoke-gray eyes red and devastated. The scar on his eyebrow creasing as his forehead crumpled with pain.

Fuckity fucking fuck.

"Sage," Priya says, just above a whisper. "Do you really believe in your heart that he could do that to you—betray you? That everything you guys shared was a lie? Because if you do, I won't push you to have another conversation with him."

The thing is...I *don't* believe it in my heart. But I have to believe it *in my head*. Plus I've already ruined everything and I won't go crawling back. I'm not meant for relationships; I never was. And Alexander was fucking warned.

Maybe it's not even him *I distrust, but...me.*

I pull Priya's hand to my face and kiss her knuckles before tucking her hand under my cheek like a security blanket.

"Thank you for understanding," I tell her, doing my damnedest to sound both carefree and final. "I do appreciate your feedback. You're the best."

She makes a grumbly sound like she's unconvinced, but lets it drop. As I feign drifting off to sleep, I can't help thinking of my fake sneeze in the elevator with Alexander in Melbourne, and that Priya is a lot easier to fool than he is.

Unfortunately, there's no fooling *myself* that I'm not heartbroken.

But it's too fucking late.

24

FRANCE

ONE MONTH LATER

ALEXANDER

Of course I love France, though not as much as Americans do (to be fair, I probably don't even love London as much as Americans do). But I wouldn't be here right now if it weren't for Badrick getting married to Laurent.

For four weeks I've scarcely left my house. My hair is shaggy, I've lost nearly a stone, and I gave up on shaving… leading to the dismaying discovery that my facial hair at this length is alarmingly and undeniably ginger.

Still, when Bad called and said he and Laurent had decided to make a trip (reckless, but no one asked me) up the middle aisle, I packed a few suits and chucked them into the boot of the Austin-Healey and hit the road.

I suppose it's good for me to get out of the house, rather than mooning around playing piano and day-drinking and rereading books that made me satisfyingly depressed as a teenager. (Thank you, Graham Greene, for *Brighton Rock*.) On the Dover–Calais ferry, I leaned into my adolescent despair to such a degree that I stood on deck with my face in the wind, listening to Amália Rodrigues's "Maldição" on repeat and feeling very sorry for myself. The lyrics, *What destiny or curse commands us, My Heart?* seem written just for me.

For reasons that are probably unfair and a bit territorial, I took Laurent for a gold digger, but it turns out his parents have a small winery in Reims, where the wedding is. After making my way up the winding drive, I park near a picturesque barn that has the doors thrown open. Workers dart in and out, preparing for tomorrow's festivities.

I drove with the top down from Calais onward, so I'm all kinds of disheveled, and a little sunburned on the back of my neck. As I climb out of the Sprite, Badrick exits the house and trots over to me, arms open.

"You look terrible, mate," he says, embracing me and pummeling my back.

"And you look like an International Male cover stud, as usual." I nod sideways at the wedding preparations. "Even if you are such a cliché that you're having a barn wedding."

"Fuck off," he says with a laugh. "And the reception's in the barn, not the ceremony." When I pull my garment bag from the boot, Badrick takes it from me and leads the way to the house. "That scruff! My best man couldn't be arsed to shave?"

I rub my jaw. "You don't think it looks…virile?"

"Maybe if you weren't otherwise giving 'shipwrecked.' I'd ask where's the rest of your baggage, but it's under your feckin' eyes."

I think I must've winced, because Bad's expression goes

from piss-take to pity. His steps slow. "Brighten up, boyo." He lands a playful punch on my shoulder. "Laurent has three sisters, all with friends who'll be here. And some of the girls from his modeling agency are coming too. This time tomorrow you'll be up to your pecs in hot birds."

I give a wry sniff. "No thank you."

"All right, not that, then." He throws out a sweeping gesture at the fields of champagne grapes. "So walk a bit, touch grass, breathe the country air, remember who you are."

I stop on the path, probably looking more hopeless than I intend. "That's just it, Bad. I don't fucking *know* who I am. There's no 'real' me—I'm a box full of cheap disguises. For a few weeks, with Sage, I thought I finally had it. I had *everything*. I was becoming…fuck, I don't know, someone? Myself. My *best* self. And now…" I shrug.

He squeezes my upper arm. "*I* know who you are, bruv. You can't see it 'cause you're too close." He chuckles. "There's always been a 'real you,' Piano Twat—take it from Drum Twat." He slowly sets off in motion toward the house again. "Still haven't talked with her?"

"I think she blocked my number—my texts went green the first night, so I stopped writing them. I won't be an utter mug and send my pathetic pleas into a void." I shove my hands into my pockets as we walk, and even a small gesture like that makes me think of her; she once told me it looks sexy when a man wearing a suit has his hands in his pockets.

The setting sun is throwing beautiful long shadows, fringing the ground beside the stands of grapes, and I think of all the pictures Sage and I exchanged just weeks ago.

Hers from Miami: an amusing misspelled sign, a flower she saw growing out of cracked pavement, the pillows on her bed with Wish you were here.

Mine from London: a broken umbrella in a puddle, a wound on a tree where the branch sheared off and left the shape of a heart, my hand on my piano keyboard with Wish you were here.

The next morning, I stand at the window in the little slope-roofed dormer room, gazing at the sun on the grass below, the chairs set up in their tidy rows, the arbor arch hung with grapes and jasmine and honeysuckle.

"Bloody hell," Badrick mutters, faffing with his tie in front of the antique mirror, "it's still crooked. The fuck do I need a *triple* Windsor for?"

"Because it looks better, you plonker. Here—let me fix it."

"Regular knot's fine," he says, veering aside at my approach.

"If you're a pleb. Hold still, for fuck's sake." I whip the necktie into shape and smooth it down. "There, neat as a pin."

He turns to the mirror, inspecting, then eyeing me through the reflection. "Thanks."

"Cheers." I go to a rustic armoire and lean against it. "I hope you know I really am happy for you and Laurent. I've taken the mick plenty, but I do like him. You two are a good couple, and I was wrong about it being 'too sudden'—you've been together over a year. I was purely being a sulky shit, and I apologize."

"No worries. Appreciate it, bruv." He focuses on affixing

his boutonniere—a purple iris entwined with a red Tudor rose. "I suppose six weeks with your little racing bird changed your mind about how soon you can know you've found your person."

His words paralyze me like an icicle to the chest. "Fuckin' hell, Bad. *Don't*."

He shrugs. "I ain't gonna go easy on you when I think you gave up too quick. Laurent has a weakness for those angsty romance books and made me read a couple of 'em myself, and there's always a 'grand gesture' in the story. A dramatic moment where you show your heart, lay it all bare."

"My heart *was* bare, pretty much from day dot."

"Then she thought you stabbed her in the back, and when she said it'd all been bollocks from the start, you told her—according to your account—'I'm not giving up,' followed by *giving up within twenty-four hours*. You think that's gonna change her mind? Make her think she's wrong about your feelings not being genuine?" He makes a disgusted scoffing noise.

"The texts I sent that night after she walked out made it clear that—"

"You said yourself she probably blocked your number, mate. She was furious." He gestures toward the window. "You think I ain't seen that shit a thousand times with Laurent? He's got a temper like a rabid badger. You let 'em cool down, then you talk it out."

I fold my arms, offering a sarcastic "Oh, and now I should organize a flash mob to do a dance outside her trailer while a fuckin' jet sky-writes 'Alexander will love you for all eternity'?"

"Not a bad place to start," he says with a crooked smile.

"She knows where to find me if she wants to talk."

"With an attitude like that, you deserve to lose her."

My arms drop and I stumble a step back, feeling like I've taken a shot to the chest. "Oi! Steady on. That's un-fucking-called for."

"The truth hurts, but maybe you need a solid kick in the arse. Because years of wondering what might've happened if you hadn't been a coward...that's much more painful." He falls silent and fusses with the boutonniere.

I walk slowly to an overstuffed chenille chair and sag into it. "She's in Montreal right now for the GP anyway. It's not like I can do anything."

"Oh, right," Badrick says, snapping his fingers. "You couldn't possibly send flowers—there are no florist shops in Canada. Well, carry on, then. You know what you're doing, clearly."

I glare at him, and he smirks back.

His tone is gentler when he says, "Are you my best man or what? So...*be your best*. Quit making excuses for why it won't work. I don't know if you're more afraid that you're right about that, or afraid you're wrong."

My shred of laughter is bitter, and I focus on adjusting the strap of my wristwatch. "Fine. Next GP is Silverstone. Maybe I'll...give her a shout and see if she's willing to get together and talk in London."

"You'll 'give her a shout'? Not much of a grand gesture."

"Don't push your luck. The flash mob can wait until I see whether she's receptive."

"Fine, but at least don't make her come to you. It's an hour or two up the M1 to Silverstone. Go to *her*, you feckin' bellend. Christ." He shoots his cuffs with an expression of pure wedding-day jitters, then comes to offer me a hand up. "Right, it's go time."

I stand and he pulls me into a brief, back-thumping hug. "Love you, bruv. I just want you to be happy, you know that, yeah?"

"I do. And you're not wrong about any of it." I gnaw at my lower lip and admit, "The stakes are just so fucking high."

"They are." He grins, glancing at the window. Outside, the sound of Laurent's distinctive laugh rises on the golden morning sunshine. "But the higher the stakes, the bigger the payoff."

LONDON

It took a while to decide whether I would execute revenge on CJ Ardley. If that was my plan, I'd need access to my blog again. It has over a hundred thousand subscribers and gets a healthy amount of non-subscriber traffic as well. I asked my mother (omitting mention of a revenge plot, of course), and she reinstated my admin control because she felt sorry for me and said a bit of writing would give me something to do until the new job at *Caterwaul* starts. Between the beard, the weight loss, and the shadows beneath my eyes, Mum was genuinely distraught by my appearance.

For a week, I started drafts of a post detailing what Ms. Ardley had done, painting her as the worst kind of embittered, striving, sleazy hag. I looked at the screenshots I'd saved in the secure photo-vault app on my phone, texts from her in which she said incriminating things. There were even a few where she mocked her powerful benefactor and paramour, Gavin Yates. I knew those were pure gold. He's a vain monster, and if I published messages in which she called him "a clod with all the sex appeal of a crow eating roadkill," their alliance would be over.

But dammit, I couldn't do it. *Who am I now?*

All I could think of was how such poisonous gossip had hurt Sage. CJ Ardley may deserve payback, but I won't stoop to her level and be the one to bestow it. I'm not that man anymore. Whatever my future holds—with or without my Salvia officinalis—knowing Sage (and knowing *myself* a little better) has changed me.

When I do publish my first *In the Mirrors* post after the hiatus, the tone is different than it's been in the past. Rather than gossip, it's more race analysis, combined with some comically self-deprecating material about my travels.

I can't help throwing in a bit of glowing praise for Sage, hoping she'll see it.

At any rate, I end up deleting the screenshots of CJ's messages, and to my surprise, I'm relieved. I feel free, like I can finally take a full breath, having removed some stifling, sweaty plastic Halloween mask after a lifetime of hiding behind it.

It turns out that CJ gets her comeuppance anyway, as tends to happen.

She calls me two weeks after Badrick's wedding. I'm back in London, picking up pastries at Forno. (I can't say a steady diet of maritozzi, pain au chocolat, and red wine is improving my performance at the gym, but at least I'm eating again.)

I pull my mobile from a pocket, balancing the pastry box on my other arm as I exit the bakery. "Ms. Ardley, to what do I owe the pleasure?"

"You're not going to get away with this," she grits out. "I know it must've been you who put my daughter up to writing those things."

I wander leisurely toward the kerb where the Austin-Healey is parked. "I assure you, I've never met your daughter. To what are you referring, pet?"

"Don't play dumb with me," she rants. "What she said on her blog, obviously! About how I've 'ruined our relationship' by reporting *entirely accurate* information about Sage and Julian Sikora, how I'm 'having a midlife crisis,' calling me a 'social climber' and saying Gavin put the moves on her when we met up with her and her husband vacationing in Croatia. Making up those disgusting things he supposedly said, proposing a threesome! And worst of all, revealing private messages, stuff I'd told her confidentially about him. I can't—"

"Carol-Jeanne, love, let me get this straight: Your child expressed that your actions, slagging off her close friends, have damaged your mother-daughter relationship. She called you out for toxic behavior. She said that the 'No Pity Chef'—a man universally recognized to be a womanizer and bully—propositioned her. Please, a moment of self-awareness. Are you claiming that *any* of this is unlikely?"

"I'm not saying it's *unlikely*. I'm saying the tone is cruel."

"Again, listen to yourself. Does it sound strangely familiar?

Like…oh, I don't know…the logical consequences of things you set in motion?"

"*You* must have set it in motion!" she seethes. "Sage dropped you cold—everyone knows it—because she figured you're the one who gave me those tidbits about Julian."

"She 'figured' it because you strongly implied as much."

"Yeah? *Good*. Because it'll take a lawsuit to get me to reveal my mole at the rehab." After a pause, she sighs, switching to the weary, chiding tone of disappointed nanny. "Oh, Al. We coulda done something great together, you and me. But you got swayed by that little tramp and lost your edge."

Reaching my car, which has the top down, I set the pastry box on the passenger seat. "I couldn't be happier to have retired my 'edge.' I've wounded enough people with it over the years. Not that you need my advice, pet, but you might be happier—and your estranged daughter certainly will be—if you spend less time sharpening yours. Best of luck to you."

I hang up and pocket my mobile. Leaning against the car, I look up at the smoochingly perfect late-June sky, streaked with clouds, and feel a wash of something like peace for the first time in five weeks. *It's going to be okay. Different, but okay. As long as Sage is happy.*

I reached out to her via email (though I can't be sure it's the right one—I think she has several accounts) after Badrick's wedding, as promised, but got no reply. I then made the mistake of trying to get a message to Sage through Phaedra Morgan, and she shut me down handily, responding, *You know what it means when a woman won't reply to your overtures, right? Fuck off and leave my driver alone.*

So that's it. My Salvi is no longer *my* Salvi. It's over.

I have Google alerts set for her, of course. I haven't seen any paparazzi snapshots of her hitting the clubs yet, but it's just a matter of time. I'm steeling myself for the pain that will come the first time I see pics of her on someone's arm.

As I take out my car keys, my attention is drawn to a young boy dragging his mother by the hand over to the window of the bakery, pointing and pleading. She looks harried, trying for stern but telegraphing grief as she tells him, "It's too expensive! We have buns at home."

For some reason, the pale, lanky, dark-haired tot reminds me of the one in Bahrain to whom I gave a biscuit just before he swiped my mobile. I remember striding into Sage's driver room later that day, confronting her about her practical joke sending me out to the shops for those ridiculous items. The frustration I felt that she already had the upper hand where my heart was concerned. The electricity between us when I touched her sternum with a fingertip. How she boldly held her ground, eyes glittering.

Taking the pastry box from my seat, I hold it out to the boy and his mother as she hauls him away from the bakery window. "Please, take these. My treat."

"Can we?" the boy begs his mother.

Her eyes narrow with suspicion, so I manufacture a quick white lie to make the offer seem less dubious. "It was the wrong order, so they gave it to me for free." I lift the box another inch toward them. "It'll just go to waste, truly."

The boy hangs off his mother's sleeve. "Pleeeeeease?"

Her arms lift, and I hand over the box.

"Maritozzi, lemon curd buns, and cornetto al pistacchio," I tell her. "You're doing me a favor."

"Thank you," she manages. The boy gazes at me like I'm the Saint Nick of sweets.

On the drive home, I feel lighter. Not just because I've divested myself of a kilo of baked goods and am vowing I'll have muesli and fruit for breakfast, but because in this moment, after CJ's call, I have a sense of closure. The breakup with Sage hasn't stopped hurting and may never heal completely. She will always be the ideal to me.

I'll never have that again—the love I felt with her. No stepping in the same river twice, as it's said. Once an unrepentant player, I now can't stomach the thought of spending time with any woman other than Sage. But one day, perhaps, I'll meet someone else…and deserve to.

25

ENGLAND

SAGE

Predictably, my drive in Spain was shit. I made the mistake of trying to "soldier through" with the back pain because I was afraid of looking weak. But winging my arm out like a pissed-off chicken when Alexander touched my elbow, the night we broke up, I tore the muscle.

During the Spanish GP, I was breathing shallowly when I needed every fucking cubic centimeter of air, and my right hand had poor grip and was twitching. It was a miracle I came in twelfth. My back was so locked up by the end of the race that I literally had to be lifted out of my car, and…yeah, I took endless shit about that online from everyone who hates women drivers. It didn't matter that it was reported soon after the race that I was playing hurt.

Phae and the team batted around the idea of me sitting out Monaco and having our reserve driver Kalle take my place, since it was only a week later and I wasn't at 100 percent. But

I was desperate to prove I could do it. I'll admit, I just didn't want Alexander to see that I was struggling. So I got a shot in my back on race day, and it did help with the pain, but I wasn't moving naturally and my drive was compromised. I only squeaked out a point in tenth place because Akio Ono and João Valle had a dustup and retired.

The two weeks' break before Baku helped a lot, both for my fucked-up back and my emotional state. I was worried about lagging so far behind Cosmin in the points, since we have that 100-point-gap contract clause. But Aoife, my manager, told me there's an exception for injury, which in my cluttered, pain-exhausted, grief-addled brain is something I'd forgotten. I finished P8 in Baku, then P6 in the Canadian GP ten days ago, despite a dramatic crash during quali that caused me to start pretty far back on the grid.

Healing up from this injury (okay, *injuries*, if you include the broken heart) has ruled out any kind of socializing or partying. I've been tempted to go out to a club and get my freak on and have pics splashed all over the internet of me dirty dancing with a gorgeous stranger, tongue down their throat, not a care in the world. But even if I were in shape to flail around on a dance floor, the vengeful impulse to show off for Alexander is always short-lived—a pulse of spitefulness that gets swallowed up the next second by the pain of missing him.

And I *do*. So much I almost can't stand it. Especially because it now appears I fucked up and accused him when he wasn't guilty.

Julian earned landline phone privileges a month ago and we've been talking every other day, and one of the first things he told me was that he'd revealed in group therapy meetings his guilt over what happened in Thailand. It was such a relief to clear the air with him about all that and apologize for assuming the worst for years. Our talks have been amazing, honestly. I can't wait to see him when he's done with his program.

Anyway, clearly someone at the treatment center passed that shit on to the *Sports and Tortes* harpy. But there was no way I was gonna call Alexander up and tell him, *Oh, my bad.*

I did what I'd always hoped *not* to do: showed him my worst self. Realistically, he'll get over me. He's probably relieved to go back to his "three-shag limit" with the haut monde A-listers. I blocked his number the first night because I was mad, but… to be honest, it *stayed* blocked because that way I don't have to know and be hurt by it if he doesn't ever try to call. I'd be checking my phone constantly for messages.

This way I can tell myself he *can't* text, rather than he just doesn't care to.

But yeah…I miss his voice, his scent, his freckles, the scar on his eyebrow. I miss the thing he'd unconsciously do with his mouth—tilting his lips and biting the inside of his cheek—just before saying something that made him nervous, like admitting an embarrassing secret or a vulnerable detail. I miss the way he'd put one ankle between mine when we'd fall sleep, and how later when he'd change position, he'd kiss my shoulder and whisper, "Salvi…" before turning away, like he was reassuring me that he was still there.

I even miss how after we'd get a coffee, he'd chew on the stir stick and make me nuts and I'd have to tell him, *For fuck's sake, knock it off—stop chewing on wood like a beaver.*

I guess I'm not okay.

And I don't want to sleep with anyone else. Like, *ever*. How lame is that?

So my heart got broken, something I never thought would happen to me. But this race week it's eyes on the prize, no distractions, no regrets. Physically I'm in fighting form again, and best of all, Julian is getting out of rehab—two weeks early, but he swears he's ready—and is coming to England to stay with Pri and me and attend the race at Silverstone.

I'm *so* ready to hit the reset button on years of pointless feuding. All I can think about now is how great he actually is, and how dumb I've been. He's transformed, in my esteem, from a shiftless, pampered fail-son slutting around the globe rock climbing and draining his trust fund to…well, I guess how everyone else has seen him all along (especially Pri): a generous, good-hearted golden retriever who's a skilled climber and a curious, adventurous person.

Flawed, yeah. But aren't we all?

It's Thursday, and I've just finished the press meeting, feeling as close to "on top of things" as I've been since the bust-up with Sandy. Julian flew in this morning and Pri drove down to London to pick him up. I'm looking forward to seeing them both tonight. Phae is lending us her family's house in Towcester, and Pri and Jules probably arrived there hours ago. After, uh, "catching up" with each other (not gonna think about that one, but I wish them well), they're gonna cook a big dinner for us all.

When Pri calls me in late afternoon, I'm assuming it's to ask me to pick something up on my way to the house—a bottle of wine, dessert, whatever—but when I open the call, the sob in her voice stops me like I've run face-first into a wall.

"What the fuck is going on?" I demand, my scalp prickling. "Why are you crying?"

She sniffles, and in the pause, I hear an unmistakable soundtrack: the background noise you hear in a hospital.

"Oh, Sage—it's Julian," she chokes out.

I detour into an empty meeting room and sag into a chair, my legs suddenly so weak that I almost miss it completely and slide onto the floor. "Is he...?" I rasp.

"He's alive," she says quickly. "But we're in St Thomas' Hospital and you need to get down here. He—"

"What happened?" I interrupt, too loud.

"Sage, don't be mad. Not at him and not at me. I only lost sight of him for a little while," she explains in a rush, her voice breaking.

She's phrasing it like someone talking about a toddler who's dashed into the street. I suspect what's happened, but I don't want to believe it. *Not now, after months of progress. Not now, when we're going to be a family again.*

"We stopped for breakfast in a café," she continues, "and he told me he needed to go get gifts for me and you, and I should hang at the coffee place and read or whatever, that he'd be back soon. But then it'd been *three hours* and he wasn't answering texts. I thought maybe he'd lost his phone, and couldn't find his way back? Then I got a call from him and...it was actually someone I didn't know on his phone and they said Julian was at St Thomas' and he'd overdosed."

I roar down the M1 in the Mercedes, keeping it around 145 kph anywhere possible, slicing through traffic like a scalpel. I've always thought it'd be a little fun to get caught speeding and pull an Ayrton Senna, who when stopped by police while speeding was asked, "Who do you think you are—Nigel Mansell?" and replied, "No, I'm faster." But today I can't afford the delay just for the sake of being a quippy sass-box.

When I approach the hospital, I groan at the sight of press, milling around just outside the range where they could be shooed away. How did they get wind of this so fast? *Fuuuuuuuuck*. There are only three of them, but it's three too many.

I park and hunt around the car for anything I could use as a half-assed disguise. There's a rumpled hoodie squished between the seats, but it's Emerald F1 gear, so obviously that won't help. My sunglasses are useless too. How many blue-and-green-haired, neck-tattooed girls are going to be walking into St Thomas' right now? I'm pretty much fucked.

I'm desperate to get out of the car and hurry to Jules and Pri, but I take a minute to collect myself, since there won't be any avoiding the press. I'm so frustrated and overwhelmed that I almost dissolve into tears. The only thing stopping me is knowing that pics of me crying in the car would be media gold.

I rub both hands over my face, releasing a slow, shaky sigh. At a tap on the window, I jump. I'm expecting some journalist vulture has spotted me, but when I look up, it's Alexander.

Holy shit, he looks different. He has a short beard, bright

as a shiny new penny, but it's the only thing about him that's shining. His gray eyes are smudged with shadows and he's lost probably ten or fifteen pounds. His hair is longer—it's gone from *I paid a fortune for this do* to *I live in a cave and hunt woolly mammoths.*

We stare at each other for a long moment, then I open the door and he steps aside while I climb out of the little sports car.

He opens his arms. "Salvi," he murmurs simply.

I allow the hug, both comforted and disturbed by how right it feels to have his arms around me again. "How'd you find out?" I ask against the lapel of his blue plaid suit.

"Alerts on my mobile."

"For me?"

He holds me tighter. "You, Julian, Emerald, *everyone*. You're…very missed."

When we finally pull apart, I study his face. "You look kind of awful."

He gives a sad smile and chucks me under the chin with a fingertip. "I reckon so." Nodding sideways toward the hospital, he says, "Couldn't let you do this alone, however you may feel about me. And I'm terribly worried for Julian. How is he?"

"I don't know yet." As we start toward the entrance, I reflexively take Alexander's hand, then drop it. "Sorry," I mutter.

The knot of journalists catch sight of us, and Alexander drapes an arm protectively around my shoulders. As all three of them crowd me, blurting out questions, Alexander shoves away the extended arm of one who gets his phone too close to my face.

"Off you fuck, then," he tells the man in an efficient tone. "There's a good lad."

In seconds, we're past and inside, where I practically run to the reception desk, pulling free of Alexander. As we get into the elevator, two other people are about to step in with us. Alexander again puts an arm out, warding them off and earning an indignant sputter from the two older ladies. I smile, looking down at my feet as the doors close, remembering us in Melbourne when I told that old couple to take the next elevator because Alexander and I were going to have sex in that one.

I try for a weak joke to break the silence. "We're, uh, not gonna fuck in here this time."

"More's the pity." He leans against the wall. "Though we didn't that time either. Not until hours later."

We watch each other as the elevator hums upward.

"How are you?" he asks quietly.

"Oh, great, *great*. Thanks, yep." I do a slow nod. "I mean, my brother might be—fuck, I don't even know—like, in a coma? And my last four races were varying degrees of garbage, and…oh! I also got my heart broken. So it's been a gas. And you? How's tricks?"

I want to sink into the floor and disappear, because I wasn't going for "rant"; I was hoping for wry and irreverent. But my voice got louder with each sentence and cracked like a twelve-year-old boy's, and my eyes are stinging and I want *so bad* to throw myself into Alexander's arms. The fact that he rushed here to be with me is a little swoony.

His eyebrows lift and it draws my attention to that tender white scar and I want to cry.

"Well," he says, sounding tired, "Badrick got married, so that's lovely. As for me, I turned into, erm..." He waves a vague hand at himself.

I scowl. "Are you eating? Your cheeks are hollow, though the beard covers it a little. You're a cross between eighties goth-band skinny and pale and...uh, Grizzly Adams."

He smiles cautiously. "I've no clue who that is. This?" He touches his profusion of facial hair, and I can almost feel my hand there too.

"Mmm-hmm. Hokey TV show about a mountain man with a pet bear. My mom liked it."

The elevator chimes and I squeeze out the barely open door. I race-walk down the corridor with Alexander at my heels, and as I zero in on the room, my stomach is trembling like it's full of ice—I'm so scared of what I'm going to see. Will Jules be all limp and gray with tubes sticking out? Beeping machines and a hysterical Priya draped over his legs?

As I round the corner, I stop so quickly that Alexander runs into my back, then grasps my shoulders to steady me.

Jules is sitting up in bed, Priya in a chair beside him, and they're both looking at their phones.

"Got it in three," Jules says with a teasing smugness. He turns his phone screen to show Priya, and *he's playing Wordle*, for fuck's sake. "In your face," he adds.

She snorts. "More like *your* face," she returns. "Which of us has another black eye, hmm? And I guessed it in four." She leans to look at his phone. "*Tsk!* You just got lucky."

"Um, hello?" I say.

They swivel to look, and Priya jumps up and hurries to me,

yanking me into an embrace. Once she lets me go, I make eye contact with Jules, who offers a nervous fingertip-wave.

"Hey, Sage," he says, voice tentative.

"Hey, fuckwit." A wave of sorrow and relief and just plain love crashes over me and the next thing I know I'm on the edge of the bed, holding him hard. "Don't you ever scare me like that again. Do you hear me? *Never…again.*"

A shiver passes through him like he's trying not to cry. "I really fucked up. I didn't mean to. I didn't have it planned or anything, and—"

"I know," I breathe against his cotton-gown-clad shoulder.

"And I'm not asking you to trust me, because I haven't earned it."

"Oh, fuck that, Jules." I pull back, and yeah, now *I'm* crying. I swipe my tears away. "Of course I trust you. And I love you. Just don't die, okay?" I look at Pri. "If you do that to my best friend, I'll kick your ass."

She lets out a small sob of a laugh. "Take a number. I told him I'd kick his butt too."

Standing inconspicuously to one side, Alexander watches us with a kind smile. Julian finally notices, and he sits up and practically shouts out, "Shit, dude! You're here! Bring it in."

Alexander goes to exchange a fist bump and one of those guy hugs, then gets a chair from by the window and drags it over, sitting down. When he does, I notice that *oh my God, he's wearing the fly fishing socks from the suit I gave him in Italy.* My shocked gaze goes from his ankles to his eyes, and he gives me a cute helpless shrug, and my heart clenches.

Pri and I perch on either side of Jules's bed and we all chat and I'm brought up to speed on what happened. Long story short: Jules told an old pal (um, *drug pal*) he'd be in London, the friend asked him to drop by, he thought he'd prove to himself how "over it" he was by seeing the friend, and…obviously he was wrong about being over it. I'm not dense enough to buy his story completely, because if the thought of using never crossed his mind, he would've taken Priya with him and wouldn't have lied to her about where he was going.

So it's a process. We're not there yet, but I believe in him. I prepared for the 40 to 60 percent possibility of a relapse, and I've educated myself with the tools to help Julian to help himself more effectively as we move forward.

I'm not giving up. And I won't let him give up either.

"Sage, no way am I letting you pay for treatment again after I failed," he tells me upon hearing that I'm sending him right the fuck back to rehab.

I take his jaw in one hand, pinning him with a stern look. "We'll do this as many times as it takes," I insist. "*I'm driving for you now*, got it? You didn't save me the first time you went back to look for me in Thailand. I didn't save you the first time you went to rehab. We keep trying. We're family, Jules."

There's a discreet tap on the open door, and I look over to find Maya Ardley leaning in. "Is this an okay time?" she asks.

"Meems!" Julian calls out with a happy laugh, using his years-ago nickname for her. "What the hell are you doing in London?" He beckons her over, and as they exchange a hug, she glances at Priya like she's checking to see if it's okay.

"Technically I'm in England to attend the British GP,"

Maya says, adding in an amused deadpan, "Your sickbed is just a detour."

I know Pri doesn't feel weird about Maya. But Maya still seems self-conscious, probably aware that it lands different that she's here for Jules. She mentions her husband, Tau, a few times, and I suspect it's not only because she's nuts for the guy but also to make it clear to Priya that she doesn't have designs.

After we've all been talking awhile, Julian falls asleep, and I feel like I understand the contentment my mom once described to me when she'd see us kids sleeping, knowing we were somewhere safe for a few hours, where nothing could hurt us. I examine the relaxed lines of Julian's face and I want him to get better *so much*...I don't think I've ever even wanted to win a race as much as I want him to win this fight.

Alexander—who's mostly been quietly listening to the conversation—gets up and makes his way subtly to the door, meeting my eye and pointing to indicate that he's leaving. Pri and Maya are chatting, so I stand and follow him into the hall. We wander to the recess of an empty doorway where there's some privacy, and he takes both my hands in his.

"I'll shove off, then," he tells me. "I know you can hold your own with the press. I just, uh...I didn't know what we'd find—Julian's condition, that is to say—and I wanted to be here for you in case it was quite bad. But you're fine."

There's a sinking feeling in my chest. "Yep, that's me. Totally fine."

He squeezes my hands, staring at our dovetailed fingers. "I told myself I wouldn't say this and look gauche, as if I'm taking advantage of this situation to get near you when you want nothing to do with me. But…" He looks up cautiously. "Salvi, I love you. I always will. And I know you may still not believe that I had nothing to do with that shite Maya's mum wrote. But part of me is always going to be waiting for you, too lovesick to let go."

I can barely breathe, and I know my eyes are wide. I can't even manage to pull on my aloof mask—this hurts too much. *God, he's beautiful.*

He emits a breath of a laugh, rueful. "If ever I were to marry someone else," he goes on, "I'll insist that it's written into my vows, 'But if Sage comes back to me, it's straight into the bin with you.'"

I choke out a snort-laugh, then clap a hand over my mouth. "Oh, your hypothetical future wife will *love* that."

He shrugs with a weak smile. "Needs must."

I know I should let his hands go, but I can't. "Sandy, I do believe you didn't tell CJ that stuff about Jules. Like, I've known that for a month. It just seemed like I'd probably burned the bridge with you. The things I said were *really* mean. I didn't give you a chance to defend yourself. I did pretty much every single step of that whole scene wrong."

"Your assumptions weren't unjustified, however fierce you were in the delivery. I've always been a careless twat, and this is the result when personal growth happens too late. I've no one to blame but myself. My behavior, historically, has been far from above reproach."

"We made plenty of mistakes," I mutter, my head dropping.

There's a long pause where we stare at our feet, squeezing each other's hands.

"I don't suppose," Alexander ventures, "that we might consider that to have been our first quarrel? We did it badly, but… maybe we both learned a lot and the next one will go better."

Everything in my torso makes a roller-coaster jump, and when I meet his eyes, I know mine are probably borderline pleading. "You don't think we fucked it up too majorly to be repaired?"

He hums a small laugh. "After the crash during qualifying in Montreal, your car looked like a fuckin' wadded kebab wrapper and I thought, 'How will Emerald get that wreckage fixed overnight?' But it happened."

"The team was highly motivated."

He pulls my hands to his lips and presses a kiss to my knuckles. "We could be just as motivated, could we not? My fuckin' God, Salvi. It took me so long to find you, I don't know how I can walk away. I've spent all my life so far up my own arse I couldn't have found my way out with satnav. You changed me. I won't give up if you won't."

A sound of footsteps headed our way causes us to lean and peek around the corner. Maya stalls in her steps when she spots us, then rushes over.

"I was worried you'd both left! I came here to see you too, Sage. And I'm glad I ran into *you*, Alexander. I wanted to talk to you about what happened with my mom."

I give him a suspicious smirk. "Wait, what'd you do?"

He holds his hands up as if about to deny something when Maya goes on. "No, nothing bad," she tells us with a laugh. "I just need to thank you for what you said to her when she called you, and then for making that recommendation to your mom for the job."

He looks almost sheepish, and I give him a playful sock on the arm. "Okay, spill it. There's obviously a helluva story here."

When he hesitates as if trying to find the words, Maya tells me, "My mom called him and lost her marbles because she thought he'd convinced me to write in my blog about, y'know, all the bad blood."

"What the fuck?"

"Right? And he shot straight with her and said the problem between her and me was, like, her own fault—*duh*. Something about how she should tone down her 'edge' and she'd have more friends? Anyway, it hit home. I guess she was in the right place to hear it, since we'd had the big fight and she was mega sad."

Alexander pulls me closer with his arm across my shoulders, and it feels so natural I could cry. I snake a hand around his waist, and he looks down and flashes a hopeful smile.

"But then the best part," Maya says, looking from Alexander to me, "is that he told his mother to hire my mom to write for *Pâte à Pâtisserie Magazine*. He got her a job, Sage! Can you even?"

I angle a stunned look up at him. "I cannot, no. Holy shit, Sandy. Why?"

"A little something I learned from Nefeli Laskaris herself. When I was making mischief, as a boy, rather than punishing me she'd give me something 'important' to do. A task to keep me busy and give me the attention I'd been craving. Go out and help the gardener pull weeds, wash dishes for our cook, hoover my father's car—that sort of thing." He shrugs. "It worked. So I reasoned that Ms. Ardley just needed a better outlet for her admittedly engaging writing skills."

"And that was *perfect*," Maya says, "not only because it was a dream of hers to write for a magazine but also because you doing her a favor after she acted like a flaming B made her feel pretty guilty." She laughs. "It's like a reward but with a tiny punishment wrapped inside, just to keep things balanced."

I think of how Priya often does something kind for me when I've been a jerk and realize it's a little of both too: an olive branch, but also a reminder to me that I should be nicer.

"Pretty clever, Sandy-boy," I tell him, stepping closer in his embrace and patting his chest.

Maya's phone rings in her bag and she pulls it out. "Oop, it's Tau. Gotta take this." She backs up a few steps, swiping the screen. "Let's all get together for dinner after the race!" she calls in parting. "Monday maybe?"

She waves before turning away and walking down the hall, and I watch her retreat. I shoot a side-eye at Alexander. "Hey, Sandy?"

"Yes, my seraph?" He brushes a knuckle along my jaw.

"You keep surprising me. I love it. And I love *you*. Can we have do-overs?"

"Hell yes. And I love you too, unreservedly and immoderately." He combs his fingers into my hair and kisses my forehead. "I'm overjoyed that it all got sorted out."

"Hmm, you're pretty chill right now for a guy who's 'overjoyed'..." My other hand goes to his waist and I pull him tight against me. "Shit, you *did* get skinny."

His lips close in on mine. "Then feed me."

EPILOGUE

FRANCE

THIRTEEN MONTHS LATER

ALEXANDER

Over in the wide, grassy area by the house, a few grape rows away from where Sage and I are strolling, we can hear Laurent calling to the dog in strident French: "Viens, Chouchou…non non non…Lâche!" Sage and I exchange an amused look.

"Bloody hell," I say, "between the different names—Gaston or Chouchou—and commands in two languages, that poor feckin' confused mutt doesn't stand a chance of obedience. No wonder it's so horrid."

"How dare you say that about our godson," Sage mock-scolds. "Or…uh, god-dog?"

She takes my hand and does a little pirouette, and I reel her in close, wrapping her in my arms. In the low August light, her pupils are dark pools ringed in sultry gold, and she tips her head up in invitation. I tease her lips in light brushing passes before squeezing two handfuls of her now fully emerald-green hair and going in for a deep kiss.

Lost in each other for a long minute, our hands explore as we map each other's hunger with our mouths. The scent of grapes and earth and sun mingles with Sage's sugary warmth, and I'd pull her down on this shadowy row of dirt and undress her right now if six other people weren't roaming this French vineyard.

As if on cue, I hear a foot scuff against the ground as someone rounds the row we're in.

"Oop, sorry—as you were," Maya says with a giggle, looping an arm through her husband Tau's and dragging him away. Somewhere in the orchard, Priya and Julian are wandering too, all of us invited by Badrick and Laurent to a late one-year wedding anniversary gathering. Laurent and Sage are thick as thieves now, so he and Bad delayed the party by two months to coincide with the F1 summer break, specifically to give Sage the chance to spend several days vacationing in the French countryside with no work pressure.

Last year, Emerald F1 took third place again in the Constructors' Championship, but didn't rise any higher due to Sage's dip in performance during her injury (to say nothing of the drama between us, and Julian's struggles). But this year, roughly two-thirds of the way through the season, they're flying high, locked in a solid fight for *second* place.

Next season there are some regulation changes coming to the sport—aerodynamics, chiefly—and Sage and Cosmin and Phaedra and the entire Emerald F1 team think they have a chance at *winning* Constructors' for the first time. Basil

Rowley has more skill, experience, and engineering artistry than anyone at Allonby Racing, the current champs.

This vacation feels especially celebratory, because Sage got her history-making win two weeks ago at the Belgian GP. I'm not ashamed to admit I cried more than she did, seeing her atop the podium.

We're "shacked up" now, as she puts it, splitting our time between her flat in Monaco, my place in London, and a San Francisco loft we bought together last Christmas, in the same neighborhood Julian and Priya call their home base.

So much has happened. For the first time in my life, I feel like part of a true friendship group—Sage and I, Badrick and Laurent, Priya and Julian, Maya and Tau. My life used to be more like trying to hoard Badrick to myself (and shut out Laurent) while flitting from one blink-and-you'll-miss-it affair to the next. I'm surprised at how different friendship is with a diverse group, each member bringing their own context and quirks. It feels like we're hollowing out a deep pool of experience and memories together, floating confidently on the trust we all have in each other.

I knew *love* would change me, but to be honest...I never anticipated to what a degree friendship would as well.

Another big change to come: Priya and Julian are expecting a baby in four months. It was a surprise, but a welcome one. Julian was already doing well, health-wise, but with this development he's quite transformed; not only is he recovered from his opiate dependence but he also doesn't drink. In consideration for his upcoming role as a father, and respecting the limits of his body, he's no longer globe-trotting to the most dangerous climbing destinations. He founded a rock-climbing club for at-risk youth, and regularly takes groups to Castle Rock State Park once they've graduated from his indoor climbing gym to outdoors.

The assistant editorship of *Caterwaul* was offered to me this year, but I opted to stick with overseeing the jazz section of the magazine. My work is mostly remote, aside from visits to the London offices every few months. Just the right speed, as I feel my most important work is supporting Sage in her career.

When I switched the focus of my blog from F1 to vinyl record collecting, I lost 90 percent of my subscribers, but I really don't mind. I don't need an audience anymore—with my sweet Salvia officinalis, I always feel seen.

We turn at the end of the rows and walk perpendicular to them, getting farther from the house, voices and laughter and barking growing dimmer behind us. Sage lets go of my fingers and trails a hand along a stand of champagne grapes, picking one and popping it into her mouth, then cracking up and unabashedly spitting it onto the ground.

"Shit, *no*," she chokes out, wincing. "Not quite ready yet."

After the words, a funny anxious look passes her expression. She examines me, then spins away and dances down the path in her capering way, always energetic, always physical, always singing—this time, the Kinks' song "Strangers," one of her favorites. The first time we slow-danced together, it was to that song.

She peeks back at me, and when I take a few quick steps to catch up, she eludes me with a laugh, skipping farther away.

"Wicked girl," I tease. "Where are you taking us? Did you find a private spot for us to make love amongst the butterflies?"

She catches my outstretched hand and pulls me the last few yards to a huge old tree, then flops down on the warm dirt. I settle beside her and we gaze up toward the house, where we can see Badrick playfully wrestling a stick from the dog's mouth with Laurent standing by, hands on hips, surely scolding him (as we've all heard so many times), "You make him frantic! Is not good for him!" like a fussy parent.

It's so beautiful here—the grapes, the perfect clouds, the hum of insects, the peace of being together. I snap off a blade of grass and poke it into my mouth, then lean back on my elbows. Seeing me do it, Sage affects a frown of feigned disapproval and plucks the grass from between my lips.

"Stop chewing on everything. I'll find something for you to do with those," she jokes, straddling my hips and leaning to kiss me. When she sits up again, the silvery clouds are behind her like a halo.

"This is so picturesque," I tell her with a smile, "that it'd be a perfect place for me to propose to you, if you wouldn't just immediately take the piss."

Her eyebrows dart up. "Who says I'd make fun of a proposal?"

My own eyebrows mirror hers. "Well now, Ms. Sikora. Full of surprises, you."

A slow grin blooms on her face, and she removes one of her silver handcuff-shaped earrings. "I am. Because actually I brought you here so *I* could propose. You know I have to be in the driver's seat." She pulls me upright and scoots back a bit on my thighs, holding my left hand, the earring poised near it. "Whaddya say, Sandy? Wanna get hitched?"

A thrill goes through my pounding heart. I inspect her expression, my lips parted.

She tilts her head. "Wait, do you think I'm messing with you? Because I'm totally serious." Her lower lip pulls between her teeth and she nibbles at it. "I mean, unless you think it's a stupid idea…"

"It's the fucking *best* idea. Though I suspect if you wedge that onto me"—I nod at the earring—"I'll lose a finger." I pull her against my chest. "It might be worth the sacrifice," I say into her hair with a laugh that's just broken enough to betray my emotion. She adjusts herself to meet my lips and we collide rather ungracefully.

After a volley of kisses, she sinks the earring onto my pinky finger to the first knuckle. "There—close enough," she says, satisfied.

We watch each other quietly, both fairly beaming. "*Yes*, by the way," I tell her. "In case you need something definitive, I accept."

"You'd better. Because I can't imagine life without you."

She strokes a fingertip over my eyebrow where the scar is. I made up a half-dozen fictional origin stories for it after we got back together—katana battle with a ninja assassin, attacked by a vicious hedgehog, that sort of nonsense—before admitting that I went face-first into a park bench trying to learn skateboarding as a teen.

A prosaic truth, but as it turns out, the truth—the "real me"—is more than enough.

ACKNOWLEDGMENTS

Creating the Frontrunners trilogy has been such a wonderful experience, and I am grateful to everyone who made this journey possible.

Massive thanks to the team at Forever: my dazzling editor Leah Hultenschmidt; fellow F1 fangirls publicist Caroline Green and senior production editor Mari C. Okuda; editorial assistant Jordyn Penner, production coordinator Xian Lee; and copy editors Shasta Clinch and Carrie Andrews.

So much gratitude to my agent Melissa Edwards at Stonesong—you spied the potential in the Frontrunners series and, through your belief, helped to turn it into a reality.

Thanks to Fernanda Suarez for this gorgeous cover!

Big thank-yous to my author friends who beta read and gave me priceless feedback and encouragement: Carman Webb, Elin Corva, Lisa Larkins...you are absolute inspirations.

Amanda North, bestie, you're still my favorite warrior princess after all these years.

To my family—Mumsy, Dad, Linda and Beau, Aunt Taddy—thank you for believing in me. I love you all.

To my awesome sons, I hope your ol' mom made you proud.

I love you both eternally. Now please, never read any of these smutty books. (They're pretty okay—just take my word for it.)

Sean, my heart, my "Is same mop," my world. You are the reason I believe in romance. "O King, live forever!"

And finally, infinite thanks to my readers. I have loved creating this fictional world to share with you all.

ABOUT THE AUTHOR

Josie Juniper is a Pacific Northwest native who has worked chiefly in mathematics and journalism. She writes romance featuring STEM, sass, spice, smart women, and angsty, wicked-talking men. She lives in Portland, Oregon, with her artist husband and a flock of rescue turkeys. In addition to weird loud birds, she's a fan of Formula 1 racing, prime numbers, tattoos, rain, crochet, and lost causes.

Find out more at:
josiejuniper.com
Instagram @JosieJuniperAuthor
TikTok @JosieJuniperAuthor

RAISING READERS
Books Build Bright Futures

Dear Reader,

We'd love your attention for one more page to tell you about the crisis in children's reading, and what we can all do.

Studies have shown that reading for fun is the **single biggest predictor of a child's future life chances** – more than family circumstance, parents' educational background or income. It improves academic results, mental health, wealth, communication skills, ambition and happiness.[1]

The number of children reading for fun is in rapid decline. Young people have a lot of competition for their time. In 2024, 1 in 10 children and young people in the UK aged 5 to 18 did not own a single book at home.[2]

Hachette works extensively with schools, libraries and literacy charities, but here are some ways we can all raise more readers:

- Reading to children for just 10 minutes a day makes a difference
- Don't give up if children aren't regular readers – there will be books for them!
- Visit bookshops and libraries to get recommendations
- Encourage them to listen to audiobooks
- Support school libraries
- Give books as gifts

There's a lot more information about how to encourage children to read on our website: **www.RaisingReaders.co.uk**

Thank you for reading.

---

[1] OECD, '21st-Century Readers: Developing Literacy Skills in a Digital World', 2021, https://www.oecd.org/en/publications/21st-century-readers_a83d84cb-en.html

[2] National Literacy Trust, 'Book Ownership in 2024', November 2024, https://literacytrust.org.uk/research-services/research-reports/book-ownership-in-2024